Praise for Su

T0082195

After She V
(**previously published as** *Crossing the Lines*)

2018 Winner of the Ned Kelly Awards, Best Crime Fiction

"A pure delight, a swift yet psychologically complex read, cleverly conceived and brilliantly executed."
—Dean Koontz, *New York Times* bestselling author

"A tour de force! A brilliant blend of mystery, gut-wrenching psychological suspense, and literary storytelling. The novel stands as a shining (and refreshing) example of metafiction at its best—witty and wry, stylish, and a joy to read."
—Jeffery Deaver, *New York Times* bestselling author

"A delightful, cerebral novel featuring a crime writer who grows dangerously enamored with her main character. As the interplay between creator and created reaches Russian-nesting-doll complexity, it forced us to question the nature of fiction itself."
—Gregg Hurwitz, *New York Times* bestselling author

"This is an elegant exploration of the creative process, as well as a strong defense of the crime-fiction genre, as Gentill illustrates the crossing of lines between imagination and reality."
—*Booklist*

"In this intriguing and unusual tale, a stunning departure from Gentill's period mysteries, the question is not whodunit but who's real and who's a figment of someone's vivid imagination."
—*Kirkus Reviews*

"Fans of postmodern fiction will enjoy this departure from Gentill's 1930s series. It's an exploration, as one character puts it, of 'an author's relationship with her protagonist, an examination of the tenuous line between belief and reality, imagination and self, and what happens when that line is crossed.'"
—*Publishers Weekly*

"Literary or pop fiction lovers will enjoy."
—*Library Journal*

A Dangerous Language
The Eighth Rowland Sinclair WWII Mystery

"A thrilling eighth mystery."
—*Publishers Weekly*

"Fans of historical fiction and murder mysteries will consider her treasure trove of novels to be a rich discovery."
—*Bookreporter*

Give the Devil His Due
The Seventh Rowland Sinclair WWII Mystery

"This is a great addition to a fun Australian mystery series…a fast-paced and captivating novel set during a turbulent period in Australia's history. Containing an intriguing mystery, a unique sense of humour, and a range of historical characters, this is a highly recommended read for lovers of Australian fiction."
—*Sydney Morning Herald*

"[D]evil of a good read"
—*Herald Sun*

"This 1930s Sydney is vibrant and authentic, and the inclusion of a relevant newspaper cutting at the beginning of each chapter is a neat touch... In order to get the best value out of this highly original series with its quirky characters...seek out the earlier titles and follow them in sequence."

—Historical Novel Society

A Murder Unmentioned
The Sixth Rowland Sinclair WWII Mystery

Shortlisted for the Davitt Award for Best Adult Novel for 2015
Shortlisted for the Ned Kelly Award for Best Crime Novel 2015

"Each chapter begins with a brief excerpt from an Australian publication, such as the *Camperdown Chronicle*, that offers insights into the popular culture of the times. Fans of historical mysteries will find a lot to savor."

—*Publishers Weekly*

"A charmingly complex hero whose adventures continue to highlight many worldly problems between the great wars."

—*Kirkus Reviews*

"This sixth entry in the Rowland Sinclair series, which blends historical figures seamlessly with fictional ones, clarifies and advances the family dynamics of its appealing protagonist, which should delight fans and win new readers."

—*Booklist*

"Sulari Gentill likes to tease, blithely slotting real people and events into a crime series set in the 1930s relating the fictional adventures of artist and gentleman of leisure, Rowland Sinclair... The sixth book in the series and by far the most interesting... As always, every chapter opens with a relevant snippet from a periodical of the time. Once again, telling the fictional from the real is part of the fun... Clever Gentill. Investigating the past has never been more fun."

—*Sydney Morning Herald*

Gentlemen Formerly Dressed
The Fifth Rowland Sinclair WWII Mystery

"This book has it all: intrigue among the British aristocracy, the Nazi threat, and a dashing Australian hero. I didn't want it to end!"
—Rhys Bowen, author of the *New York Times*
bestselling Royal Spyness and Molly Murphy mysteries,
and the #1 Kindle bestseller, *In Farleigh Field*

"Rowland's determined attempts to open British eyes to the gathering storm combine mystery, rousing adventure, and chance meetings with eminent figures from Churchill to Evelyn Waugh."
—*Kirkus Reviews*

"The pleasure of this novel lies...in observing Rowland at dinner with Evelyn Waugh, trading insights with H. G. Wells, and setting Winston Churchill straight on the evils of nationalism. Fans of upper-class sleuths will be in their element."
—*Publishers Weekly*

"With fast pacing, madcap characters, and intriguing histori-cal personages like H. G. Wells, Evelyn Waugh, and Winston Churchill making appearances, *Gentlemen Formerly Dressed* is historical mystery at its most fun. Sulari Gentill has managed to capture the odd decadence of the British upper classes, in stark contrast to the rising fascist factions in both Germany and England. Fascinating history, entertaining characters, and a hint of romance make *Gentlemen Formerly Dressed* irresistible."
—*Shelf Awareness*

Paving the New Road
The Fourth Rowland Sinclair WWII Mystery

Shortlisted for the Davitt Award for Best Adult Crime Fiction for 2013

"The combination of famous historical figures, detailed descrip-tions of a troubling time, and plenty of action makes for a tale as rousing as it is relevant."
—*Kirkus Reviews*

"This installment takes the aristocratic Sinclair into a much darker place than did the previous three entries in the series but does so without losing the stylish prose and the easy way with character that have given the novels their appeal."
—*Booklist*

"Stylish, well-paced murder mystery...cheeky plotline... This tale is told with such flair and feeling for those extraordinary times... Verdict: thrilling."
—*Herald Sun*

Miles Off Course
The Third Rowland Sinclair WWII Mystery

"Gentill's third reads like a superior Western, alternating high adventure with social and political observations about prewar Australia."

—*Kirkus Reviews*

"Set in Australia in 1933, Gentill's entertaining third mystery featuring portrait artist Rowland Sinclair will appeal to fans of Greenwood's Phryne Fisher... Gentill matches Greenwood's skill at blending suspense with a light touch."

—*Publishers Weekly*

"Rowland is an especially interesting character: at first he comes off as a bit of a layabout, a guy who feels he's entitled to a cushy life by virtue of his aristocratic roots, but as the story moves along, we realize he has a strong moral center and a compulsion to finish a job once he's started it. A great addition to a strong series and a fine read-alike for fans of Kerry Greenwood's Phryne Fisher novels."

—*Booklist*

A Decline in Prophets
The Second Rowland Sinclair WWII Mystery

Winner of the Davitt Award for Best Adult Crime Fiction for 2012

"I thoroughly enjoyed the glamour of the ocean voyage, the warmth and wit among the friends, and yet all the time, simmering beneath the surface, was the real and savage violence, waiting to erupt. The 1930s are a marvelous period. We know what lies

ahead! This is beautifully drawn, with all its fragile hope and looming tragedy. I am delighted this is a series. I want them all."
—Anne Perry, *New York Times* bestselling author

"Set in late 1932, Gentill's lively second mystery featuring dashing Australian millionaire Rowland 'Rowly' Sinclair takes place initially aboard the luxury cruise ship *Aquitania*, as it steams along toward Sydney... The witty and insightful glimpses of the Australian bourgeoisie of this period keep this mystery afloat."
—*Publishers Weekly*

"A delightful period piece."
—*Kirkus Reviews*

"Rowland Sinclair is a gentleman artist who comes from a privileged background but whose sympathies are with bohemians, lefties, and ratbags. It's a rich political and cultural era to explore, and Gentill has a lot of fun with a hero who is always getting paint on his immaculate tailoring."
—*Sydney Morning Herald*

A House Divided
(formerly *A Few Right Thinking Men*)
The First Rowland Sinclair WWII Mystery

Shortlisted for Best First Book for the Commonwealth Writers' Prize for 2011

"As series-launching novels go, this one is especially successful: the plot effectively plays Sinclair's aristocratic bearing and involvement in the arts against the Depression setting, fraught with radical politics, both of which he becomes involves in as he turns sleuth. And Sinclair himself is a delight: winning us over completely and making us feel as though he's an old friend."

—*Booklist*, Starred Review

"While the vintage Down Under settings might make this debut...comparable to Kerry Fisher's Melbourne-based Phryne Fisher 1920s mysteries, Gentill works in historical events that add verisimilitude to her story. There are more political machinations going on here than Phryne could ever contemplate. VERDICT: Thanks to Poisoned Pen Press for bringing another award-winning Australian crime writer to U.S. shores. Her witty hero will delight traditional mystery buffs."

—*Library Journal*, Starred Review

"It takes a talented writer to imbue history with colour and vivacity... *A Few Right Thinking Men* more than matches its historical crime contemporaries... It is rare to find such an assured debut. The novel deserves to be both read and remembered as an insight into the Australia that was; its conflicting ideologies, aims, and desires; the hallmarks of a country still maturing."

—*Australian Book Review*

"Fans of Kerry Greenwood's Phryne Fisher series, rejoice: here comes another Depression-era Australian sleuth! Along the way there is plenty of solid discussion of politics and social status, with enough context to both draw in those new to the era and keep those more well-versed in their history interested."

—Historical Novel Society

Also by Sulari Gentill

The Rowland Sinclair WWII Mysteries

A House Divided
Murder in the Wind
Miles Off Course
Paving the New Road
Gentlemen Formerly Dressed
A Murder Unmentioned
Give the Devil His Due
A Dangerous Language

The Hero Trilogy

Chasing Odysseus
Trying War
The Blood of Wolves

Standalone Novel

After She Wrote Him

SHANGHAI SECRETS

SHANGHAI SECRETS

A Rowland Sinclair WWII Mystery

SULARI GENTILL

Poisoned Pen
PRESS

Published by Poisoned Pen Press, an imprint of Sourcebooks
P.O. Box 4410, Naperville, Illinois 60567-4410
(630) 961-3900
sourcebooks.com

Originally published as *All the Tears in China* in 2019 in Australia by Pantera Press.

Library of Congress Cataloging-in-Publication Data
Names: Gentill, Sulari, author.
Title: Shanghai secrets / Sulari Gentill.
Other titles: All the tears in China
Description: Naperville, Illinois : Poisoned Pen Press, [2021] | Series: A
  Rowland Sinclair WWII mystery | "Originally published as All the Tears in
  China in 2019 in Australia by Pantera Press"--Title page verso.
Identifiers: LCCN 2020027640 (paperback) | (epub)
Subjects: GSAFD: Mystery fiction. | Historical fiction.
Classification: LCC PR9619.4.G46 A79 2021 (print) | DDC 823/.92--dc23
LC record available at https://lccn.loc.gov/2020027640

Printed and bound in the United States of America.
SB 10 9 8 7 6 5 4 3 2 1

Chapter One

The Woman's World

Conducted by Winifred Moore

DEAR READERS OF MINE

Though eavesdropping as a habit is not regarded with favour in the best society, it is an amusing and sometimes instructive occupation when the matters overheard are of a general and not a personal nature.

Indeed, if one's sense of hearing is acute it is almost impossible not to collect a few items of other people's business when going about the city even if they are not sought deliberately. As the poet might have said: 'A little eavesdropping now and then is relished by the wisest men...'

—*Courier Mail*, 31 May 1934

Rowland Sinclair's Chrysler Airflow was a magnet for attention, both admiring and aghast in equal measure, and so the presence of three men loitering curiously by the motorcar was not particularly unusual. The automobile's revolutionary design and all-metal body, not to mention its yellow paintwork, made it distinctive amongst the black Austins and Ford Tudors also parked in Druitt Lane.

Rowland handed his seven-year-old nephew the key to the Airflow's door. "Let yourself in, Ernie, while I have a word with these gentlemen."

Rowland had become accustomed to explaining his automobile to inquisitive strangers. He was, himself, still enamoured enough with the vehicle not to find the interest tedious. Still, on this occasion, he was in a hurry, and the men in question had placed themselves in the way of the car... They'd probably want him to show them the engine.

Ernest Sinclair ran directly to the driver's side door with the key clutched tightly in his fist while Rowland strode over to the men leaning on the Airflow's bonnet.

"Afternoon, gentlemen."

"Flash car. She yours?"

"She is."

The man who'd asked glanced at his companions. "You Sinclair?"

At the mention of his name, Rowland tensed instinctively. Apparently, the reaction was reply enough, and they fell upon him, fists leading. In the face of the onslaught, Rowland gave no quarter and responded in kind. He'd been in this kind of situation often enough that he knew to keep the three men in front of him—if one was to grab and hold him from behind, the situation would become grim indeed. His assailants, too, were clearly not novices in the dubious arts of street fighting. They forced him away from the car, raining blow after blow and using their number to bypass his defences. Eventually Rowland went down.

The surface of Druitt Lane was warm and hard against his

face. He used it to steady the world, to focus on fighting back. Rowland wanted to shout at Ernest to run, but he was not sure if that would simply alert what might be a band of kidnappers to the boy's location.

He was almost relieved when one of the men—he could not see which—called him a "Commie-loving traitor." This was about him, not Ernest. Whatever their purpose, it was probably not child abduction. The jagged impact of a boot against his ribs drove the breath from his lungs. And then another.

"Oi! What the hell's going on here?"

From the ground Rowland knew only that it was a voice he'd not heard before, followed by several moments when he could almost hear the indecision, and then the pounding feet of men in flight.

"Are you all right, mate?" A concerned hand on his shoulder.

Rowland pushed himself gingerly off the road. "Yes, I think so."

"Mongrels! Bloody mongrels! Did they rob yer?"

Rowland shook his head slowly.

The Samaritan—a large man with a strong and steady grip—helped him stand. "They were giving you one hell of a kicking, you sure you're—"

Rowland's head began to clear. "Dammit! Ernie!"

"I beg yer pardon, mate?"

"Ernie, my nephew. He was…" Rowland stepped unsteadily towards the Airflow, panicked now. He couldn't see the boy. "Ernie!"

A tousled head rose hesitantly above the dash, blue eyes wide.

Rowland stopped to breathe. He opened the front passenger door. "Ernie, thank God!"

Ernest was pale and obviously shaken. "I wanted to help, Uncle Rowly, but you told me to stay in the car."

"I'm glad you did, mate." Rowland leant against the doorframe still trying to get his breath.

"You're bleeding, Uncle Rowly." Ernest remained in the protection of the Airflow's cabin.

"It's just a scratch, Ernie. I'll be all right."

"Who were those men?"

"To be perfectly honest, I'm not really sure."

"Why were they cross with you?"

To that, Rowland did not respond. He could guess why, but there was no point frightening Ernest. "We should get home to Woodlands."

"Are you up to driving that contraption, mate?" The man who'd stopped the attack regarded first the Airflow then Rowland Sinclair with equal scepticism, before drawing back sharply. "Hold your horses there a minute..." He rummaged inside his jacket to extract a newspaper.

Rowland grimaced. He really didn't want to get into another fight, but at least there was only one man this time.

The man held the front page beside Rowland's face. "That's you!" he said. "That's you with that fella, Keesch."

Rowland glanced back at Ernest in the car. Egon Kisch was regarded as either a peace advocate or a dangerous Communist subversive. The three men who'd just tried to pound Rowland into the ground were indisputably of the latter opinion. Still, Rowland had never been a man to deny his friends. "Yes, that's me."

"Well, whaddaya know, from the front page! The wife will never believe it."

Rowland smiled and put out his hand. He introduced himself, relieved that the gentleman seemed more starstruck than offended by the picture. "I appreciate your assistance, sir."

"Barry Love," he said, shaking Rowland's hand solemnly. "Always pleased to help a gentleman. You'd best be on your way, lest those jokers come back. There's some folk pretty worked up over your mate Keesch."

"It would seem so."

Rowland farewelled Love with more thanks and slipped behind the steering wheel, wincing as he settled.

Ernest watched him intently.

"I'm sorry you had to see that, Ernie. But I'm fine, you know."

"You were on the ground."

"Yes, that was a little undignified—but I was about to get up."

"Pater said that half of Sydney wants to kill you."

Rowland smiled faintly. Wilfred hated being called "Pater" but Ernest was rather enthusiastic about learning Latin. "He told you that?"

"He told Dr. Maguire. I was leavesdropping."

"I believe the term is eavesdropping, Ernie."

"Even if we were in the garden?"

"Even then."

"Oh."

"And eavesdropping is not generally the done thing, old boy, not if you're a gentleman," Rowland added, keen to distract Ernest from the subject of who might want to kill his uncle.

"You're not going to tell Pater, are you?"

"No, I won't tell your father. But perhaps you should try to do less of it anyway."

"What if they're talking about me?"

"Especially if they're talking about you."

"What if I was there first and they walk in talking afterwards?"

"Well you should leave or let them know you're there."

"Pater says I shouldn't interrupt."

By the time young Ernest Sinclair had thoroughly defined the parameters of eavesdropping, the Airflow had turned into the long drive of Woodlands House and pulled up at perhaps the grandest and stateliest home in Woollahra, which was not a suburb lacking in magnificent abodes. Ernest jumped from the car to greet the misshapen, one-eared greyhound that leapt down the entrance stairs to greet them.

"Sit, Lenin, sit, sit, sit!" Ernest shouted. The greyhound licked his face but otherwise ignored him.

Rowland climbed out of the motorcar, and called his dog to heel. He was only slightly more successful than his nephew. The emergence of two men from the house did little to abate the hound's excitement.

Milton Isaacs threw open his arms and declared, "I am sir Oracle, and when I ope my lips, let no dog bark."

Lenin barked.

"Clearly Len has no respect for Shakespeare," Rowland said, reflexively attributing the words. A self-proclaimed poet, Milton seemed to consider that repurposing the verse of the great bards with passion was creative effort enough. To Rowland's knowledge, his friend had only ever composed one original line—more akin to a nursery rhyme than verse—though that was not something that bothered any of them unduly.

"Lay down, Len!" Clyde Watson Jones's attempt to silence the hound was more effective if less elegant. Raised in the country, Clyde was as direct and practical as Milton was theatrical. Years on the wallaby track, scavenging for work and survival, had infused a necessary pragmatism into his otherwise romantic soul. Lenin settled beside Rowland's feet, eyeing them all resentfully.

Clyde turned to Rowland, his arms folded across his chest. "What's happened? You look like you've gone a couple of rounds."

Rowland glanced uneasily at his nephew who was, as usual, listening intently. "Ernie, why don't you be a good chap and take Len into the kitchen? I'm certain Mary was saving a ham bone for him."

"Yeah, go on, mate," Clyde added. "She's been baking those little jam cakes."

Any reluctance to leave thus overcome by jam cakes, Ernest set off into the house with Lenin in tow.

"So?" Milton asked as they watched boy and dog disappear.

"Three chaps grabbed me as I was getting into the car. They must have been waiting."

"Ernie?"

"He was already in the car. I don't think they realised he was there."

"So they just gave you a kicking?"

"Yes," Rowland admitted ruefully.

"Do I need to ask why?"

"The gentlemen objected to my association with Egon Kisch, I believe."

"God, if Egon knew—"

"There would be nothing he could do, so telling him would be pointless," Rowland said firmly.

"You're going to have one hell of a shiner," Milton observed.

"I suppose I should clean myself up. I promised Ernie we'd—"

"Hello!" Milton interrupted as a racing-green Rolls-Royce Continental came through the gates and negotiated the sweeping drive. "Isn't that your brother's motor?"

Chapter Two

"THANK YOU, MR. MENZIES!"

Agitator's Debt of Gratitude

A KISCH'S...FAREWELL

KISCH has gone! At long last. But before he left the West he gave a farewell message to Australia and some words of advice to Mr. Menzies, whom Kisch apparently considers to be about the funniest man he ever met. Anyway, he thanks the Federal Minister most cordially for the splendid publicity he gave both him and his cause during his stay in Australia. Without Mr. Menzies' aid he would have been powerless.

"IN this last hour I will spend in Australia for probably some time, I thank 'Smith's Weekly' for agreeing, to give my farewell message to your Commonwealth." This was Herr Egon Kisch's statement just before he rejoined the "Orford" at Fremantle on Monday after addressing gatherings in Perth. "I think Australia a most beautiful continent, with the best people and the worst politicians in the world," he continued. It would be impossible in Europe for a man to do anything like Mr. Menzies has done in my case without being killed by ridicule..."

—*Smith's Weekly*, 16 March 1935

———————————————⚭———————————————

They watched the Continental make its way down the long driveway and pull to a stop beside the Airflow. A chauffeur stepped out to open the door for a gentleman in his midforties. Wilfred Sinclair was shorter than his younger brother and his hair fair in comparison. Indeed, their only resemblance lay in the deep blue eyes which seemed common to all the Sinclair men. He was dressed immaculately in a dark three-piece suit, his shirt crisp and starched.

Rowland shook his brother's hand. "Hello, Wil. We weren't expecting you till tomorrow."

Wilfred frowned as he assessed the darkening bruise on Rowland's face, the traces of blood on his cheek. "Clearly. I'd like a word with you, Rowly."

"Of course."

"Would you like us to keep Ernie occupied for a while?" Clyde offered uncertainly.

Wilfred nodded curtly. "Yes, that would be very helpful, Mr. Watson Jones."

"Not at all, Mr. Sinclair. We'll take him out for a game of cricket."

Rowland accompanied his brother into the house, and Wilfred led the way into the library. Rowland braced himself. The library was possibly the only part of the mansion that had not been touched in any way during his reign as master of Woodlands. In its traditional conservative opulence, it spoke of a different time and attitude. It remained the domain of their father. Rowland hated the room, but Wilfred seemed to prefer it, particularly for conversations of gravity, one of which it seemed they were about to have.

"Would you care for a drink?" Wilfred took charge of the well-stocked decanters arranged on the drinks cabinet. "You look like you could use one."

"I could, actually." Rowland eased himself into one of the leather armchairs. Perhaps gin would deaden the pounding in his head.

Wilfred handed him a glass. "What the devil have you been doing this time?"

Rowland told him of the attack. Wilfred tensed with the realisation that Ernest had been present.

"Ernie was in the car, Wil. I doubt they even knew he was there—it was me they wanted."

"And who were these chaps?"

"Self-appointed defenders of something, I expect."

Wilfred shook his head. "Bloody hell, Rowly, your friend Kisch has left you in a fine mess."

"This isn't Egon's fault."

"The devil it isn't! This is the third time you've been assaulted in the last two weeks! It's only a matter of time before you're seriously injured."

"It'll pass, Wil. I'll be more careful, and people will calm down."

Wilfred shook his head. "Ernie might have been hurt this time."

Rowland let his head fall back against the chair and closed his eyes. He was all too aware that his nephew had witnessed three thugs pummel him into the ground; that Ernest might well have been hurt if he'd left the car. "I'm sorry, Wil. I really am."

Wilfred removed his spectacles and polished the lenses with a handkerchief. "Rowly, I know you'd do everything in your power to protect Ernie—God knows you've proved that—but this is simply getting out of hand. This current animosity towards you may pass, but right now, it means neither you nor anyone around you is safe. Not Ernie, not Mother, not even your layabout Communist friends!"

"I'll speak to the police."

"Kisch is making monkeys of the police, Rowly. They will not be kindly predisposed to you." Wilfred pointed at his brother. "Bob Menzies is determined that you should answer for your part in this Egon Kisch affair, one way or another."

"As I said, Wil, I'm not sure who those chaps were, but I'm fairly certain Robert Menzies was not one of them."

"Don't be smart, Rowly."

Rowland stared at his gin. Wilfred was right. He'd made an enemy of the Commonwealth attorney-general. Menzies had not taken his own failure to keep the Communist peace advocate from setting foot in the country well. And like many people, he believed Rowland had betrayed his country by helping Kisch get in. It was probably only due to Wilfred's influence that Rowland Sinclair had not been charged with anything thus far. But that could change. There were, he knew, Federal Police surveilling his house even now, watching for any transgression for which they may conceivably arrest him.

Wilfred lit a cigarette. "I want you to go to Shanghai."

"What?"

"I want you to go to Shanghai. It's in China."

"I know where it is! Why the dickens do you want me to go to China?"

"Sinclair Holdings is represented in Shanghai by the legal firm of Carmel and Smith. Gilbert Carmel is an old chum—we served together in France." Wilfred smiled fleetingly. "Kate and I have been planning to take the boys to Shanghai—to introduce the baby to his namesake, and so I can meet with some wool brokers."

"You want me to accompany you?"

"No. I want you to go in our place."

"Me?" Rowland put down his glass and stared at his brother. He had always maintained a studied disinterest in the machinations of the Sinclair fortune; the maintenance, expansion, and control of which had traditionally been Wilfred's remit alone. Over the years, Rowland had simply signed whatever Wilfred told him to sign, content to allow his older brother to do whatever he saw fit with the Sinclair assets. "You can't be serious."

"I'm afraid I am. I can't leave at the moment."

"Surely there must be someone else you could send."

"These chaps can be easily offended." Wilfred's explanation was characteristically blunt and brusque. "Believe me, you'd be the last man I'd send if your name wasn't Sinclair."

Rowland tried to extricate himself. "Wil, I don't know anything about wool markets—how on earth am I supposed to negotiate?"

"Under no circumstances are you to negotiate, promise, or agree to anything. Say as little as possible."

"But—"

"Your purpose is to hold our place in these meetings," Wilfred said. "Just listen and be pleasant. For God's sake, don't sign anything."

"Wouldn't you be better sending someone who understands the—"

"If I actually intended to do business—yes. But, for now, I simply wish to assure our potential trading partners that I value them enough to send a blood relative."

Rowland's brow rose. Blood seemed a dubious qualification. "Who are these potential trading partners?"

Wilfred said nothing for a moment. "The Japanese. As you know, there is talk of a trade embargo against Japan."

Rowland hadn't known. Whilst he was more aware of international politics than he had once ever wanted to be, his attention had been focused on Europe and not the East.

Wilfred continued carefully. "I am not predisposed to conducting business that may be counter to government policy, but neither do I wish—for reasons about which you need not concern yourself—to show my hand."

Rowland's eyes narrowed. Wilfred Sinclair had always operated the grand machines of commerce, in which any part Rowland played was at most a tiny cog. It made him wonder. "You're sending me as some kind of political subterfuge?"

"I am sending you because it is not in our interests to commit either way," Wilfred corrected. "I don't intend to inform them in advance that you will be attending in my stead."

"Why?"

"Best they don't have time to devise some strategy about how to deal with you." He paused and then added impatiently, "Take your unemployed lefty friends with you, if you must."

The suggestion roused Rowland's suspicions. Whilst Wilfred's opinion of Rowland's friends had softened in the last year, he was unlikely to propose they accompany him on a business trip unless it was to make sure that Rowland went. "Why do you want me out of the country, Wil?"

"Don't be absurd, Rowly. Although, it wouldn't be a bad idea to go abroad if only to give Menzies an opportunity to calm down."

"I didn't break any laws."

"That's a matter of perspective." Wilfred exhaled. "I would go to Shanghai myself, but Kate needs me here."

"Kate?" Rowland asked, alarmed. His sister-in-law rarely made demands on Wilfred. "Is there something—"

Wilfred shook his head. "Issues with her father's estate. The Bairds are circling for an almighty stoush. I can't get away."

Rowland nodded. There was nothing Wilfred would not do for his young wife and sons. It was the soft underbelly of the otherwise impenetrable Wilfred Sinclair. And it was this that caused Rowland to relent, albeit unenthusiastically.

"Very well then, I'll go to bloody Shanghai. But if I ruin us all by accident, remember that this was your cockeyed idea."

Wilfred nodded. "Good man." He opened his mouth to begin

but stopped. "Go and get yourself cleaned up, Rowly." He glanced at his pocket watch. "I'll have your housekeeper organise some coffee, and then we can get to work."

"To work?"

"There are a few things you should be across before you go, or else you may well indeed ruin us all."

"Can't it wait? I just—"

"Don't whine, Rowly. You're a grown man, for God's sake. We don't have much time—you'll have to leave soon."

Rowland groaned. His head was pounding as it was without a crash course on wool or economics or whatever else his brother had in mind.

"I'll say hello to Ernie," Wilfred continued, "and inform your friends that you won't be joining them for dinner." He frowned. "Perhaps we should call a doctor and have you checked over."

"No need, I'm fine." Rowland stood, resigned. Resistance was obviously going to be futile.

He met Edna Higgins on the staircase. In overalls, with her hair tied up and a stray smear of clay on her cheek, the sculptress had obviously been working, although her hands were now clean. She held the sixteen-millimetre Bell and Howell movie camera Rowland had recently given her for no reason in particular but that he'd hoped it might suit her. Rowland was a man of such means that generosity needed no reason. Edna had embraced the new medium with a child-like zeal, filming their day-to-day lives at first—Rowland and Clyde at their easels, Milton skylarking, even Lenin, the greyhound, and the cats that lived at Woodlands House. She'd recorded Egon Kisch's speech at the Domain and his private visits to Woodlands House. In the last few weeks, she'd graduated to making short films, persuading the men with whom she lived to take roles in her productions, which, despite jeers and complaints, they had done with good humour.

She stopped mid-step, able to look directly into Rowland's

face by virtue of her place on a higher tread. "Again?" she said, raising her hand to gently touch the darkening bruise on his temple.

"I'm all right, Ed," he said, smiling. "I just haven't had a chance to clean up." He looked down the stairs. "Wil's here."

"You go up," she said, frowning. "I'll bring you up a compress, or a poultice or something, for your face."

"That's very kind. But don't trouble yourself. Wilfred is expecting me back directly."

"Expecting you back where?"

"The library."

She grimaced. "Is he cross?" The sculptress had lived long enough at Woodlands to be familiar with Wilfred Sinclair's preference for the library as a venue for battle.

"No more than usual."

Edna turned Rowland's face to look more closely at the bruise. She noticed the blood on his collar, the tear in the shoulder of his jacket. "We're going to have to do something about this, Rowly. This is the third time…"

He grabbed her hand and squeezed it as he proceeded up the stairs. "Don't worry, Ed. Wil has a solution."

Wilfred Sinclair spent most of that evening educating his brother on the very basics of the wool trade and commercial negotiation. He coached Rowland on words and phrases of which to be wary, and those he should use in order to appear interested without committing to a course of action, the broad principles he could enunciate to avoid answering a direct question, and the judicious use of the term "utmost good faith."

"Bloody hell, you'll want me to kiss babies next!" Rowland muttered.

Wilfred ignored his grievances. He was relentless in his

instruction. Indeed, he seemed to be relishing the opportunity, and eventually Rowland said as much.

For a moment Wilfred did not reply and then said, "When I came back—after the war—I always imagined that we would run the business together, Rowly."

"Really?" Rowland didn't hide his surprise. Wilfred might as well have said he'd expected his brother to join the Royal Ballet.

Wilfred sighed. "I understood, of course, that you had oats to sow—you're not the first young man to...paint."

Rowland smiled.

"But I always hoped that eventually you'd settle down and show an interest."

Rowland's brow rose. "I'm afraid I've been something of a disappointment then."

"More a frustration than a disappointment." Wilfred sat back in his chair and regarded Rowland thoughtfully. "You're barely thirty. It's not too late."

"I'm afraid it is."

"You're a Sinclair, Rowly. You can't ignore who you are."

"I know. It's why I paint."

The task of briefing Rowland to Wilfred's satisfaction took most of that night. By the time Rowland was allowed to retire, he had at least an idea of the nature and size of the Sinclair holdings, and quality of and quantity of its wool clip, both seasonal and stockpiled. Rowland could not understand why he needed to know anything at all, given that he had been forbidden to make any commitments or enter into any agreements. But Wilfred was determined that he should nevertheless seem competent to represent the Sinclair marque. Perhaps Wilfred hoped that his efforts would somehow ignite a real interest. Perhaps he had not yet given up on the idea of Rowland working at his side.

By the next morning, preparations and necessary arrangements were already underway so that appointments in Shanghai could be kept. Passages were booked and trunks packed. Rowland's Aunt Mildred was persuaded to move temporarily into Woodlands House to keep his elderly mother company.

Elisabeth Sinclair had resided with Rowland for the past year, though she believed him to be his brother, the son she'd lost to the Great War. Rowland had long learned to live with this malady of his mother's mind and heart. Despite her age and background, Elisabeth relished the bohemian company he kept and had somehow come to regard them as her contemporaries. Consequently, she was less than happy with the proposed companionship of her sister-in-law.

"Millie is so old," she complained.

"Aunt Mildred is two years younger than you, Mother," Wilfred reminded her.

"Nonsense!" Elisabeth would not have it. She had recently decided that she, like Edna, was twenty-eight years old. Rowland and his friends did not try to convince her otherwise, and nothing Wilfred said would change her mind.

Eventually, however, she was reconciled to "looking after Millie" for a couple of months. Elisabeth Sinclair had, after all, been raised with an understanding of family duty.

Edna and Milton decided immediately that they would accompany him to Shanghai, though it amused them that Wilfred Sinclair would send the black sheep to trade wool. The sculptress saw the expedition as another chance to explore the world, in the company she most liked to keep, and perhaps, this time, to capture their travels on film. She was, in any case, glad to quit Sydney for a while. Milton simply sensed adventure in the sudden call to Shanghai.

Clyde, too, was inclined to join the sojourn to the Far East, but for the job he had taken just the week before.

"Maybe I can catch up with you," he said somewhat despondently.

"Just resign," Milton urged. "It's not the Sistine Chapel."

"I can't. I said I'd do it." As much as he did not relish being left behind, Clyde was man of his word.

"What's the job?" Rowland asked. He hadn't realised Clyde had taken on a new commission. "Is it a portrait?"

Clyde looked embarrassed. "Murals. I'm painting murals."

"Really? Where?"

"For the new amusement park they're building at Milsons Point. Luna Park," he mumbled. "They've hired a few artists to paint murals around the attractions."

"What exactly are you painting?" Edna asked, intrigued.

"Monsters."

Milton sniggered.

Edna shoved the poet. "I beg your pardon?"

"I've been assigned the mural at the entrance to the ghost train." Clyde folded his arms defensively. "It's honest work. I can't just leave them in the lurch."

"Of course you can't," Rowland agreed. "How long will it take you to finish this monster mural?"

"Two weeks, perhaps three."

Rowland frowned. Wilfred was insisting they leave as soon as possible. "What if I help?"

"That's a tremendous idea, Rowly!" Edna jumped to her feet. "I can help too."

"I'm not sure they'll allow—" Clyde began.

"You just tell them that Rowly and I are your assistants," Edna directed. "We'll have your mural done in a few days, and you can sail with us."

Clyde hesitated. He looked at Rowland. Edna didn't care about painting one way or another but Rowland was wealthy enough to confine himself to works of fine art, to paint only those subjects that inspired him. "Are you sure, Rowly? It's a mural...in an amusement park."

Rowland shrugged. "A gallery by any other name."

Chapter Three

LUNA PARK NEAR SYDNEY BRIDGE

PROTEST AGAINST PROPOSAL
"Lack of Aesthetic Taste"

SYDNEY, Tuesday—"The people of Sydney have a deplorable lack of aesthetic taste," said the acting president of the Parks and Playgrounds Movement (Mr. A J Small) to-day, when as a member of a deputation to Mr Ryan, Honorary Minister, he protested against the granting of a lease of the site of the Harbour Bridge workshops at Milson's Point for the establishment of an amusement park. The lease was granted recently to Messrs Phillips Bros, of Melbourne.

Mr Small said that it made him despair of local government when he heard that a council had consented to the introduction of a cheap-jack show.

The honorary secretary of the moment (Dr. C W Bean) said that the proposal was akin to putting Coney Island under the Tower of London.

—Argus, 1 May 1935

———————————⟨◦◦⟩———————————

Rowland consulted the plan Clyde had drawn up. The mural was taking shape more quickly than they'd dared to hope. Clyde was an excellent foreman, directing Edna and Rowland's contributions to the fresco in a manner that took advantage of both their stature and strengths as artists. Rowland's height meant that he could reach the upper edge of the painting with little difficulty, and his natural style allowed him to block in general shapes at speed. Edna was happy to sit cross-legged on the ground to paint the lower detail. Although she was a sculptor, or perhaps because of it, Edna painted with a particular eye for dimension and perspective. Clyde managed the middle territory himself and sequenced the specific areas of work so that they were not tripping over one another.

When the amusement park's representatives raised concerns on the third day that the mural was too frightening for a children's ride, Clyde had responded calmly, instructing his assistants to put broad smiles on the faces of every monster in the composition. The result was distinctly unnerving—werewolves, phantoms, and vampires grinned down from the wall like they were sharing some ghoulish joke—but after only four days, the mural was nearly complete.

Rowland dabbed a highlight on the upswept brows of the vampire. They were simply enjoying themselves now, including personal touches into the detail of the composition for their own amusement.

Clyde shook his head. "People are going to recognise your vampire," he warned. "It might be defamation."

Rowland smiled. "I have no idea what you're talking about."

Clyde laughed. "Ed's ghoul is carrying a bowl of tripe for some reason."

Edna pulled a face. "I would have thought the reason perfectly obvious."

"Eddie!"

Rowland recognised the voice, though he was surprised to hear it. He turned.

A man in a cream linen suit ran towards them with an enormous bouquet of roses held out before him. Bertram Middleton. Rowland frowned. The last time they'd met, he'd punched the journalist. That was several weeks ago now, but not enough time had passed to make him regret it.

Edna stood. "Bertie. What on earth are you doing here?"

"I'm looking for an answer." He smiled.

"An answer for what?"

"The most important question in the world, my darling. I got that job at the *Sydney Morning Herald*. I hope you realise what that means."

"I'm sure I have no idea."

Middleton laughed too loudly. "My new position carries with it a substantial increase in salary and prospects."

"I'm happy for you, Bertie."

"For us, Eddie." Middleton smiled. "I've made a reservation at Romano's for this evening."

Edna shook her head. "I'm sorry, Bertie, I can't—"

"Tomorrow."

"No."

"Next week then."

"We're going to China."

"China?" Middleton's eyes narrowed and moved to Rowland. "Why the devil are you going to China?"

"Because I want to," Edna said evenly.

"Is Sinclair going to China?"

"Yes, I am." Rowland's voice hinted at impatience.

The smile faded from Middleton's lips. "Eddie, darling. I don't think you'll want to go once I've asked my question."

Clyde cleared his throat and looked away. Rowland was equally unsure of what to do. This was not the first time an optimistic swain had tried to press his case with Edna. In normal circumstances, they would have given the poor fool privacy for his impending disappointment.

"Don't ask the question, Bertie." Edna's voice was clear but there was compassion in her face. Rowland moved to make a discreet exit, but a momentary flash of fury in Middleton's face stopped him. Perhaps Clyde, too, had seen it, because he also remained where he was.

Middleton took a breath and smiled again. Too broadly. "I understand," he said. "It would be unfair to spoil your trip when you can't change your plans." He handed her the flowers. "Perhaps you'll be able to pick up a few things for your trousseau in Shanghai."

Edna shook her head. "Bertie—"

Middleton cut her off. "Let's go dancing, Eddie. We should celebrate."

"There's nothing to celebrate," the sculptress said firmly.

"Don't be like that, Eddie." Middleton laughed. "I'm sure you'll have a lovely time. We'll miss each other, of course, but I'll be waiting for you when you return, and we can—"

"No!" Edna said loudly now. "Listen to me, Bertie. Don't wait. There's nothing to wait for."

"Believe me, I don't want to wait either." He grabbed her wrist.

Rowland moved immediately. His hand clamped down on Middleton's shoulder and wrenched him back. "Perhaps you should leave, Middleton."

"Perhaps you should mind your own business!" Middleton snapped back. He attempted to shake Rowland off. "Unhand me before I knock you flat."

Rowland's brow arched sceptically. Middleton became enraged. "I know what you're trying to do, Sinclair. And I won't allow it!"

Clyde stepped in now. "Settle down, mate."

Middleton appealed to Edna. "Tell them, Eddie. Tell them about us."

"There's nothing to tell, Bertie. I'm sorry, but I don't want to see you again."

"I don't believe you, Eddie." He turned to Rowland. "He's making you say that—"

Rowland had had enough. He pulled Middleton away from Edna. "For God's sake, man, you're making a bloody a fool of yourself."

"She loves me, Sinclair," Middleton hissed. "Always has. She just doesn't know how to tell you."

"Don't be absurd, Bertie!" Edna said furiously.

"You can't protect him forever, Eddie," Middleton replied. "It's time to tell him that you are not for sale!"

Some of the other artists working on murals nearby came over now. "What's the trouble, mate?"

"This chap wandered in by mistake," Rowland replied calmly. "He's just leaving."

Middleton hesitated, but faced with a wall of men, he stepped back and stalked out towards the entrance gate.

"Are you all right, Ed?" Rowland asked as they all drifted back to work.

The sculptress nodded. She seemed uneasy as much as angry. "I've refused to see him since I discovered what he did last year."

Rowland picked up his paintbrush, touched by her loyalty. Edna's lovers were temporary, but her friends weren't. To them, she was fiercely protective and unwaveringly steadfast. The previous year Middleton had passed certain information to the papers in an effort to publicly discredit Rowland Sinclair, whom he saw as a rival for the sculptress's affections. Wilfred had used his influence to successfully keep the scandal and its accompanying photographs from being published, but it might otherwise have ended very badly indeed.

"I've not replied to his letters; I've returned his gifts unopened and lately his letters too. I can't understand why he thinks I might even consider marrying him," Edna whispered, frustrated.

Rowland resisted an absurd impulse to take her into his arms and suggest she marry him instead.

While many men had fallen in love with Edna Higgins, most seemed to accept that she would not belong to any of them.

"I should have a word with him," Rowland murmured. "Make sure he understands that his attentions are not welcome."

Edna declined firmly. "We'll be leaving for China soon. By the time we get back, Bertie will have forgotten about me."

They stayed late that night, determined to finish the mural to thereby guarantee Clyde's release, returning exhausted to Woodlands House, which was now in the midst of final preparations for their impending absence.

At Wilfred's insistence, Rowland's studio was locked, and many of his paintings removed from the walls in other parts of Woodlands House. Rowland bore this without protest. As much as his artistic reputation had been built on the manner in which he painted nudes, those depictions were also very likely to offend his Aunt Mildred.

With Clyde's place in their party now secured, they made the necessary arrangements for an extended stay in the Far East with renewed vigour. Having travelled with Rowland previously, his friends already possessed wardrobes that belied their own stations and befitted the first-class accommodations to which Rowland Sinclair was accustomed. Rowland's high street tailors attended the Woollahra mansion to see to any clothing repairs, alterations, and replacements, and trunks were packed with tailcoats, dinner suits, evening gowns, hats, ties, gloves, and every other form of attire they might need.

It was in the midst of all this that Clyde introduced Rowland to a businessman from his hometown, Batlow, in the Snowy Mountains. Danny Dong had travelled to Sydney after he'd heard through one of the local Watson Joneses that Clyde was going to China. He brought with him an ornate chest, which he asked his old friend to take to Shanghai.

Clyde raised the matter with Rowland, who was amused and a little uncomfortable that Clyde had felt the need to ask his permission at all. "We'd be very happy to take it, Mr. Dong."

Dong was effusively grateful. "My cousin will collect it from you," he promised, shaking their hands warmly as he took his leave.

"Rowly, I'm sorry," Clyde began after the door had closed behind Dong. "It's a hell of a request, but I've known Danny and his family all my life."

"Don't be daft, Clyde." Rowland dismissed his friend's concern. Clyde never took generosity for granted and was occasionally unnecessarily grateful for what Rowland considered the smallest thing. Rowland glanced at the growing collection of trunks being readied for their departure. "We're not travelling lightly, after all. Mr. Dong's box of souvenirs will be neither here nor there in the sum of things."

And so the beautifully carved chest was added to their luggage.

Lenin was taken back to Oaklea and placed under the care of Wilfred's younger sons and the gardener. Wilfred muttered about the imposition of "Rowly's bloody dog," but the hound was not unwelcome.

Wilfred called twice to further supplement Rowland's knowledge of commerce. Rowland tolerated his brother's efforts with something akin to goodwill. Perhaps it was a good time to be despatched to China. It seemed both he and Edna had reason to get away while passions cooled.

Chapter Four

"DON'T GO TO SHANGHAI."

The Prime Minister (Mr. J. A. Lyons) stated yesterday that the British Minister in China had reported that unemployment amongst British subjects in Shanghai was so serious that persons who were known to contemplate proceeding there should be warned not to do so.

He understood that Australian stowaways had been arriving at Shanghai.

—*Newcastle Morning Herald and Miners' Advocate*, 3 January 1934

Rowland Sinclair cast his eyes across an Eastern Babylon.

Colour was muted by fog, which seemed also to soften the cacophony of sound. On the water, Chinese junks fluttered around steamships like exotic birds, light and graceful against the lumbering momentum of the liners. The port was busy this morning, disembarking passengers and cargo. The waterfront teemed with movement and purpose, scuttling rickshaws, traders, locals in both traditional attire and the Western fashions, amidst the grand buildings of the international settlement. Taxicabs vied for customers, but the Australians had already been warned about the dangers of bandit drivers. The hotel had, in any case, arranged cars to collect them.

Edna leaned against Rowland, her arms folded tightly against the cold. Stray tendrils of hair, which had escaped the confines of her cloche, had become copper coils in the damp wind. Rowland placed his arm about her shoulders.

"We should go," he said. "There'll be time to gaze at Shanghai later."

The sculptress glanced up at him and smiled. "Still, it's breathtaking, isn't it?"

Rowland laughed. The catch in his breath had nothing to do with the city. Even after all this time, the sculptress had that effect. He pointed out the hotel which would be their base.

The Cathay Hotel was located in the magnificent gothic-styled Sassoon House which overlooked the Huangpu River. The pyramidal copper-sheathed roof distinguished it among the colonial grandeur of the buildings along the waterfront district known as the Bund, and made it plainly visible from the dockside.

"We've got a bit of a space problem, Rowly." Milton held open the back of the Packard which had been sent to collect them. The back seat was piled with trunks and bags.

"Why don't we walk?" Edna suggested, unwilling to retreat from the vibrant reality of the Bund just yet. This was Shanghai, the Far East. The hotel would still be there when they'd finished exploring.

"Ed, it's freezing." Clyde stood behind the Packard, his sun-lined face almost hidden behind the folds of his scarf. "That wind is brutal."

They had boarded an Imperial Airlines flight in the last burst of an Australian summer, flying to Singapore and taking a ship from there. The entire exercise had taken a mere ten days. For Clyde, Shanghai's sharp spring was too sudden a change.

"You chaps take the motorcar back to the hotel with the luggage," Rowland offered. "Have them send another car back for us. I'll keep Ed company."

Milton hesitated for a moment between the car and a gallant urge to insist Edna take his place. A blast of wind helped him decide for the relative warmth of the Packard's cabin. "Ah, bitter chill it was! The owl, for all its feathers, was a-cold."

"Keats," Rowland replied.

The local driver was clearly unhappy with the plan. He shook his head emphatically and spoke first in Cantonese, and when that proved fruitless, in the pidgin by which the various cultures of the treaty port communicated. "No joss. Not safe, Missy. Cathay side, chop chop."

Edna smiled at him. "It's kind of you to worry, sir, but I'll be with Mr. Sinclair, and we can't all fit."

The driver shook his head and said something in Cantonese that perhaps could not have been adequately expressed with the simplified lexicon of pidgin.

"How about I stay with Rowly?" Clyde offered, shivering uncontrollably.

"Your need is clearly greater than mine, Clyde darling." Edna took Rowland's hand. "We'll be fine—we'll wait right here so the driver knows where to find us. Honestly, I'm not cold."

"The sooner you set off, the sooner we'll all be out of the wind," Rowland added as Clyde hesitated.

Clyde conceded. "Fair enough. If you're sure. We'll send a car for you as soon as we get to the hotel."

And so they parted ways. Rowland and Edna stood in fog, watching the activity on the pier in companionable silence. They were accosted from time to time by taxi and rickshaw drivers in search of a fare. They refused politely and then firmly, as the invitations to ride became more insistent.

When an overzealous driver grabbed Edna's arm to pull her into his vehicle, Rowland intervened sharply. The man backed off smartly, but it left them both uneasy in the chaotic jostle of the dockside.

"I'm beginning to think standing here is not the best idea," Rowland murmured. He checked his watch. It had been nearly half an hour since Clyde and Milton had left.

"We could have walked there by now." Edna was more cross than concerned.

Rowland glanced at the nearby taxi drivers who stood watching for the next opportunity to make their case.

"Perhaps we should start walking; the hotel's less than a mile away."

Edna nodded. "Yes, let's. There's probably been some mix-up about where exactly we're waiting."

They set out into the fog, from which the sun seemed to rise into a sky still stained red by dawn. Despite the frenetic, congested activity of the port, traffic on the Bund was light at this early hour. At every intersection, bearded Indian policemen directed horse-drawn, man-drawn, and motorised vehicles with expansive gestures. The background babble was multilingual—Rowland recognised French, Russian, English, and German in amongst what he guessed was Cantonese, Mandarin, or perhaps one of languages of the Indian subcontinent.

They wove through the bustle, dodging the blind hurtle of trams and crossing the Bund to the sparser foot traffic on the other side. People were dressed in the tailored clothes of the West, the looser styles of the East, and unique fusions that would be outlandish anywhere but Shanghai.

A roadside stall selling painted fans caught Edna's eye, and she begged for a minute to browse. Rowland stood by as she searched through its wares. He was a little bemused that the sculptress would be attracted to fans when the Shanghai wind cut to the bone. They purchased three silk and ebony pieces before they continued. Edna's excitement was contagious, and Rowland found himself less resistant to this sojourn in the East. Perhaps it would not be as bad as he feared.

They made their way quickly past the stately headquarters of banks and consulates, and the baroque towers of the *North China Daily News* Building. Rowland turned up the collar of his overcoat against the wind while Edna purchased hot chestnuts from a cart. He was glad his friends had decided to accompany him.

"*Entschuldigung sie.*" Someone tapped his shoulder from behind.

He might have turned if Edna had not screamed. As it was, the butt of the gun glanced off his shoulder, rather than knocking him unconscious, and he was in a position to resist the assault that followed. There were half a dozen of them, solid men in dark western suits. They said nothing as they grabbed Rowland and tried to force a hood over his head.

"Ed! Run!"

The sculptress did so, but towards him, shouting for help at the same time.

"Oi! What the hell do you think you're doing?" Clyde's voice. He dragged two men off Rowland and smacked their heads together.

Rowland struggled to free himself from the others. Milton joined the fray. They were outnumbered, but assisted by the fact that resistance had not been anticipated.

A black Buick screeched to a halt beside the skirmish, and its doors were flung open. Rowland's attackers scrambled for the idling motorcar. More help arrived now—security guards from the buildings on the Bund, the Indian traffic policeman, and the chestnut vendor. Rowland attempted to hold onto one of his assailants, but the man twisted and kicked and leapt into the waiting vehicle. The Buick's wheels squealed as it sped away.

Clyde straightened, panting. "Well, that warmed us up."

Rowland picked up Edna's handbag, which had been dropped in the scuffle, and returned it to her. "You all right, Ed?"

She nodded. "It's jolly lucky that Milt and Clyde turned up."

"Bit of a problem checking in without Rowly," Milton said, dusting off his hat. "They eventually sent another car, but it returned without you."

"We figured you'd given up and taken shanks's pony," Clyde added. "So we left our trunks with the porter and came out to find you."

"Damn. Of course." Rowland grimaced. The reservation was under Sinclair—he should have realised before he'd sent them on ahead.

"As Ed said, it was lucky." Clyde shook his head. "Were they trying to rob you, Rowly?"

"Kidnappers, sir," the traffic policeman interrupted. "There have been several incidents in the past weeks. Targeting Europeans generally."

"Oh, I see." Rowland thanked him and the other men who had come to their aid, a little unsure as to what to do next.

Edna pulled the chestnut vendor aside and purchased hot chestnuts in paper cones for all. The security guards thanked her in Russian and returned to their posts, while the policeman advised Rowland to report the incident to the relevant authorities, for what it was worth, from the comfort of Cathay. "You should proceed there as soon as possible, sir. The Bund can be a dangerous place to stroll."

They were met at the hotel entrance by the concierge—a sleek, fat man in a tailcoat who introduced himself as Mr. Van Hagen. He gave sharp instructions in Mandarin and pidgin, sending the young Chinese porters scurrying to see to the luggage, and apologised profusely for having refused Milton and Clyde earlier.

"Not at all, Mr. Van Hagen," Rowland said as he signed the guestbook. "It was my mistake."

Van Hagen checked them in and handed Rowland a thick envelope of China's new currency. The not-inconsequential sum had apparently been arranged for their convenience and use by Wilfred. Van Hagan explained the exchange rate and assured Rowland that the Copley would be happy to cash his cheques as required. Once this was done, he personally took the Australians up to the ninth floor, to one of the hotel's apartments deluxe on the side of the building which overlooked the Bund.

"Oh my, how beautiful." Edna peered through the doorway into the drawing room of the "Chinese Suite." Designed for visiting aristocracy, the apartment included servants' quarters to accommodate ladies' maids and gentlemen's valets. Of course the party from Sydney had neither.

"Shall we go in, Ed?" Rowland said, amused by the manner in which she lingered on the threshold.

Edna laughed. "It's so grand and exotic, Rowly. I forgot for a moment that we weren't just sightseeing."

Rowland Sinclair was accustomed to first class travel and accommodation. Indeed, in his company, his friends, too, had become so. But they, unlike Rowland, had at least a memory of humbler circumstances.

"After you," he said enjoying the sculptress's undisguised delight.

Edna stepped into the drawing room, her face lifted towards the oxblood red ceiling and the lanterns which hung therefrom. A chaise longue upholstered in pale gold brocade rested along one wall, a picture window overlooking the Bund on the opposite. Through a semicircular moon gate was the formal dining room—silk panelled walls, a round table surrounded by chairs of lacquered blackwood. Intricately carved jade lions guarded the partition.

Milton's gaze was more utilitarian, directed at locating the drinks cabinet rather than admiring the furniture. Rowland spoke to the concierge about reporting the attempted abduction.

Van Hagen nodded gravely. "Yes, of course, Mr. Sinclair. I shall call the police immediately." He cleared his throat. "And as you are travelling without servants on this occasion, sir, I shall send up some chambermaids to see to your unpacking."

"Please don't trouble yourself, Mr. Van Hagen. I'm sure we'll manage."

"It'll be no trouble, sir. This is the Cathay. We pride ourselves on the fact that our guests are not required to manage."

Chapter Five

ABDUCTED!

Shanghai Doctor
ARMED BANDITS

SHANGHAI, January 31

The foreign community here was rocked to its founda-
tions yesterday afternoon, when Dr. Cecil Robertson,
President of the Shanghai Medical Society, was abducted
by a gang of armed kidnappers in broad day light...a
wheelbarrow was trundled in front of Dr. Robertson's
car and was immediately followed by the appearance of
four armed men. These ejected the Chinese chauffeur,
took the wheel and menaced the doctor with pistols.
They then raced at breakneck speed through the city.
The doctor, who was taking the Chinese child to the
hospital, had a desperate struggle with the kidnappers,
one of whom fired three shots, one of which penetrated
the white man's arm. Even this failed to prevent the
doctor from resisting. On the outskirts of the city, the

robbers attempted to take Dr. Robertson's gold watch and 250 dollars, but he made a last desperate effort and wrenched open the door. Gathering the child in his arms, he leaped for safety. The police are baffled as to the motive of the crime, which is the most desperate attempt to kidnap a foreigner ever made here.

—*Maitland Daily Mercury*, 1 February 1934

When the concierge left to call the police and organise refreshments and chambermaids, they explored the suite properly, uninhibited now with their excitement and awe. Each room seemed more exquisite than the one before.

"It's immensely kind of Wilfred to book this for us," Edna murmured as she looked around one of the vast bedrooms. "Clearly he's not cross with you anymore, Rowly."

"I wouldn't go quite that far." Rowland surveyed the congested Huangpu from the window. The Bund was busier now as the commercial day began. "Wil made the reservation for himself, Kate, and the boys. I expect they would have come across with the boys' nannies, if Kate's father hadn't passed away."

Edna tested the carved bed in the room, bouncing gently on the mattress. "Poor Kate. The time away might have done her the world of good. It's such a shame they had to cancel their trip."

"Old Mr. Baird's estate is in a bit of mess, from what Wil tells me," Rowland replied. "Kate's brother died in the war, and so there are no male heirs to take over the farm. It's resulted in something of a brawl."

"Oh, dear." Edna blanched. They had all met the hot-blooded Bairds a couple of years before.

"At least the proletariat can die quietly without a family scrap over their worldly goods," Milton murmured. "Believe you me, no one's going to fight over the Isaacs family heirlooms, such as they are."

"I wouldn't be so sure." Clyde inspected the craftsmanship on the elaborate carved bedposts. "When my grandmother passed away, there was one helluva battle over who got the old lady's collection of preserving jars. Aunt Bessie still won't speak to us."

Edna smiled. "Well, even if Wil hasn't forgiven you completely, Rowly, he trusts you enough to take his place here."

"Yes." Rowland elected not to disillusion her by pointing out that he was there merely to bear the Sinclair name into meetings. If it was confidence, it was of the barest kind.

Edna lay back, staring up at the serpentine dragons carved into the top of the headboard. "May I have this bedroom?"

"Are you asking us to leave?" Milton settled into the lion-footed armchair to demonstrate that he had no intention of doing so.

"Not at all. I just like this bed, and the room's only got one window." Edna sat up and wrapped her arms around her knees. "If we took down that painting, we'd have a beautiful blank wall."

Rowland laughed. "I see."

"You've created a monster, Rowly," Clyde grumbled. "She thinks she's DeMille."

Edna had brought a projector, as well as the Bell and Howell, to Shanghai. As they expected the sojourn to extend for some months, the sculptress was determined to use the time, as well as the inspiration of the exotic trading port, to best effect. Already she could feel dragons evolving from clay beneath her fingers, towering hybrids of modern commercial ferocity and ancient ritual, creatures of many and varied faces... Perhaps she would cast them in bronze, then, in time, her dragons would develop a green patina like the pyramidal roof of the Cathay. But sculpting would have to wait until they returned to Sydney. She would instead capture the detail and movement of this city of dragons on film.

A knock at the door to the suite interrupted them. Rowland

made his way out and duly admitted a uniformed officer, who introduced himself as Constable Bethell of the Foreign Branch of the Shanghai Municipal Police.

Among the four of them, they gave the policemen an account of what had happened. Rowland did his best to describe his attackers. "They might have been German," he said. "They spoke German at least."

Bethell made notes, but it was clear that he did not anticipate that there was any personal nature to the crime nor hold out much hope of apprehending the culprits.

"I'm afraid attempts to abduct Europeans are far from unusual in Shanghai," he informed them. "They are usually entirely opportunistic. You say you arrived in Shanghai only this morning, sir?"

"Yes."

"And who knew of your arrival, sir?"

"Any number of people I suppose. The hotel was told to expect us, I have a meeting later today, and many people would have seen us arrive, though they wouldn't have known our names."

"And you walked from the port?"

"It's barely any distance."

"It's enough, Mr. Sinclair. Kidnappers in Shanghai are organised and systematic. They probably had a lookout watching the liners who noticed you and Miss Higgins leave the port on foot and somehow signalled the others. Of course, they wouldn't have anticipated the arrival of Mr. Isaacs and Mr. Watson Jones."

"But how would they have known Rowly and Ed were worth kidnapping?" Clyde asked.

Bethell glanced around the elegant drawing room. "Can I assume you disembarked with the first class passengers, Mr. Sinclair?"

Rowland grimaced. "I see." Put like that it seemed they'd been almost inviting abduction.

The policeman took his leave, promising to notify Rowland of any developments. "You'll find the Bund is quite safe during the day," he said in parting. "Villains don't seem to keep ordinary business hours. In any case, sirs, madam, welcome to Shanghai."

Waiters arrived as Bethell left, with the trays of tea and cakes Van Hagen had ordered on their behalf, and a sheaf of correspondence. Most of the letters and telegrams were for Rowland, with one for Edna.

"It seems kidnapping here is as ordinary as fish on Friday," Clyde said as they sat to partake the mid-morning repast.

"We're on the other side of the world, I suppose," Edna said, frowning as she looked at the envelope in her hand.

"We'll have to remember to be more careful." Rowland helped himself to a pastry.

Edna curled up on the couch beside Rowland as she opened her letter. "I wonder what kind of ransom they would have demanded for us?" she said distractedly.

"There's probably a going rate," Rowland murmured.

"They only grabbed Rowly," Milton pointed out, grinning wickedly. "Clearly they didn't think you were worth the trouble."

Edna called the poet an idiot as Clyde chuckled. Rowland, too, smiled, though he did wonder if there was anything to Milton's observation. Perhaps the gang in question only targeted men. It seemed unlikely that they could have been after him particularly. He'd not been in Shanghai long enough to have enemies.

Edna had fallen silent beside him. Rowland sensed a disquiet in her manner and asked her gently for its cause.

She folded the letter she'd been reading. "It's from Bertie."

"Good lord, that's a bit keen. He must have posted it before we even left!"

"How did he know where we'd be staying?" Clyde asked.

"Perhaps he guessed." Milton helped himself to a cucumber sandwich and pointed it at Rowland. "It wouldn't be too wild a supposition to assume that a Sinclair would stay at the best hotel in Shanghai. What does he say?"

Edna handed him the page, and the poet read quickly. He drew back in surprise. "Blimey Charlie, Middleton thinks the two of you are going to settle down when you return from Shanghai." He laughed loudly. "The poor bloody fool."

Edna took the page back and folded it into its envelope.

"What are you doing?"

"I'm sending it back."

"Perhaps you should tell him you don't intend to marry him." Milton regarded her disapprovingly. "After what he did to Rowly last year, I'm surprised you're even speaking to the mongrel!"

"Steady on, Milt." Rowland came instinctively to Edna's defence. "Middleton's a buffoon, but it's not like he tried to kill me."

"You very nearly ended up married!"

"They were desperate times," Clyde agreed.

"You need to tell the bloke to sod off, Ed!" the poet warned. "Stop leading him on."

Edna bit her lip. "Oh Milt—I have, many times. But it's like he can't hear it."

Milton's face softened as he heard the hint of despair in her voice, and he continued more kindly. "Well, he has time now to get over his deafness," he said. "If he's still carrying on when we get back, Rowly, Clyde and I will sort him out."

Edna smiled wistfully. "It's just a letter, sent nearly two weeks ago. He will have seen reason by now."

Rowland left his opinion of the journalist unspoken. But perhaps the sculptress's optimism was sound. If Middleton's current insanity was induced by passion, a couple of months away from the object of it might see him return to reason.

The chambermaids and room boys Van Hagen had insisted upon arrived, escorted to the suite by a man in a morning suit which bore the crest of the Cathay Hotel. His black hair was parted and slicked back from a round, boyish face that dimpled when he smiled; his collar was starched and folded crisply over a grey cravat held in place by gold pin bearing the double lion crest of the Cathay. He introduced himself as Wing Zau and explained that he had been assigned to the suite and Rowland Sinclair, with Mr. Van Hagen's compliments.

"Please thank Mr. Van Hagen, Mr. Wing, but I don't think—"

"Rowly," Milton pulled him aside before he could finish. "I think we should keep him."

"He's a gentleman's valet, not a stray puppy," Rowland whispered. "I don't need someone to hold my cufflinks."

"I know that, comrade, but he looks like a local. It could be handy."

"I know Shanghai very well, sir, and I'm fluent in Cantonese, Mandarin, Shanghainese, pidgin, and Old Norse," Wing offered hopefully. He spoke slowly but clearly, with an accent that was carefully British.

"Really?" Edna was intrigued. "Old Norse?"

Wing Zau nodded. "Alas, I have not had as much call to practise my Old Norse as I would have liked, but should a Viking take a room at the Cathay, I shall be ready to converse with him."

Rowland's brow rose. Wing seemed very unlike the professionally reserved manservants he'd encountered from time to time.

"Come on, Rowly," Milton whispered. "You'll offend him if you refuse."

Rowland wavered. Having someone on hand who could speak the languages he couldn't might indeed prove useful. But the thought of engaging a butler seemed ridiculous.

Wing spoke up. "I understand, Mr. Sinclair. I only hope that Mr. Van Hagen will not be too disappointed with my inability to please you—or angry; he's often angry." He sighed, his shoulders slumping despondently.

"Good Lord!" Clyde blurted. "Don't forget to tell him about your sick mother, mate."

Edna giggled, delighted with the transparent appeal to Rowland's sense of compassion.

Regardless of its lack of subtlety, Rowland relented, turning back to the valet. "Thank you, Mr. Wing. We'd be very pleased of your help."

Wing bowed. "Excellent, sir." He began immediately— enthusiastically directing the maids and boys, who spoke only Shanghainese, in the task of unpacking. Clyde jumped up to ensure that the contents of Danny Dong's chest did not get caught up in Wing's efficiency. After enquiring after their plans, the valet arranged for luncheon to be delivered to the suite and ensured the gentlemen's dinner suits were pressed for the evening meal. As he did so, he advised them of Shanghai's sights and places of interest further afield.

"Why thank you, Mr. Wing," Edna said, touched that in addition to everything else, he'd found time to set out her hairbrush and perfume on the dresser in the bedroom she'd chosen. "That was very thoughtful."

"Gratitude is kindest when it is unnecessary, Miss Higgins. I merely do my duty," Wing replied. "I am, after all, here to anticipate and accommodate your every want."

"In that case, do you know anything about the abduction of Europeans in Shanghai, Mr. Wing?"

"I'm afraid we're not permitted to abduct people."

Rowland laughed.

"Forgive me," Wing said. "I make a small joke."

Edna smiled. "What I meant was: have you heard anything about who might be abducting people? The police didn't tell us a great deal."

Wing frowned. "It's a bad business, but not one that's owned by one man."

"What do you mean?"

"There are many in the business of abduction." Wing shrugged. "Sometimes ransom is asked, sometimes not."

Rowland glanced at his watch. "I'd better get on. I'm supposed to meet some chap from the Grazier's Association at three."

Clyde stood. "We should go with you, in case someone tries to snatch you again."

"I don't think anyone was actually trying to abduct me, Clyde." Rowland reached for his hat. "No more than any other foreigner, anyway."

"Even so."

Rowland shook his head. "I'm not leaving the hotel, Clyde." He smiled as he added, "And as Mr. Wing has just explained, the staff are not allowed to abduct people."

Chapter Six

"Loved It"

WE are indebted to a daily for publishing a letter from
a Brisbane society girl holidaying in Shanghai, in the
war zone. It reads like this, in part:

'We were in the Cathay Hotel when the first
Japanese bomb hit the city. We did not take the slightest
notice, and when we came out the streets were full of
armoured cars and Japanese soldiers, and a man was
killed a few yards from where we were standing. It was
awfully thrilling and I just loved every minute of it.'

—*Truth*, 21 February 1932

The Jasmine Lounge on the ground floor of the Cathay Hotel
was a tribute to its founder's very British fondness for tea and
prided itself on offering every blend of tisane known to man. A
kaleidoscope of guests was seated at tables draped in crisp white

linen. Westerners, Chinese, and Indians in their various styles of dress, an American woman in what looked like a modified sari, young Chinese men in boaters and spats, a European man in the robes and skullcap of a Chinese monk. Waiters took orders, and a sommelier advised patrons on the various fusions and brews.

Rowland scanned the tables for the gentleman he was to meet here. Immediately he spotted Alastair Blanshard, whose imposing stature and bright red hair were as distinctive here as they had been in Munich eighteen months before. They'd last parted in distinctly tense circumstances. The man with Blanshard was greying at the temples and his sandy hair cut short in military style: Andrew Petty, of Highland Mercantile, according to the message which had been left at the reception desk. Petty was the wool consignor with whom Wilfred had been dealing. What Blanshard was doing in Shanghai, let alone why he joining them, Rowland had no idea. Both men were drinking cocktails rather than tea.

Rowland made his way to the table. Petty looked up first.

"Mr. Petty," Rowland began, offering his hand.

Petty looked bewildered. "I don't believe I've had the pleasure."

Blanshard groaned. "This, old boy, is Rowland Sinclair."

Petty looked back at Rowland, clearly alarmed. "Rowland? Where the hell is Wilfred?"

"My brother was unavoidably detained, gentlemen," Rowland said evenly. "He's sent me in his stead."

"For pity's sake! We're talking about international trade, high-level negotiations, not his spot in the local batting lineup." Petty slammed down his cocktail and stood.

"Clearly you underestimate how seriously Wilfred takes cricket," Rowland said, smiling faintly.

Petty stared at him.

"Andrew..." Blanshard cautioned.

Petty sighed. "Yes, very well. Sit down, Sinclair. What will you drink?"

"Gin."

"So," Blanshard began as they waited for the drink to arrive, "you're looking well, Sinclair."

Petty's eyes narrowed.

"This particular Mr. Sinclair and I met in Munich," Blanshard explained briefly. He turned to Rowland. "I believe you ran into a spot of trouble before you left Germany."

"You might say that," Rowland replied.

"All's well that ends well, I suppose."

"I'm afraid we're unlikely to see an end to it until Germany is no longer in the grip of the Nazis."

Startled, Petty glanced over his shoulder. "Mr. Sinclair, this is a treaty port. All the great trading nations are represented here. You would be well advised to be a little more circumspect with your political opinions."

"I didn't realise you were in the wool business, Mr. Blanshard," Rowland said carefully. When last they'd met, Alastair Blanshard had been a spy of sorts. They'd worked together to thwart Eric Campbell's attempts to meet Adolf Hitler and bring European fascism to Australia. They'd succeeded, but the cost had been high, for Rowland at least.

Blanshard smiled. "I'm not. I just happened to join Andrew for a drink." He drained the last of his cocktail. "In fact, I think I might leave you chaps to it." He stood and pushed in his chair. "Welcome to Shanghai, Sinclair. Don't let Andrew here lead you astray."

They watched him leave the lounge. Then Petty cleared his throat. "Well then, it seems we're in a bit of a pickle, Sinclair."

"How so, Mr. Petty?"

Petty sat back. "Your being so woefully inexperienced in matters of commerce and diplomacy, not to mention the particular vagaries of Shanghai. The Sinclair seat at these meetings is one of great influence and import."

"I see."

"It's jolly fortunate we have a few days before the first meeting. I'll do what I can to school you, as it were."

"That's very kind of you, but—"

"Don't look so appalled, Sinclair. I'm not proposing to teach you geometry—simply how things work over here. I daresay you'll enjoy the experience." He signalled a waiter and ordered another round of drinks. "I'm otherwise engaged tomorrow, but what say I collect you after breakfast the following day—Wednesday? About ten o'clock? We should start by introducing you to Shanghai."

"I'm travelling with a party," Rowland said, unsure what it was that Petty felt he needed to teach him.

"I'm sure they'll be able to spare you. I'd like to make sure we understand each other, and that you understand how things are done here."

And so, while Rowland did not actually agree, he was herded into acquiescence. They finished their drinks as Petty spoke to Rowland about the wool market and the potential for Australian pastoralists to profit in the current climate. Rowland set his face in a show of attention. For a moment, he wondered if he should tell Petty that he would not be making any decisions on Wilfred's behalf, but perhaps such a confession would undermine whatever value his presence would achieve. Wilfred had assured him that there would be nothing that he could not take on advisement. He was relying on that being the case.

"*Heil* Hitler!"

A sharp, loud Fascist salute caught Rowland's attention a couple of tables away. A young man joining a table. More subdued greetings in return from those already seated, and the newcomer was hastily found a chair.

Petty grimaced. "Gauche, isn't it? The young like to bring attention to themselves. In my day we were taught the value of discretion."

Rowland's eyes darkened as he bit back comment. The presence of Nazis outside Europe disturbed more than surprised him. Shanghai was a treaty port, to which each nation brought its own interests, culture, and politics. And Hitler's was an expansionist regime.

***

Originally and officially named the Horse and Hound, the bar at the Cathay Hotel had been designed to have the character of an English pub. A mecca for touring jazz bands, it had taken on a different identity and was now called simply the Jazz Bar. On this night, the Jazz Bar was busy—an after-dinner crowd who'd come to drink and dance and revel. The clientele was racially diverse but uniform in its elegance. Europeans and Shanghainese in evening gowns and dinner suits, in cheongsam or Mandarin-collared jackets, sipped cocktails at tables around the dance floor. Reminiscent of the most exclusive private clubs, the venue currently boasted the talents of a touring jazz band from Chicago and featured the vocal talents of a Chinese artist. The music was a mix of American and Shanghai's own brand of swing.

Rowland sat at a table, drawing idly in the notebook he always carried. He sketched the dark-skinned band members in their white jackets in sparse lines that captured the energy and movement of each musician. The Chinese vocalist, in particular, drew the eye. Rowland was looking forward to unpacking the small trunk of paints and brushes that he and Clyde had brought with them. Wing Zau had already procured easels from somewhere; the valet seemed to have a talent for preempting their requirements.

A waiter arrived bearing cocktails, which he set down on the low table. The drinks proved a clarion call for Milton, who detached himself from a conversation on the other side of the room to claim his vodka martini.

"Where's Ed?" Clyde asked, removing a cherry from a concoction of gin and pineapple juice.

Rowland motioned towards the dance floor. The sculptress was easy to spot, her black cheongsam striking against the cream of her skin. Her hair had been arranged into an elaborate twisted knot by Wing Zau, whose skills, it seemed, were many. Edna was at that moment in the arms of a fair-haired gentleman attired in what appeared to be a military dress uniform.

"Who's the bloke?" Clyde asked.

"I'm not sure," Rowland replied. "He cut in about a bracket ago." He frowned. "Do you think Ed needs rescuing? Maybe I should—"

"She doesn't look unhappy, comrade." Milton squinted over the rim of his glass. He pointed at the line of men gathered on the edge of the floor. "There are plenty of chaps waiting for the opportunity to cut in. Jump the queue, and you'll probably start a fight."

"Excuse me, gentlemen." They stood hastily as a young woman in a deep red gown approached. Her hair was a silvery blonde, and her eyes wide and blue. She smiled. "I haven't seen you gentlemen here before."

Rowland introduced himself and his companions. "We arrived in Shanghai this morning."

"I bid you welcome then, gentlemen. My name is Alexandra Romanova."

"Would you like to join us, Miss Romanova?" Milton asked.

"I only came to ask if you would care to dance."

The Australians glanced at each other a little awkwardly. It was not so much that the young lady was issuing the invitation—they lived with Edna and were accustomed to the gentler sex dragging them onto the dance floor in a manner that might have been considered too forward in certain circles—it was that they were unsure to which of the three of them the invitation was directed. In the end, Milton sought clarification, in his fashion.

"The one red leaf, the last of its clan, that dances as often as dance it can."

"Coleridge," Rowland murmured. He smiled apologetically at Alexandra. "Mr. Isaacs is concerned that you might find it too much of an imposition to dance with all of us."

"Oh no." She turned to look at a group of young ladies gathered near the stage. "I have friends if you all wish to have tickets."

"Tickets?"

"Dance tickets."

"You have to buy tickets to dance?"

"With a taxi girl, yes."

For a moment there was silence, as they individually contemplated what it was that a taxi girl did. Rowland broke it. "Why not? We'll all have tickets."

"It'll be one pound for each dance," Alexandra said sweetly over her shoulder as she went to fetch two more girls.

Clyde choked. "For God's sake, Rowly, what are you doing?"

"I seemed a bit rude to say we didn't want to dance with them."

"Rowly, I hate dancing. You're going to pay some girl an entire pound to torture me."

Milton laughed. "Money well spent, if you ask me."

"When they say dance, they do mean *dance*, don't they, Rowly?" Clyde said uneasily.

Rowland stopped. He hadn't thought of that. He glanced at the three women making their way over. Undeniably attractive, they walked with a kind of high-heeled purpose. "I'm pretty sure they won't be able to overpower us…"

Milton laughed. "I may not put up much of a fight."

Chapter Seven

RUSSIAN REFUGEES

PATHETIC CIRCUMSTANCES

Pathetic details of the flight of Russian refugee women in Shanghai are given in a report of the Nansen International Office for Refugees, issued in Geneva. After appealing to the League to supply funds for the relief of the Russian exiles, the Nansen Office presents the report of its Shanghai representative, who, referring to the large number of Russian women in disreputable houses, contends: "I cannot but add the general complicity, not only of residents, but often also of distinguished travellers."

—*Singleton Argus*, 2 November 1934

In the course of the first dance, Alexandra Romanova chatted gaily about music, the club, and her favourite drinks. At the end of the song, she politely informed Rowland that the next dance would cost him another pound. Somewhat relieved that the nature of the transaction was at least now clear, Rowland paid for another turn about the floor.

"Were you born in Shanghai, Miss Romanova?"

"No, we—my family—fled Russia during the revolution. I was a little girl."

"I see."

"Papa was a soldier, loyal to the tsar. They fought the Red Army, but, in the end, there was nothing left but to run. Now we must work in small jobs, as taxi girls and security guards, but one day, Mr. Sinclair, we will return and reclaim what was ours from the filthy Bolsheviks."

Rowland led into a turn. Milton and Clyde, both of whom were Communists, seemed to have quit the dance floor. He couldn't see either. "Do you remember much of Russia?"

Alexandra looked up at him, her sky-blue eyes moistening. "I remember a big house and servants. I had a pony called Mischa. My brother played violin, and I wanted to dance with the ballet." She laughed bitterly. "Now we are without a country, Sergei teaches fat, tone-deaf children to play, and I dance here."

Rowland hesitated, unsure how to respond, guilty now for dancing with a girl who clearly resented having to do so. In the end he said simply, "I'm sorry."

"No, Mr. Sinclair," she said hastily. "You dance beautifully! You don't haggle about price! The Italians haggle—'I have only two shillings,' they say. You are polite and handsome, and you smell very nice."

Embarrassed now, Rowland laughed. Alexandra seemed to relax. She told him about the Russian theatre opening in the French Concession—that part of Shanghai which had been conceded for French settlement. "There are more Russians than French people living there now."

When the song finished, Rowland suggested a drink. They

returned to the table, and found Milton and Clyde already there.

"Did you not wish to dance again?" Alexandra looked for her friends. "Anya and Natalia are excellent partners and very pretty."

"Anya's toes took a bit of a battering dancing with Clyde," Milton replied. "Natalia's card was booked, I think."

"Do you work here every day?" Rowland handed Alexandra a cocktail of champagne and cream.

"In the evenings, yes." She sipped the drink, and then accepted Rowland's handkerchief to wipe the froth from her upper lip. "You did not say, Mr. Sinclair, why do you come here?"

"We're staying in the hotel," Rowland replied. "The Jazz Club was recommended by the valet."

"No, no, I mean Shanghai. What brings you all to Shanghai?"

"Rowly's here on business," Milton said. "We just tagged along."

Alexandra locked her eyes on Rowland's. "Perhaps you will come back tomorrow."

Before Rowland could reply, a gentleman interrupted to present his ticket and claim the dance for which he'd paid. Alexandra reacted with professional courtesy, detaching herself immediately to attend to this new client.

As the taxi girl disappeared into the crowd upon the dance floor, Edna returned—the man with whom she'd been dancing earlier in tow: a handsome, if slightly heavy man who looked to be about thirty-five. His hair was fair, parted cleanly, and slicked back, his attire evocative of the uniforms worn by the European military elite. She introduced him as Count Nickolai Kruznetsov. He nodded stiffly.

Rowland offered the count his hand. For a moment Kruznetsov stood motionless, and then he accepted the handshake warmly. "Yes!" he said. "Let us do away with formalities. You must call me Nicky. I will call you..." He looked at Edna questioningly.

"Rowly," she said.

"Rowly! I will call you Rowly!"

He shook Clyde and Milton's hands in turn, and for a few minutes they exchanged the usual pleasantries. Kruznetsov was in flamboyantly high spirits, buying drinks with a generosity that was commensurate with his title.

Even so, it seemed the count worked as a private security guard for a Shanghainese businessman.

"Are you good gentlemen filmmakers?" he asked. "Shanghai is popular in Hollywood films now."

Milton shook his head. "I suppose Ed's been telling you about her camera—it's a bit of a stretch to call her a filmmaker."

"Oh no, Edna belongs in front of the camera. She is too beautiful to be otherwise."

Clyde groaned.

"I do act, as it happens." Edna smiled at Kruznetsov. "I even had a part in a film back home."

"You were sacked," Milton reminded her.

"The director and I had a difference of opinion." Edna tossed her head indignantly. "He was entirely unreasonable."

"Clearly the man was a buffoon," Kruznetsov declared. "My cousin Ivan drives for Warner Orland. I could arrange an introduction; perhaps he might find you a part in the film he is making here."

"Who's Warner Orland?" Clyde asked.

"He's the actor who plays Charlie Chan, I think," Rowland said. Kruznetsov nodded. "He is what they call a Hollywood star."

"That would be wonderful, Nicky," Edna said enthusiastically. "I saw Charlie Chan in London at the cinema last year. I'd love to meet him."

Kruznetsov puffed a little. "I will speak to Ivan tomorrow. He will tell this Warner Orland that he must find a part for you."

Milton shook his head. "You know not what you do, comrade."

The count's face clouded. His eyes flashed dangerously. "Do not call me comrade, sir! That is the title of red vermin traitors."

Milton shrugged. "Well, I could call you sweetheart," he said airily, "but we hardly know each other."

Kruznetsov pulled back a clenched fist. Rowland stepped between the two. "Steady on there, Nicky."

Edna moved to defray the tension by taking Kruznetsov back onto the dance floor.

"Our friend Nicky is a White Russian I expect," Rowland said under his breath as he watched them embark on a quickstep.

"I gathered," Milton replied quietly. "You know, once upon a time I would have said bugger it—his type deserved everything they got in the revolution."

"Once?"

Milton shrugged. "I'm no longer as hostile to the privileged upper classes as I once was."

"Why?"

Milton grinned and nudged Rowland companionably. "Let's just say my standards have slipped."

Rowland laughed.

"Don't get me wrong, I still believe in the revolution, I just find myself more able to have some sympathy for the usurped." He grimaced. "I'll try and remember not to call him comrade."

"I'm not sure it'll make a difference." Clyde scowled. "He looks pretty bloody dark."

Milton folded his arms. "Well, it's not as if Ed's likely to marry the bloke. He's probably just one of her passing fancies."

"Yes." Rowland's eyes were still on the dance floor. "It's not necessary that Count Kruznetsov likes us."

Clyde and Milton stood by him sympathetically. Rowland's torch for Edna was well established, as was her determination to keep the men she loved separate from those she took as lovers. Her reasons were complicated and probably irrational, but her resolve was absolute. Edna Higgins would be known for her art, and not by the name of a husband. It was, to be honest, not an uncommon decision among the free-minded suffragists of the modern age. It was probably more unusual that her passion for an independent life seemed only to strengthen Rowland's passion for her.

When Edna and Kruznetsov finally left the dance floor, the sculptress had managed to mollify the Russian. He apologised for any bad temper on his part and ordered champagne for them all. Milton called him Nicky loudly and often and it seemed all was forgiven.

Alexandra Romanova found Rowland again. "I have a gap in my card. Would you care to dance with me again?"

"It would be my pleasure." Rowland took her into his arms for a jazz waltz. She asked him about London, and once he'd corrected her misapprehension that he was English, he told her about Sydney and the grazing property near Yass on which he'd been born.

Edna waved as she and Kruznetsov whirled past.

"Is that your wife?" Alexandra enquired. "She is very beautiful."

"No, she's not my wife, but yes, she is very beautiful."

"Your wife is not here?"

"I'm afraid I don't have a wife." Rowland was somewhat bemused by the question.

She frowned slightly, then shook her head, laughing. "I am sorry. So many men take a wife and then will not admit to having done so, and do not behave as if they have done so. Especially when they are dancing with another."

"I see." Rowland met her eye. "I'm not married. I give you my word."

At the end of the dance, Alexandra declined to take her fee. "No, that time was my gift to you. You may return it by inviting me to the take tea and cakes with you, tomorrow."

Rowland smiled. Perhaps this was why she had wanted to establish that he was unmarried. "Would you do me the honour of joining me for tea and cakes tomorrow afternoon, Miss Romanova?"

"I do believe I'm free at four, Mr. Sinclair."

"Shall I send a car for you?"

"No, I'll call here at the hotel. The Cathay's tearoom is the best in Shanghai."

———

Edna stood at the window of the Chinese Suite filming the awakening Huangpu. The river came gradually to life in the soft light, many thousands of stories floating on its waters. Engrossed in trying to capture the vista on celluloid, the sculptress was humming along before she fully registered that someone was singing "Honeysuckle Rose," belted out with a gravelly volume of which Fats Waller would have approved. Intrigued, she placed her camera on the window's wide sill and peered quietly around the moon gate into the dining room. Wing Zau danced as he filled the warming trays on the sideboard in preparation for breakfast. He took the plates from the traymobile and shuffled to the sideboard, crooning "Goodness knows, Honeysuckle Rose" like he was centrestage at the Tivoli.

When finally he noticed Edna, he froze, the song dying suddenly on his lips, an embarrassed stutter in its place.

"Oh don't stop, Mr. Wing." Edna walked over to take the plate of bacon from his hands and place it in one of the silver dishes. "I love this song."

"I apologise, Miss Higgins." Wing looked mortified. "I was just humming, and then I sang a couple of bars, and then...I didn't intend to become so loud."

"I do that all the time." Edna closed the lid of the warming tray. She collected the teapot from the traymobile and sang, "Every honeybee fills with jealousy, when they see you out with me," as she poured tea into two of the cups set out on the table. "Sit down and have a cup of tea, Mr. Wing. The others won't be up for ages."

Wing hesitated.

Edna reached for the sugar bowl. "Please?"

Wing took the chair beside hers reluctantly, sipping his tea stiffly. Edna peppered him with questions, searching for his opinions about the city. It was not long before Edna's complete disregard for the proper way of things thawed the manservant's reserve. They talked about Shanghai and Sydney and the world in between. Wing told the sculptress of his Australian-born cousins who, fearing persecution, had returned to Shanghai when Australia's immigration laws made it clear the Chinese were not welcome.

Wing nodded sadly. "As civilised as we have become, it is still skin we see first. The tiger recognises his own kind and devours all others."

"Is that an old Chinese saying, Mr. Wing?"

"Chinese—yes, but not old. I just now made it up." He smiled. "Still, I'm sure my honourable ancestors would have agreed."

Edna laughed.

Rowland was the first of the Australian men to venture out. He paused by the moon gate, taking in the scene framed within its circular perimeter—Edna and Wing chatting like old friends over tea. At first neither the sculptress nor the valet noticed him, engrossed in their own conversation. "Did you have a good time at the Jazz Club, Miss Higgins?" Wing asked Edna.

"Oh yes. I danced with a Russian count!"

Wing clicked his tongue disapprovingly. "Every second Russian in Shanghai seems to be a count or a duke, Miss Higgins. I do not mean to be cynical, but I do not wish you to be disappointed."

"I shan't be disappointed, Mr. Wing. I only danced with him."

"You must be careful. Wealthy foreigners are often targeted by unscrupulous men with spurious titles."

"I'm afraid my wealth is as spurious as their titles, Mr. Wing." Edna sipped her tea as amused by the valet's concern as she was by the notion that she was wealthy.

"Good morning." Rowland announced his presence.

Wing Zau stood hastily, guiltily. "Mr. Sinclair, I did not realise you were awake, sir. You didn't ring—"

"Sit down, Wing. I really don't need anyone to help me dress."

The butler remained on his feet. "Mr. Isaacs and Mr. Watson Jones..."

"Can also dress themselves."

Wing remained standing. The pause became slightly awkward.

"Taxi girls—are they all Russian?" Rowland asked suddenly.

"Many are. Despite their titles, the Russian refugees are penniless." Wing was clearly relieved to have something asked of him. "As taxi girls, they can earn a living, which, if not respectable, is not shameful."

"Nicky didn't seem penniless," Edna said, glancing at Rowland. The Russian had been insistently generous.

Wing nodded knowingly. "Russians!" he said, throwing up his hands. "They will spend a month's wages in a single night. It is as if they have not realised that their circumstances have changed."

"I see." Rowland grimaced, now uncomfortable that he had enjoyed Kruznetsov's largesse.

"It is difficult for the refugees." Wing was warming to his subject. "The better jobs are reserved for the expatriate population, the labouring jobs for the Chinese. It is not so bad in Shanghai because there are rich people here who need guards and music teachers, but north of the wall I have heard that many Russians have starved to death."

"Oh how dreadful," Edna said. "Those poor people."

The look on her face seemed to startle Wing. "I apologise, Miss Higgins. I should not speak of such things. I apologise."

"Nonsense. We want to know." She turned to Rowland. "Maybe we could help somehow...some of them at least."

"Oh, you cannot venture north of the wall, Miss Higgins. The Japanese control most of Manchuria now. It is not safe."

Rowland frowned. Having invaded Manchuria almost four years ago, the Japanese had been consolidating and expanding their control of northeast China. International condemnation seemed to have had no effect. Japan had left the League of Nations and continued on its own course. News of Japanese atrocities and the plight of the White Russians, as well as the Chinese, in Manchuria had been widely reported in Australia, sparking a kind of removed outrage and occasional fits of fundraising. He shared Edna's impulse to help, but he wasn't sure how exactly they could, on a large scale at least. "I believe the Red Cross is active in Manchuria. I'll see what I can find out," he said in the end, hoping that it would be something.

"I fear that Manchuria is beyond even the magnanimity of the West," Wing said quietly.

Chapter Eight

The Little Things

Nearly every man will tell you that if he had in hand all the time he has spent in waiting for unpunctual ladies, he might conquer the world. And he will complain that it is precisely the unpunctual ladies who are transformed into dangerous furies if they themselves are kept waiting for the tenth of a second; for they astoundingly assume that the other partner or partners to the rendezvous will stand already booted and spurred in advance until the moment of their glorious appearance. Unpunctuality (by no means the monopoly of women) has the air of being a trifle; but it is possibly more prolific than anything else in social friction, and social friction is the arch enemy of happiness.

—*Advocate*, 26 April 1934

When Alexandra Romanova failed to keep her appointment with Rowland Sinclair, he was a little disappointed but not unduly concerned. He had, after all, only met the young lady the previous evening, and perhaps in the sober light of day, she had simply reconsidered pursuing their acquaintance.

He'd left his companions exploring the French Concession, where they'd all spent the afternoon at the Russian Theatre, returning alone to the Cathay. At five o'clock he concluded that Alexandra was more than just late, and gave up. Doubting that he would be able to find his companions in order to rejoin them for the evening, he decided he would spend the time attending to correspondence, including two telegrams received from Oaklea. He had yet to report back to Wilfred of his meeting with Petty and Blanshard, and he had promised his mother and his nephew that he would write when he'd reached Shanghai. He stopped in the gift shop to purchase postcards and proceeded up to the suite.

Rowland let himself in. They'd told Wing Zau not to expect them back till after dinner, and so he anticipated he would have the suite to himself.

He removed his coat, hanging it with his hat on the rack in the marble vestibule. It was not yet completely dark. The suite's expansive windows allowed in enough twilight to make the room navigable. Rowland might have searched for a light switch had he not been intrigued by the view of the Huangpu in half light. The water seemed purple, and the junks glowed softly as they came into shore. He loosened his tie as he crossed the room to the window. The sky was streaked with crimson—Rowland presumed the sun was setting on the other side of the building. He looked down at the play of shadow and life spread out below him. One seemed always to look west at sunset, and yet there was a less spectacular but equal beauty on the eastern horizon where darkness began. He gazed out of the window for several minutes idly wondering if he should try to paint landscapes again.

Rowland put the thought firmly aside; he had never painted landscapes well.

When finally he was able to drag himself away from the view, it had become almost completely dark. He fumbled for the switch on the standard lamp by the secretaire.

It was only then, in that limited light, he noticed the figure lying on the chaise longue at the back of the room. A figure stretched out gracefully in slumber.

Rowland knew immediately that she was too still. Even so, he called her name before seizing her wrist to check for a pulse. There was none. He tried to revive her regardless, loosening the scarf around her neck. His hands came away sticky with blood "Miss Romanova, Alexandra." Nothing. She was cold. With the scarf pulled away, her throat gaped open, slashed almost to the bone.

Rowland moved back, horrified. He comprehended that the taxi girl was dead, but nothing else seemed to make any sense. Pulling himself together, he picked up the telephone and rang the reception desk.

"Yes, hello…I'm afraid… Look, a young woman's been killed in my suite. Would you mind calling the police?"

"I do beg your pardon, sir?"

Rowland repeated himself, realising even as he did so that he must sound mad or drunk or both. Right then, he wanted to be drunk.

"Please, send someone up immediately."

Within minutes the Cathay's manager arrived at the suite to ascertain the precise nature of the problem—he clearly expected it was alcohol or some kind of prank. Wealthy men often had juvenile senses of humour. He walked in, looked from Rowland to the body and then backed slowly out of the suite.

Rowland sat down to wait. There was nothing else he could do. He thought about trying to wipe the blood from his hands, but it seemed an indecent thing to do in the presence of Alexandra

Romanova's body. Her eyes were open, China blue, and seemed fixed in death upon him. The scarf he'd removed from her throat was on the floor. Without thinking he picked it up. The silk was soaked in blood and the stylised lions of the Cathay's crest embroidered upon it seemed stained a darker red.

The police did not take long to arrive. It was only when he heard the scrabble and click of the key in the lock that Rowland realised that the manager had locked him in.

The members of the Shanghai Municipal Police Force who attended the incident at the Cathay were officers of the Foreign Branch. Chief Inspector Randolph took charge of the scene, directing his men to secure it immediately.

"Am I to understand you discovered the young lady's body, Mr. Sinclair?" Randolph clasped his hands behind his back as he spoke in a fashion that was distinctly military.

"Yes."

Randolph's eyes dropped to Rowland's hands, the blood-stained cuffs of his shirt, the soaked scarf still in his hands. He signalled a man to take the scarf as evidence.

"I wasn't certain she was dead at first," Rowland said. "I thought..." He shook his head.

"Was the deceased known to you, sir?"

"Her name is Alexandra Romanova. I met her for the first time last night."

"Where?"

"The Jazz Club downstairs."

"And the nature of your relationship?"

"We danced."

"I see." Randolph rocked back on his heels. "I assume you were hopeful of becoming better acquainted, and so you brought her up to your suite."

Rowland stared at him. "Absolutely not. I left Miss Romanova at The Jazz Club."

"So you found her disagreeable?"

"I found her charming. I invited her to have tea with me this afternoon, but she didn't keep the appointment."

"I imagine you were offended and very angry that she didn't arrive as agreed?"

"Not at all. It was merely tea."

"Can you tell me what she's doing in your suite, Mr. Sinclair?"

Rowland shook his head. "Perhaps she misunderstood where we were to meet... I really don't know."

"Did you let her in, Mr. Sinclair?"

"No."

"Was there anyone else in the suite when you discovered Miss Romanova's body?"

"I don't believe so."

"Chief Inspector—" A young policeman interrupted. "There are two gentlemen and a young lady outside who insist this is their suite."

Rowland nodded. "Miss Higgins and Messrs. Isaacs and Watson Jones."

"Detain them, but do not let them in. I'll speak to them in a few minutes—I have a few questions for Mr. Sinclair first."

"Would you please let them know I'm all right?" Rowland asked the constable, or whatever it was the lower ranks were called in the Shanghai Police Force.

"Why would your friends believe otherwise, Mr. Sinclair?" Randolph's eyes narrowed.

Rowland sighed. "I don't know that they would, Chief Inspector. I just don't want them to worry."

Randolph glanced at Alexandra Romanova's lifeless body on the chaise. "Clearly, it is not you they should worry about."

It was, in fact, another two hours before the chief inspector finished questioning Rowland Sinclair. He conducted the interrogation on site rather than taking the Australian into the station. It was more a convenience than a courtesy. If the murder weapon had been discovered in the suite, he might have arrested Rowland. There were razors of course, as one would expect with three men in residence, but each was clean and stowed neatly in the bathroom beside the shaving mirror. Sinclair might have cleaned his implement—true—but a man cold enough to calmly wash the murder weapon and return it to its place would surely think to also change his bloody clothes. Randolph was a cautious man. One did not arrest a man wealthy enough to take a suite at the Cathay over the death of a penniless taxi girl unless one was very sure.

Van Hagen hastily arranged another suite for the use of the Sinclair entourage that evening. It was not as lavish, but neither was it a crime scene. Rowland showered and changed while he waited for his friends to return. By the time each of them had given statements, it was quite late in the evening.

"Rowly—" Edna opened the door of the new suite just as Rowland was pulling on a fresh shirt.

"Just a minute, Ed, I'm—"

Edna burst into the bedroom. "Rowly, are you all right?" She scrutinised him for signs of injury. Clyde and Milton were behind her. "We saw them take you out, you were covered in blood, they wouldn't tell us—"

Rowland grabbed her hand to slow her down. "I'm perfectly all right, Ed. It wasn't my blood."

She looked into his face and embraced him impulsively. "God, Rowly. We thought—"

"Didn't Inspector Randolph tell you?"

"No," Milton replied. "He's an officious sort of chap, isn't he?"

"All he'd say was that you were involved in an incident in the suite." Clyde shook his head. "Wanted to know about your movements, mostly."

"What the hell's happened, Rowly?" Milton asked.

Clyde nodded. "Unhand him, Ed. Let the man tell us what's going on."

Milton studied Rowland for a moment, before he walked out of the bedroom, beckoning them all to follow. "Rowly looks like he could use a drink." The poet located the appropriate cabinet in the sitting room and decanted generous glasses of Scotch for himself and Clyde. He poured gin for Rowland and enquired of Edna what she fancied.

"Sherry." The sculptress slipped off her shoes and curled up on the couch beside Rowland. "What happened, Rowly? Who was hurt?"

"Alexandra Romanova."

"The girl you were meeting?"

"Yes. I'm afraid she's dead."

Edna reached up and turned Rowland's face towards her own. "Start from the beginning, Rowly. What happened to her?"

Rowland shook his head. "To be honest, I don't really know." He told them how he'd come to find the body on the chaise longue. "I had hoped she was just asleep or unconscious...until I saw the blood." He bit back a curse. "Someone had cut the poor woman's throat."

"Oh, Rowly." Edna grasped his hand. "How simply ghastly!"

"It was. It took me a while to realise there was absolutely nothing I could do for her." Rowland stopped, remembering the moment too clearly. "I called the reception desk, and once they'd sent someone to establish I wasn't drunk or playing some kind of lunatic prank, they sent for the police."

"How did you not notice her immediately?" Clyde asked incredulously.

"It was getting dark and I was...watching the sunset...God." Rowland groaned as he recognised how absurd it sounded.

"I wonder what she was doing in the suite." Milton topped up Rowland's glass.

"Someone must have let her in," Clyde said. "Perhaps one of the staff."

"Where's Mr. Wing?" Edna asked suddenly.

"I don't know." Rowland frowned. They had told the valet that they'd be back after dinner, and whilst they had no particular need of him, it seemed odd, given his earlier declarations of commitment to duty, that he was not there.

"Perhaps he let Miss Romanova in and—" Milton stopped short of accusing the valet.

Edna followed the poet's train of thought to a different place. "Perhaps whoever killed Miss Romanova abducted Mr. Wing. We should tell the police—he may be in danger."

Rowland stood. "Perhaps we'd better make sure Mr. Wing's not simply late," he said, picking up the telephone. Ringing down to the reception desk, he noted wryly the new note of trepidation with which his call was received, as if he might be ringing to report another body. He inquired instead after Wing Zau. There was an embarrassed delay as the hotel manager was duly consulted. It was Van Hagen who took the call in the end.

"I'm afraid Mr. Wing has left us, Mr. Sinclair. Of course, a replacement valet will be assigned to you immediately."

"That's not necessary, Mr. Van Hagen. It was Mr. Wing with whom I wished to speak. What exactly do you mean that he's left you?"

"Mr. Wing is no longer in the employ of the Cathay."

"Why?"

"I'm afraid Mr. Wing was unable to continue with us for personal reasons. He tendered his resignation this morning. We do, of course, apologise for any inconvenience."

Rowland probed further, but Van Hagen would not elucidate.

"Do you, by any chance, have a forwarding address at which I might write to Mr. Wing? There is a matter about which I must consult with him rather urgently."

"Is it something with which we might assist, sir?"

"No, I'm afraid not."

Rowland clamped the receiver to his ear with his shoulder and extracted the notebook he kept in his breast pocket. He scribbled the address details below a sketch of a rickshaw and its driver.

"You're going to write to Wing?" Milton asked sceptically once Rowland had hung up.

"Of course not. But I didn't think they'd give me the address for anything less benign than correspondence." Rowland sat down again and recounted the conversation he'd just had with the concierge. "It appears Wing resigned suddenly."

"He didn't seem unhappy this morning," Edna said, frowning. "I do hope we haven't offended him somehow."

"It may not have been anything to do with us," Rowland said. "Perhaps some family emergency required his attention."

"Or perhaps our man Wing is on the run." Milton poured himself another drink.

"Have the police spoken to him?" Clyde asked cautiously.

Rowland shrugged. "I'm not sure. Randolph didn't mention the servants."

"Should we tell him?" Milton asked. "Wing could very well be involved in Miss Romanova's murder."

Rowland considered their options. "Perhaps we should talk to him first? I don't really want to set Randolph on him unnecessarily."

Edna sighed. "I miss Detective Delaney."

Rowland nodded. It had, in the past, been convenient to have an ally in the police force. But this was Shanghai, and they had no friends among the authorities in the treaty port. He looked again at the address jotted into his notebook. Huoshan Road, Hongkew District.

"Shall we go find Wing, then?" Milton stood and grabbed his hat, taking a moment to adjust the feather just so.

"Now?" Clyde asked, startled. "It's ten o'clock."

"No time like the present."

Rowland offered a compromise. "Why don't you and Ed stay here to make sure our trunks are brought down from the other suite after the police have finished going through them—"

"Going through them?" Clyde jumped to his feet. "They're going through our trunks? All of them?"

"I expect it's just routine, Clyde. They're still looking for a murder weapon I believe."

Clyde collapsed back into his chair and buried his face in his hands. He groaned.

"Whatever's the matter, Clyde?" Edna asked, concerned for him now.

"The trunk I brought over for Danny." Clyde looked up at Rowland. "I tried to tell you."

Rowland picked up on Clyde's panic now. "What was in it?"

"Old Mrs. Dong."

"I beg your pardon?"

"Mrs. Dong. Danny's grandmother, her remains anyway. She wanted to be buried in China, so Danny had her exhumed and... she was in that trunk."

Milton and Edna stared at Clyde incredulously. Rowland blinked. "I see."

"Jesus, Mary, and Joseph." Clyde was grey. "They're going to find human remains in our suite and they'll think... God knows what they'll think, but it won't be good. What if they take her as evidence? What am I going to tell Danny?"

"Steady on, mate." Rowland tried to stem his friend's agitation. "I presume Mrs. Dong didn't die recently, so we're just talking about bones."

"Yes, but—"

"When they ask, we'll explain. Did Danny give you any paperwork?"

"Yes, yes, he did." Clyde was beginning to calm down. "There are some letters to his cousins with the trunk in my room."

"Well, then." Rowland braced Clyde's shoulder reassuringly. "It'll probably be a little awkward to explain, given the circumstances, but there is a perfectly legal reason."

Edna moved to sit with Clyde. "You two go find Mr. Wing,"

she said. "Clyde and I will stay here and wait for them to find Mrs. Dong. It's probably better if you know nothing about it, Rowly."

Rowland hesitated.

"Come on, Rowly." Milton handed him his hat. "Let's go talk to the butler before he disappears entirely."

Chapter Nine

TROUBLE BREWING

Japanese In Shanghai
("Sun" Special)

THE turbulence of Japanese gangs is causing some anxiety and two disquieting incidents occurred today.

Mr. A. Thompson, a British subject, was seated on a bench, together with some Japanese marines, in Quinsan Gardens, a small park in Hongkew. He pushed a marine's knee aside and an altercation arose. Thompson was carried off by a Japanese naval patrol but was subsequently rescued by the international police. Later, believing that a Russian who reached for his handkerchief was really getting out a pistol, the Japanese gave chase. The Russian sought refuge in a local journalist's motor car, whereupon the Japanese wrecked the electrical gear and assaulted the journalist, who, however, was saved from serious injury by the arrival of patrols. Japanese crowds and "toughs" are turbulent throughout the district, seeking British or foreign victims, but the situation seems well in hand.

—*The Sun*, 2 July 1934

———————————————⚘———————————————

The air outside the hotel was bracing and damp. Despite the late hour, the ground floor of the Cathay was busy as patrons arrived in their furs and silks to drink and dance at the Jazz Bar. A Buddhist monk monopolised Van Hagen's attention at the reception desk. It made it easy for Rowland and Milton to slip out unnoticed, despite the police presence. Electing not to take a hotel car, they risked a motor-taxi instead. They climbed into a gleaming Buick, judging the good faith of the Sikh driver by the immaculate presentation of his vehicle. It was probably not scientific, but they did not have the time to be more rigorous.

Milton took the seat behind the driver, Rowland, the one beside.

Hongkew was in the northern part of Shanghai, an older precinct of the International Concession. Boasting a significant Japanese population, the area had been at the centre of the most recent escalation in Sino-Japanese tensions. The taxi pulled up outside a dilapidated tenement plastered with Chinese Communist Propaganda posters bearing sinister depictions of Japanese invaders. As Rowland paid the fare, he asked the driver to wait.

"We might be a little while," he said peeling off a number of additional notes. "But we will return."

The driver pulled a newspaper and a torch from under his seat. "Do not be worried, sir. I will wait."

The building on Huoshan Road might once have been a better address. Its fittings, though old, were fine. The doorman wore no uniform. Indeed, the ancient man may not have actually been employed to open the door, but he did do so, informing them in creaking, stilted English that the elevator no longer worked. Rowland thanked him with a gratuity which was accepted with a bow.

They climbed the stairs to the third floor and knocked on the door of number 303.

There was no answer.

Rowland banged harder until Milton gripped his shoulder. "I heard something."

The poet held out his hand. "Give me your pocketknife, Rowly."

It took Milton about two minutes to breach the lock. They could hear scrambling and a series of clatters as the door swung open. They entered the darkened apartment warily. The corridor was narrow and finished in a quite tiny sitting room.

"Bú yào guòlai!" It was Wing Zau's voice.

Rowland turned. Milton found a light cord and pulled it. The electric bulb flickered momentarily before coming on. Rowland ducked as something flew past his head. The blade embedded in the wall with a thud.

Wing Zau stood in the galley which adjoined the sitting room with a knife in one hand, scrabbling for a kitchen cleaver with the other. He looked confused and quite terrified.

"Wing, it's us—Rowland Sinclair and Milton Isaacs. You brought us breakfast this morning." Rowland tried to calm the man and to remain calm himself.

"What are you doing here?" Wing demanded, the knife still poised, though his hand shook.

"Miss Higgins was concerned about you. The Cathay said you'd tendered your resignation—"

"I did not resign!"

"Come on, Wing." Milton closed the apartment door. "We mean you no harm; you can put down the knives."

"Can't we discuss this like gentlemen?" Rowland suggested, stepping back into the living room. "If you didn't resign, perhaps we can help sort this out."

Slowly, Wing put down his weapons. "I apologise, gentlemen."

"No harm done." Rowland nodded encouragingly. "So, if you didn't resign?"

"The Cathay sacked me. I was not at my post."

"I beg your pardon?"

Wing sighed. "I was your valet, Mr. Sinclair, assigned to your suite. That was my post."

"Even when we weren't there?"

"It seems someone broke into your suite while I was out. The police were questioning you when I returned. Mr. Van Hagen was furious. If I hadn't left my post, I would have been present to prevent the murder, or at the very least to prevent it taking place in the Cathay and compromising the hotel's reputation."

"So you didn't let Miss Romanova in?"

Wing shook his head. "No. I wasn't even in the hotel."

"Why the knives, Mr. Wing?" Milton asked. "What are you afraid of?"

"I owe money. My creditors are insistent." He rubbed his face wearily. "And now I don't have a job."

"Cards or horses?" Milton prodded.

"Cards." Wing looked at Rowland. "I'm sorry I threw a knife at you, sir. I thought it was them."

Rowland shrugged. "Considering you missed, I'm inclined to overlook it."

Milton pulled the knife out of the wall. "Who, other than you, would have been able to let Miss Romanova into the suite?"

Wing frowned. "The chambermaids, the room boys, the concierge, the manager. There are many people involved in looking after guests of the Cathay, particularly those in the better suites."

Rowland glanced out of the window. He could see the taxi still on the street below, but he did not know how much longer they could expect the driver to wait. "We should get back."

Wing nodded. "Of course, sir."

"We can't leave him here," Milton protested. "Not with some loan shark looking to break his legs."

"No, we cannot," Rowland agreed. He turned back to Wing. "How much do you owe, Mr. Wing?"

"With interest...twenty-five pounds."

"Right—you'd better come back with us tonight. We'll sort out something about your debts tomorrow."

"The Cathay has dispensed of my services, sir. I can't go back."

"You won't be working for the Cathay; you'll be working for me."

"You still want me to be your valet?"

"I never wanted you to be my valet, but I could use someone who speaks the languages I don't, someone who knows and understands Shanghai. Especially now."

For a moment Wing said nothing, and then he nodded. "Yes, thank you. I will serve you to the best of my ability, Mr. Sinclair."

They waited in the small living room as Wing packed a bag. Milton kept a wary eye on their taxi through the window, lest the driver forget his promise. Rowland leaned against the one chair. Wing Zau's apartment was sparsely furnished. In the corner was a shrine of sorts. Rowland's eyes lingered on the framed photograph of a Chinese woman in a traditional silk cheongsam, before which burned two sticks of incense.

Wing emerged from the bedroom with a battered valise. "My mother," he said sadly, noticing the direction of Rowland's gaze. "She died a few months ago."

The Australians offered their sympathies.

"My mother was a very moral lady." Wing took the picture from its place and reverently wrapped it in cloth before slipping it into the suitcase. "She would be deeply distressed to know what I have done, and ashamed."

"We all make mistakes, comrade," Milton said sympathetically. "In my experience mothers are the most likely to forgive them." He frowned suddenly, his attention still fixed out of the window. He beckoned Rowland and Wing over. Three men in suits walked past the taxi and stopped before the building. "Are those fellows by any chance your creditors, Wing?"

Wing was ashen. "You must get out of here. It's me they want."

Milton glanced at Rowland.

"They'll have to come up the stairs." Rowland turned to Wing. "Is there another way down? A fire escape?"

Wing shook his head.

"Rowly, there's a ledge below the window and a drainpipe about ten yards to the left." Milton pointed.

Rowland opened the window and looked out. It wasn't impossible. He grabbed the chair, moving to the door and wedging it under the handle. "That might buy us a little time."

"They just walked into the building," Milton said.

"Right, Milt, you go first. Mr. Wing, follow him. I'll be right behind you."

Milton climbed out of the window onto the ten-inch ledge, pressing himself against the outside wall as he sidled towards the drainpipe.

A knock on the door.

"Now, Mr. Wing!"

Wing clambered out of the window, clinging to the side.

The knocking grew louder.

"Who is it?" Rowland called out, trying to stall.

The response was Shanghainese and shouted. A thud as someone ran at the door.

Rowland looked out of the window. Wing had reached the drainpipe; Milton was on the ground.

"Milt!" Rowland dropped Wing's bag to the poet. Milton missed the catch, and the valise fell open as it hit the road. Rowland climbed out as Milton and now Wing retrieved its contents.

The door to the apartment crashed open as Rowland made the journey along the ledge. He could hear the angry confusion as the intruders found the place empty and searched the rooms. Then the cries as they spied the open window. Rowland reached for the drainpipe as a head poked out the window and spotted him. Wing's creditors tore down the stairs as Rowland shimmied down the pipe. He reached the ground first, shouting for Wing and Milton to get into the taxi. Rowland sprinted after them. Someone grabbed his jacket from behind. He turned and swung in the same movement, connecting with a face and following with a second blow. But by then another man had caught up. The taxi, with its passenger door still open, cut across the road towards them in reverse. As it approached, the driver reached out the window, grabbing Rowland's assailant and reefing the man to the ground with the momentum of the still moving cab. Rowland leapt in.

"Go!" he shouted before he was entirely on board. The obliging driver slammed the accelerator pedal to the floor.

Chapter Ten

Woman Mining Engineer

A NEWCOMER to Australia, who proposes to exploit a new field of vocation for women, is Miss Emilie Hahn, a B.M.E. of Wisconsin, U.S.A., who has adopted mining engineering as a profession. She wishes to see what opening there is for her unique qualifications in the Australian mining fields. Most of her practical experience has been in the oil industry, a branch of mining upon which many Australian hopes are built.

—*Queenslander*, 16 January 1930

Rowland allowed his head to fall back, as the taxi accelerated.

"Bloody hell!" Milton peered through the rear window at the three diminishing men venting their frustration in the street.

"I'll say," Rowland muttered. He turned to the driver, who

seemed entirely unperturbed by the evening's activity. "May I ask your name, sir?"

"Ranjit Singh, sir."

"You've been a tremendous help tonight, Mr. Singh. Thank you."

"Very good, sir."

"It's become apparent to me that I will need a motorcar and a driver that I can trust while I'm in Shanghai. I don't suppose you'd be interested in hiring out your taxi and your services to me for the next few weeks?"

As it turned out, Singh was very interested in the proposition. So the deal was struck, and Ranjit Singh and his taxi became Rowland Sinclair's private driver and car.

Singh took them back to the hotel and, after making arrangements to return the following morning, left to finish his shift before joining Rowland Sinclair's employ. The Australians walked with Wing into the hotel's foyer and made their way to the lift. Despite the discreet presence of police officers, the Cathay maintained the refinement and decorum for which it was famous.

Van Hagen intercepted them.

"Mr. Sinclair," he said pleasantly, "I didn't realise you'd left the hotel."

"An errand, Mr. Van Hagen. I hoped to convince Mr. Wing to rescind his resignation."

"I'm afraid Mr. Wing's position has already been filled, sir."

Rowland nodded. "I expected as much. Which is why I've retained Mr. Wing personally as my...my private secretary."

Van Hagen glared at Wing, who shrugged and smiled.

"Of course." Van Hagen turned back to Rowland. "Mr. Sinclair, could I trouble you for a private word?" He motioned to the door behind the reception desk. "We could step into my office for a few minutes."

"Certainly, Mr. Van Hagen."

"We'll wait here for you," Milton said uneasily.

Rowland shook his head. "Head up to the suite before Clyde and Ed start to worry."

"I promise you gentlemen," Van Hagen spoke to Milton's reluctance, "I will not detain Mr. Sinclair for long."

As Milton and Wing Zau made their way to the elevator, Van Hagen ushered Rowland into his office. Like the rest of the hotel, it was decorated in the style of a British gentlemen's club—wood panelling, studded leather, and restrained opulence.

Van Hagen directed Rowland to a chair and picked up the telephone.

"Van Hagen. Penthouse, please. Thank you."

Rowland waited.

"Sir Victor...yes, he's with me now. Right away, sir." Van Hagen returned the receiver to its cradle and turned back to Rowland. "Mr. Sinclair, could I trouble you to come with me?"

"Where?"

"Sir Victor Sassoon has invited you to join him in the penthouse for a few minutes."

"Who is Sir Victor Sassoon?"

"Sir Victor owns the hotel. He'd like to speak to you himself."

"I see." Rowland shrugged. "Very well, Mr. Van Hagen. Lead on."

They took a private elevator from the reception to the penthouse, which occupied the entire tenth floor of the Cathay. They were admitted into a drawing room that was as elegant as it was modern. Every piece of furniture was of itself beautiful and complemented every other piece. The lines of the club lounge were echoed in the inlaid patterns on the wall panels. The design of the rugs mirrored the elaborate plasterwork of the recessed ceiling. The woman reclining on the chaise, smoking a cigar, was young—well, no older than Rowland—dark featured, and strikingly beautiful. Rowland's gaze might had lingered longer there had it not been drawn by the unexpected presence of a monkey, a gibbon, sitting in the armchair. It wore some kind of napkin and a little red jacket.

"Victor's just placing a telephone call." The woman's accent was American. "He won't be a moment." She coiled and then unfurled off the longue, standing as she switched the cigar to her left hand and offered Rowland her right. "Emily Hahn. How d'you do, Mr.—?"

"Sinclair. Rowland Sinclair."

"This is Mr. Mills," she said as the gibbon scurried into the position she'd just abandoned on the chaise. "He's a monkey," she added as if Rowland might have overlooked the fact.

Rowland nodded politely at the creature, who smiled...or bared its teeth—he couldn't quite tell.

"Can I fix you a drink, Mr. Sinclair?"

"Gin, if it's not too much trouble, Miss Hahn." Rowland watched as Emily Hahn dragged on her cigar and sent a perfect ring of smoke into the air between them.

"Mickey, you must call me Mickey—everybody does," she said firmly. It was a direction rather than an invitation. "You're Australian?"

"Yes, I am."

"I visited your country about five years ago now, en route to Africa."

"I trust you enjoyed your stay."

"Such as it was. I had hoped to find employment in the Antipodes. I was a mining engineer then."

"And you're not anymore?"

"I suppose one doesn't stop being qualified...but I'm a journalist now. I'm with the *North China Daily News*."

"I see," Rowland said carefully.

"Don't look so alarmed, Rowland. I'm not here to cover your little...incident. Victor and I are friends. I was here modelling for him when all hell broke loose."

"Modelling?"

"Victor likes to take photographs. I'd show you, but they are somewhat intimate in nature, and we are barely acquainted."

Rowland wasn't entirely sure how to respond, so he sipped his drink instead.

Emily's smile was mischievous, and Rowland wondered if she'd hoped to shock him.

"Mr. Sinclair, please forgive me for making you wait." The gentleman who entered the room with his hand outstretched wore a dinner suit. His hair was receding and slicked back, his moustache thin and waxed. A monocle was held in place by a distinguished brow, and his smile was broad. "I trust Mickey's company has been ample in my absence."

Rowland shook Sir Victor Sassoon's hand. "It has."

"Why don't you have a seat, Mr. Sinclair." Sassoon motioned towards an armchair, which was promptly occupied by the gibbon.

Rowland hesitated, unsure how exactly to urge the monkey to give up the seat.

Emily Hahn intervened. "Mr. Mills, come and sit with me, darling." She patted the chaise beside her.

The monkey's head tilted, its black eyes bright, as it considered the invitation. Eventually it accepted, leaving the armchair for a position on Emily Hahn's shoulder, from which it observed the proceedings.

"I'm afraid, Mr. Sinclair, that the incident earlier this evening leaves us with something of a quandary."

"How so, sir?"

"It's something of a delicate matter." Sassoon adjusted his monocle. "I must, you see, be able to guarantee the safety of my guests."

"I appreciate your concern, sir, but I assure you that I was never in any danger."

"Oh it's not your safety about which I am concerned, Mr. Sinclair. Though the Cathay is genuinely happy that you are unhurt."

"I'm not sure I follow, Sir Victor."

Sassoon sighed. "This is a little awkward." He took a deep

breath. "Your residency at the Cathay you see…our other guests may be concerned…"

Emily Hahn interrupted. "What Victor is trying to say, Mr. Sinclair, is that he can't allow a man who might be a murderer to be a guest of his hotel. It's not good for business."

"I see," Rowland said evenly. "I assure you, Sir Victor, I had nothing to do with what happened to Miss Romanova. I don't know how she came to be in my suite."

"Be that as it may, Mr. Sinclair, the Cathay's guests expect a certain standard of personal safety within our walls. Until you are cleared of suspicion—and perhaps not even then—they will be uncomfortable sharing these premises with you and your party. And, as you can understand, the comfort of our guests is paramount."

Rowland's eyes flashed angrily. "Are you asking me to move to another hotel?"

"I'm afraid you'll find it difficult to book into another hotel given the circumstances."

"Fortunately, I have a booking at this hotel," Rowland replied coldly.

"Calm down, Mr. Sinclair." Emily took the olive from her drink and handed it to the monkey on her shoulder. "Victor isn't proposing to throw you out onto the streets."

"Then what exactly are you proposing, Sir Victor?"

"I have a house in Kiangse Road which is presently vacant. It is not as luxurious as your current suite, nor is it in the most salubrious of districts, but I am sure you and your companions will find it adequate."

"And if I refuse?"

Sassoon shook his head. "I am trying to help you, Mr. Sinclair. In all fairness you cannot expect me to allow you to stay on here. For one thing, your suite is a crime scene and the Cathay is fully booked."

Rowland's eyes narrowed. "What about the suite we're currently—"

"It is reserved for the French Ambassador who was delayed in Singapore. We expect him to arrive tomorrow morning."

"Kiangse Road is not so bad, Mr. Sinclair." Emily sucked on her cigar as she curled her legs up onto the chaise. "In actual fact, I have an apartment there myself."

Rowland groaned. He didn't have much of a choice but to accept. They were unlikely to be accepted by another hotel.

"Allow me to extend the Cathay's apologies for the inconvenience," Sassoon said. "I'll arrange for your trunks to be packed and taken to the house this evening."

"This evening?"

"Mr. Van Hagen informs me that you have retained Wing Zau personally. I'm afraid, in the circumstances, I cannot send any of the Cathay's chambermaids with you, but perhaps you'll be able to employ—"

Rowland glowered at him. "Thank you. We'll make our own arrangements."

"I'm sure that in time you'll come to see that I'm being more than reasonable, given the situation."

Rowland exhaled. "Perhaps." He smiled faintly. "In time."

Sassoon laughed. "For what it's worth, Mr. Sinclair, I have come to the conclusion that you had nothing to do with what happened to Alexandra Romanova."

For a moment Rowland wondered why Sassoon had come to that conclusion, but he decided that he was not in a position to challenge the reasoning of allies. He placed his glass of gin on the coffee table. "What do you know about Miss Romanova, Sir Victor?"

Sassoon looked surprised. "My dear Mr. Sinclair, I do not personally hire the taxi girls."

Chapter Eleven

BUTTLING IS AN ART

The Super Gentleman's Gentleman

The secret of the Perfect Butler is to be found in the pads of his feet, writes a special correspondent of the London 'Daily Mirror'. I learned this secret when I went to Bretson, superman's man, late butler to Lord Bethell and the Marquis of Headfort, for a lesson on How to Buttle.

Bretson gave up buttling to open a school—the only one of its kind—where he could train raw youths in the art of manservantry.

He estimates that he has trained more than 500 valets and butlers, who have been taught that the only path to success in buttling has to be trodden on the pads of his feet. They are now successfully padding their way up and down the corridors of England's stately homes. Bretson's first look when I presented myself was at my feet. "The pads of your feet are the most important things about buttling," Bretson began.

"Once your arches fall, the days of your stewardship are numbered."

—*Chronicle*, 26 November 1936

Sassoon's terrace on Kiangse Road was just a couple of blocks from the Cathay Hotel. The area was congested and vaguely seedy, boasting many sing-song houses and opium dens among noodle shops and apartment buildings. Merchants wearing traditional garb and long pigtails smoked and bartered on the street corners with modern Chinese and Shanghailanders from various nations in double-breasted suits or saris or turbans. Human voices, motors, and livestock conglomerated into a background din. The air hung with spice and smoke and human sweat, creating a cacophony for all the senses. The terrace itself was distinctly French in style. It was in good order, though not luxurious and, in comparison to their vast suite at the Cathay, relatively small. On the ground floor was a drawing room, dining room, and kitchen with a large fireplace and hearth; a narrow staircase led to bedrooms and bathrooms on the floors above. The furniture was traditional and a little worn.

Amongst the luggage that was moved from the Cathay was the trunk which contained Mrs. Dong. There had, of course, been a little initial excitement when the human remains were found, but Clyde's explanation had apparently been deemed acceptable. The remains were, after all, by no means fresh, and it seemed it was not unusual for Chinese who'd died abroad to be returned to rest in the country of their birth. The authorities had, however, retained the Australian men's razors. Despite the time, Wing Zau had procured replacements so that they would be able to shave the next morning. And so it was in the early hours of the morning when they walked through the bright red door.

They were greeted by hothouse flowers in every room, courtesy of their host, and a well-stocked pantry and drinks cabinet. Edna claimed the tiny converted garret, captivated by the view of the road afforded through its round window. Clyde, Milton, and the remains of Mrs. Dong shared one bedroom on the second floor. Rowland directed the Cathay porters to put Wing Zau's bags and his own trunks in the second large bedroom. There were, at least, enough beds to accommodate them all separately.

Wing protested the allocation. "I am your servant, Mr. Sinclair."

"I'm afraid there appear to be no other sleeping quarters, Mr Wing," Rowland replied. "And until we can sort out your financial difficulties, you can't return to your apartment."

"But it's not done, sir, not in Shanghai. It is an unacceptable imposition on you."

"I suspect it would be a great deal less acceptable for either you or me to share a bedroom with Miss Higgins," Rowland said, mildly amused by Wing's horror. "I do regret the inconvenience, but with any luck we'll be able to move back to the Cathay in a short while."

Wing hung his head. "All this is my fault. I do not understand why you are being so kind."

"Did you kill Alexandra Romanova, then?" Milton asked blithely.

"No, sir." Wing stepped back, shocked. "I didn't, I swear I didn't!"

"I believe Milt is trying to point out that whoever killed Miss Romanova is responsible for our current difficulties, not you," Edna said gently. "We know you didn't kill her, Mr. Wing."

Milton grinned. "Well, to be honest, we don't know, but despite rumours to the contrary, it's never the butler."

Wing seemed confused.

"I'm afraid you'll have to get used to Milt's sense of humour." Edna sighed.

Clyde nodded. "It makes him easier to ignore." He yawned.

"Right now, I'll take any bed I can get." He looked at Rowland. "Chin up, mate. This might seem less of a mess in the daylight." Rowland grimaced. "I somehow doubt it."

———

Rowland slipped out of bed just before sunrise. Sleep had been elusive and, when found, troubled. Dreams of the sparkling girl with whom he'd danced, twisted by images of her body in death, had broken every fitful rest. He was careful not to disturb Wing Zau, who lay facedown on the other bed.

There was sufficient light to make out the fresh clothes hung neatly on the teak valet near the door. Rowland made a note to remind Wing that he did not need help dressing, but at this hour it was convenient not to have to rummage through the trunks. He bathed and dressed quickly, managing to do so without waking his roommate, who apparently slept very soundly indeed.

He was descending the stairs before he noticed the aroma of frying bacon and the sound of activity. Clyde was cracking eggs into a frypan when Rowland entered the kitchen. He grinned. "Morning, Rowly."

"What are you doing?"

"I was too hungry to sleep any longer," Clyde replied. "I figured I was probably the only one of us who knew how to cook anything, so I started on breakfast."

"Oh."

"Don't look so surprised. I didn't always live with you and your cooks and maids and footmen—"

"Footmen?"

Clyde waved a spatula. "Of course, I can't do much other than eggs and bacon." He handed Rowland a knife and pointed to a loaf of bread which sat on the middle of the kitchen table. "Cut us a couple slices... You do know how to cut bread, don't you?"

"I'm sure I can work it out." Rowland was suddenly ravenous himself.

"Is it just the two of us up?" Clyde asked.

"I believe so."

Clyde instructed Rowland to search for cutlery, whilst he piled eggs and bacon and thick slices of bread onto two plates which he carried through to the dining room.

Rowland slipped the knives and forks into his pocket so he could carry the pot of coffee and a couple of cups as well. They ate silently and with singular purpose for the first few minutes.

"So, Rowly old mate," Clyde began, once their most urgent pangs of hunger had been addressed, "what are we going to do?"

Rowland swallowed. "I'll go see Wil's chum Carmel today. Fortunately he's a lawyer."

"This is hardly a wool contract."

"No." Rowland poured coffee. "But any port."

"What about our Mr. Wing?"

Rowland shrugged. "His creditors are less likely to find him here, so that should buy us a little time. I'll settle his debt and hopefully that'll be the end of the matter."

"You trust him?"

"Well, he slept in the next bed and didn't murder me in the night; that's got to count for something."

Clyde laughed. "You have exceptionally low expectations of your friends, mate."

"Fortunately, my friends keep exceeding them." Rowland took up his fork and resumed the meal.

"I can put together a passable breakfast, Rowly, and I could do a damper in a pinch, but that's it." Clyde grumbled, "If Ed's crazy parents hadn't been so determined that she never marry, she might have been able to boil an egg!"

Rowland picked over his bacon, preoccupied. The events of the previous day were present and distracting. Who had murdered the beautiful taxi girl, Alexandra Romanova? Why had she been slain in the suite of a man she'd met only the night before? How had she got in? None of it made any sense.

Clyde watched him for a moment. "Are you all right, Rowly?"

"Yes, of course. I was just thinking about Miss Romanova."

Clyde shook his head. "It's a terrible business."

"I just can't imagine why anyone would—"

"You barely knew her. She may have been in some sort of trouble."

"Perhaps."

Clyde regarded him thoughtfully. "Have you asked Mr. Wing about her?"

"Wing?"

"Since she worked in the Jazz Club at the Cathay, there's a chance he knew her."

"I did."

Wing Zau stepped into the room through the open door.

"How long have you been standing there?" Rowland asked, startled.

"A short time, Mr. Sinclair."

"Why didn't you—"

"A good servant does not insert himself into the conversations of his masters."

Rowland smiled faintly, reminded of his nephew's valiant defence of eavesdropping. He'd promised to send Ernie a post-card. "I didn't employ you as a butler, Mr. Wing."

"Yes, pardon me, Mr. Sinclair." Wing sighed. "I confess I'm a little uncertain as to the precise nature of my role. I hoped I would overhear something which might help me understand what you expect of me."

"We need an interpreter and a guide, Mr. Wing." Rowland glanced at Clyde. "And I may need you to ask a few questions for me…"

"Of course," Clyde muttered. Rowland's propensity to become involved in investigations was not something of which he wholly approved.

"What kind of questions…of whom?" Wing nervously took the seat Rowland drew out for him.

"It'd be quite useful to know a bit more about Miss Romanova… perhaps one of the chambermaids noticed something."

Wing tried to understand the request. "Are you a detective, Mr. Sinclair…in Australia?"

Clyde laughed.

"No," Rowland admitted. "But she may have been coming to see me when she died. I found her. I feel I should do something."

Wing nodded.

"Not to mention the fact that the police seem to believe you're involved," Clyde added, resigning himself to the fact that Rowland's interest was inevitable. "You said just now that you knew her, Mr. Wing?"

"Not so well, but yes. I'd see her in the kitchens. Sometimes the chef would give her leftover food. The Russians are poor, you see. She talked of going back someday, and of ballet." Wing's eyes were sad and sombre. "She'd beg for scraps for the stray dogs and feed them in the alley after she finished work. We'd take turns to accompany her, lest…" He stopped.

"Do you know where she lived?"

"Many Russians live in the French Concession, sir. The Cathay would know exactly where."

"I'm not sure they would give us that information."

Wing nodded. "I still have friends who work at the hotel. I shall find out. I would like to help you in this."

Rowland sat back. "First we're going to have to sort out this financial difficulty of yours. How much did you say you owe, Mr. Wing?"

"Twenty-five British pounds."

"To whom?"

"Du Yuesheng. He's a businessman."

"Will he call off his thugs if you pay the debt?"

"I don't know. He is angry."

"If he's a businessman, he'll get over it to have the debt paid. Do you think you could arrange a meeting?"

"A meeting?" Wing paled.

"We'll go with you," Clyde said. "Just to make sure they don't take the money and break your legs anyway."

Wing swallowed. "You don't understand. Du Yuesheng is a powerful man."

"All the more reason to sort it out now, man to man," Rowland replied. "They'll find out where you are in time."

Edna and Milton entered the dining room then, laughing over some thing or other. They were clearly delighted to find that Clyde was capable of making breakfast and worked together to coax him back to the kitchen.

Clyde relented eventually. "I'll fry some more eggs," he said, rising. "Rowly, why don't you and Mr. Wing get the fires going— it's flaming cold in here. There's wood stacked outside the back door. Milt, you clear away these plates and set new places. Ed, you might like to make another pot of coffee."

Milton shook his head as Clyde disappeared into the kitchen. "He cooks one meal, and he thinks he's our mother."

Milton went to answer a knock at the door as they were cleaning up after breakfast under Clyde's direction. Edna had retrieved her camera to film the event, impishly delighted with the sight of Rowland Sinclair at domestic chores and managing to avoid them herself in the process.

Rowland attempted to snatch the camera from her, and she squealed, darting out of his reach.

The hall door flew open, and Edna screamed in earnest as Inspector Randolph and two officers barged in, their weapons drawn and ready to prevent another young woman from being murdered. The Australians stared at the invasion, astounded. Rowland stepped in front of Edna. "What the devil—"

"Are you all right, Miss Higgins?" Randolph demanded.

"Yes, perfectly well."

"We heard you scream—"

"Rowly and I were just being silly. Would you mind lowering your gun, Inspector?"

"I see." Randolph returned his weapon to its holster. His colleagues did likewise.

"What can we do for you, Inspector?" Rowland put down the fire iron he'd being using to scrape out the hearth and took out a handkerchief to wipe the soot from his hands.

"Sir Victor informed me that you had left the Cathay Hotel. I called to verify your address."

"You do understand that we decamped at Sir Victor's insistence?" Rowland said cautiously.

"While this investigation is ongoing, Mr. Sinclair, we'd like to be regularly informed of your whereabouts and immediately apprised of any change of residence."

"Of course." Rowland didn't argue. "Have you made any progress with what happened to Miss Romanova, Inspector?"

"She was murdered, Mr. Sinclair." Randolph was curt.

Rowland bristled, but he replied calmly. "I beg your pardon, Inspector. I meant what happened to lead to her being murdered."

"I expect you'd know as much about that as any of us, Mr. Sinclair."

Rowland's eyes flashed, but his face remained impassive. Randolph was clearly trying to goad him into some kind of outburst. "I have told you everything I know. I had hoped you might have discovered something more."

"We will, Mr. Sinclair. Be assured of that." The inspector signalled his officers and turned on his heel.

"Right," Clyde said as the red door slammed. "You'd better see those lawyers now, Rowly."

Chapter Twelve

RIOTING IN SHANGHAI
Rickshaw 'Blacklegs' Wounded

The 10,000 public hire rickshaws in Shanghai's international settlement almost entirely disappeared from the streets today, to the accompaniment of riots and acts of sabotage. This was a climax to the prolonged dispute between the municipal council and the rickshaw owners, whereby the latter were ordered to improve the conditions of the pullers of the vehicles. The rickshaw pullers naturally are supporting the council, but the gangsters engaged by the owners and middlemen, who stand to lose most, are desperately endeavouring to maintain the services in their former conditions. The 'blacklegs' engaged for this purpose ruefully withdrew this afternoon, nursing wounds inflicted by the legitimate pullers. It is estimated that between 50,000 and 70,000 pullers and their dependants are involved.

Hundreds were arrested, fined, and cautioned, but further and more serious trouble is expected.

—*Courier Mail*, 11 August 1934

The offices of Carmel and Smith were in the International Concession, on the Bund a block or so from the *North China Daily News* building. The firm was large and prestigious enough to boast three storeys behind a gothic façade featuring arches and gargoyles.

Gilbert Carmel was in a meeting when he received the message that Rowland Sinclair had requested to see him. Carmel checked the slip of paper. The lawyer had learned just the previous day that his old chum, Wilfred Sinclair, had not come to Shanghai as planned. The telegram had said only that he was unavoidably delayed, but that in his place he was sending this Rowland Sinclair who would take over his booking at the Cathay. The news had been a blow. Carmel had looked forward to seeing his old chum again—there were reminiscences to indulge and business opportunities to discuss. The Japanese were looking for wool and willing to pay a king's ransom. With talk of a trade embargo afoot, they were anxious to secure supply now.

The lawyer brought his meeting to a hasty close, on the pretext of being called away by a matter of urgency.

And so it was merely minutes later that he welcomed Rowland into his office. "Mr. Sinclair." Carmel looked for a resemblance to Wilfred in the young man who entered. He was too old to be Wilfred's son, surely. But the eyes were strikingly familiar: dark blue, unusual in shade and intensity. "Sir, I must confess I am a little perplexed. I was expecting—"

"Wilfred," Rowland finished for him. "I'm afraid my brother is unable to visit Shanghai right now. Private matters have waylaid him at present. He sent me in his stead." Rowland offered Carmel his hand. "Rowland Sinclair. How d'you do, sir?"

"Well, well, Rowland Sinclair. A pleasure to meet you, dear fellow. I had been looking forward to seeing your brother again, but no matter. I'm sure you and I shall be firm friends soon. Indeed I am inclined to transfer all the warmth I feel for Wilfred directly to you, without dilution or restraint. I'm sure you're on the level."

Rowland hesitated, a little concerned that any response in the affirmative would see him expected at some Shanghai Lodge meeting as a visiting Brother. Still, denying his membership would possibly be taking Freemasonic Secrecy too far. "I am. Thank you, sir."

"Now, Rowland, how can I help you? We"—Carmel gestured with flourish at the elaborate brass plate above the door, emblazoned with the name of Carmel and Smith—"are at your service, and that of your good family."

Rowland smiled, already growing accustomed to the solicitor's florid style. Gilbert Carmel was about Wilfred's age, solid and broad. There was a faint, faded Scottish brogue to his accent. The lawyer favoured double-breasted suits and spats and, despite being completely bald, compulsively smoothed some ghost of the hair he might once have had. Rowland told him of the murder of Alexandra Romanova, of how he'd found her body in the drawing room of his suite at the Cathay Hotel and of the investigation which followed. All this Carmel recorded on a legal notepad, asking questions—small clarifications—from time to time.

"You must understand that we generally work with purely commercial matters," he said when Rowland had finished.

"Yes, of course."

"But we will represent you in this matter with our very best offices." He looked over his notes. "I will be in touch with Inspector Randolph today."

"Thank you."

"Not at all, my boy, not at all." Carmel sat back, beaming as he stroked his glossy scalp. "You just get about the business for which Wilfred despatched you, and Carmel and Smith will manage the police. And of course, we'll be at your service should you wish us to oversee any contractual arrangements arising from the meetings you will have in Shanghai."

They talked socially then for a few minutes. Rowland answered friendly enquiries about his brother's health and growing family, particularly Wilfred's youngest son, Gilbert, who was the lawyer's namesake. Carmel spoke of serving with Wilfred Sinclair in the Great War and invited Rowland to attend the next meeting of the Northern Lodge of China. Eventually Rowland took his leave and rejoined the party waiting for him in the reception area.

"I've asked Mr. Carmel to arrange an appointment with Du Yuesheng, as soon as possible," Rowland said as they left the building. "Once Mr. Wing's debt is settled, we'll no longer need to worry about the gentleman's thugs."

"And in the meantime?" Clyde asked, glancing at Wing Zau.

"We carry on," Rowland replied. "But we keep a weather eye out for debt collectors."

Milton slung an arm about Wing's shoulders. "Don't you worry, comrade; they'll have to get through us to lay a hand on you."

They waved away his thanks, as they did his apologies for the trouble he had brought them. There was much to do to address their changed circumstances, which had raised unexpected inconveniences.

"Andrew Petty was meant to call for us at the Cathay this morning," Rowland said, glancing at his watch. "It was only when Mr. Carmel reminded me why Wilfred had sent me to Shanghai that I remembered."

"You have had rather a lot to distract you." Edna entwined her arm in his. "It's still morning—we might yet catch him."

"Rowland! Hello—have you come to see me?" Emily Hahn emerged from the *North China Daily News*'s premises, waving. She was svelte and sophisticated in a black coat and a fur-trimmed red pillbox hat.

Rowland introduced his companions. "Miss Hahn and I met last night in Sir Victor's penthouse."

"Mickey," she insisted. "British formality is considered quite

odd and rude in China, so you simply must call me Mickey."
She turned to Rowland. "And how do you find Victor's house
on Kiangse Road?" She held up her hand before he could reply.
"I'll hear no complaints. It's a thousand times better than my
ugly little apartment, and you cannot find the real China at the
Cathay Hotel."

Rowland smiled. "We're perfectly happy in our new lodgings,
and though I'm afraid we've not yet had time to search for the real
China, I'm sure it's there somewhere. In fact, we were just on our
way to the Cathay to thank Sir Victor personally."

Emily Hahn extracted a cigarette from a silver and enamel case
and waved it expectantly. Clyde provided the light.

"Would you care to join us, Mickey?" Edna asked, almost shyly.

"I may as well," she replied, beaming. "I have an appointment
to lunch with Victor in any case."

And so the journalist strolled with them. Though it seemed she
had not been long in Shanghai herself, Emily Hahn appeared to
have an affinity with the city. She walked confidently, sidestepping
rickshaws instinctively, all the time chatting gaily as she pointed
out buildings of significance along the way, like a tour guide of
sorts. The day was bright and sunny, though the spring was not
yet warm—to Australians anyway. The streets were busy and
vibrant, a weaving parade of colour and diversity. With midday
approaching, delivery men picked through the traffic on bicycles
stacked precariously with tiffin tins. Rowland fell back a little,
extracting the notebook from his breast pocket to sketch the strain
and movement of the rickshaw men. When he looked up again
he saw his companions had stopped, waiting for him.

"Probably best not to wander off after everything that's happened, Rowly," Clyde said almost sternly.

Rowland put away his notebook. "Sorry. Old habits."

"We should be careful, mate. Someone's already tried to snatch
you once."

"That wasn't personal."

"We can't be sure." Clyde glanced sideways at Wing Zau, who was watching the road nervously.

Rowland nodded. "Hopefully Du Yuesheng's thugs won't try anything in broad daylight, but you're right."

They remained within a step of each other as they made for the Cathay with neither haste nor undue delay. It was not till they saw the taxi stopped on the street outside the hotel that they remembered Ranjit Singh.

Rowland groaned. "I wonder how long the poor man's been waiting."

Milton peered into the taxi. "He's not here."

"Are you sure it's the right taxi?" Edna asked.

"No," Rowland admitted.

"Come on." Edna took his hand and pulled him towards the building. "We'll ask at the reception desk. Perhaps your Mr. Singh enquired there."

The mystery of the missing taxi driver was solved the moment they entered the hotel foyer. Ranjit Singh was at the desk arguing with the concierge. In the daylight and standing, the Sikh was noticeably tall and immaculately attired in a dark three-piece suit which contrasted the deep red of his turban.

"I'm afraid Mr. Sinclair is no longer a guest of the Cathay Hotel," the concierge insisted.

"I don't understand. The gentleman assured me—"

"Mr. Singh, I'm so sorry to have kept you waiting." Rowland stepped in to explain the change of plans. He pulled Singh aside and slipped him the address of Sassoon's house on Kiangse Road. "It's only a couple of blocks away," he said.

"Never mind, sir," Singh said. "I will wait."

Rowland checked his watch. "We were going to have lunch in the restaurant here. We'll be at least an hour, probably two."

"Then if you don't mind, sir, I will go home and come back. Tiffin time, you know."

"Of course, Mr. Singh. Thank you."

Emily Hahn also took her leave. "I'll call on you all soon," she promised as she stepped into Sassoon's private elevator.

"Welcome back, sir." Van Hagen eyed the Australians warily. "Will you be—"

"We escorted Miss Hahn to her appointment with Sir Victor," Rowland said pleasantly. "The rest of us hoped we might take a table in the Cathay Room, since we're here." Over Van Hagen's shoulder he could see Wing Zau slip, as agreed, through the staff entrance which led to the service corridors.

Van Hagen seemed flustered. "I'm not sure the restaurant has any tables available."

"I'm sure there's something."

"No, sir, I'm sure there's not. Perhaps if you'd made a reservation..."

"Give Mr. Sinclair and his friends my table." Sassoon emerged into earshot with Emily Hahn on his arm. "Miss Hahn and I will be dining elsewhere." He winked at Rowland. "After all, we can't throw the man out and then deny him basic succour."

"As you wish, Sir Victor." Van Hagen's face was unreadable. "There have been a number of messages for your party, Mr. Sinclair," he added as Sassoon and Emily Hahn departed. He took several metal discs from a compartment under the desk and placed them in a large envelope, which he handed to Rowland.

"What on earth are these, Mr. Van Hagen?"

"Phonographic discs, sir." He pointed to a number of booths along one wall of the foyer, which Rowland had assumed contained telephones. "Messages are recorded in the cubicles and left for guests. There's a gramophone in the drawing room at your new address, I believe."

Rowland thanked the concierge and slipped the discs into his pocket. He expected that at least one disc contained a message from Petty. He wondered if the businessman knew about the murder of Alexandra Romanova.

Before they proceeded into the Cathay Room, Rowland

cashed a cheque large enough to ensure they would not run out of yuan for some time, and handed Van Hagen the letter he'd drafted to Wilfred, taking a moment to add a note about his meeting with Carmel and Smith before arranging for it to be despatched as a telegram.

"Probably a good thing you'll be on the other side of the world when Wilfred receives it," Milton observed.

"True." Rowland offered Edna his arm.

The Cathay Room was busy feeding Shanghai's elite. After a word from Van Hagen, they were escorted to Sassoon's table on the balcony. The Huangpu and Shanghai's skyline were laid before them, and for several moments, they disregarded their menus, mesmerised by the vista of colliding civilisation below.

They were seated before fine china and silver service, Irish linen napkins, and moist, warmed towels to refresh their hands. They were offered fine wine and sparkling champagne, and recommended a selection from the menu.

Wing joined them just as the entrées were being served.

"I took the liberty of ordering for you, Mr. Wing," Edna said as he took his seat awkwardly. "I do hope you like lobster bisque."

Wing stared at the elegantly set table and hesitated.

"I'm sure we can reorder if it isn't to your liking," Edna added.

"Not at all, Miss Higgins," Wing said hastily. "You must forgive me, as much as it seems an Australian custom, I am unused to sitting down with my master."

"Please don't call me that, Wing." Rowland passed the salt to Milton. "You make me sound like Stoker's Dracula."

Edna laughed.

"We must find a way of working together, Mr. Wing, that doesn't render either of us uncomfortable." Rowland began on his salmon croquettes.

"Even so, sir—"

"Can you not think of us all as colleagues?" Milton said in an attempt to be helpful.

"Colleagues?"

Milton beckoned Wing closer and lowered his voice. "We're working together to find out who killed Miss Romanova and how she ended up in our suite. I would say that made us colleagues at least."

"For the love of God, we're not—" Clyde began, alarmed.

"Actually, I think we probably are," Rowland interrupted. There was no point in pretending. He couldn't just carry on as if nothing had happened, as if a young woman had not danced with him one evening and died in his suite the next day.

Wing stared at his plate. "Yes," he said, finally lifting his head. "We are working together—as colleagues." He smiled. "I will not call you master again."

Milton raised his glass. "Words to live by, comrade."

"Did you learn anything, Mr. Wing?" Edna asked. "From your friends on the staff?"

Wing nodded. "Miss Romanova lived on Nanjing Road in the French Concession. She had a brother."

Rowland nodded. "Sergei. She mentioned him. He teaches music, I believe."

"About that, you know more than I." Wing started nervously on his bisque. "The chef believes that there was man, a suitor."

"Does he know this man's name?"

Wing shook his head. "He only saw him waiting for her. They would walk together. A black-skinned gentleman. Chef thought he was one of the musicians perhaps."

"Might this have been a crime of passion?" Milton mused. "If this man was jealous of Rowly, leaving her body in his suite might have been an act of revenge."

Rowland said nothing.

Edna glanced at him. "If he was...if he did...you couldn't have known, Rowly."

"Of course," Milton said quickly. "You were just the poor sucker she danced with."

"Miss Romanova needed money." Wing looked up from his meal. "She borrowed from the barman who worked at the Jazz Club and from the other taxi girls."

"Do you know why she needed money?"

"No one seemed to know. But she had asked many of them for loans. The barman said he gave her what he could because she seemed desperate. Perhaps she too..." Wing trailed off self-consciously.

"If so, would she also be in debt to Du Yuesheng?"

"Perhaps, but there are others who lend."

"Would they kill her for an unpaid debt, as they tried to kill you?"

"They would not have killed me, Mr. Sinclair—not while there was a chance I might pay the debt. They might have encouraged me to pay as a matter of urgency, but they would not have cut my throat."

Rowland nodded thoughtfully. It made sense. "Thank you, Mr. Wing. At least now we have an idea of where to begin."

Chapter Thirteen

FASCIST TERROR RAGES FROM WEST TO FAR EAST

Appalling Slaughter
BY NAZI HEADSMEN CHINESE
EXECUTIONERS & BRITISH BOMBERS

The Communist International Executive Committee, at the conclusion of its thirteenth Plenum in Moscow last month, issued the following manifesto:-
PROLETARIANS! WORKERS OF THE WHOLE WORLD! COMMUNISTS! The blood of the best sons of the working class is being shed in all capitalist countries.

...Chiang Kai-shek, who has called into his service German, British and American generals and Social-Democratic police presidents of the Grzeszinski stamp, is chopping off the heads of Chinese revolutionary workers and peasants by the thousand. In Shanghai in the autumn of last year, workers at an anti-war meeting were arrested. All were shot on the spot. In the summer of 1933 the Kuomintang hangmen arrested 150 participators in the Anti-Fascist Congress, shipped them to Nanking, and wreaked their bloody vengeance on them. In Japan, the ruling Fascist clique during the past two years has thrown 15,000 revolutionary workers, peasants and soldiers into its dungeons. Dozens of Japanese Communists have been killed. In Manchuria, Korea and Formosa, tens of thousands of people have been tortured for resistance to Japanese imperialist violence...

—*Workers' Weekly*, 2 March 1934

The telephone affixed to the hallway wall rang as Rowland unlocked the red door and held it open for Edna. She stepped in and ran to seize the Bakelite receiver in time. She handed the receiver to Rowland.

Rowland spoke to the solicitor Gilbert Carmel briefly before returning the receiver to its cradle. "Mr. Du Yuesheng will meet with us this evening."

Wing looked quite ill.

"Take heart, comrade," Milton braced his shoulder. "You said yourself, they will not kill you while there is a chance you will pay... Rowly is that chance."

Wing hung his head. "I don't know how to thank you—"

"You already have. I'd rather you stopped." Rowland tossed his overcoat at the stand by the door. He smiled, both surprised and triumphant when it caught on the hook.

Edna laughed. "When you come to know Rowly a little better, Mr. Wing, you'll learn that he really doesn't like to dwell on things like that."

"Why?"

"I expect it's because our dear Rowly has never been completely comfortable with his unearned, capitalist wealth," Milton said gravely. "His blood may be blue, but his heart is red through and through!"

Rowland ignored the poet, opening a copy of the *North China Daily News* as he settled into an armchair.

Clyde reached over and clipped Milton across the head. "You're an idiot." He turned to Wing. "Don't look so alarmed, Mr. Wing. Rowly's not a Communist."

Wing sat down. "The Communists have not fared well in Shanghai," he said, looking directly at Milton. "When I was a younger man, there were many Communists in the city, but they have since fled or been found."

"Found? By whom?"

"The Municipal Police. Some were imprisoned, others executed."

"Without trial?"

"Yes."

Milton sat forward. "And this is what's happened to all the Communists in China? I was wondering where the blazes they'd gone."

Wing paused. "I have heard that the army and the taipans have the Communists on the run in the north. They are all but defeated."

Milton and Clyde both winced in sympathy for their Chinese comrades.

"So the Communists are hated here?" Edna perched on the arm of Rowland's chair, concerned for Milton and Clyde, who were not always discreet about their philosophic convictions.

"Shanghailanders consider them subversives. Dangerous."

"To whom?"

"To business. Shanghai is all about business."

"What about the Chinese people? Do they hate Communists too?"

"The Communists have strength in the rural areas, amongst the poor. There are many poor. But the taipans and the rich fear them."

"As they do in Australia," Milton murmured.

Wing frowned. "You must understand, Mr. Isaacs; Du Yuesheng is not an ordinary businessman. He is a friend of Chairman Chiang Kai-shek."

Milton sat back in his chair, unperturbed. "So he's a well-connected businessman."

Wing shook his head. "Du Yuesheng won this friendship, this allegiance, for his help in the purge of Communists from Shanghai."

Rowland lowered his paper. He'd still been in England when news of the Shanghai massacre had broken. The counter-revolutionary coup had seen Chiang Kai-shek's Nationalist Party, the KMT, conduct a ruthless purge of thousands of Chinese Communists. Of course, the fact that the victims had been both Chinese and Communist had dampened outrage in the West. Indeed, some had applauded the firm action taken to stem the red tide. "Fortunately we are calling on Mr. Du to settle a debt, not to discuss politics."

Wing swallowed. "You do not understand. Du Yuesheng is the *zongshi*—the grand master."

Milton grinned. "That's all right then. Rowly here is a Freemason too." He glanced at Rowland, stuck out his right hand, wiggled his fingers and added a series of claps and a wink. "Rowly'll give him the secret handshake, and they'll be the best of mates."

"Of what exactly is Mr. Du the grand master?" Rowland said, trying not to laugh. He gathered by Wing's bewilderment that they were not talking about membership of the Lodge.

"Qīng Bāng—the Green Gang. It is a secret society."

"Like the Freemasons?" Clyde asked hopefully.

Wing shrugged. "The Green Gang controls the opium trade

in Shanghai, as well as gambling and many"—he glanced at Edna embarrassed—"sing-song houses."

Rowland frowned. It seemed they were about to call upon some kind of criminal gang lord. Considering the reason for which they were doing so, it was probably not surprising. Still, in his experience, even gangsters didn't kill people trying to give them money.

Edna moved to sit on the arm of Rowland's chair. "Don't go, Rowly—it's too dangerous."

"The martial courage of the day is vain," Milton murmured.

"Wordsworth," Rowland replied.

Edna persisted. "Just have the lawyers send Mr. Du his money and be done with it."

Rowland pressed her hand gently. "I suspect it's too late for that, Ed."

Wing nodded despondently. "Master Du does not tolerate disrespect. We must keep the appointment."

"Ed should stay here," Clyde said suddenly. "Just in case—"

"I'm not sure about leaving her alone," Milton interrupted before Edna could protest. "Not after everything that's happened."

Rowland nodded. They could not be sure that Alexandra Romanova's murder had nothing to do with them beyond the scene of the crime. "You chaps stay here with Ed." He folded his newspaper. "Mr. Wing and I will keep the appointment."

The voices of dissent were immediate in reply.

"Not a good idea, Rowly." Clyde folded his arms across his chest. "We need a show of force at least."

"What about Ed? We can't—"

"Of course we can't," Milton agreed. "We just have to figure out where we're going to stow her."

"Stow?" Edna stood. "I'm not a stick of old furniture."

"Du Yuesheng is a traditional man, and superstitious." Wing looked at the sculptress apologetically. "He may be offended if you bring a lady to a business meeting."

"What if Ed stays in the taxi with Singh?" Clyde suggested. Rowland turned to the sculptress. "What do you think, Ed?"

Edna rolled her eyes. "I suppose I'll be able to do something if you don't return."

"Yes," Wing said. "That may be required."

"What exactly do you propose to do?" Milton asked suspiciously. "You can't march in there and—"

"Don't be absurd. I'll go directly to the police, and if they do anything, I'll go see Victor Sassoon."

The answer satisfied the men. Edna instinctively resisted all attempts to protect her, but she was not a fool.

"You will just pay the man and leave, won't you?" she said. It was more an order than a question.

Wing groaned and Rowland sensed that the erstwhile butler was gripped as much with guilt as fear. "If it makes you feel any better, the police will be on hand to rescue us rather smartly, should that be required. They've been following us since we left the Cathay."

Milton agreed. He too had noticed the police car parked rather blatantly outside the house. "We'll just tell Singh to drive slowly so there's no chance we lose them between here and this bloke Du's pile."

"This is probably not going to look good for you, Rowly," Clyde warned quietly. "Meeting with a gang lord will probably promote you to the top of Inspector Randolph's list of suspects."

Rowland nodded. "It can't be helped."

Milton pulled a deck of cards from his breast pocket and proposed a hand of poker to pass the time.

"No!" Wing backed away as if the deck were on fire. "I cannot play."

Milton smiled sympathetically. "Too soon? Come on, Wing— we'll teach you how to play properly. Gambling's only a problem if you lose."

But Wing would not be moved, declaring that he would never

play cards again, a decision the Australian men thought a trifle melodramatic.

"Leave Mr. Wing alone." Edna fetched her camera from the shelf on which she'd left it that morning. "You can come for a walk with me, if you'd care to, Mr. Wing. I want to film Kiangse Road."

"It might be best if you waited a day before you ventured out, Ed," Rowland said carefully. "We don't know that Mr. Du has called off his dogs."

"Oh, I forgot. How very vexing!"

Wing stared at his feet. "I am so sorry, Miss Higgins. This is all trouble I have caused."

Edna's face softened. "It's nothing at all, Mr. Wing. I'll simply film out of the window in the garret. It'll be a lovely perspective."

Milton laughed as he dealt cards to Rowland and Clyde. "Just don't slip—there's no way Randolph will believe Rowly didn't throw you out."

Du Yuesheng's house was situated on the waterfront of the French Concession. The building was new, constructed as a demonstration of its master's power. It was not the opium baron's only property, but it was probably the grandest and the one in which he housed his three wives, each on a separate floor. Its sprawling rendered façade, its colonnades and western styling spoke of a progressive sensibility despite the traditional Chinese details. The towering wings of the structure were connected by colonial verandahs which provided views of the water and the concession. Several cars, including three police cars, were waiting in the sweeping drive when Ranjit Singh's taxi pulled up.

"The local police deliver Master Du's opium," Wing explained. He spoke urgently to Singh and Edna. "If help is required, seek it from the international police. There may be one or two of them not in Du's pay."

Singh nodded, his eyes bright and wide. The taxi driver had lived in Shanghai for many years. He understood the reach of Du Yuesheng. "Do not worry; I know where to go."

"Good man." Rowland grabbed Edna's hand and kissed it. "I hope you won't need to do anything. Give us half an hour."

Edna checked her watch. "Not one minute more. Do you understand?" She looked to Clyde, who had always been the least reckless of the men she lived with.

He winked. "Don't worry, Ed, I'll scream 'Run' as soon as it gets hairy."

They left Edna and Singh in the taxi, and walked up to the iron gates. Wing informed the gatekeeper of their business, and they were admitted. Two men leaned against the columns of the portico smoking. They said not a word, motioning them to the entrance with a flick of bored eyes.

The floor of the portico featured golden roundels emblazoned with five-claw dragons, a motif once reserved exclusively for the Imperial family. Rowland wasn't sure whether Du could actually claim Imperial descent—perhaps the dragons simply attested to the new reign of the drug lords.

A servant answered the door and brought them into a foyer of white marble and gold gilt, so bright that it was, for a moment, dazzling. They waited, taking in the richly decorated walls, the fusion of Chinese design and modern art deco sensibility, whilst the servant disappeared into the dimly lit hallway.

Music and muffled chatter reached down the hallway to the foyer—there was a party in swing somewhere in the house. The servant returned and invited them to follow. They passed several darkened rooms in which men and women clustered in giggling groups or languished stupefied on chaise longues. Rowland recognised the paraphernalia of opium being passed among them. He wondered if Du Yuesheng was an opium addict.

Wing Zau walked before them, directly behind the servant. His back was straight and determined, but his forehead glistened with perspiration, and his normally immaculate hair was falling out of place. Milton caught up with him and placed a hand on his shoulder.

They proceeded up the wide staircase to the first floor. A set of double doors was opened, and Rowland Sinclair and his associates were announced into a large room. Mentally, Rowland sketched, making notes with the lines he might have drawn. A young woman plucked at what looked like a banjo and sang long, quavering notes for a man who reclined in a chair so ornate that it might have been a throne. The musician was beautiful, her attire traditional, her hair cut short in the latest style. The man, whom Rowland assumed was Du Yuesheng, was dressed in the white gown of a scholar. He was not old, but there were years on his face, a kind of ancient, formal civility. He had prominent ears, which had given rise to the moniker "Big-Eared Du." But it was to the opium baron's mouth that Rowland's eye was drawn—Du's lips were controlled, and in the set of them, the artist saw a ruthless intelligence.

There was a kind of perimeter guard stationed around Du. European men whose stances hinted that they were armed. They remained in the shadows of the room, watching. Six in total. Rowland recognised one: Count Nickolai Kruznetsov.

Rowland tensed. But Kruznetsov showed no sign that he recognised any of them.

Du waved his hand languidly, and the music stopped immediately. The woman lowered her head and retreated from the room, leaving the *zongshi* with his visitors.

Wing fell to his knees, bowing forward in a kowtow. The Australians remained standing as Wing introduced them, though they understood nothing of what he said save their own names.

Du began softly, but his words became progressively sharper and clipped. And he spoke for what seemed a long time.

Wing looked so pale, he was possibly safer on his knees.

"What did he say?" Rowland asked when the gangster finally

drew breath. "Did you tell him that we are here to settle everything you owe?"

Wing nodded. "Master Du is displeased that I have caused him so much trouble. That I have involved strangers and that we have come as four men. He says it is unlucky and that I have brought bad luck to his door. For this he says we must pay a special penalty."

"What kind of penalty?" Rowland asked calmly as he tried to identify their best chance of escape. He could see Milton and Clyde also sizing up the room and the Russian guards. The situation was somewhat bleak.

Du spoke again. His voice was cold.

"He says my debt is now forty pounds."

Rowland struggled to keep the relief from his face. He was allowing the man's reputation to get to him, imagining barbaric retribution for what was essentially a financial transaction. "If that's what it must be, then I agree," he said with a show of reluctance. He sensed that Du required his penalty to be felt to some degree.

Wing translated.

"He wants to know if you brought the money."

Rowland smiled faintly. He was not some simpleton. "Please inform Mr. Du that I will write him a cheque on the Shanghai International Bank. I'll telephone when we get back to ensure that they honour the amount without any fuss."

Licking his lips nervously, Wing conveyed Rowland's response.

Du's eyes flashed, and then he too smiled. And so the deal was done.

"Mr. Wing, would you please ask Mr. Du if Alexandra Romanova owed him money?" Rowland extracted a cheque book from his breast pocket and, moving over to the desk Du offered him, proceeded to fill in the requisite details. "Tell him I will pay her debt too."

Wing swallowed. And then he asked.

Du looked closely at Rowland before he spoke.

"Master Du asks if she was the girl found dead at the Cathay."

Rowland nodded. Clearly Du expected an equal exchange of information.

"Master Du says that if she owed him money, he would have been offended by her murderer. He is not offended."

Du sat back in his chair and ventured another question.

"Master Du wishes to know if Miss Romanova was a—" Wing was already shaking his head—"a sing-song girl."

Rowland bristled. He gathered that sing-song girls were prostitutes of some sort. "Tell him no."

Perhaps Du noticed his ire, because he offered information next.

"Master Du has never heard of Alexandra Romanova. He does not believe she is a gambler or an opium addict. He would know her name otherwise."

Rowland nodded. Then Du posed another question.

"Master Du wants to know if Victor Sassoon knew Miss Romanova."

"I don't know. I don't think so," Rowland said uneasily. The opium baron seemed to be plying him for gossip. "Would you thank Mr. Du and tell him we will not take up any more of his time?"

Wing did so.

Du nodded thoughtfully.

"Master Du says he will meet you again."

Chapter Fourteen

CHINA WILL CALL WHITE MAN'S BLUFF

Western Civilisation Forced its Way in, and the Chinese Hope to Force it out

Inscrutable Orientals No Longer Regard Europeans as Kings of the Earth

Though China is too busy squabbling with Japan at the moment to look for trouble elsewhere, there is no doubt that China is preparing to call the white man's bluff. For years the Europeans have lorded it over the patient Orientals, but the Chinese have been biding their time. Were it not for the fact that they are so divided among themselves and have been always so distrustful of Japan, they would have swept the white man out long ago. The whites won by force most of what they hold in China and many who are watching the situation very closely are satisfied that it is by force that the white man will so out.

When the white man in the early years of the

century, burst upon the Chinese with all the evidence of invincible Western civilization—moving pictures, chewing gum, telephones, Scotch whisky, machine guns, and other fascinating gadgets—he easily awed the modest Orientals by his superiority, his wealth, his prodigious brain. The white master slapped the cook for serving underdone breakfast bacon and delivered a kick to accelerate his rickshaw coolie's speed. Glorified, the white man swaggered through China confident of his supremacy. But today the story is different. Every racial group in Asia, from the Japan Sea to the Indian Ocean, is endeavouring to

EXPEL ALL WESTERN INFLUENCES

which conflict with native tradition. China in particular seeks freedom from foreign control. However they may appear to have adopted Western manners, the Chinese will never permit themselves to be weaned from their own culture, tradition, and habits...

—THOMAS STEEP, American
newspaper correspondent.
—*Mirror*, 28 December 1935

There had, it seemed, been no false modesty to Clyde's declaration that he could only cook bacon and eggs. And so they finished the day with the same meal as that with which they started it. Ranjit Singh was warmly invited to join them for this festive, if makeshift meal.

The taxi driver accepted readily, in the mood to celebrate the emergence of his employers from the lair of the gangster. Indeed, he was decidedly pleased to have played a small part in the caper. Working for Rowland Sinclair was already proving an excellent diversion. Ranjit did not dislike driving his taxi, but at times during the fifteen years he had been doing so, he'd longed to participate in the intrigues of Shanghai, to move with businessmen and power brokers—the dazzling, clever wealthy people who came east to play. Of course, he was a taxi driver, and that sort of life would only ever be the subject of daydreams whilst he was waiting for a fare.

Over the years, Ranjit had driven all manner of person from all manner of place, but he found the Australians particularly intriguing. Sinclair had clearly always had money; there was a depth to his polish which eluded more recent millionaires. But his friends hadn't. They were erudite enough, but there was a competency about them, a knowledge of everyday tasks like brewing coffee and lighting fires, that gave away humbler origins.

He had never before been invited to dine by a client, but neither had he been asked to drive a getaway vehicle. It was all rather thrilling. The only person about whom he wasn't entirely sure was the Chinese butler. The man, it seemed, was a gambler, and though the Australians appeared to have no issue with that particular failing, Singh did not entirely trust Wing Zau. He resolved to keep a close and wary eye on him.

As they gathered about the table, Milton filled their glasses from a random assortment of liquor bottles he'd gathered from the drinks cabinet while he recounted what exactly had transpired in the house of Du Yuesheng. "Tell you what, I thought we were done for when he started talking about penalties!" The poet shook his head. "But it turns out the crims here simply impose fines. It's quite civilised really."

"We were lucky," Wing said. "I am lucky."

Milton laughed. "If you were lucky, comrade, you wouldn't have lost your shirt in the first place."

Even so, Wing showed them how to raise a toast to his good fortune, Chinese style, turning over their glasses to show that they were drained after declaring *"kanpei,"* then Clyde came in with a simply enormous platter. "This is the last of the eggs and bacon... We might have to restock the pantry or buy a few hens if we're going to eat tomorrow."

Milton helped himself. "Don't worry, Mum; one of us will go to the market for you tomorrow."

"I suppose we might have to take all our meals out," Rowland suggested. Whilst he quite liked bacon and eggs, he expected that they would tire of it eventually. And poor Clyde looked exhausted and harried by the exertion of frying.

"My sister is a most accomplished cook," Ranjit said. "Women are better cooks, I think."

"Not this one." Edna buttered bread.

"Perhaps Harjeet could cook for you?" Ranjit ventured. "Her husband is away, so she is just at home."

Rowland hesitated.

Ranjit withdrew. "What am I saying? If you wanted a cook, there any number of qualified chefs whose services you could hire."

"It's not that, Mr. Singh." Rowland put down his knife and fork. "You see we left the Cathay under somewhat rushed and difficult circumstances."

"Financial difficulties?"

"I'm afraid not. A young woman was found murdered in our suite."

"The taxi girl in the papers? That was your suite?"

"Yes."

"How—"

"We've no idea." Rowland explained the situation as plainly as he could, as well as the fact that he was under suspicion. Singh deserved to know who exactly he was working for.

The driver took it all in, lips pursed thoughtfully.

"As you can understand, Mr. Singh, we seem to have found ourselves in the middle of something unsavoury."

Singh frowned. "You wish to find out who murdered the girl? A private investigation?"

"We're not detectives, Mr Singh," Edna said carefully. "But we need to know what she was doing in the suite, and how she came to be murdered there."

"Why?"

"Because we care. And, of course, we need to make sure the police know it was nothing to do with Rowly."

"Naturally, we'll understand completely if you wish to end your agreement with us," Rowland said. "I really should have told you at the outset."

Singh shook his head. "No, no, no—I am happy to drive you, Mr. Sinclair. Sikhs have no fear of death, and even less of men. Perhaps I could help you in other ways too. We taxi drivers, we overhear many things."

"Have you heard something?" Clyde made a sandwich of his eggs and bacon.

"Nothing, but I could let it be known that I'm interested in anything that may concern the young woman who died at the Cathay." He nodded enthusiastically. "Many of Shanghai's taxi drivers are my relatives one way or another."

Milton nodded. "Could be useful, Rowly. Miss Romanova's death is in all the papers; maybe one of the drivers heard something."

Bolstered, Singh continued. "And perhaps my sister could come work for you, if you like—to cook and to clean. She's a very good cook."

"Would she want to work here, all things considered?" Rowland asked.

"Yes, yes. She would not be frightened. I could bring her every morning and take her home when she is done. If that would suit you, sir?"

Rowland glanced at his companions. "Yes, I believe that would suit us very well—if she agrees, of course."

"If you'll permit me, sir," Wing ventured, "it is the butler's duty to manage the household staff. I could receive the lady tomorrow morning and settle all the details." Despite Rowland's protests, Wing insisted upon leaving the table to make an inventory of the pantry immediately.

"Let him do this, Rowly," Edna whispered.

"It's really not necessary—"

"Even so. I know you paid this Mr. Du, but Mr. Wing still feels he's in debt."

Rowland left it. Edna understood people better than he did, and she and Wing seemed to have a rapport. They could hear him singing now: "In the shadows when I come and sing to you…"

"Mr Wing sings beautifully don't you think?" Edna said as they all stopped to listen, amused.

They returned to their meal, and before they were finished, Wing had belted out a very commendable rendition of Bing Crosby's "Shadow Waltz" and compiled a list of what needed doing to keep the household running to his satisfaction. Purpose, however small, seemed to have steadied him somewhat. They retired to the drawing room for coffee and brandy, and over these Ranjit Singh told them stories from the streets of Shanghai, tales of the opium trade, warlords, and clashing tradition. The driver had come to Shanghai just after the end of the Great War.

"You were a soldier?" Edna asked.

"Yes. I fought in Turkey, at Gallipoli, and then in France. After it was all over, I didn't want to go home."

"I lost a brother at Ypres," Rowland said quietly.

Singh's black eyes were sympathetic. "I remember the Australians. The British generals used them almost as badly as they did us coloured troops from the subcontinent."

Rowland said nothing. He had heard it said before that the English commanders were careless with colonial lives. And he was not so naïve as to expect that there were not more levels to that lack of regard.

"I lost brothers too," Singh said sadly. "We were not afraid of death." Singh stood. "If you'll excuse me, good people, I will say good-night. My wife will be worried if I stay out much longer, and she will already be cross that I have no appetite for her curries this evening."

"Of course. I'm terribly sorry if—"

"Do not be sorry, Mr. Sinclair. I have very much enjoyed this evening in your company. Rarely do I disembark on arrival, the lot of a driver, you know."

Rowland walked Singh out to the Buick, so that he could thank the driver again. Singh assured him that he had not been at all alarmed by his part in the excursion and was prepared to discharge more dangerous duties if the need arose.

Amused, Rowland waved Singh into the late-night congestion of Kiangse Road and returned to his friends. Wing Zau, who had been noticeably quiet in Singh's presence, reanimated somewhat and told them of Shanghai during the war, emptied of Englishmen and Europeans who had returned to fight for king and country on both sides of conflict. He spoke of the Chinese labourers who had dug the allied trenches. "After the war, the Shandong Peninsula, Chinese land, was given to the Japanese. Many Chinese believe that our allies betrayed us."

Rowland frowned. "They probably did. The spoils of war don't often bring out the best in men."

"No, no...I apologise Mr. Sinclair." Wing shook his head. "A wise man does not allow past wrongs to poison the friendships he makes today."

"An ancient Chinese saying?" Milton topped up Wing's glass with Sassoon's cognac.

Wing shrugged. "Perhaps. I read it on a restroom wall in Boston, but I'm sure my honourable ancestors would concur."

Rowland laughed. "When were you in Boston, Mr. Wing?"

"I was a student at the Massachusetts Institute of Technology, Mr. Sinclair. My dear father had a great deal of faith in western education."

"Had? Did MIT disappoint him?"

"No, it's not that. Father was arrested and executed in the purge of Communists from Shanghai."

Edna gasped. "Oh, Mr. Wing."

Clyde shook his head. "We're truly sorry to hear that, Wing."

Wing nodded sadly in the wake of their condolences. "They were difficult years. All the tears in China might have flooded the Huangpu. For my mother's sake, I went to work for Sir Victor. There is a certain protection afforded to the Cathay."

Rowland frowned thoughtfully. Sassoon did seem to wield a great deal of power and influence in Shanghai, and he had gone to great lengths to distance the investigation of Alexandra Romanova's death from the hotel itself.

"Shall we have some music?" Edna suggested before the conversation became too sombre. "Where do you suppose Sir Victor keeps the records? Perhaps he has some Fats Waller... Rowly, what's wrong?"

He grimaced. "Nothing really." He felt inside his pocket for the silver discs Van Hagen had given him that morning. "I just remembered that Mr. Van Hagen had given me these."

Rowland placed the first disc on the gramophone's turntable, and they all stood around to listen, intrigued by the Cathay's elaborate method of taking messages.

The voice that came out of the bell was scratchy, but it was that of Andrew Petty. He spoke smoothly and without awkwardness, but possibly he had left recorded messages at the Cathay Hotel before.

"I say, old boy, where on earth are you? I heard about this awful business in your suite, quite outrageous if you ask me. My condolences, old bean. A dreadful, positively dreadful introduction to Shanghai. Now they tell me you've checked out—I don't wonder! But the jumped-up little demagogue behind the counter won't tell me where your digs are now. So I shall have to leave that to you. Telephone me via the exchange, and let me know where you're staying. I don't suppose you've had someone show you the sights yet. And there are, of course, matters of business aside from pleasure.

"Well then...toodle-oo old boy."

Rowland stifled a yawn. "I'll call him in the morning."

"Who made the other messages?" Edna asked, looking closely at the silver discs.

"Put them on and let's see."

Edna chose one and exchanged it with the one already on the turntable. She set the needle.

"Mr. Sinclair..."

Rowland stiffened and stepped closer to the gramophone. The voice was Alexandra Romanova's.

"Mr. Sinclair...is this working? Oh yes. Dear Mr. Sinclair, I'm afraid I won't be able to keep our appointment for tea and cakes today. I hope you will forgive and you will come find me at the Jazz Club this evening. I must talk to you, to explain, though I cannot come this afternoon... He will know. I think you are kind, Mr. Sinclair...Rowland, so I hope you will understand, that you will help me."

The recording became faint—barely audible.

"May God protect you..."

The gramophone scratched silence.

Rowland lifted the needle and played it again.

"Oh, Rowly." Edna grabbed his hand before he could play it a third time. "That poor girl." The sculptress's voice was unsteady. Even on the recording, there had been a palpable fear in Alexandra Romanova's voice. And just hours later she would be dead.

Rowland nodded. "God, if we hadn't stepped out..."

Edna pulled him down to sit beside her. "We don't know that, darling. You would have helped her if you'd been given the chance."

Milton cursed. "What the hell is going on here? Did she say anything to you, Rowly—that night at the Jazz Club?"

Rowland shook his head. "We talked about music and books. She spoke of returning to Russia one day with her brother. She made sure I wasn't married before she suggested I ask her to tea. She was charming and confident... There was nothing."

"She made a beeline for Rowly," Clyde said thoughtfully. "It was as if she had singled him out."

Edna frowned. "That's hindsight. She might just have found Rowly particularly handsome."

"Perhaps," Clyde conceded, "but considering what's happened... She did say she wanted to explain, that she wanted him to understand. That sounds like she wanted to talk about more than standing him up for tea."

Rowland nodded. "Clyde's right. She'd already apologised for breaking the appointment. What could she have possibly wanted me to understand?"

"She used the recording like she was writing a letter," Edna observed.

"Many people do." Wing Zau poured another round of brandy. Despite the roaring fire, Alexandra's voice had chilled them all. "Most people find leaving a spoken message quite awkward and uncomfortable at first. Some people shout, others giggle, and some speak as if they are dictating a letter or a telegram. Mr. Petty's obviously left messages at the Cathay before, but I doubt Miss Romanova has."

Milton rested his elbows on his knees, sitting forward and swirling the brandy in his glass. "We need to decide what we're going to do with the recording."

"What do you mean?"

"Randolph will use it against you, Rowly."

"How could he?"

"He could well use it to allege that your relationship with Miss Romanova was much more than merely dancing with her the night before she was killed. You could read almost anything into what she said."

Rowland exhaled. He could see Milton's point. But still. "We can't withhold it, Milt. It may be a clue to who killed Miss Romanova."

"I agree," the poet said carefully. "Or I would, if I thought Randolph was actually investigating who killed her. As far as I can tell, he's already decided it was you. I say we don't help him lock you up."

Chapter Fifteen

CHRISTMAS MESSAGES

BY PHONOGRAPH RECORDS

LONDON, Nov. 12.

A number of Australians living in London are taking advantage of the opportunity of sending messages to friends in Australia at Christmas by means of personal phonograph records. The novelty allows of a 90 seconds record for one shilling. The record is delivered to the customer before he leaves the shop.

Sir Edward Macartney (Agent-General for Queensland) is sending greetings to the Brisbane Golf Club in this manner.

—*Sydney Morning Herald*, 14 November 1930

They argued and drank well into the night. Milton was adamant that handing over the disc to Randolph would be a mistake; Rowland and Clyde were reluctant to withhold evidence that might lead to Alexandra Romanova's killer. Edna did not want to do anything that might make matters worse for Rowland, and Wing would say nothing but that he would do or not do whatever they wanted him to.

"Right," Milton said finally. "What say you take the recording to your lawyers, Rowly? Let that fellow, Carmel, decide what to do with it. At least then they can prepare your defence first."

Rowland glanced at Clyde. It seemed a reasonable compromise. "Very well, that's what we'll do."

Edna leant drowsily against Rowland's shoulder. "Thank goodness that's sorted."

"What about the other message, sir?" Wing picked up a third silver disc.

"I guess we'd better listen to it," Rowland said half-heartedly. It was already one in the morning.

Wing placed the disc carefully on the turntable, wound the gramophone's handle, and set the needle.

"Yes...Sinclair...Sinclair? How does this infernal contraption work? Oh yes, then. Alastair Blanshard here. Look, Sinclair, I'm leaving Shanghai for a couple of days. I'll be in touch when I return. There are a couple of things you should know. In the meantime, I want you to be particularly careful. Do not take any chances. I'll explain when I get back. With regards and so forth—Blanshard."

Rowland groaned, suppressing a curse. Blanshard and his ridiculous obsession with cloak and dagger! He had no idea what exactly the Old Guardsman was doing in Shanghai, but it appeared he was at least still playing at being a spy.

For a few moments they contemplated the recording, and then Clyde broke the somnolent silence.

"So, Rowly, what do you think?"

Rowland shifted, trying not to wake Edna, who had fallen asleep on his shoulder. "It's my considered opinion we should go to bed and deal with it in the morning."

Milton stretched. "I'll second that." He poked the sculptress. "Wake up, Ed. You're too fat to carry up to bed."

Edna was not so deeply asleep that the poet did not get a fitting response.

Rowland laughed as he helped her to her feet. "Our troubles will still be here in the morning... Perhaps by then it will all make a little more sense."

Rowland was the first to wake the next morning. He had again slept fitfully, haunted by Alexandra's last message. What had she wanted to speak to him about? What could she have needed to explain? Surely it had to be something more than why she couldn't meet him for tea. He showered and dressed and slipped downstairs, still contemplating the recording. Kiangse Road was already busy though it was barely light, the clatter of rickshaws passing the louvered shutters, the faint cacophony of languages.

Rowland stared at the silver discs beside the gramophone. They were all marked simply "Sinclair." He'd have to play them again to determine which was which. Bracing himself, he wound the gramophone. Alexandra's message was the second, and as chilling and tragic in the light of day as it had been the evening before. Rowland ran a hand through his hair as she signed off, allowing the disc to run while he mentally replayed everything she'd ever said to him. Another voice caught his attention, a man's voice. Faint, speaking what sounded like French.

"*Votre Majesté!*"

Rowland looked up sharply. Your Majesty?

Alexandra's voice. "I'm sorry. Don't. Please, I'm coming."

And then nothing. Rowland moved the needle and listened

again. He let the disc play out in case there was anything else. There was not.

Edna came down the stairs in pyjamas. "Rowly? What on earth are you doing up so early? It's barely six in the morning."

He beckoned her over and played her the end of the recording that they'd missed the night before.

"*Votre Majesté*? She's not—"

"I don't know. It seems unlikely."

"Still, Romanova."

"There are probably thousands of Romanovas. Ed—it doesn't mean... The Russian royal family was executed by the Bolsheviks."

Edna pushed the oversized sleeves of her pyjamas up to her elbows. Though she'd awoken only shortly before, her eyes were bright. "There are rumours that the youngest princess escaped."

Rowland rubbed the back of his neck absently. He had of course heard the widespread speculation that the Princess Anastasia had survived. There were even stories that both Anastasia and her brother, the tsarevich, had been spared or escaped the slaughter of the Romanovs—a romantic hope more than anything else. "Surely if she was a princess in hiding from the Bolsheviks, she wouldn't call herself Romanova?"

"Perhaps the Romanov name is all she has left."

Rowland began to wonder now. There had been a sense of divine right to Alexandra's determination to return to Russia... but that was possibly common to all aristocrats. "She sounded terrified."

"Of someone who called her 'your Majesty.'" Edna reset the needle and listened again. "I'm certain he's not a Frenchman," she said. "His accent isn't right."

Rowland nodded. Edna's mother had been French, and her mother's language had been her first. He could hear it now, himself. An unnecessary heaviness in the r...not obvious, but the man was probably not French.

She took him by the hand. "Come with me, I'm going to teach you how to make a pot of tea."

"Why?"

"Because a grown man should not be quite so helpless without servants."

Though he did not think making tea could possibly be that complicated, Rowland allowed her to lead him into the kitchen and show him how to scald and warm the pot, measure out the leaves, and steep the brew. He was, in the end, surprised that the task was so involved. But by the time the rest of the household descended to the lower floor, he had made tea for them all.

Edna ran upstairs to dress, while Rowland played the men the end of the recording.

"Do you have any inkling as to who that might be, Mr. Wing?"

"There are a great many people in Shanghai who speak French, sir."

"Including you, Rowly," Milton noted.

"Still, it's something." Clyde sampled the tea. "Not bad, Rowly. You'll be pressing your own suits next."

"Let's not get carried away."

The notion was rendered unnecessary by the arrival of Ranjit Singh and his sister, Harjeet. Harjeet Kaur Bal was a physically substantial woman, strong and cheerful. Her children were now grown and married themselves. She missed organising their day-to-day lives, being busy and needed, and so she had responded enthusiastically when her brother had told her of the hapless Australians who were in need of help. Their difficulties with the police aside, Harjeet trusted her brother's assessment that these were good people, modern and a little wild in the way that Westerners were, but decent. They would pay well, he assured her, and he would be nearby. And so she arrived at Kiangse Road ready to take over the running of Victor Sassoon's house.

She liked Rowland Sinclair immediately. His British reserve was mitigated by an easy smile, and his manners were impeccable.

Milton Isaacs was a rascal, Harjeet thought, but not a bad boy. Clyde Watson Jones seemed a little older and perhaps wiser, but he was very respectful. Harjeet might have been scandalised by the easy familiarity with which Edna Higgins dealt with the men, but the young woman was a Westerner, and Western women in Shanghai were often unconcerned about their reputations. In any case, Harjeet felt a creeping admiration of the utter lack of self-consciousness in Edna's manner. It was endearing more than shocking.

Wing Zau attempted to apprise Harjeet of the contents of the pantry and her duties, but she shooed him away, declaring that she had run households since before he wore trousers. He made a rather futile attempt to exert his authority, and the exchange became somewhat heated before Wing emerged from the kitchen defeated. In twenty minutes Harjeet Baal served them a breakfast of savoury pancakes and vegetable curry, accompanied by coffee and fresh fruit.

"Right." Rowland stood, having eaten his fill. "I'd better take Alexandra's recording to Mr. Carmel, and then see if I can track down Andrew Petty. I've probably missed a couple of meetings already."

"Give us a moment to finish breakfast—"

"There's no need for you all to come—I expect it'll be rather dull. We've barely had a chance to look around Shanghai properly. Why don't you take the taxi and explore? I can walk to the Bund from here."

"Shouldn't I come with you, sir?" Wing rose.

"No, Mr. Carmel speaks English quite well for a lawyer. The others may need you more than I."

"Rowly, are you sure that Du chap—" Clyde began.

"Mr. Du is no longer a problem. I telephoned the bank this morning." Rowland glanced at his watch. "I don't expect I'll be all that long. What say I catch up with you somewhere?"

"I think I'll go with you anyway." Clyde snatched the linen

napkin from his collar and motioned towards Edna, who had left the table to fetch her camera from the drawing room. "I'm a bit fed up with being Ed's leading man."

Milton snorted, lifting his chin haughtily. "Believe me, my friend, while I'm in the frame, you've a supporting role at best."

Clyde stood to retrieve his hat from the hook by the door. "Righto then, Rowly, we'll leave Ed to make 'An Idiot in Shanghai' and go deliver this recording."

Rowland laughed. "Fair enough. If Ed can spare you." He stopped, turning back to Milton and Wing. "Shall we meet at the Cathay tea rooms—let's say half past two? I'd like to have a look at the recording booths."

His mouth full, the poet waved his fork in agreement.

The sculptress was already rolling film, and so their farewell and departure was captured on celluloid.

The red door was barely closed behind them when Clyde raised the issue of Mrs. Dong, whose remains were still hidden beneath Clyde's bed.

"What exactly were you supposed to do with Mrs. Dong?" Rowland asked.

"Danny wrote to his cousins to tell them to come to the Cathay, but since we're no longer there..."

"Perhaps we should give Mrs. Dong into Van Hagen's keeping."

"We can't just leave her there for collection like a lost hat. What if Van Hagen gives her to the wrong people?"

"How many people will come to the Cathay asking for human remains?"

"I don't know, mate, but I promised Danny that I would look after the old girl." Clyde sighed. "I was terrified of her when Danny and I were little tackers, but still..."

Rowland smiled. "Of course. We'll sort something out—I'm sure the Cathay can simply alert us when Danny's cousins turn up."

"I hope they don't take too long," Clyde grumbled. "There's

only so long you can be expected to keep someone's grandmother under the bed."

They made their way down Kiangse Road, towards the Bund, picking their way through the press of people, dodging the occasional erratic rickshaw.

"One helluva job," Rowland murmured as they watched a barefoot driver drag grown men in his cab.

"It's opium, you know."

Rowland and Clyde turned to see Emily Hahn skipping to catch up with them. They stopped and she stepped between them, hooking her arms through theirs. "Most of the rickshaw drivers are opium addicts. Deadens the pain I expect."

"Good morning, Mickey," Rowland said, moving his head to avoid being hit by the feathers in her hat.

"I was just about to hail a rickshaw to work."

"You don't mind that the drivers are opium addicts?" Clyde asked.

She smiled up at him. "Opium is part of the real China, not to mention the muse of men like Coleridge and Cocteau. I've always wanted to be an opium addict myself."

"We're on our way to the Bund." Rowland decided to leave the declaration alone. "We'd be pleased to escort you if you have the time to walk."

"Well, thank you, I think I will." She turned to look at Rowland, hitting Clyde in the face with the feathers in her hat. "Are you going to see your lawyers?"

"How did you—"

"I'm a journalist, Rowland. I'm not covering the murder but, you know, old habits."

"I see."

"The dead woman's brother called by the Cathay looking for you, you know."

"I didn't."

"Yesterday evening. He seemed quite agitated. Victor and

I had just come in from the boat. Of course, the staff has been instructed to tell no one where you are. Poor chap. Inspector Randolph intercepted him, took him for questioning there and then."

"Why did Randolph want to question him?"

"Beats me."

"And afterwards?"

"I don't know. Victor and I went dancing."

The conversation fell into matters less consequential then. Emily told them a little of her time in the Congo, where it appeared she had developed a love for primates.

"What exactly brought you to Shanghai?" Rowland asked.

"A broken heart. Shanghai's the kind of place that helps you to forget."

"I see. I'm terribly sorry."

"Victor advises against throwing sentiment away on self-pitying drunks." She sighed. "He's right, of course. He's been very kind and attentive…but then Victor does have a soft spot for girls with broken hearts. And what about you gentlemen? I have bared my soul now you must do the same."

"Rowly is here on family business," Clyde replied. "The rest of us just came along for the ride."

The feathers slapped Rowland's chin now. "That's hardly baring your soul. Try harder, Mr. Watson Jones!"

"Well, I'm afraid…"

"That's really all there is to it, Mickey." Rowland came to Clyde's rescue. "We're utterly dull."

"Well, we'll just have to do what we can to make you more interesting!"

Rowland laughed. "That's very kind of you."

"You can start by coming to Bernadine's salon tomorrow evening."

"Bernadine?"

"Mrs. Szold-Fritz. A dear friend from Chicago who's settled

here. Bernadine is one of nature's catalysts, like manganese dioxide. She makes things happen!"

"I'm afraid we haven't had the pleasure."

"I'll arrange for invitations if you must hang on such formalities."

They had by then reached the steps of the *North China Daily News*, where Emily Hahn bid them farewell.

"Do you think she meant what she said about wanting to try opium?" Clyde whispered as they watched her walk up the steps.

"I believe she said she wanted to be an opium addict."

"But do you think she meant it?"

"Yes."

Chapter Sixteen

"Detestable"

English Pudding

In 1658 Chevalier d'Airieux wrote of the English Christmas pudding: Their pudding was detestable. It is a compound of scraped biscuits, as flour, suet, currants, salt, and pepper, which are made into a paste, wrapped in a cloth, and boiled in a pot of broth; it is then taken out of the cloth, and put in a plate, and some old cheese is grated over it, which gives it an unbearable smell. Leaving out the cheese, the thing itself is not so very bad.

—*Daily Mercury*, 19 December 2939

Rowland and Clyde arrived at the Pudding Club in the International Concession a little before midday. The recording of Alexandra Romanova's last message that they'd presented to Gilbert Carmel had caused the solicitor some mild concern, but he had agreed to take it to the authorities himself. He gave them an undertaking that he would see what he could find out about the murder of the taxi girl. The wool broker, Andrew Petty, met them as arranged at the door. He pumped Rowland's hand.

"Rowly, how perfectly wonderful to see you, old man! You're looking well despite this dreadful business at the Cathay. You must tell me about it over a drink."

Rowland introduced Clyde.

"Mr. Watson Jones? I say, you're not perchance related to the Toorak Watson Joneses are you? They were in timber I believe."

"No, I'm not…in timber or related."

"Well, come in. The boy will take your coats. Rather traditional establishment this, founded to uphold the English tradition of pudding in Shanghai I believe."

"Do the Chinese not have sweets?" Clyde asked.

"Oh yes, they have those infernal mooncakes and the like, but nothing like a jam roly-poly or a spotted dick—good British puddings. It's that sort of harmless indulgence for which one finds oneself homesick more often than not."

He led them into the gentlemen's club, a bastion of studded leather and oak panels. Aided by the smog of cigar and pipe smoke, the lighting was dim enough to evoke the gloominess of an English day. There was little evidence in the club's décor of its location in Shanghai. It was thoroughly and intentionally British, with the exception of the Chinese waiting staff.

Petty ushered them to seats and duly ordered drinks.

"Now suppose you tell me about this dreadful business with the Russian girl."

Uncomfortable with Petty's interest, Rowland told him as little as he could without being obviously evasive.

"My giddy aunt! Your hotel room? Did you give the young lady your key?"

"No."

"Good Lord! And now Sassoon's stowed you at digs somewhere appalling I expect? Why that's outrageous!"

"I'm afraid our suite was designated a crime scene, and no others were available."

"Still, it's convenient for him."

"I beg your pardon?"

"Old Sassoon has quite the reputation, you know. A patient of Dr. Voronoff, I'm told."

"I'm sorry?"

"Dr. Serge Voronoff who came to international attention for a certain surgical method."

Rowland, who had a vague idea of the procedure for which the Russian surgeon was notorious, did not ask further. Sadly Clyde had never heard of Voronoff, and did.

Petty grinned gleefully. "Voronoff specialised in transplanting thin slices of baboon testicles into human scrotums."

"Whatever for?" Clyde asked weakly.

"In the hope of rejuvenating the gentleman concerned."

Rowland flinched, Clyde looked decidedly pained. Petty carried on.

"Sir Victor has quite a reputation for…voraciousness. If it wasn't for the fact that the poor girl was found in your suite, I've no doubt that the police would be looking carefully at him."

Rowland's face was unreadable. "Sir Victor has been very accommodating—a perfect gentleman and host."

"Well, I suppose you could say that. He's given you somewhere to stay and, in doing so, conveniently severed your connection with his hotel. He's wily, I'll give him that."

"Are you saying you think Sir Victor killed Miss Romanova?" Clyde blurted.

"Good Lord, no! I'm merely ruminating on the likelihood that Victor Sassoon would have a key to every nook and cranny within the hotel, including your suite."

Rowland refused to be drawn further on the subject. "I expect the police have it all in hand, Mr. Petty."

"No doubt." He signalled the waiter to replenish their drinks. "You'll be very pleased to know I've arranged for you to meet some influential gentlemen from Japan."

"I see."

"With all this talk of a pending trade embargo, the Japanese are eager to secure a reliable supply of wool, and what's more, they are prepared to pay very handsomely for it. As you may be aware, your brother has been stockpiling the portion of the Sinclair clip for a number of seasons."

Details of the Sinclair wool stockpile, accrued since the early twenties, was not something of which Rowland would normally have been aware had it not been for the intensive briefing to which Wilfred had subjected him before they'd left Sydney. He was, as a result, able to look unsurprised.

"This is an exciting opportunity, Rowland. You, old boy, have every chance of returning to Sydney having secured a very lucrative deal indeed."

Momentarily, Rowland considered confessing that he had been strictly directed to commit to nothing while in Shanghai, but decided against it. "I look forward to meeting these gentlemen."

"They've invited us to join them for a banquet at the Paramount Ballroom in Little Tokyo." Petty glanced anxiously at Rowland. "It's something of an elaborate affair, I believe. I could arrange a suitable young lady for you—"

"That's very kind of you, Mr. Petty," Rowland replied. "But I can make those arrangements myself."

"Yes, of course…a young man with your breeding and prospects—of course you can."

"I must say I was rather surprised to see Alastair Blanshard the other day. I don't suppose you know what the old dog's doing in Shanghai?"

"Alastair? Goodness me! I believe he's just taking in the sights…grand tour of the East or some such thing."

"So he's not here on business?"

"Not any of which I'm aware."

They finished their drinks then, over conversation about cricket and weather. Unaware that Rowland had no intention of making any deals, Petty did try to impart some wisdom on commercial negotiation. "Even if their proposition seems an excellent one, it is a better strategy to approach it with a blend of poise and reserve. We're British after all. Under all circumstances, Rowly, my boy, you must not allow excitement to win the day. Follow my lead—I'll subtly signal you if the offer is good enough to accept."

Eventually they made their excuses and took their leave of Petty, setting out from the Pudding Club to return to the Cathay Hotel.

"Your friend Petty doesn't seem to have much time for Sassoon," Clyde said as they made their way back towards the Bund.

"I noticed."

"Even so, he may have a point."

"Why would Victor Sassoon kill a taxi girl?" There was more speculation than scepticism in Rowland's question.

"Perhaps he knew her, Rowly. Miss Hahn did say Sassoon had a yen for girls with broken hearts—it might have been a crime of passion."

"Possibly." Rowland frowned. He didn't know about a broken heart, but there had been a wistful sadness about Alexandra. "Sassoon is putting us up."

"That doesn't mean we shouldn't suspect him."

"No…but it does seem rather ungrateful."

Clyde grinned. "Not to mention impolite."

Rowland grimaced. He had just been thinking that accusing their host would be rude.

It took them about half an hour to make their way back to the Cathay, but even so, they arrived at the hotel with twenty minutes to spare. Rowland spoke to Van Hagen, making him aware that they were holding a package for which the owners might call.

"Do you wish me to give these men your new address, sir?"

"No," Rowland said after a moment's thought. "But perhaps if you could take their details and get in touch with us as soon as possible?"

"Very good, sir." The concierge returned to his duties.

"Let's have a closer look at these recording booths," Rowland said, beckoning Clyde to follow.

The booths were along one wall of the foyer, individual cubicles equipped with a phonograph. There was a glass window in the door of each booth which allowed one to ascertain if it was in use. Rowland let himself into an empty booth and closed the door. He was impressed by the silence within. The cubicle was well sealed for sound. The French-speaking man would have had to have come into the booth to have been caught on the recording. He beckoned to Clyde through the window. Clyde opened the door and stepped in. It was a tight fit with two grown men. Alexandra was smaller than him, of course, but Rowland was struck by the necessary proximity of anyone within the booth. Alexandra had sounded terrified. As it turned out, with good reason.

A rapping on the glass and Milton's face pressed against it. Clyde opened the door to find the poet and the sculptress outside.

"Where's Wing?" Clyde asked.

"In the kitchens," Edna replied. "He wanted to talk to the chef again. He'll meet us back at Kiangse Road."

They found a table in the Jasmine Lounge in which to take tea and share reports of the day. Milton and Edna had spent the morning exploring the French Concession and had taken seats at a matinee show at the Cathay Theatre, which apparently was also owned by Victor Sassoon.

Rowland recounted their meetings with Gilbert Carmel and Andrew Petty, being careful to keep his voice down as he repeated what Petty had told them about Sassoon.

"Do you think it's true?" Edna heaped sugar into the cup she'd filled with Russian Caravan tea.

Rowland shrugged, taking a finger sandwich from the multitiered silver platter of savouries and cakes placed on the table between them. "I get the impression that Mr. Petty does not particularly like Sir Victor, so it might all be vindictive gossip."

"But the fact remains," Clyde said quietly, "Sassoon could have killed Miss Romanova."

"Steady on, Clyde. We don't even know if he knew her."

"She worked in his hotel. He's bound to have run into her, seen her around…"

"Maybe."

"What was he doing when Miss Romanova was killed? Was he even in the hotel?"

"I don't think anyone's asked him," Rowland said, choosing another sandwich.

"Perhaps we should."

Rowland considered it. "Mickey—Miss Hahn—might know. She seems to spend rather a lot of time with him, and we could probably ask her less offensively."

"Why do you suppose Miss Romanova's brother wishes to see you?" Clyde asked, reminded by the mention of Emily Hahn of what she had told them that morning.

Rowland grimaced. "I presume the poor chap's been told that she was found in our suite. He probably wants to know what she was doing there. I would."

Clyde nodded. "What are you going to do?"

Rowland checked his wristwatch. "Thanks to Mr. Wing, we have Alexandra's address. She lived with her brother, I believe. I'll call on him this afternoon and offer my condolences."

Clyde and Milton exchanged a glance. "We'll come with you, comrade," the poet declared. "Clyde and I met her too."

"We'll all go," Edna added determinedly. "Perhaps there's something we can do."

Alexandra Romanova had lived in one of the less fashionable districts of Shanghai. The European architecture gave way to humbler Chinese-style dwellings and rundown tenements. There were few cars here, the roads ruled by rickshaws.

"Russians live here predominantly, and the Chinese," Singh informed them as they waited for a rickshaw to give way. "A very poor area. A lot of crime." He pulled his taxi up beside a butchery. "This is the address. I think she must have lived above the shop." He pointed to the rusted iron stairs around the side. "Shall I wait for you all here, sir?"

"I'm not sure how long we'll be," Rowland said apologetically.

"Not at all, sir. I'll do my meditation while I wait. It will be time well spent."

Though Milton was curious to witness Singh meditating in the taxi, they left him to it and climbed the creaking iron stairs to a small landing outside a weathered door. They could hear music from within, a melancholy violin. Rowland knocked. At first it seemed the knock was unheard against the music, but when Rowland pounded more loudly, the violin stopped. A few moments later, the door was thrown open by an enormous young man. Sergei Romanov was at least as tall as Rowland and about twice as wide. His hair was the same silvery blond as his sister's had been, swept back from a broad, bearded face. The violin seemed small and toy-like in his large hands. He reeked of sorrow and alcohol, and swayed a little as he stood.

"Sergei Romanov?"

"Who asks?"

"I'm Rowland Sinclair. We've come to—"

Perhaps Rowland's eyes were lowered as he prepared to offer condolences, for what came next caught him completely by surprise. He reeled as Romanov broke the violin against the side of his head. Divested of their burden, the Russian's hands closed around Rowland's throat. Clyde and Milton jumped in, trying to pull the man off, but lack of space aided the white-hot fury of Romanov, who was trying to throw Rowland off the landing. Clyde managed to pry one of the Russian's hands away from Rowland's neck. Undeterred, Romanov used it to punch Rowland in the jaw instead, elbowing Milton in the face at the same time.

"Murderer!" he hissed. "*Ubiytsa!*"

Rowland fended off another blow and wrenched himself, gagging, from Romanov's grip. The Russian turned on Milton. Clyde scrabbled to prevent the poet falling backwards down the steps. Flattened against the doorway, Edna cried a warning as Romanov lowered his head and charged. "Rowly!"

Rowland lunged out of the way. The landing shuddered.

Edna screamed as the corroded railing gave way under Romanov's momentum. Rowland grabbed the Russian's shirt as he fell, and Clyde, his arm. For a few panicked moments Romanov flailed. Then Milton managed to grasp his other arm, and slowly the Australians heaved him back onto the landing. Milton sat on him, lest he see fit to attack again, and they stayed there, all trying to catch their breaths.

A few people had gathered to watch the commotion, but only a few, and they soon dispersed. A scuffle between Europeans was apparently not, in this part of Shanghai, sufficiently interesting to distract people from the necessities of their day. From the landing, they could see the taxi, but Singh's meditations had obviously rendered him insensible to the fracas above.

"Mr. Romanov," Rowland said, touching the side of his head gingerly. His fingers came away covered in blood. He winced. "I didn't kill your sister, sir. I only came because I was told you were looking for me."

From his position pinned to the landing floor, Romanov glared at him and cursed.

Edna intervened. "We came to offer our condolences, Mr. Romanov. Couldn't we talk inside?"

"You want me to invite my sister's murderer into my home?" His words were slow and slurred.

Edna picked up the remains of the violin. Her eyes softened as she looked at the grieving musician. "Rowly didn't kill Alexandra. He just happened to find her body." She told Milton to let Romanov up. "We'll go if you want us to, Mr. Romanov, but you should know that we are just trying to find out what happened to your sister."

Romanov said nothing for a moment, clambering unsteadily to his feet. The Australian men stood tense and ready should he explode again.

Instead, the Russian's great shoulders collapsed. He shook his head and walked into the apartment. "Come."

Inside, the dwelling above the butchery was sparse and dim—essentially a large single room. A primus stove on an upturned crate beside a sink served as a kitchen. There was a bed in the corner, unmade and piled with blankets. A couple of dresses on hangers hung ad hoc on the picture rail. Rowland recognised the red gown Alexandra had been wearing the night he'd met her. An old couch and another wooden crate topped with a cushion were positioned by the dirty window; a shelf fashioned out of bricks and a plank of wood held a few old books and a small porcelain ballerina. Three empty vodka bottles sat beside the ballerina.

Romanov slumped onto the upturned crate and dropped his face into his hands and sobbed.

"We are dreadfully sorry for your loss," Rowland said quietly after a while. "If there's anything we can do for you—"

"You can tell me what happened. Why Sasha was in your room?" Romanov was more despairing than angry now. "Were you her lover?"

"No."

"Why is she dead?" The question was childlike, grief and loneliness wrapped in bewilderment.

"I really don't know. I wish I did." Rowland sat opposite Romanov and told the man everything he could about that night.

"She did not keep your appointment for tea and cakes?"

"No. I waited for about an hour and then I went up."

"Sasha loved cakes...the pretty fancy cakes. And you found her in your bedroom...dead?"

"Yes, but it was not a bedroom," Rowland said firmly. "She was in the drawing room of our suite."

"Of course, of course. A suite." He looked about the meagre room and shame coated his misery. "We didn't always live like this you know."

Rowland nodded. "Is there anything at all we can do for you?"

"*Nyet, nyet*...I will endure. My heart is broken and that is all. I have had a sister since I was five years old. A pretty little sister who danced like a butterfly..."

"At least let me replace your violin." Rowland was desperate to help in some way.

Romanov looked at the splintered pieces of wood Edna had retrieved. "Ah yes, you broke it with your head." He threw his arms in the air. "No matter...I do not want to play anymore."

Edna beckoned the Australians aside. "Clyde, why don't you and Milt see if you can get him decent food?" she said, glancing back at the makeshift kitchen. "I don't think he's had anything but vodka in a while. Rowly and I will stay with the poor man."

"What if he—?"

"We'll be fine." Rowland handed Clyde his pocketbook. "Make sure you get him some coffee."

"Are you sure?" Clyde looked pointedly at Rowland's bloody brow. "He's just attacked you."

"He was drunk."

"It'll be a while before he's sober," Milton observed.

"Let Mr. Singh know we might be longer than we thought," Edna said impatiently. "I don't think the poor man has any fight left in him."

"I wouldn't count on it," Clyde murmured, but he followed Milton out.

Chapter Seventeen

Chinese Revolution

UPRISINGS ALL OVER MANCHURIA
Fresh Successes of Anti-Japanese Struggle

SHANGHAI, Nov. 17.—The Chinese Press continues to be full of reports on the movements of the insurgents in Manchuria. Especially sharp conflicts have taken place near Tunchua, in the East of Manchuria. In October alone the insurgents made 158 attacks in this district, in the course of which 337 Japanese were killed.

The summer operations of the Japanese troops against the insurgents, writes the *China Weekly Review*, ended in victories for the partisans. In actual fact, there is not a single town, not a single railway line in Manchuria safe from the attacks of the insurgents. The most important centres, as Mukden, Harbin, and Chanshun, were attacked during this time. The impossibility of suppressing the armed struggle against the present regime in Manchuria is due, according to this newspaper, to the armed resistance of a considerable section of the population, especially the peasantry.

The *North China Daily News* reports from Harbin that a group of partisans, 10,000 strong, has been formed on the banks of Ussuri and has proclaimed an independent republic. Cannon and reserves of ammunition have enabled this group to repulse all attacks by the regular troops. The partisan troops have amalgamated all the units which have been fighting in Manchuria for the last three years and have been arousing the rebellions in the army of Manchukuo.

—Workers' Weekly, 4 January 1935

By the time Clyde and Milton returned with supplies of eggs and bacon, tinned beans, mooncakes, bread, sugar, and coffee, both Rowland and Romanov had cleaned themselves up a little. Romanov had stopped weeping, expressing his grief instead with music. As he had destroyed his violin attacking Rowland, he sang instead—hymns and Russian folk songs rendered in a resonant baritone. In the confines of the apartment, it was a little startling but not unpleasant.

As there was just the single primus, it was decided that coffee was the most urgent need. They let Romanov sing until it was brewed, and then stopped him mid-chorus to drink. Clyde found a frypan and set about cooking the man a meal.

Sobriety seemed reluctant to return to the large Russian, but he did at least have food and coffee to dilute the vodka in his stomach. He became tearfully grateful.

"Only Sasha looked after me so well," he said. "She would laugh at me, call me useless bear locked out of forest, but she would look after me. She was the in…int…the clever one."

"Do you have any ideas as to who might have wanted to harm her, Sergei?" Edna asked. "Did she have any enemies?"

"Bolsheviks, only the Bolsheviks." He lapsed into a string of vehement Russian, which Rowland chose not to translate. Even so, it was apparent to Clyde and Milton that their own Communist affiliations were best left unmentioned.

"Anyone else?" Edna pressed. "Was there anyone with whom she'd fallen out?"

"Fallen? She did not fall."

"Was there anyone with whom she'd argued?"

"*Nyet*, everyone loved Sasha!"

"Did Alexandra have a suitor?"

Romanov looked at Rowland. "Him! He suited her. Her rich foreigner with blue eyes!"

"She met Rowly only a few days ago. Was there anyone before him?"

Romanov shrugged despondently. "There were many men in love with Sasha. She was beautiful." He looked at Rowland. "No?"

Rowland nodded. "She was lovely."

Romanov sighed. "If she had a lover, she might not have told me… She would not have wanted me to frighten him away. A bear, she called me."

"What did Inspector Randolph tell you?" Clyde put another pot of coffee on to brew. "When he interviewed you yesterday?"

Romanov swiped his hand in Rowland's direction. "He wanted to know about him. It was as if Sasha was of no importance apart from what she was to him…"

"What specifically did he ask you about Rowly?"

"Was he Sasha's lover, he say. Rowland Sinclair killed her, he say… Rowland Sinclair is a Communist, he say!" Romanov began to anger again. So too did Milton.

"What the hell is Randolph playing at? He can't run around telling people Rowly's a murderer—that's flaming slander!"

"Inspector Randolph is wrong," Rowland said calmly. He looked Romanov in the eye. "I found your sister. I tried to help her, but it was too late. I had no reason to kill her. I didn't kill her."

"But she is dead even so," Romanov said miserably. "And I tell you this, my friends, no one cares about a poor Russian girl in Shanghai... Once the tsar himself would have demanded justice for Alexandra Romanova!"

Edna reached over impulsively and pressed his hand. "We'll demand justice for her! We won't let them forget about her."

Romanov's eyes welled again. He tried to speak, and when the words would not come, he reached over and seized the sculptress in a mighty hug. The move was so sudden that Rowland instinctively stood and Clyde armed himself with the frying pan. But Edna returned the embrace, and her friends held back, though they remained wary lest the Russian crush the sculptress in his inebriated enthusiasm.

"You are kind," he said when he finally let her go. "Like Sasha. You must be careful."

"Careful? What do you mean?"

The Russian closed his eyes. He did not answer. Edna did not press him but spoke instead to Rowland. "We should let the poor man get some rest. He's exhausted."

Rowland retrieved the notebook from the inside pocket of his jacket. He flicked through in search of a clean page, pausing just briefly when he came to a sketch he'd made of Alexandra a couple of days before. He continued until he found an unused page. On it he wrote the telephone number at the Kiangse Road house and tore it out of the book before leaving it on the improvised shelf under the porcelain ballerina. "You can contact us on that telephone number or through the Cathay."

Romanov had by then stretched out on the worn couch.

Edna pulled a blanket off the bed and threw it gently it over him. She tucked him in like a child.

"*Spasiba,* Sasha," Romanov murmured half asleep. "You are a good girl. *Izvinee,* Sasha, *Da svidahnia mladshaya syestra...*"

Ranjit Singh delivered them home to a house fragrant with the spices of the dinner his sister had prepared. She fussed at the sight of them, bringing all the men into the kitchen to attend to their injuries with warm water and iodine while she reported on her day. Romanov's violin had left Rowland's temple and brow grazed and bruised, and Clyde and Milton, between them, sported a split lip and a black eye.

"This was all inflicted by the one man?" Harjeet asked, almost admiringly as she checked the abrasion on Rowland's face for splinters.

"He got the jump on us," Milton admitted.

"It is a pity." Harjeet wiped the dirt off the shoulder of Rowland's suit with a damp cloth. "The boy had just collected your other suits for cleaning and pressing. I have arranged for him to come once a week. I will of course launder your shirts and Miss Higgins's frocks myself. Mr. Wing constructed a very nice drying line for me at the back of the house... Goodness knows how the previous residents dried their clothes."

Rowland thanked her. He hadn't actually thought of laundering, but then he rarely had call to do so.

"No trouble, Mr. Sinclair. You did not want luncheon, so I have had plenty of time to organise the house and do the marketing. I've been very careful not to use too much spice today as I expect you are not at all used to it, and tomorrow I will make a Western meal." She smiled proudly. "I can cook anything."

"A loaf of bread, the Walrus said, is what we chiefly need," Milton replied.

"Who is this Walrus?" Harjeet asked, confused.

"An evocation of absurdity, dear lady," the poet said blithely. "The magnificent aromas of your cooking have moved me to verse."

"Lewis's verse," Rowland noted.

Milton continued nevertheless. "If what you've prepared tastes half as good as it smells, I shall be compelled to compose ballads in its honour and yours."

Harjeet giggled, clearly pleased. "What nonsense! If you are hungry, I shall serve."

Over a dinner of curries and rice, served with rotis and sambals, they talked of the day's events. Ranjit joined them at the table though he refused to eat, declaring that his wife would be angry if he was not hungry. Instead he took it on himself to explain the meal Harjeet had placed on the table, advising on how it was best eaten and detailing the differences between the way his sister and wife prepared each dish.

Wing Zau arrived just as the taxi driver was explaining how coconut was scraped to make a sambal.

Milton caught sight of him first. "What happened to you?"

Wing's face sported a rather spectacular black eye, though the stain of iodine revealed that he had entered through the kitchen and encountered Harjeet.

Rowland's eyes darkened. Had Du Yuesheng reneged on their deal?

Taking the seat they'd left for him, Wing tried to explain. "Please do not be concerned, Mr. Sinclair. My dishevelment is nothing to do with the difficulties through which you have already helped me."

"Then what happened?" Singh asked sharply. He eyed Wing Zau suspiciously.

Wing ignored the driver and addressed his reply to Rowland. "I was trying to help."

"Help whom, Mr. Wing?"

"You, sir." Wing grimaced. "I thought I would try and find out about this black man who has been seen with Miss Romanov from time to time."

Singh snorted derisively.

"I see." Rowland vaguely noted the growing animosity between the two men in his employ.

"I attempted to question the men in the band that plays at the Jazz Club." Wing glowered at Singh. "The Americans."

"I take it they were less than forthcoming."

"They were positively standoffish, sir."

"What on earth did you say to them?" Edna asked.

"I asked if any of them had anything to do with the murder of Alexandra Romanova."

"That was possibly a little too direct, Mr. Wing."

"I didn't have much time—Mr. Van Hagen had seen me. I believe I must have offended them."

"I expect you're right." Rowland frowned. "Still, attacking you was unnecessary. I think I might call on them myself tomorrow."

"Are you all right, Mr. Wing?" Edna asked. "Perhaps we should send for a doctor?"

Wing shook his head. "I am perfectly well." He squinted his good eye at Rowland, and then Milton and Clyde. "Did you go see the band too?"

They recounted what had happened when they called on Sergei Romanov. Harjeet, who'd been bringing in yet another dish, turned on her brother. "What were you doing when this was happening, Ranjit? Why did you not help?"

"I did not know." Singh held up his hands. "Or else I would certainly have done something."

It was Wing's turn to snort.

"We were on the landing above the street." Edna came to Singh's defence, exaggerating the truth a little to protect him from Harjeet's ire. "Mr. Singh was parked miles away."

"What use is a driver who parks the car miles from where you must be?" Harjeet shook her head.

But Singh refused to be offended by his sister's barbs. "Next time you must call me," he told Edna. "I will make sure no harm comes to any of you. I am good for more than driving the getaway vehicle."

Edna smiled. "Sergei was just mad with grief, Mr. Singh. He's quite sweet really...just terribly sad."

"May I remind you he clocked Rowly with a flaming violin!" Clyde insisted.

Edna's brow furrowed as she thought of the Russian. "I forgot about the violin—I expect he won't be able to work without it."

Clyde's eyes narrowed. "Yes. Bit odd that he would be so reckless with his only means of employment."

"I don't believe he was thinking clearly at the time," Rowland said.

Still, Clyde was uneasy. "I dunno know, mate. You've been drunk before. You've never hit anyone with one of your paintings."

Rowland shrugged. "I don't generally open the door with a canvas in my hands. I may well have otherwise. In fact, I have a few landscapes that would be better weapons than they are paintings."

"A painting wouldn't really be the best thing for that purpose." Milton helped himself to more rice. "Not unless it was framed. You'd be much better belting someone with your easel."

"Or a paintbrush." Rowland launched an imaginary dart in the poet's direction. "A well-aimed paintbrush could do some damage."

Clyde gave up. Clearly the conversation was going nowhere sensible. Instead he raised their meeting with Andrew Petty and the ball which would be hosted by the Japanese wool buyers.

"A ball?" Edna looked up. "Would you like me to come with you, Rowly?"

"I was rather hoping you would. It might be easier to avoid talking business if I have someone with whom to dance."

Edna smiled. "How could I turn down such a gallant invitation?"

Rowland laughed. "I'd rather dance with you than do anything in the world, Miss Higgins, and I'd be honoured, not to mention eternally grateful, if you'd allow me to escort you to this party. If you consent I have no doubt I shall be the envy of every man in the room."

Edna rolled her eyes. "Now you're being silly."

"Not as much as you think."

"Mr. Wing?" Edna noticed a change in Wing's demeanour. His shoulders were tense and his face rigid. "Is there something the matter?"

"I am Chinese. I do not trust the soldiers of the sun." He turned to Rowland. "You must not deal with Japanese, Mr. Sinclair!"

Singh's brow rose. "Who are you to tell Mr. Sinclair who he may deal with?"

"Who are you to speak to me like that?" Wing demanded.

"I am an employee who knows his place!"

Clyde glanced at Rowland and attempted to placate Wing before he retaliated. "These are businessmen, Mr. Wing, not soldiers."

Wing glared at Ranjit Singh. "Every Japanese is a soldier, whether or not he wears a uniform."

Singh rolled his eyes.

"My mother's family was from Changtu in Manchuria," Wing continued angrily. "Most of them were murdered when the Japanese invaded."

Edna's face softened. "Oh Mr. Wing, how horrible. I'm so sorry."

"The sun soldiers conducted an illegal war, created without cause or honour. They bombed civilians and fired on survivors." Wing's jaw hardened as he recounted the destruction that had been visited upon his cousins, his uncles, and grandparents. "My ancestors are interred in Changtu, and they cannot rest with the feet of the sun soldiers on their necks," he said bitterly. "The Japanese are not finished. They will not be satisfied with Manchuria."

"Do you believe they want more of China?" Rowland asked.

"I believe they want more of the world, Mr. Sinclair."

Chapter Eighteen

Did She Escape?

Did the Princess Anastasia, the youngest daughter of the late Czar of Russia, escape assassination at the hands of the murderers of her father, mother, sisters, and brother? Did she, disguised as a peasant, manage to work her way through the country to Germany? These are questions being asked in Berlin, in connection with a certain young and attractive woman who has been accepted by the former Crown Princess Cecile of Prussia, who was on very intimate terms with the old Russian Court.

Some time ago the young woman referred to visited Berlin and gained audience of Princess Cecile, to whom she unfolded a wonderful story, circumstantial in every detail. She drew graphic word pictures of that dread morning when, in company with her mother and sisters, she helped carry the invalid Tsarevitch down the narrow stone steps into the cellar which was to become the death chamber of the Romanovs. Then she went on to tell how the bodies were bundled into a cart and taken to a spot in some forest far away, where they were to be destroyed, and how she alone of the entire family was not dead and was taken away by a sympathetic peasant.

—*Mercury*, 31 December 1925

Rowland noticed the gleaming black Cadillac limousine parked in the street outside the house when he first entered the drawing room to work on the painting he'd started late the evening before. After the mayhem of the past few days, it had been a relief to lose himself in line and shape, to tackle problems that he actually knew how to resolve.

He'd set his easel up by the window in anticipation of catching the morning light, and so he noticed the motorcar immediately. Of course there were many vehicles parked on Kiangse Road, even at that early hour, and he did not initially think anything of it, concentrating instead on bringing life to his portrait of Alexandra Romanova. He painted her dancing—the way he saw her when he could force the image of her corpse from his mind. It was how he wanted to remember her.

He'd been working for an hour or so, when he noticed that though the Cadillac had not moved, its chauffeur was outside the car, leaning on the bonnet with his eyes fixed on Victor Sassoon's house. Rowland wiped his hands on a rag and looked more closely. He recognised the man in the chauffeur's cap.

Rowland grabbed his jacket from the back of an armchair and slipped it on as he opened the front door.

The chauffeur straightened.

Rowland wove through oncoming traffic and crossed the road to where the Cadillac was parked.

Kruznetsov extended his hand. "Rowly."

Rowland accepted the handshake. "What are you doing here, Nicky?"

Kruznetsov smiled awkwardly. "I was hoping to see Edna."

"Why didn't you just knock on the door?"

"It's only seven o'clock. I did not wish to wake your household."

"Then why did you come this early?"

The Russian shrugged. "I was excited."

Rowland frowned. "Did Du Yuesheng send you?" he asked bluntly.

"No. I work for Master Du in the evenings. During the day I drive for an American lady."

Rowland glanced at the Cadillac. "Where is she?"

"I am to collect her from the hotel at nine o'clock. I took the motor out early in the hope of seeing Edna first. I have been thinking of her every moment since fate brought us together."

"I see."

"You left the hotel, and they would not tell me where you had gone."

"How did you find us then?"

"When you left Master Du's house, I followed." Kruznetsov shifted uncomfortably. "I could not talk with you at Master Du's house—he would think I was working with you, perhaps against him. It would not have been good for you or me." He drew Rowland's attention to the bouquet of flowers on the front passenger seat. "I thought I would call on Miss Higgins this morning and explain that I cannot arrange for her to meet Warner Orland—I promised I would, you remember."

"I'm sure Ed will understand."

"You all must think me a fool," Kruznetsov said.

"Why would we think you a fool?"

The Russian shook his head. "He played a joke, my cousin. We like the Charlie Chan films you see." Kruznetsov spoke with confessional haste. "We heard that they were making a film called

Charlie Chan in Shanghai, and my cousin Ivan he tells me he will drive Charlie Chan himself."

Rowland listened, bemused.

"And I think, of course, if Warner Orland is in Shanghai filming, then Ivan could drive him, and the film is called *Charlie Chan in Shanghai*. But it is made in Hollywood on a set and Warner Orland has never been to China. And everybody knows this but Nickolai Kruznetsov!"

Rowland smiled. "Actually we didn't know either, Nicky. One would expect a film called *Charlie Chan in Shanghai* to be made in Shanghai."

"Ivan—he thinks he is a funny, funny man."

"Ed will understand, Nicky, and she will appreciate that you tried to keep your promise."

"I would like to take her dancing instead," Kruznetsov said. He hesitated, studying Rowland. "If I could ask her father for permission to court her, I would do so, but in his absence I ask you."

Rowland laughed. "Why would you ask me?"

"You are her patron, are you not?"

"No."

The Russian's face fell. "You do not consider me worthy. You refuse your blessing."

Rowland dragged a hand through his hair. This was uncomfortable for many reasons. "You'd better talk to Ed yourself, Nicky." On the other side of the road, Harjeet Bal alighted from Singh's taxi and let herself into the house. "Do you have time for breakfast?" Rowland asked Kruznetsov. "You could give Ed your flowers."

"Yes, yes, I will come." Kruznetsov embraced him. "Thank you, my friend. You will not regret this."

"I rarely regret breakfast," Rowland said, mildly alarmed by the intensity of Kruznetsov's gratitude. "Before we go in, may I ask you a question?"

"Anything, my friend."

"Did you know the young lady I danced with at the Jazz Club? She was beautiful. Her name was Alexandra Romanova."

The smile slipped from Kruznetsov's face. "Her name is not Romanova!" he spat.

"Is it not?"

Kruznetsov took a silver case from his inside breast pocket. He offered Rowland a cigarette before lighting one himself and continuing. "Some years ago, here in Shanghai, a young woman claimed to have survived the Bolsheviks' murder of our beloved tsar and his family. She claimed to be a Russian princess. She did, indeed, resemble the Grand Duchess Anastasia and spoke with knowledge of the Romanovs. Some believed her; they rejoiced and gave her everything they had…but in time it became clear she was an imposter."

"What exactly made it clear?" It was a question not a challenge. Rowland had no wish for Alexandra to be Anastasia Romanova. The taxi girl's life had been wretched enough without adding to it the tragedy of the Romanovs…but perhaps that was why she was murdered.

"She could not have been as old as she claimed. And there was a brother. A big man—strong. He could not have been the tsarevich—who was known to have been sickly and frail. She said, of course, with the cunning of a rat, that the man was not her brother but a loyalist who had helped her escape, that she called him brother out of gratitude only. There were many little things that were not right. Eventually, she was denounced as a fraud and discarded as such."

"But she still called herself Romanova."

Kruznetsov shrugged. "I recognised her at the Jazz Club, a taxi girl." He shook his head in disgust. "But I never spoke with her so I know not what she called herself."

"You know that she's dead? That she was murdered?" Rowland asked.

"So, that was her? The woman in your suite?"

Rowland was surprised. Kruznetsov obviously knew about the murder and its connection with them. And yet it did not seem to have given him pause. "Yes. That was why we were forced to leave the Cathay."

Kruznetsov's lip curled. "Even in death, she causes trouble."

"You disliked her?"

"My mother believed her. She gave the grand duchess her ruby brooch, proud that the last of the Romanovs would wear the only jewel she managed to bring with her from Russia."

"But when you recognised her, you said nothing?" Rowland asked sceptically.

"What point was there? She was working as a taxi girl—clearly she no longer had the brooch or riches of any sort. In time I might have said something...but not that night."

Rowland paused. "That was the first night you saw her at the Jazz Club?"

"I do not go dancing every night, my friend. But yes, I had not seen her before."

Edna was surprised but not displeased by Kruznetsov and his flowers. Wing, on the other hand, regarded him warily. Perhaps this circumspection was rooted in Kruznetsov's association with Du Yuesheng and the bodyguard's consequent knowledge of the debt from which Rowland had rescued his erstwhile butler.

Kruznetsov joined them for breakfast and ate as heartily as he complimented Edna. The sculptress dealt graciously and lightly with his tributes. Eventually the count gathered enough courage to confess that he was unable to introduce her to Warner Orland. "I am sorry, Edna. I am a fool."

"Nonsense. It was a mean trick." She smiled at him, and Rowland saw Kruznetsov's posture buckle a little under the power of it.

"The film, *Charlie Chan in Shanghai*, is showing at the theatre in Frenchtown next week. Will you do me the honour of being my guest, Edna? I will take you dancing afterwards."

Wing grabbed Rowland's arm and whispered in his ear. "No, Mr. Sinclair. It is too dangerous. Do not allow it."

Edna had, by that time, accepted.

Wing shook his head desperately at Rowland.

Rowland grimaced. This was going to be awkward. "My nephew Ernest is a great fan of Charlie Chan. I don't suppose you'd mind if I came too, Nicky? It would give me something interesting to fill my letters home."

Kruznetsov looked startled. So too did Clyde and Milton. As much as they were aware of Rowland's torch for Edna, they had never known him to insinuate himself into her romantic trysts with other men before. Certainly not so clumsily, anyway.

Edna seemed to find the notion amusing. "Oh yes, it would not do for me to join you unchaperoned, Nicky. That would be most improper."

"Of course," Kruznetsov replied finally. "You must join us, Rowly."

After breakfast, Edna walked her Russian count to the door and waved him on his way, before turning back to Rowland. "Tell me, has Ernie ever seen a Charlie Chan film?"

"It's quite possible that he has," Rowland replied.

"I told Mr. Sinclair that you should not go alone," Wing volunteered.

"Why? Do you know something about Count Kruznetsov that we don't, Mr. Wing?" Edna was more curious than cross.

Wing blinked nervously. "It's more what we don't know, Miss Higgins. Like whether he is really a count, whether his relative really drives for this film director, whether that's where he intends to take you."

"Wing's right," Clyde agreed. "Considering that Miss Romanova's murderer is still at large, we should be careful. For all we know, it could be Kruznetsov."

"Now you're being ridiculous," Edna protested. "Nicky didn't know Miss Romanova."

"Actually he did." Rowland told them of his earlier conversation with Nickolai Kruznetsov.

Milton whistled. "She was a charlatan?"

"Either that or she really was the Grand Duchess Anastasia."

"And the good count had a reason to kill her," Clyde said.

"It sounds like many people did," Milton observed. "In the Russian community at least. She used their loyalty to steal from them."

Edna folded her arms, turning away from the conversation. Rowland sensed her uneasiness. "Ed?"

"Alexandra can't defend herself!" Edna replied so fiercely that she startled them all, herself included. She took a breath and continued more evenly. "I'm not saying Nicky's a liar, but she can't defend herself. It seems wrong to decide she was a fraud and a thief."

"We'll speak with her brother," Rowland offered. Edna was right; it was wrong.

Edna's face lifted. "Yes. Sergei will know."

"He can at least tell us what happened," Clyde added. "Not every victim is innocent, Ed."

"No, but nobody deserves to die the way Alexandra did. I don't care if she tried to sell them the Sydney Harbour Bridge, she didn't deserve to die like that."

Rowland placed his arm around the sculptress's shoulders. "We'll call on Sergei this morning."

"And after that we speak to Inspector Randolph," Clyde said firmly. "Tell him what Kruznetsov said. Even if it isn't true, it shows that someone might have had reason to kill her. It might point at someone other than Rowly."

"What's in heaven's name is going on?" Edna asked, craning her head out of the taxi window as the Buick approached the butchery above which Sergei Romanov lived. The street was more congested than normal and at a standstill in front of the butchery. People ran in all directions shouting. "*Quiming a! Sa fla!*"

"There's a fire," Wing said as they climbed out. The translation proved unnecessary. Smoke billowed from the windows above the shop as people ran out of the butchery. There was no fire service in sight.

Rowland caught the arm of an aproned man who had just run out of the shop. "Mr. Wing, please ask him if the tenant upstairs got out?"

Wing complied. "He says he does not know. He has not seen him."

Rowland cursed.

"We'd better see if we can force the door," Clyde said, heading towards the iron stairs.

"Would you stay with Ed?" Rowland called over his shoulder to Wing as he followed.

The Australians took the steps two and three at a time to reach the landing outside the burning building. They could hear the oncoming bells of Shanghai fire trucks in the distance. The smoke was thick and acrid, but the breeze took it out towards the street, and they were able to see and breathe well enough to make out the door.

"Sergei? Are you in there? Sergei!"

They put their shoulders to the door in an attempt to force it.

The explosion was unexpected. It blew the door back and them with it.

Chapter Nineteen

EXILED GERMAN JEWS

SEVERAL HUNDRED IN SHANGHAI.
THREE FOREMOST MEDICAL MEN.

Shanghai, Nov. 6.

The first effect of the anti-Jewish policy of the Hitler Government is expected in Shanghai today, with the arrival of the first batch of several hundred German Jews, who were forced to leave their country following the persecutions. Twenty-six scientists, doctors and other highly skilled professional Germans arrived with their families for the purpose of making their home in China, stating that they would be followed by several hundred others...

—*Kalgoorlie Miner*, 8 November 1933

Edna stifled a scream as flames surged out of the doorway. In the frenzy that followed, firemen manned hand pumps and hoses, and sent a deluge onto the landing. Others took to the stairs with buckets. Wing pulled the sculptress back. "No, Miss Higgins, it's too dangerous."

"Can you see them?" Edna tried desperately to glimpse some sign of her friends through the smoke.

Wing shook his head.

Edna pulled away from him and jostled her way through the crowd towards the stairs.

"Miss Higgins!" Wing pushed after her.

"Ed!" Rowland and Milton hobbled down the stairs with Clyde supported between them. Battered and coughing, they were nevertheless upright.

"The door protected us from the worst of it," Rowland explained as Edna spluttered her relief. "Clyde seems to have done something to his leg though."

They moved out into the road away from the burning building.

Wing waved for Singh and his taxi. "Mr. Watson Jones needs a doctor," he shouted over the rising din. "I'll stay and find out what happened."

Edna opened the back door of the Buick.

"Will you and Ed be all right to get Clyde back to Kiangse Road?" Rowland asked Milton as they eased Clyde into the car.

"I'm all right, Rowly, honest to goodness," Clyde said through gritted teeth.

Rowland pressed his friend's shoulder. "We won't be long. I'd better speak with the authorities—make sure someone knows to look for Sergei Romanov."

Edna reached up to touch Rowland's face. "Rowly, are you sure you're—"

"I'm perfectly well, Ed," he said, suppressing a fit of coughing. "Just a bit sooty." He looked up at the building, which was fully ablaze now. "God, I hope he wasn't in there."

"I'll be back for you, sir," Singh called out of the window as he pressed the car's horn and inched the Buick through the milling crowd.

Rowland and Wing joined a bucket line passing pails of water for a time and then watched as the Shanghainese firemen brought the fire under control. The upper storey was a smouldering ruin, but the fire had been defeated before the flames spread to neighbouring tenements. Wing found the fire captain and spoke to him of Sergei Romanov.

"They have no idea whether he was in the building," he said, returning to Rowland. "There was some kind of fuel stored in the apartment which caused the explosion that blew the door off its hinges, but he says it's too early to tell anything else. They haven't found any remains, but there may be some in the rubble."

"Do they know what caused the fire?"

"Well that depends on whether they find any remains."

"Why."

"If they don't, if the apartment was empty, they will conclude arson. If not, carelessness."

"I see."

By the time they'd left the necessary contact details with the fire captain, Singh had returned for them in the Buick.

"How's Clyde?" Rowland asked, getting in.

"Doctor stitched his wound," Singh replied. "He is not too bad. The doctor is waiting for me to return with you."

"Me?"

"Miss Higgins insists."

The physician was having a cup of tea when Rowland and Wing walked through the door. Edna introduced him as Dr. Rubenstein.

"Rowland Sinclair. How'd you do, sir?"

"Please sit down, Mr. Sinclair, and let me examine you." The physician's accent was thick. He spoke slowly to compensate.

"It's quite unnecessary, Dr. Rubenstein. I just need to clean up."

"Allow me to be the judge of that, Mr. Sinclair." Rubenstein was already checking Rowland's eyes. He took a stethoscope from his bag. "Would you mind removing your jacket and opening your shirt?"

"Is that really necessary? I wasn't hurt."

"Just let him examine you, Rowly," Edna said.

"I'd like to listen to your chest. Smoke inhalation can be dangerous."

Rowland did as he was asked, albeit reluctantly.

Rubenstein stopped for just a moment longer than necessary before he placed the stethoscope on the swastika-shaped scar on Rowland's chest. The physician was visibly tense. "You have been in Germany," he said.

"Yes."

"And this scar? It is an insignia of some sort, a badge."

"It is a violence," Edna said fiercely, protectively.

Rowland reached out and took her hand. "It's all right, Ed. I can assure you, Dr. Rubenstein, this scar does not represent my own views or politics in any way. The injury which left it was inflicted when I was unable to fight back."

"Are you, by any chance, Jewish, Mr. Sinclair?"

"No, sir. Mr. Röhm's objection to me was based on something else entirely."

Rubenstein's eyes widened. "Ernst Röhm?"

Rowland nodded, hoping Rubenstein would ask no more. He didn't like talking about the night the Brownshirts had tried to kill him. Even after nearly two years, and though Röhm was now dead, it was a memory mired in pain and fear. The swastika Röhm had branded into his chest with lit cigarettes was still humiliating; it still burned.

Rubenstein paused. "I am terribly sorry for what happened to you."

"Thank you. But I suspect there are many people who have suffered more than I have at the hands of the current German government."

"Yes. I expect there are. I expect there will be. Would you cough for me, please, Mr. Sinclair?"

Rowland did so.

Rubenstein checked his lungs, allowing the other scars on Rowland's upper body to pass without comment. He examined and cleaned the minor lacerations and contusions sustained in the blast and then told Rowland he could redress. "You and Mr. Isaacs have come out of the incident very well."

"And Clyde?" Rowland asked, worried by the omission.

"Mr. Watson Jones has a cut on his lower leg—shrapnel from the blast, I believe—which required cleaning and several stitches. As long as he keeps the wound clean and stays off the leg for three or four days, I expect him to make a complete recovery."

Rowland slung his tie back around his collar. "Thank you, sir."

Rubenstein's face was thoughtful. "What is your business in Shanghai, Mr. Sinclair?"

"Wool, Dr. Rubenstein. I'm here to trade wool."

"You be careful, Mr. Sinclair. Shanghai is not entirely beyond the reach of the Third Reich."

They were interrupted by Milton, who came down the stairs that led to the second floor bedrooms. He went directly to the drinks cabinet and poured a large glass of scotch. "Clyde sent me down to fetch him a cup of tea… Not all that stoic, our Clyde."

"I'll ask Harjeet—" Edna turned towards the kitchen.

"No need. I've got it right here." The poet held up the glass.

"You can't—"

Rubenstein smiled. "A small medicinal drink will not do any harm and may alleviate discomfort."

Milton grinned triumphantly. "There you go, doctor's orders! I don't suppose you'd care for a medicinal scotch, yourself, Dr. Rubenstein?"

Rubenstein glanced at his pocket watch. "I do believe I may have time—for just one."

Milton handed the glass he'd already poured to Edna. "Take this little pick-me-up to Clyde will you, old thing? You're much better at dispensing sympathy than I am."

Edna rolled her eyes, but she took the glass, calling into the kitchen for a plate of Harjeet's oil cakes before she ran up the stairs.

Milton poured and distributed drinks. He lifted his glass in toast. "To that bloody door."

"Have you arrived recently in Shanghai?" Rowland asked Rubenstein as they took seats in the drawing room.

The doctor nodded. "Yes. I had been trying to leave Germany with my family for a year, but the world does not want Jews. Shanghai is a free port."

"Well, comrade," Milton said sombrely. "I expect you'll be glad you left Germany when you did!"

Rubenstein regarded the poet carefully. "They are presently many Jewish refugees in Shanghai. Of them, the greater number are fleeing the Bolsheviks, my young friend."

Milton faltered. He was not oblivious to the excesses of the Bolsheviks, the stories of life in Stalinist Russia as revolutionary idealism became a totalitarian regime. But he was not yet ready to abandon his ideals, his hope that it could be done better.

Rubenstein redirected the conversation himself, asking politely about Australia. It seemed it was one of the countries that had declined his application to migrate. He was curious about the wool business, and thanks to Wilfred's schooling on the matter, Rowland was able to answer most of his questions.

Rubenstein finished his drink. He stood and replaced the stethoscope into his bag. "I shall return tomorrow to change the dressings on Mr. Watson Jones's leg."

Rowland paid him for the house call and walked him out to Singh's taxi. "Thank you, Dr. Rubenstein," he said as he shook the physician's hand.

"You're welcome, Mr. Sinclair. I hope I did not upset Mr. Isaacs. Young men and their ideals. Sadly, age shows you how ideals may be repurposed by evil men."

Rowland smiled. "I wouldn't worry, sir. Both Milt and his ideals are fairly robust."

Rubenstein's eyes narrowed. "You do not share them?"

"On the contrary. I'm not a Communist, but Milt and I believe in many of the same things."

"Yes, of course." He handed Rowland a card. "Should you have need of me before tomorrow."

Rubenstein climbed into the waiting Buick, and Ranjit Singh closed the door after him. He hesitated. "Mr. Sinclair, may I have a brief word?"

"Is something the matter, Mr. Singh?"

"I want to ask you to be careful of Wing Zau, sir."

"I'm not sure I understand."

"I do not trust him, sir. Gamblers are not so easily reformed, and you have simply taken him on his word. This is Shanghai—the truth is only one of many languages spoken here. He comes and goes… Who does he meet? And he sings. Are you sure about him, sir?"

"Do you have any specific reason to distrust him, Mr. Singh?"

"Beyond the fact that he is a gambler, that he was in league with gangsters…"

"He was in debt rather than in league." Rowland glanced at Rubenstein waiting in the car.

Singh inhaled and set his lips. "I suspect that he's a Communist, Mr. Sinclair. It is a terrible accusation I know, but I have been watching him—"

Rowland interrupted. "I appreciate your concern, Mr. Singh, and I assure you I will be careful, but to be honest, I rather like Mr. Wing."

Singh's lips kneaded for a moment. "You will excuse me if I keep an eye on him, Mr. Sinclair? For my own comfort."

"If you must, Mr. Singh."

———————————❦———————————

Rowland stood for a minute watching as Singh's Buick pulled out and drove off to return the doctor to his home. He wondered if he should do more about the animosity between his employees, but he couldn't very well order Wing and Singh to get along. This was not something he'd had cause to deal with before—at Woodlands the staff was so ably managed by his housekeeper that he had no idea of their personal frictions. Milton was still in the drawing room brooding over his whisky when Rowland walked back into the house.

"Are you all right, Milt?"

"Me? Dandy. Just thinking about what Rubenstein said." He paused thoughtfully. "The good doctor's right, you know."

"About what exactly?"

"As much as the Fascists are wrecking the world, my lot isn't exactly covering itself in glory in Russia."

"No, it's not."

Milton shook his head. "The principles aren't wrong... How could they be wrong?"

Rowland sat opposite him. "Perhaps they're not. Perhaps they're just in the hands of the wrong people."

"Is that true of the Fascists as well?"

Rowland paused and then shook his head. "As far as I can tell, Milt, there are no ideals behind the Nazis. Just the rantings of a madman."

"For all we know, Stalin may be just as mad, Rowly." Milton spoke so quietly he was barely audible, and Rowland was aware of what the admission, the realisation, must have cost him. In many ways, Milton had always been the most certain of them, anchored by his beliefs.

"Quite possibly." Rowland rubbed his face. "Democracy has elevated lunatics and persecuted people before, too... Still, I'm not ready to abandon the idea."

Milton shook an accusing finger at him. "But you, Rowland Sinclair, are a hopeless romantic."

Rowland smiled. Perhaps he should have found the poet's politics as offensive as he did the Fascists', but he didn't. There was nobility and compassion in Milton's belief in the Communist cause—it just relied on an overestimation of human nature. As much as his friend accused him of being a romantic, Rowland suspected that Milton and Clyde were the true idealists. "Where did you find Rubenstein?" he asked.

"Ed telephoned the hotel's switchboard—told them we needed a doctor. Victor Sassoon sent him." Milton's eyes narrowed. "Why do you ask?"

"He was just very interested in what we were doing in Shanghai. It made me wonder."

"You suspect he's an undercover policeman?"

Rowland laughed. "No. Nothing like that. I just find it incredible that anyone could be that interested in the wool business."

Milton pulled at his goatee as he considered the physician's manner. "Now you mention it, he was very inquisitive about what you were doing here. And he did ask Clyde and me rather a lot of questions too."

"What kind of questions?"

"How long we'd been in Shanghai, what business were we in, how long we planned to stay—that sort of thing."

"What did you tell him?"

"I said I was your poet—that you always travelled with at least one."

"Naturally. Did he believe you?"

"He wrote it down. I don't suppose he's reporting back to Sassoon."

Rowland exhaled. "It could simply be that he's nosey," he said in an attempt to be fair. "Perhaps it's just his bedside manner. Talking of which—" Rowland stood. "I should check on our fallen comrade."

Clyde was resting comfortably with his bandaged leg elevated on a pillow. Wing Zau had brought up a more conventional pot of tea, and he and Edna sat with the injured artist playing gin rummy.

When Rowland came in, Wing put his hand down hastily.

"I've no objections to cards, Mr. Wing. Just deal Milt and me into the next hand."

"We're not playing for money, Mr. Sinclair," Wing said guiltily.

"Probably wise. Ed's a ruthless creditor."

"Well she would be, if she ever won," Milton added.

Edna replied by taking the hand.

"How are you feeling, Clyde?" Rowland asked, pulling up a chair beside the bed.

"I'll live. Did Romanov?"

"I don't know. If he was in the apartment, he didn't escape, but we can't be sure he was in there at all."

Wing recounted his conversation with the fire captain.

"So someone may have tried to kill him?" Edna said, moving from the end of Clyde's bed to the arm of Rowland's chair.

"I'm afraid someone might have succeeded," Rowland replied.

"Oh...no."

Rowland rubbed her hand. "All I mean is that we don't know yet, Ed. With any luck he was out when the fire started, however it started."

"If the fire was started to kill Sergei Romanov." Milton lay back on his own bed. "Then that puts what happened to Alexandra in a different light."

"What do you mean?" Clyde asked.

"Well, surely it shows that these murders are something to do with the Romanovs...their past or current activities; that Alexandra's death was nothing to do with Rowly."

"Yes, but we always knew it was nothing to do with Rowly," Clyde said.

"We always knew that Rowly didn't kill her, but Rowly's acquired some powerful enemies. It may have been that Alexandra's murderer was waiting for him," Milton said thoughtfully. "But," he added before anyone could protest, "this attempt on Sergei, whether or not it was successful, does indicate that Alexandra wasn't just some poor girl in the wrong place at the wrong time."

Harjeet appeared at the open door with a tray bearing a larger teapot and several cups. The uninjured gentlemen rose to relieve her of the tray. Harjeet handed the tray to Wing and turned to Rowland. "There was a telephone call, just now, Mr. Sinclair. An Inspector Randolph. He did not wish to speak to you, sir, only to ask whether you were in."

"I expect he intends to call," Rowland said.

Edna looked him up and down, wrinkling her nose. "You and Milt better clean up," she said. "I'll call Mr. Carmel now, and Mr. Wing and I will keep the inspector occupied until you both look less like you started a fire."

Chapter Twenty

MIRACLES ARE CHEAP TO-DAY

Home Movies for Tenpence

THE name for cheap stores in America is the Five and Ten, meaning five and ten cents, though many articles are sold in them costing twenty cents, or tenpence in English money.

The very latest of those is a real kinematograph projector, which gives moving pictures on a safety film by its own electric light. A new lamp costs twopence halfpenny! Remarkably good little moving pictures can be displayed with these projectors, and their invention is of very real interest. The two new films which enable amateur photographers to take home moving pictures in natural colours have given a tremendous stimulus to domestic kinematography, and the little tenpenny marvels are just one more step toward an age in which the film will reign supreme in the fields of both entertainment and education.

—*Telegraph*, 24 October 1935

Rowland washed the soot from his hair and body, and changed quickly. There was little he could do however to disguise the dark bruise to his left temple left by Sergei Romanov's violin. He made his way down the staircase. He could hear Edna in conversation with Chief Inspector Randolph as he approached the drawing room.

"Are you sure you won't have a cup of tea, Inspector? I'm sure Rowly won't be a minute."

"Miss Higgins, I must ask you again, is Mr. Sinclair on the premises?"

"And I tell you again, Inspector, he is upstairs. Harjeet has told him you're here, and he'll be down directly."

"Inspector." Rowland stepped into the room and offered Randolph his hand. He nodded to the four constables who stood behind the chief inspector. "I do apologise for the delay," he said without giving any reason for it.

Randolph accepted the handshake coolly.

"What can I do for you, Inspector?"

"We have received, via your solicitors, a certain phonographic disc containing a voice recording by the late Miss Romanova." Randolph returned his hands to their customary position behind his back. "Can I ask you, Mr. Sinclair, why you didn't turn that particular evidence into the police immediately?"

"I didn't receive the disc until the day after Miss Romanova died, and I didn't think to listen to it till later," Rowland said carefully. "I took it to my solicitors the following morning."

"And the reason you didn't bring it to us directly?"

"That was on my advice." Milton entered the room in an immaculate cream linen suit and emerald cravat. The poet's long black hair glistened, still wet. "The recording corroborated Mr. Sinclair's statement that Miss Romanova did not keep her appointment with him. I thought it prudent that Mr. Sinclair's solicitors were made aware of the recording and had a chance to listen to it, before it was surrendered to the police."

Randolph's moustache bristled. "I see." He took a breath. "Can I ask what happened to your head, Mr. Sinclair?"

"Sergei Romanov took a swing at me with his violin," Rowland said evenly.

"Why?"

"He was upset about his sister's death and under the impression I had something to do with it. An impression you seem to have given him."

Randolph's face registered nothing in the way of chagrin. "And what did you do when he hit you with his violin?"

"As you might expect, Inspector, I tried to defend myself. Fortunately, Messrs. Isaacs and Watson Jones were present to restrain Mr. Romanov. Once he'd calmed down, he seemed to accept that I had not murdered his sister."

"Why would he accept that?"

Milton intervened. "Perhaps because he knew that there were other people who actually had a reason to want his sister dead."

"What people?"

Milton recounted what Kruznetsov had told them. "According to the good count, there were several people who were swindled by Alexandra when she was claiming to be the Grand Duchess Anastasia."

Randolph frowned, but for a moment he seemed less hostile. "If this is true, then Sergei Romanov had as much to fear for his part."

"I expect he did."

Randolph turned back to Rowland. "Are you aware, Mr. Sinclair, that there was a fire at Mr. Romanov's residence this morning?"

"Yes, I am. We called on Mr. Romanov this morning. The building was on fire when we got there."

The thaw in Randolph's manner disappeared. Rowland continued regardless. "We tried to force the door in case he was still inside, but there was an explosion of some sort."

Randolph looked from Rowland to Milton. "You both look very well for men who've survived not only a fire but an explosion."

"The explosion was strong enough to blow the door off its hinges on top of us. It seems to have shielded Mr. Isaacs and me. Mr. Watson Jones was less lucky."

"Where is he?"

"Upstairs. The doctor ordered bed rest."

Randolph despatched one of his constables to verify that was the case.

"Inspector Randolph," Edna said calmly, "I'm sure if you spoke to the firemen who responded to the blaze, they will be able to confirm what Rowly's told you. There was a crowd of people outside the butchery who saw Mr. Sinclair, Mr. Watson Jones, and Mr. Isaacs trying to break down the door."

"Be assured that we will be doing just that."

A pounding on the front door announced the arrival of Gilbert Carmel, who discreetly adopted the pretext that he was there to speak to Rowland on an unrelated business matter. Indeed he'd brought a sheaf of papers "for execution" and expressed surprise at finding Chief Inspector Randolph there.

"Miss Romanova's residence has burned down," Rowland said. "Her brother is missing, feared dead."

"And the inspector came to let you know—how very thoughtful!" Carmel turned to Randolph. "Naturally, you know that my client is very eager to see the young lady's killer brought to account and is willing to do—nay, has done—everything within his power to assist."

"What has he done to assist?" Randolph almost snarled.

"Why, he had me deliver that phonographic disc your men had failed to discover in your investigations at the Cathay Hotel. The recording, as you know, corroborates my client's statement that he did not see Miss Romanova that afternoon and is also evidence that there was another man with her that day." Carmel smiled again. "That's a fair bit of assistance, I'd say!"

For several moments there was silence as Carmel and Randolph locked eyes. Rowland glanced at Milton, unsure if he should say something himself. The poet grimaced.

"As much as I appreciate your client's assistance," Randolph said finally, "I ask you, Mr. Carmel, to advise him of the dangers of interfering with an ongoing investigation by the local constabulary."

"Thank you for the suggestion, Inspector. I shall of course do so at the first available opportunity."

Randolph and his men departed shortly thereafter. Carmel took a seat and perched a pair of spectacles on his nose. "Well then, gentleman and lady, perhaps you should tell me precisely what's happened since last we met."

"In that case, Mr. Carmel," Edna said, "you should stay to luncheon. We have rather a lot to tell you."

Carmel took the watch from his fob pocket and studied it. "As it happens, it's just gone tiffin time, and far be it from me to allow my clients to go hungry."

So Gilbert Carmel joined them for lunch, during the course of which they told him of what they had learned through Count Kruznetsov and Sergei Romanov. The solicitor took notes, posed the occasional question, and complimented Harjeet on the piquancy of her roast duck.

"Well," he said in the end. "Your introduction to Shanghai has certainly been less than ideal. Please allow me to extend my apologies on behalf of this great city. Chief Inspector Randolph is not the easiest man with whom to have dealings, but I have not yet abandoned hope of winning him over."

Rowland also mentioned his meeting with Andrew Petty and the invitation to the banquet hosted by the Japanese wool brokers.

Carmel nodded. "That is how business is done here. I'm

surprised no one has banqueted you already. The Japanese will be especially keen to secure your wool stocks."

"Why?" Rowland asked. He gathered it was well known in wool trading circles that the Sinclairs had a substantial quantity of wool stockpiled, but they weren't the only producers in Australia.

"Your brother is an influential man, Rowland. I expect the Japanese wool buyers feel that dealing directly with him would see other Australian producers follow suit, allowing them to procure enough wool to withstand any possible trade embargo which might be imposed by the League of Nations."

Rowland glanced at Wing. "I see."

"But I presume Wilfred has already briefed you on his intentions in that respect," Carmel said without giving away whether or not he knew what those intentions were.

"Yes."

"And Carmel and Smith remains at your service."

"Thank you, Mr. Carmel."

Carmel tapped his head thoughtfully. "As a precaution, avoid speaking with the inspector unless I'm present. I'll notify my secretary that your calls are to be taken immediately and at all times." He smiled. "Just in case Inspector Randolph proves inured to our obvious charms."

With Clyde immobilised, they stayed in that afternoon. Edna set up a film set in the drawing room, and Rowland and Milton helped Clyde down the stairs into the dining room so that they could play cards in between takes.

"What exactly is this film about?" Clyde grumbled. Edna seemed to be filming a series of unrelated scenes calling on each of them to play villains, heroes, ghosts, servants, conspirators, drunks, and even romantic leads. "It doesn't seem to have any kind of plot."

"It doesn't, not yet—I'm filming as many interesting scenes as I can think of, first," the sculptress replied. "And then I'll patch them together into a story...like a collage."

"That's very avant-garde, Ed." Rowland sat up from the floor after the fistfight Edna had just had him and Milton simulate. They'd flipped a coin to decide which of them would lose.

Edna handed the camera to Wing Zau, instructing him to film while she fainted into Rowland's arms.

"Why does Rowly get to catch you?" Milton asked.

"Because he will catch me." Edna directed Rowland into position.

"Won't the uncertainty add a little something to your performance?" Milton grinned wickedly.

The sculptress ignored him. "Now, Rowly, look towards the door...no, the window—that'll work better. Try to look frightened."

"Frightened? By something at the window?"

"Well, at least alarmed—no, you can't just raise an eyebrow. There's something monstrous at the window. Ready, Mr. Wing? Right. Action!"

As it turned out, Rowland did not struggle to feign an expression of alarm—that came naturally when Edna screamed. He was, in fact, so startled that he nearly forgot to catch her as she fell backwards into his arms and it was the relief on his face when she did so and he realised the scream was part of the pretence, that compromised the take.

Milton roared with laughter. "I reckon a 'thank God she's finally shut up' expression is entirely appropriate, Ed."

"Sorry, Ed," Rowland said. "I had no idea what you were doing."

"I was acting," Edna declared, exasperated.

"We can try it again."

"I think we'd better." Edna moved them both back into position. "Ready, Mr. Wing? Action."

This time Edna's scream was more a gasp of surprise and a gleeful squeal.

Rowland wasn't sure what to do—was she still planning to faint?

"I could swear I saw a monkey," Edna said as she ran to the window.

"Is this part of the scene?"

"No. I really saw a monkey."

A knock on the red door.

"That'll be the police again, wanting to know why Ed's screaming," Clyde muttered.

Rowland answered the door.

"Rowland! Hello...I'm finally keeping my promise to visit." Mickey Hahn stood on the doorstep in poised splendour. The deep indigo of her long, tailored skirt was offset by an orange bolero jacket and cloche. A kid-gloved hand held a thin gold chain on the end of which was Mr. Mills attired in a matching indigo jacket and orange fez.

"A pleasure to see you again, Mickey."

She accepted his invitation to come in, proceeding into the drawing room and taking a seat. The monkey, too, found himself an armchair. Mickey introduced Mr. Mills as if he were an old acquaintance with whom she'd stepped out that day.

Edna was delighted. She had been, if truth be told, disappointed that at their last meeting, Emily Hahn had been *sans* monkey.

Milton offered the journalist a drink and, since it would have been rude to allow her to partake alone, mixed cocktails for them all.

"What on earth are you all up to?" Mickey noted the film camera and the furniture cleared to make room.

"Ed's making a film." Rowland and Milton returned the couch to its original place while Wing helped Clyde into the drawing room.

"Gracious! What happened to Clyde?"

For a moment there was silence as they all waited for Rowland to take the lead.

"Are you enquiring as a journalist?" he asked carefully.

"Oooh…is it something that would interest a journalist?" Her eyes glistened.

Rowland said nothing.

Mickey sighed. "Oh, very well then. Off the record. What happened?"

They told her.

"Have you heard any mutterings about people impersonating members of the Russian royal family in Shanghai, Mickey?" Edna asked, reaching out gently towards Mr. Mills.

"Be careful—he bites," Mickey warned. "I've not been in Shanghai much longer than you. I'll ask at the *News*…maybe someone covered the story. Victor will be appalled to learn there was a fraudster working in his hotel."

"We don't know that she was," Rowland said.

"A fraudster or the Grand Duchess Anastasia?" Mickey's tone was sharp. She regarded him curiously.

"Either… We only have Count Kruznetsov's word that she was the same girl who defrauded his mother. He might very well have been mistaken."

"Could she have possibly been telling the truth?" Clyde asked. "About being a princess?"

"It's possible, I suppose," Mickey mused. "Anastasia would have been in her thirties now. Did Alexandra look that old?"

Rowland shrugged. "There is Sergei. He said she was his little sister. The grand duchess didn't have an older brother, only a younger one."

"You're right," Mickey said. "If she was as innocent as you seem to want to believe she was, it is more likely that this chap—the count—is mistaken or lying." She frowned. "Still, what a story—even without the murder! The sole surviving heir to the Russian throne working as a taxi girl in Shanghai!"

"You wouldn't—"

"I said it was off the record, didn't I?"

"Yes, of course."

"Anyway, I've come with a purpose." Mickey dug into her bag and fished out an envelope, which she handed to Edna. "My dear friend Bernadine would like the four of you to attend her salon. You must come; they are simply the most fabulous occasions in Shanghai."

"But we haven't even been introduced."

"Bernadine finds such social conventions tiresome. I've told her all about my new Australian friends, and she is simply desperate that you accept her invitation. Do say you'll come!"

Edna opened the envelope and extracted an exquisitely illuminated card. "Oh, it's for this evening." She handed the invitation to Milton, who glanced at it and passed it on to Clyde. He studied the summons to an evening of culture and poetry, and the look on his face possibly reminded Rowland that his friend was not well.

"I'm not sure Clyde's up to—" Rowland began.

"I'm afraid I'm not," Clyde agreed quickly. "But that's no reason for you all to stay by my bedside… I'm not dying."

"Perhaps if we found you some crutches or a walking stick," Milton began, his lips twitching into a smile.

"No. I suspect I've already overdone it just getting out of bed." Clyde was definite. "Wing will keep me company, won't you, mate?"

"Of course, sir."

"Bernardine will be sorely disappointed that you cannot attend, Mr. Watson Jones," Mickey said. "But considering the severity of the injury you sustained in such a heroic manner, she will understand…and she will of course have your companions to console her."

"Not to mention an evening of poetry and culture." Clyde was clearly a man reprieved.

Milton shook his head sadly. "But words are things, and a small drop of ink, falling like dew upon a thought produces that which makes thousands, perhaps millions, think."

"More likely to make me drink," Clyde muttered. "Who was he robbing that time, Rowly?"

"Byron, I believe."

Chapter Twenty-One

CHINESE VERSE

"The Jade Mountain" is a Chinese anthology, edited by Mr. Witter Bynner and Mr. Klang Kang-Hu, and is the result of ten years' collaboration. It consists of 300 poems of the T'ang Dynasty, A.D. 618–906—the golden age of Chinese poetry. Mr. Bynner has done the translations from the texts of Mr. Klang Kang-Hu, and each editor contributes an introduction. Mr. Bynner thinks that, of English poets, Wordsworth has the closest affinity with Chinese poets. He resembles them in his simplicity, in his sense of spiritual kinship with nature and his capacity for discerning beauty in the commonplace. But Mr. Bynner holds that Chinese poetry cleaves even nearer to nature than his.

—Sydney Morning Herald, 28 June 1930

Bernardine Szold-Fritz's banquet was to take place at a Chinese restaurant in Yangtzepoo, beyond the Soochow Creek, which marked the border of the international settlement. The waterway was only a few hundred yards from the terrace on Kiangse Road and was spanned by the impressive double arches of the Garden Bridge.

Their hostess sent a car to collect them, a gleaming white Packard with a smartly uniformed chauffeur.

Rowland offered Edna his hand as she descended the narrow staircase in a shimmering grey gown, which clung to the curves of her figure and highlighted the burnished copper tresses she'd gathered into a loose knot at the base of her neck. The wrap hanging loosely over her elbows was sheer and embroidered with peacocks, her only jewellery a silver locket embellished with seed pearls. She smiled as she took Rowland's hand. The sculptress was not oblivious to the way in which he looked at her. It was perhaps simply that he had always regarded her thus, that she was not alarmed by the intensity of his admiration. She would not have tortured him for the world if she had known she was doing so.

"You look pretty, Ed," he said quietly.

Her brow furrowed just slightly. "I do hope this is appropriate for dinner over here. I wish I'd thought to ask Mickey. We might be completely at odds with Shanghai fashion."

"I'm sure they'll make allowances." Rowland's eyes lingered on the graceful line of Edna's neck. He could capture it in a portrait from behind, a composition which had her glancing over her shoulder.

She recognised the look on his face and laughed. "You're painting me!"

"I wish I were." He glanced at his watch. "I wonder if it would be too late to send our regrets."

"Yes." The sculptress was firm. "Where's Milt?"

"Trying to add some note of personal flair to his dinner suit," Rowland said, wincing.

"We'll say goodnight to the others, and perhaps by then he'll be down."

Clyde had recruited Harjeet and her brother to make up a four for cards. Rowland had been a little surprised that Singh had agreed to join the party given the tension between the driver and Wing Zau, but perhaps he'd simply done so to keep an eye on the butler as he'd pledged. Harjeet had prepared a feast of finger food for the evening, and the card table had been moved so that Clyde could play from reclined comfort on the couch. There was already a hand dealt and underway when Edna and Rowland came in to wish them a good evening.

Harjeet gasped. "Miss Edna, you look lovely."

Clyde sat up, considering Edna appreciatively as she twirled for his benefit. "Won't you be cold?"

Edna ignored his concern. "We're off," she said. "Well, as soon as Milt can drag himself away from the mirror."

"I resent that." Milton strode in and stood so they could take in his splendour. He had accessorised his dinner suit with a silk brocade waistcoat to match the red fez on his head.

Rowland sighed. Still it was less ridiculous than he'd feared.

Clyde groaned. "You look like Mickey Hahn's monkey."

Milton frowned. "I'd forgotten about that stylish primate... Do you think she'll bring it? Perhaps I should wear the beret instead to avoid embarrassing the poor creature."

"We don't have time." Rowland walked over to look out of the window. "The car is waiting. You could, of course, just leave the fez here."

"Don't be absurd, Rowly. Colonials or not, one can't step out half-dressed!"

Edna shook her head. "We'll have to risk you and the monkey turning up in the same outfit then." She turned back to the gathering at the card table. "*Mintzowe.*"

Wing smiled. "*Chin la ke xin ye.*"

"Mr. Wing's been teaching me a little Shanghainese," she told the rest of them proudly.

"Indeed," Rowland said, impressed. "What did he say?"

"I've no idea, but I said goodbye."

—————————————— ✦ ——————————————

On the drive to the restaurant, Edna imparted the remainder of her knowledge of Shanghainese to Rowland and Milton, teaching them to say "Good evening," "Pleased to meet you," "Thank you," and "Call the police."

"Mr. Wing thought it would be a useful phrase to know, all things considered," she explained when Rowland expressed surprise at the last.

"He's probably right," Milton murmured.

They collected Mickey Hahn from her apartment only a block away. She met the car in a black jacket tailored to fit her curves and worn over a crisp white blouse and a grey tie—the androgynous style of Parisian streets and Bohemian haunts.

"Hello," she said, squeezing in beside Edna. "Bernardine will be delighted to have secured three Australians for her dinner party. Utterly delighted!"

"Are we on the menu?" Milton asked.

Mickey laughed. "In a manner of speaking."

"Is Mr. Mills not invited?" Edna was clearly disappointed by the monkey's absence.

"I'm afraid not. He's spending the evening with Victor, who was also an omission from the guest list. They'll be able to complain to each other about the slight."

Kiangse Road became more congested as they neared the Garden Bridge. Here terraces and houses gave way to vast, overcrowded tenements, subdivided and extended in a manner that was almost organic to accommodate the masses of urban poor who worked in the factories of Shanghai. Clotheslines spanned every gap, creating a disordered web in which was snared daily life.

"They are called *sikumen*," Mickey said. "People atop people—this is the real China."

The Packard travelled past slums and shanty towns on the shores of the Soochow as they rode over the bridge to the Japanese districts.

"And here lives the proletariat of Shanghai," Milton murmured. Mickey looked at him curiously, but she said nothing.

The restaurant at which the Packard pulled up was architecturally Chinese, a series of pagodas joined by open walkways, decorated with serpentine dragons and lit by strings of lanterns. The tables were laid with snowy linen and golden cutlery. The largest pagoda had been reserved for the Szold-Fritz party and was already crowded with guests. They were greeted at the entrance by a woman whose carefully cultivated exoticism tipped into the outlandish. Bernadine, as she insisted they all address her, wore a silk long coat embroidered with koi, an elaborately folded silk turban, and several pounds of jade. Rowland estimated the society doyenne to be about forty years of age. Her features were quite birdlike: a small mouth, an inquisitive nose, and bright, round eyes. She welcomed Mickey first, handing her on to a conversation with an Austrian novelist before she gave her attention to the Australians.

"Mr. Sinclair! How very kind of you to accept my invitation!"

Rowland introduced his companions, and Bernadine gushed over each of them in turn. She took Edna's hands. "Why, my dear, you are a picture. Come with me; there is a gentleman you simply must meet."

Rowland glanced at Milton. It appeared they were not to be included in the impending introduction.

Bernadine returned within a minute. "Mr. Isaacs, may I compliment you on your fez? I must find one for Chester, though I'm not sure he would wear it as well as you. Is the fez popular as headgear in Australia? You simply must meet Mollie Smethurst; she's wearing the most darling hat." She hooked her arm through

Milton's to lead him away. "I'll deal with you in just a minute, Mr. Sinclair."

Rowland watched, bemused as Bernadine ushered Milton towards a young woman in an elaborately feathered hat seated at one of the tables. There was a large birdcage on the seat beside her which housed what looked like a macaw. As she turned her head to look at Milton, so too did the macaw. Rowland smiled, struck by a vague similarity between the features of the bird and its mistress. The notion of painting birds and women entered his mind, and for a time he played with a composition of feathers and figures.

"Your turn will come."

Rowland turned. A young man, Chinese, though his accent was discernibly Oxbridge. His hair was parted and slicked back in the Western fashion, a thin wispy moustache on the edges of his upper lip. His eyes were bright and whimsical, and he wore the simple brown robes of a scholar. "Mrs. Manners will peel off your companions so that she may display you to best effect," he said.

"Display me?"

"You are the Australian gentleman, are you not?"

"Rowland Sinclair. How'd you do?" Rowland extended his hand.

"Shao Xunmei."

"I take it you've attended dinners hosted by Mrs. Szold-Fritz previously?"

"Oh yes. I am the dear lady's favourite oriental curio." Xunmei bowed.

Rowland's brow rose. "I see."

Xunmei laughed. "Do not allow me to frighten you, Mr. Sinclair. Our hostess is harmless, a little too eager to demonstrate how open-minded and cosmopolitan she is, but harmless."

At that point, Bernadine returned. "Oh how marvellous! I was just about to introduce you, and here you are already old friends."

Xunmei extracted a gold cigarette case from the inside breast pocket of his jacket and offered its contents to Bernardine and Rowland. Rowland declined, though he held a light for both of them.

"I recognise you, Mr. Sinclair." Xunmei dragged deeply on his cigarette.

"I've been in Shanghai for a few days. Perhaps—"

"It was before that...years ago. In Cambridge."

"I'm afraid I'm an Oxford man."

Xunmei shook his head. "I'm sure. Rowing...no. A boxing match perhaps."

Rowland stopped. "Yes. Actually that's possible." He had boxed at Oxford, and for Oxford in various matches against Cambridge. He was not a little impressed by the Chinese poet's recall and embarrassed by his own lack of it. "I'm sorry; I don't remember being introduced."

"Oh, we weren't. I was in the crowd." Xunmei replied. "I lost a considerable sum wagering against you, which has possibly helped me remember your face."

Rowland grimaced. It was an awkward way to be remembered.

"A boxer!" Bernadine said. "Such a brutish sport. No doubt you are fascinated by the martial arts of the Chinese—so elegant in comparison to Western fighting."

"I'm afraid I have not yet had the opportunity to see a display," Rowland replied.

"Well perhaps Xunmei could demonstrate?" The idea caught like fire in the tinder dry fuel of Bernadine's mind. "Why I'm sure we'd all love to see a demonstration."

Xunmei stepped back. "Bernadine, I am a scholar, not a common street boxer. I have no—"

"Nonsense, I insist. Consider yourself educating the foreign devils on the superiority of Chinese combat." Bernadine rushed over to a small gong on the edge of the dance floor and sounded it.

Still standing beside Rowland, Xunmei laughed quietly.

"Ladies and gentlemen," Bernadine announced, "we have a

very special treat for you tonight. My dear friend, the renowned poet Shao Xunmei, has agreed to give us a demonstration of Chinese martial arts."

The gathering gasped. Some began to clap.

Xunmei removed his quilted jacket and handed it to Rowland. "Mrs. Manners believes every Chinese should be proficient at all things Chinese." He flashed a grin. "It is easier to make something up than to argue."

The Chinese poet stepped onto the dance floor and requested a little space. He bowed and then executed several elaborate, graceful movements that looked more like ballet than combative technique. And then he stopped and bowed again, to rapturous applause.

"For what skill are Australians renowned?" Xunmei asked as he collected his jacket. "Before the night is over, you will be asked to demonstrate, my friend."

"Fortunately there's only cricket," Rowland replied. "She couldn't possibly want me to demonstrate that."

Xunmei laughed. "At least the good lady is thoughtful enough to provide a gullible audience." He flagged a drinks waiter, and they chose from a selection of cocktails and spirits.

Xunmei raised his glass. "*Bubeh bubeh!* Here's hoping she does not ask you to hop like a kangaroo."

Rowland was somewhat alarmed by the possibility.

"She is clumsy in her enthusiasm for other cultures, but at least it is an enthusiasm," the poet observed. "What business are you in, Mr. Sinclair?"

"Here in Shanghai? Wool."

"You are here to do business?"

"I suppose so."

"Forgive me for asking, but are you the gentleman who found a dead girl in your hotel room?"

Rowland looked at him, startled.

"Shanghai gossip, my friend."

Rowland drank his gin. "I don't suppose the gossips of Shanghai say anything about what happened to her."

Xunmei shrugged. "Murder is not uncommon here. Perhaps if she were not Russian and a taxi girl, there might be more outrage...but there is interest. Some believe it was you, of course. Others accuse Victor Sassoon. Still others say it was the woman who accompanies you—an act of jealous rage."

Rowland bristled. "Ed? Why that's absurd." He could feel Xunmei's scrutiny. The poet was assessing him. Murderer or unfortunate fool.

"Some say it was the Communists."

"Why would the Communists kill her?"

"She was said to be royalty. The last Romanov. Some say the Communists killed her to aid their Russian comrades, or that Stalin sent his own people to ensure there was no one around whom the White Russians in exile could coalesce."

"Do you think that's possible?"

"Revolution is a paranoid business."

Chapter Twenty-Two

Washing Dishes

Important Bit of the Work of the World

Dishwashing is like living in one respect; it is exactly what we make it. For one girl it is a dull tiresome task, for another an opportunity for a necessary service to loved ones, depending entirely on the attitude of mind assumed toward it...

GAY EQUIPMENT

Gay, colorful equipment is helpful to some. One girl replaced the old gray granite dishpan with a bright red one of different shape. Another found that the attractive little rubberised aprons, which may be bought quite inexpensively, made dishwashing far more cheerful. Attractive tea towels and gaily painted mop handles enlivened the process for still another girl...

If you wash dishes with sister or mother, make the most of the opportunity to have a good time together. In one household the dishwashing period is often gay with snatches of song. At other times mother and daughter talk about pleasant happenings, past or prospective. Sometimes they plan little surprises for father or other members of the household.

AS AN OPPORTUNITY

If dishwashing for you is a solitary affair, use it as the time to refresh yourself mentally, or, to plan usefully. One girl uses the dishwashing period for memorising verses or bits of prose which appeal to her. Another girl uses this time to review something she has recently read, to see how much of it she has really retained. Still another uses her dishwashing minutes to plan a new dress, some decorative scheme for a party, or a new way to beautify her room, and the like. All of which goes to show that one's thoughts need not be immersed in the dishwashing task which, in time, becomes largely mechanical...

—*Advocate*, 1 September 1934

"Xunmei, darling, your demonstration was wonderful!" Bernadine was back. She leant conspiratorially between Rowland and the poet. "I wanted to show them all that there is so much depth and richness to Chinese culture. I'm afraid too many Occidentals think it's all about lanterns and dragons." She fussed them towards the table, sitting between them. Also at the table was Chester Fritz— their reserved host. Beside him, an English actress who had just finished playing Beatrice in the Shanghai Theatre Company's production of *As You Like It*, a Greek acrobat, and Chao Kung, an Occidental who spoke with a heavy East European accent and wore the saffron and ochre robes of a Buddhist priest. Before the entrée was finished, the actress had been prevailed upon to perform one of Beatrice's soliloquies.

Rowland found himself wondering what it was that had singled him out for Bernadine's particular attention. Surely she had come across Australians before. What could she possibly believe he could offer by way of entertainment?

As the second course was served, Bernadine raised the incident at the Cathay Hotel, without once looking at Rowland. Of course the direction of the enquiry was clear. Chao Kung, the Buddhist cleric, looked up from his prawns, and the acrobat crossed himself. Shao Xunmei deftly changed the subject with an anecdote about his time at the École des Beaux Arts in Paris.

"You're an artist?" Rowland gratefully took the conversational lifeline Xunmei had offered him.

"More art lover than a serious artist," Xunmei replied, winking. "What with poetry and martial arts, who has time to paint?"

Rowland smiled, and the two fell into an exchange about Paris and painting and the artistic scene in Shanghai. Both men knew the French capital well, having spent time there as students. They had walked the same streets, drunk wine at the same cafes, and even painted the same scenes.

"Perhaps you will care to accompany me to a gathering of the Celestial Hound Society?"

"Greyhound racing?" Rowland ventured, a little puzzled by the invitation.

Xunmei laughed. "The society is a brotherhood of artists in Shanghai influenced by the Parisian scene."

"Oh, I see." Rowland relaxed. The thought of talking about art with fellow painters appealed a great deal. "I would—very much."

Xunmei nodded. "I'm sure my brothers would be interested to meet you."

"Rowland." Bernadine inserted herself into the conversation again. "I did want to tell you how sorry I was to hear about that frightful incident at the Cathay Hotel. It must have been a terrible shock. How are you coping?"

Rowland paused. So it was scandal that had piqued Bernadine's interest in him. "Quite well, thank you."

Bernadine continued. "When Mickey mentioned what had happened, I thought inviting you to one of my salons was the least I could do. To take your mind off the whole terrible business."

"How very kind."

"Was it dreadfully ghastly?" she whispered. "I imagine there was rather a lot of blood."

"I don't think—"

"You don't suppose it was some kind of elaborate threat, do you?"

"Threat?"

"Commercial transactions in Shanghai are a brutal business." She nudged her husband. "Isn't that right, Chester?"

Chester Fritz nodded. "Yes, dear. Ruthless."

"Perhaps the wicked fiend mistook the Russian girl for your beautiful Edna."

Rowland's expression was unreadable. He kept the horror, the cold realisation that it was possible, from showing on his face.

"It wouldn't be the first time that a businessman's family was threatened or abducted or even murdered," Chester added. "Shanghai is a place where fortunes are made and lost. The stakes are high, and extortion has been the bread and butter of many criminal elements in the city."

"It is vital to have good friends in this city, Mr. Sinclair." Chao Kung inserted himself into the conversation. Rowland paused for a moment as he wondered how one addressed a member of the Buddhist clergy. He was pretty sure that that "Father" was not correct. There was a vague familiarity about Kung which he could not at that moment place. "Fortunately, sir, my friends are travelling with me."

Kung's fleshy lips curved up. "Of course. I pray that you will require no others."

A commotion at another table interrupted all conversation. The macaw had somehow escaped its cage and was now flying around the pagoda. It flapped madly over heads, frightened by the screams it elicited in response. Rowland stood to help with the recapture, happy to have any excuse to escape Bernadine's interrogation. It seemed there were many people glad to leave the seats to which they'd been assigned. By the time the bird was recaptured, common purpose and laughter had thawed any reserve between the guests and formality was abandoned. It was Milton who eventually caught the macaw by using his fez as a makeshift hood to subdue the creature and return it, somewhat regretfully, to its cage and its mistress. The gathering cheered and, now out of their seats, did not feel compelled to return to them. Many took to the dance floor; others moved tables, disrupting Bernadine's carefully drawn seating plan. In amongst the disorder and joviality, Rowland found Edna.

"Oh Rowly, thank goodness!" The sculptress took his hand.

"Are you all right?" he asked, concerned by the sense of relief in her manner.

"The gentleman Bernadine wanted me to meet was anything but," she said, pulling a face. "And the most determinedly boring man I've ever met."

Rowland's eyes flashed. "Did he offend you?"

"No, he was just a buffoon. Stay with me and he won't return. Lord James's admiration had no courage in it."

"Point him out and I'll—"

"Don't be silly. Did you meet anyone interesting?"

Rowland told her about Shao Xunmei. He looked around. "I should introduce you and Milt."

"Is that him?" Edna directed Rowland's gaze towards the table at which Mickey Hahn sat. Beside her was an elegant man in scholar's robes. The two were sucking on orange segments as they talked, their eyes fixed on one another.

"Yes."

"I think it's best we don't interrupt."

Ranjit and Harjeet had gone home, but Wing Zau and Clyde were still awake when they returned from the restaurant in Yangtzepoo. Emily Hahn had not returned with them, but left the party with Shao Xunmei. It was an act of impropriety which had upset their hostess and scandalised other guests. It seemed Bernadine's rejection of the colour bar only went so far.

"She should be careful," Wing observed. "The Shaos are no strangers to opium. Xunmei's father was renowned for it. It comes with vast wealth and a poetic spirit. Perhaps that's why Miss Hahn was drawn to him."

Rowland was less comfortable with Mickey's fascination with opium, her conviction that the drug would open the "real China" to her, than with her choice of companion. He had heard tales of opium addiction in the dens of inner Sydney, seen the vacant, listless eyes of those who'd been enslaved by the habit. He could not understand why the journalist coveted it.

"They seemed quite taken with each other," Edna said, curling up in an armchair with a balloon of crème brandy. "And he does cut a tremendously romantic figure."

"It was quite a bizarre gathering," Milton observed. "A collection of the brilliant and odd."

"One wonders why we were invited," Edna mused.

"Well clearly, I'm the former," Milton replied. "You and Rowly...who knows?"

"Bernadine had an inordinate interest in the details of Alexandra Romanova's murder," Rowland offered.

"Why?"

"Mostly for the sake of curiosity and gossip, I expect. She must at least believe I had nothing to do with it, or she would not have invited us."

"That may not be true," Wing said. "Mrs. Szold-Fritz is famous for the people who have attended her suppers."

Clyde laughed. "Are you saying she isn't fussy?"

Wing shrugged. "About certain things she is fussy."

Rowland was quiet as he pondered over Bernadine's theory as to why Alexandra had been murdered. He didn't want to consider it, but he couldn't ignore it. It terrified him. He moved a wooden chair next to Edna's armchair and sat down. He told them of Bernadine's supposition that Alexandra had been killed by mistake; that Edna had been the intended victim.

Milton and Clyde both sat up. Rowland took Edna's hand before he continued.

"It may be nonsense," he said and he hoped. "But it is possible." He looked down at Edna's hand in his. "I think you should all go home."

"What about you?" Edna asked.

"I'm still under investigation; I can't leave."

"Then we can't either," Milton replied.

"Milt, what happened to Alexandra—"

"We don't know what exactly happened to Alexandra or who killed her. There's a lot wrong with Bernadine's theory." Milton stood and paced. "If they killed Alexandra because they thought she was Ed, it still doesn't explain what she was doing in our suite. If she wasn't murdered there, but left there, why on earth did they think she was Ed?"

"On top of that, mate," Clyde spoke up. "You're trading wool, not a kingdom."

"You're not even doing that, Rowly."

"But they don't know that." Rowland shook his head. "I know it sounds absurd. But if there's the slightest chance that you are in danger—"

"There's always a chance that we are in danger, Rowly," Edna said quietly. "Even in Sydney. Even at Woodlands. It's a dangerous world."

"More dangerous in my company," Rowland said sullenly.

Edna laughed. "This may not be all about you, Rowland Sinclair."

"Ed…"

"Oh, Rowly." Edna placed her glass on the coffee table so she could clasp his hand in both of hers. "You're panicking because Bernadine has somehow made you see me in poor Alexandra's place."

"Yes, I am. Ed, I can't risk—"

"We'd do anything in the world for you, Rowly, but you cannot order us to abandon you."

"I'm not ordering you to—"

"That's just as well then." Edna unfurled her legs and stood. "Come on. You and Milt get Clyde up the stairs to bed. We'll worry about what we're going to do next, tomorrow."

Wing jumped up. "Allow me to assist," he said, offering Clyde his arm.

"I'll be fine on my own," Clyde grumbled, but he took Wing's arm to pull himself up.

Rowland lingered downstairs, helping Edna to collect the various glasses and dishes from the drawing room and take them into the kitchen. She watched him check that the back door was locked and then tossed him a tea towel.

"I'll wash—you dry. You need to practise."

She picked up a sponge and began washing the glasses. "Well at least the chauffeur and the butler didn't kill each other while we were away."

"There is that." He told her about his conversation with Ranjit Singh on the subject of Wing Zau.

Edna laughed. "What exactly does he think Mr. Wing is trying to do?"

"I'm not sure." He frowned. "Perhaps I shouldn't disregard his suspicions. It wouldn't be the first time I was wrong about someone."

"Don't be silly, Rowly. They just don't get along, that's all."

Rowland didn't reply. He was, if truth be told, not really thinking about Wing Zau.

"What's wrong, Rowly?"

"Someone may have tried to kill you?"

"It's more than that. You seem cross, out of sorts."

"Do I?"

"Yes."

Rowland sighed. "I'm sorry. I just feel guilty I guess."

"Because someone might have been trying to kill me?"

"Yes that." Rowland hesitated. "And because I'm so appallingly glad they got the wrong woman."

Edna's face softened as she realised why he was so troubled. She wiped her hands on her skirt and looked up into his eyes. "Oh, Rowly, you wouldn't have wished what happened on either one of us."

"No...but I saw Alexandra's body, saw what had been done to her, and now I can only be glad that it wasn't you." He shook his head in disgust. "It just seems so indecent, Ed. She wasn't you, but I knew her."

"Rowly, it's natural. You're not glad she's dead, just that I'm not." She returned to the sink and washed another glass which she handed him to dry. "What have we been doing since Alexandra's body was found, Rowly?"

"I'm not sure I understand—"

She answered her own question. "We've been trying to find out who killed her, and not just to clear you. We haven't not cared. You haven't not cared." Edna handed him another glass. "You might want to dry the inside of the glass as well," she suggested gently.

He smiled. "You're right. Thank you."

She rinsed the last glass and handed it to him.

He dried the inside. "I'd still feel safer if you went home."

"I wouldn't. I've always felt safer with you nearby."

Chapter Twenty-Three

Communist Party's fight for Aborigines
DRAFT PROGRAM OF STRUGGLE
AGAINST SLAVERY

Full Economic, Political and Social Rights

...The white workers in unions, and in other mass organisations, the intellectuals, scientists, and humanitarians must all unite with the Communist Party in a common fighting front against murderous, rapacious imperialism, and help win back for the natives of Australia part of their native country and common rights as human beings. The Communist Party, speaking in the name of white and black workers of Australia, demands:

(1) Full and equal rights of all aborigines—economically, socially, and politically—with white races...

(2) Absolute political freedom for Aborigines and half-castes; right to membership in, and right to organise, political, economic and cultural organisations, "mixed" or aboriginal. Right to participate

in demonstrations and public affairs. Right to leave Australia as full citizens.

(3) Removal of all color restrictions on aborigines or half-castes, in professions, sports, etc.

Aboriginal intellectuals, school teachers, etc., not to be prevented from practising because of the "color line."

(4) Cancellation of all licenses to employ aborigines without pay

(5) Prohibition of slave and forced labor

(6) Unconditional release from gaol of all aborigines or half-castes, and no further arrests until aboriginal juries can hear and decide cases.

(7) Abolition of Aborigines Protection Boards— Capitalism's slave recruiting agencies and terror organisations against aborigines and halfcastes...

(8) Absolute prohibition of the kidnapping of aboriginal children by the A.P.B., whether to hire them out as slaves, place them in "missions," gaols or "correction" homes...

(9) Full and unrestricted right of aboriginal and half-caste parents to their children...

(10) Aboriginal children to be permitted to attend public and high schools and to sit for all examinations

(11) Liquidation of all missions and so-called homes for aborigines...

(12) Full right of the aborigines to develop native culture...

(13) Unemployed aborigines to be paid sums not less than other workers as unemployment allowance...

...Workers, Intellectuals, humanitarians, scientists, anti-imperialists fight for these demands for the aboriginal race. Prevent Capitalism exterminating this race through bare-faced murder or slavery. Struggle

with the aborigines against Australian Imperialism!
Workers and oppressed peoples of all lands, unite!
Smash Imperialism!

—Workers' Weekly, 25 September 1931

Kruznetsov arrived at the Kiangse Road house in his employer's Cadillac. It seemed the generous American woman was happy to contribute the use of her motorcar in aid of her chauffeur's romantic ambitions. Assuming that Kruznetsov had once again been too eager to see Edna to wait for a more sensible hour, Rowland was not especially alarmed. He had, to be honest, forgotten that the Russian count had invited Edna to the pictures, an invitation into which he had insinuated himself. He suggested Kruznetsov take breakfast with them.

"I'm afraid we cannot linger, Rowly."

Rowland glanced at his watch. "What time does the film begin?"

"Oh we're not going to the film... I have a much better outing planned." Kruznetsov smiled apologetically. "I'm sorry, Rowly. You were looking forward to seeing *Charlie Chan in Shanghai*—perhaps you do not wish to come now?"

Rowland groaned inwardly. Kruznetsov was obviously trying to rid himself of a chaperone. Clumsy as the attempt was, it did make it a little awkward to insist on accompanying the couple.

"Where are we going?" Edna came down the stairs in a sleeveless claret dress and a white cloche and kid gloves. "Should I change?"

Kruznetsov put his hand on his heart. "No, you are a vision. We visit Fengjing, a canal town. Ancient and very beautiful. People say it is the most romantic place in all of China."

Wing intervened. "Fengjing! Why Mr. Sinclair, that was the town of which I spoke to you yesterday. How lucky that you are visiting it today!"

Rowland cringed. This was getting worse. He decided that honesty was the only vaguely dignified response. "Look, Nicky, it may be overprotective, but until Miss Romanova's murderer is found—"

Kruznetsov bowed his head graciously. "I understand. Edna is a sister to you. I, too, would be protective."

Edna rolled her eyes. "Why don't you come along too, Mr. Wing? We might need a translator in the country. A girl can't have too many brothers!"

———

Fengjing was on the very outskirts of Shanghai, about forty miles to the southeast. The urban congestion of sikumen gave way to sparsely populated country. Rowland sat forward as a tower came into view with what seemed to be a small city of tents at its base. The red, white, and black of the Nazi flags were distinct on the landscape. Kruznetsov noticed his gaze.

"It's the German boys' club, camping and outdoor activities. Singing too. It's very popular with the Germans here."

"How long has there been a Hitler Youth in Shanghai?" Rowland could see the boys lined up in military formation. There were scores of them.

"A year, maybe two. It is a very popular organisation. My little cousin wishes he were German so he too might sleep in a tent and play war games."

"War games?"

"Yes, I'm told they teach the boys to shoot and skirmish. But what boy does not play soldier?"

Rowland said nothing. He remembered playing war as a child, until his brother Aubrey had fallen in France. He'd stopped then.

They arrived in Fengjing just before eleven. As Kruznetsov seemed to know little about the area but that it was "old" and a "water town," Wing took over as guide. Canals, cut through and around Fengjing, formed streets of water. Ancient whitewashed buildings, which seemed to float on the water's edge, were mirrored in a surface whose perfection was only occasionally disturbed by languid ripples. Locals sitting outside in the spring sunshine playing cards regarded the visitors without excessive curiosity. Wing led them through the town, pointing out the dynastic features in the architecture. Edna delighted in the wooden bridges that made the network of waterways navigable, running across and back like a child. Rowland stopped to sketch the reflected village, the children at play near the water, the boatmen on the canal with their wide-brimmed hats. At midday Wing took them to a restaurant that served the local delicacy of fried frogs' legs along with many dishes which only he could identify. They ate outdoors, overlooking the water, trying unknown foods and speaking through Wing with locals.

Rowland took out his notebook again to sketch the old men walking their songbirds by the water. Long lines: robes, beards, wiry limbs holding ornate cages. Edna and Kruznetsov played cards and drank tea while they watched a gentler, slower China.

Rowland asked Kruznetsov how he came to be working for Du Yuesheng.

Kruznetsov shrugged. "The Chinese are masters of hand-to-hand combat, but Russians know how to shoot." He formed his fingers into a gun and fired an imaginary bullet. "The Green Gang has many enemies, both Chinese and foreign. So Zongshi takes care."

His bravado was possibly for Edna's benefit. He did not know how much the sculptress loathed guns.

"And what exactly is it you do for him, Nicky?" she asked.

"Anything he wants."

Edna frowned. "Would you have killed Mr. Wing if Mr. Du had asked you to?"

Rowland kept drawing. He was accustomed to Edna's direct-ness, but Kruznetsov was clearly caught off guard. Wing seemed both intrigued and uncomfortable.

Kruznetsov squirmed. "I did not know Mr. Wing was your friend then."

"So that would have made a difference?" Edna persisted.

"Well, no." He paused. "Master Du does not ask me to do anything. He tells me."

"So if he told you to kill someone?"

"I am a soldier, Edna." Kruznetsov fingered his collar uneasily.

"A dog cannot choose not to be dog," Wing said coldly, "but he does choose his master."

"The wisdom of your honourable ancestors?" Kruznetsov's annoyance was unmistakable.

"No." Wing shrugged. "Merely an observation."

Rowland looked up from his notebook. "Mr. Du said he did not know Alexandra Romanova, that she did not owe him money," he said. "Would he lie?"

"Oh yes. But about this, I don't think he did." Kruznetsov grabbed the opportunity to change the focus of the conversation from his own actions. "He is a ruthless man but not brutal. If Alexandra Romanova owed him money, he would have allowed her to pay off the debt in one of his sing-song houses. He would not have killed her."

"You told me that you knew she wasn't the tsar's daughter," Rowland said thoughtfully. "Was that common knowledge?"

"What do you mean?"

"Did anybody still believe she was the Grand Duchess Anastasia?"

"No one has believed that for a long time."

"So the Communists would not believe her a threat?"

"The Communists are stupid, traitorous peasants! Who knows what they think?"

"It was not the Communists who were taken in by a girl pre-tending to be a princess!" Wing snapped.

"What are you saying, *podonok*?"

"Steady on, fellows." Rowland stepped in before the exchange could escalate. Edna met Rowland's eye and stood, holding out her hand to the count. "Come on, Nicky. I want to have a closer look at the water before we head back."

Sullenly, Kruznetsov took her hand and walked with her down to the water's edge.

Rowland stopped Wing before he could follow, though his eyes remained on Edna as she bent to look more closely at something in the river. Kruznetsov placed his arm around her waist in case she should fall.

Wing cleared his throat. "The Communists do not care, Mr. Sinclair."

Rowland glanced back. "I beg your pardon."

"Chinese Communists do not care about the Russian royal family."

Rowland regarded his translator anew. There was something about the way that Wing spoke…more for the Communists than of them.

"You're right, Mr. Wing. I was talking about the Bolsheviks."

"They are not the same thing, I expect." Wing glanced at Kruznetsov. "I apologise, sir. I forgot my place."

"I take it you do not like Count Kruznetsov?"

Wing paused. "I wish to repay your kindness to me by protecting you against men who do not deserve your trust. Shanghai is not a place in which you can simply trust the face of a man."

"I appreciate your efforts, but you do not need to protect me, Mr. Wing," Rowland said carefully.

"Yes, sir. I'm sorry."

"Are you also trying to protect me from Mr. Singh?" Rowland ventured.

Wing took a deep breath. "What do you really know about him, sir? He insinuated himself into your employ, and now his sister is running your household. I believe you should be more careful." He straightened his tie nervously. "I do not trust him."

Rowland smiled. The similarity between Wing's concerns and Singh's was not lost on him. "That much is clear."

Wing regarded Rowland silently for a moment. "Are the Nazis a problem in Australia?"

"Not particularly, but I fear that if they are not stopped they will become a problem for Australia...and the rest of the world."

Wing smiled. "The West perhaps. It is not all the world, Mr. Sinclair."

"You're right, Mr. Wing. It is not, but it seems the Nazis are here too."

Wing shook his head. "China has more to fear from the Japanese." He frowned, choosing his words carefully. "Every government oppresses some part of its people, Mr. Sinclair. The KMT persecutes the Communists, the Americans their Negroes, even your Australia legislates against the Chinese and disenfranchises its Aboriginal people. Why is it that the Nazis disturb you more than any other capitalist government?"

Rowland was caught off guard. He faltered. "I don't know."

Wing said nothing, giving him time to consider the question.

Rowland rubbed his face. Wing Zau seemed very familiar with world affairs, and nothing he said was untrue. "I can't tell you, Wing. I don't really know why this became my fight more than any other."

"If you don't mind my saying, Mr. Sinclair," Wing ventured. "Your dislike of the Nazis seems...personal."

Rowland shrugged. "Perhaps it is." He tried to explain—to himself as much as Wing. "We were in Germany a couple of years ago—Munich. I came to the notice of the Brownshirts and... well...it all ended rather badly I'm afraid." Rowland frowned, uncomfortable with the thought. "My brother believes I've become obsessed with the Nazis as a result."

"Is he correct?"

"Perhaps."

Wing nodded. "You must forgive my curiosity, Mr. Sinclair. I have an interest in what makes a man stand for one thing and sit quietly for others."

Rowland blanched. "I don't know, Mr. Wing. I never meant to do one or the other."

"I am not critical, Mr. Sinclair, just curious."

"What exactly did you study at MIT, Mr. Wing?"

"Philosophy."

Rowland paused. "You know, Wing, it would not bother me in the least if you were a Communist."

Wing nodded. "There are no Communists in Shanghai, Mr. Sinclair."

Chapter Twenty-Four

Paris of the East Through Michael's Eyes.

Sophistication in China.
The Gambling Spirit

Greyhound racing is a very popular sport with the wealthier Chinese, and very popular is the new Canidrome Garden cabaret, which is run in conjunction with the racing as an open-air show. Polo, too, has been enjoying a wave of popularity, partly due to the fact that Winston Guest, America's No. 2 player, stopped off here for long enough to have a few chukkas with the local lads...

They race native ponies up here, gentleman riders and all that sort of thing. Sir Victor Sassoon's stable ran away with the "Champions," which is Shanghai's equivalent to the Derby. The ponies are so small that one loses sight of them on the far stretches of the course, and has time for a little sleep before they come into view again. But one certainly doesn't lose sight of the dressing these comic little "meets." One stunning dress I saw was a tunic, cut absolutely straight another touch of the Chinese influence—pulling on over the head, with a spotted scarf knotted round the neck and showing through a slot somewhere down on the chest and tied in a bow. The frock was a kind of soft watermelon pink crepe pongee, and the scarf a hazy kind of blue spotted in white. (I hope my masculine descriptions are adequate.)

Huge cartwheel hats are all the rage here, and are seen everywhere worn on all occasions. Very shallow as to crown, the shallower the better (echoes of Princess Marina even in Shanghai).

—Michael.

—*Sydney Morning Herald*, 25 July 1935

Rowland handed three letters to Harjeet Bal for posting. One each to his mother and his nephew, full of gentle news, observations about China, and quick drawings of rickshaws and pagodas. The third letter, addressed to Wilfred Sinclair, was thicker. Rowland had spent most of the morning writing the detailed account of all that had happened since they arrived in Shanghai. Of course it would be weeks before the letter actually reached Wilfred. But it would at least explain more fully the intermittent telegrams that both he and Gilbert Carmel had sent thus far. He could only imagine what Wilfred was thinking, probably shouting, on the other side of the world.

The process of corresponding everything to his brother did make him wonder exactly what act had set him on this path. Was it that he had danced with Alexandra Romanova? Would none of this have happened if he had not gone to the Jazz Club that evening, or if he had not agreed to purchase her services on the floor? Or was it because he had asked her to take tea with him the following day? If he had not done one or any of these things, would she still be alive, or would she simply have died somewhere other than his suite?

It had been couple of days since the excursion to Fengjing. The time had been one of frustration in which their attempts to find Sergei Romanov had led nowhere. Indeed they had been unable to establish with any certainty whether the Russian was dead or alive. The Jazz Club band had apparently left Shanghai to play at a private event so they could not follow up on Wing's thoroughly unsuccessful attempt to question them.

Rowland had wanted to go to Randolph about the possibility that Edna was the intended victim, but Gilbert Carmel had been adamant that he should not speak with authorities. "Going to the police with theories only serves to make you seem suspicious, my boy. Allow me to deal with Inspector Randolph."

Rowland returned to the sanctuary and sanity of his easel and the painting of Alexandra. It was an unusual composition. Alexandra's face dominated the close foreground, her gaze fixed slightly upwards, her eyes bright with life. Behind her, couples dancing.

In the other room, Wing Zau was singing "Stormy Weather," which Ethel Waters had made a hit a couple of years before. It helped somehow to bring back details of that night at the Jazz Club.

Clyde hobbled up behind him, leaning heavily on the cane which Milton had found in one of the umbrella stands. "Bloody hell, Rowly! Blowed if I know how you do it."

"Do what?"

"Remember. It's been over a week since the night you danced with her. I can't paint my mother from memory."

Rowland handed Clyde his notebook. "I'd made a few sketches that evening after we'd returned from the Jazz Club."

Clyde flicked through the pages. "You were taken with her then?"

"Yes, I was," he admitted. "I liked her, Clyde; I felt sorry for her."

Clyde nodded. Rowland had often fallen victim to his own gallantry. Clyde handed the notebook back and leant against the back of the couch. "Something Ed said the other night got me thinking. Do you remember when she pointed out that perhaps this wasn't all about you?"

Rowland grimaced. "Yes. I do."

"Well, I was thinking, what if Alexandra didn't die in our suite?"

"I'm not sure I follow."

"We'd only just checked in at the Cathay. What if her death was connected with the bloke who had the suite before us?"

"I see." Rowland frowned. "My God, you're right! Perhaps the killer didn't realise the last resident had checked out."

Clyde agreed. "We need to find out who took the suite before us."

Rowland checked his watch. "I'll drop into the Cathay and call on Sassoon."

"But would Sassoon know something like that?" Clyde was sceptical.

Rowland shrugged. "The suites aren't generally taken by your standard guest. Whoever it was may have come to Sir Victor's attention."

"Like we did?"

"Hopefully not quite in the way we did."

"I'll come with you."

"No, you rest that leg. I'll take Milt."

———————————————

Rowland directed Ranjit Singh to the Canidrome in Frenchtown as he climbed into the Buick.

"Very good, sir."

"I thought we were going to see Sassoon." Milton leaned forward from the back seat.

"He's having drinks with Mickey at the Canidrome Club. She happened to mention the other night that they do so every Tuesday."

The greyhound racing stadium in the French Concession was vast. Located on the rue Lafayette, the stadium could seat some fifty thousand spectators. Its façade was modern—a monolithic building with a central deco tower which housed the members' club. Singh dropped them off at the portico before moving on to find a place to park and wait.

"I don't suppose you've actually thought about how we're going to get in?" Milton whispered as they approached the entrance. A sign declaring "Members Only" was mounted prominently on a stand beside a vigilant doorman.

Rowland smiled. "I say, my good man," he said addressing the doorman. "I'm afraid we're frightfully late. Rowland Sinclair and Milton Isaacs—we're joining Miss Hahn and Sir Victor."

"Sir Victor did not mention—"

Rowland smiled. "Possibly he was preoccupied with Miss Hahn."

The doorman nodded, but still he hesitated.

"I understand." Rowland produced a gilt-edged calling card from his pocket. "Would you mind giving Sir Victor my card? Just so he knows we tried to keep our appointment, despite our tardiness."

"No, no, sir. That will not be necessary. Sir Victor and Miss Hahn are in the bar." He flagged someone to replace him at the door. "I'll take you myself."

The Canidrome members' bar was a modern space. Large picture windows overlooking the stadium ensured that members missed none of the action on the track whilst they partook of cocktails in the comfort of club lounges. The bar itself was an elaborate geometric affair of mirrors and ebony in classic deco style. Framed photographs of champion greyhounds made Rowland think briefly of Lenin—not that his dog had ever been a champion. Indeed Lenin was barely a greyhound, but Rowland did miss him. The air in the club was manually circulated by servants who stood along the room's perimeter and operated fans made of cheesecloth stretched taut over bamboo frames.

Victor Sassoon and Mickey Hahn were not alone. The tycoon and the journalist stood in a cluster of feathered hats and cigarettes in long holders, a gay gathering of elegant people. The doorman approached Sassoon and pointed out the Australians. For a moment Rowland feared Sassoon would deny any appointment with them.

"There you are, finally!" Mickey intervened.

Sassoon exhaled and then followed suit. Satisfied then that they were guests of a member, as they had claimed, the cautious doorman left them to it.

"I apologise for this intrusion, Sir Victor," Rowland said quietly. "There is a matter about which I'd like to speak to you."

"And this matter couldn't wait?"

"I plan to see Chief Inspector Randolph later this afternoon." Rowland watched Sassoon carefully. "I had hoped to clarify some details first."

Sassoon drained his glass. "Well, since you have already told the concierge that you are doing so, you'd better join Mickey and me for a spot of luncheon." He clicked his fingers, and they were shown to a table by the window.

Sassoon ordered for them all, insisting that they try the beef Wellington, which was apparently the chef's speciality. Mickey spoke dreamily of Xunmei.

Sassoon told her, perhaps a little churlishly, that the poet was married.

Rowland couldn't tell if Mickey had known, or if she simply did not care.

It was not till the main course arrived that Rowland broached the subject of the suite's previous occupant.

"Am I to understand that you believe that the previous guest had something to do with the taxi girl's murder?" Sassoon asked.

"We had only just checked into that suite, Sir Victor. Perhaps the former guest had some connection with Miss Romanova?"

Sassoon's eyes narrowed. "And you wish to give that information to the chief inspector?"

"Randolph could probably find the information himself," Milton noted. "But yes, it would save time to just tell him."

Sassoon shook his head. "The previous guest could not possibly have had anything to do with it. I suggest you gentlemen look elsewhere. I certainly advise against speaking to the police about such nonsense."

Milton bristled, opening his mouth to retort. Rowland placed a cautionary hand on the poet's arm. "Thank you for your advice, Sir Victor. But you see, the previous resident's connection with Miss Romanova may not have been as her murderer but perhaps as the intended victim."

Sassoon shook his head. "No. I assure you the person in question has no connection whatsoever to the incident!"

"How can you be sure, sir?" Rowland asked calmly.

"Because Victor's rather well acquainted with her," Mickey said languidly. "The person who had your suite before you was me." She stifled a yawn. "Dear Victor was generous enough to upgrade Helen and me to a suite. I moved out into my little apartment on Kiangse Street just a couple of days before that poor girl died."

Rowland wasn't quite sure what to say. "Helen?" he asked in the end.

"My sister. It's on her account that I'm in Shanghai at all. I was intent on returning to the Congo."

"Where is she?"

"Oh, she sailed for home."

"Could whoever killed Miss Romanova have mistaken her for you?" Milton asked.

"Perhaps, but I don't see why anyone would want to kill me."

"Mickey has no enemies in China," Sassoon declared. "Not a one! Why she is the toast of Shanghai society!"

"But still…"

"Mr. Sinclair," Sassoon began angrily. "Rest assured that if you do anything to embroil Miss Hahn in this unfortunate and sordid affair, I shall be forced to withdraw the hospitality and generosity I have afforded you and your friends to date. I am not an enemy you wish to make."

"Are you threatening me, Sir Victor?"

"Yes, I believe I am."

"For goodness sake, Victor," Mickey said impatiently. "Don't be absurd!" She turned to Rowland and Milton. "You must forgive Victor, gentlemen. He's very protective of me. And he's right—there's no one in China who would wish me harm. Whoever killed Miss Romanova did not do so believing she was me, or Helen for that matter." She giggled. "Helen is even more inoffensive than I!"

"Is there anyone outside China who might wish you harm?" Rowland asked. "Someone who might have followed you here?"

A blink. A barely perceptible hesitation. "No."

"Why did you come to Shanghai?" Milton asked.

"I'd say that's none of your affair, Mr. Isaacs!" Sassoon growled.

"I've already told Rowland," Mickey replied wearily. "I'm convalescing after a broken heart. I was on my way to the Congo when I was seduced by China."

"I think we've endured quite enough of your questions," Sassoon said impatiently. "They are quite improper, and my patience is exhausted." Sassoon signalled the concierge. "I'm afraid the gentlemen will not be staying."

Milton glanced at Rowland and hastily shoved as much of his remaining beef Wellington as he could into his mouth.

"Would you mind showing them out?" Sassoon said.

"Thank you for your time, Sir Victor." Rowland stood. Milton grabbed one more mouthful before following suit.

"I hope we understand each other, Mr. Sinclair," Sassoon huffed.

Rowland didn't reply, taking his leave of Mickey instead. She smiled at him drowsily.

They were escorted out. It was an eviction, but a very civil one.

"Well, what do you think?" Milton asked as they waited for Singh to bring the Buick around.

"I don't know." Rowland frowned. "Sassoon made his feelings clear. Of course, he could be trying to protect Mickey, or something else entirely."

"Though, if someone's trying to kill Mickey Hahn, one wonders why they haven't tried again." Milton shaded his eyes against the midday sun. "She lives on her own, aside from that monkey."

Rowland smiled. "She did say he bites."

"So what are we going to tell Randolph, comrade?"

Rowland rubbed the back of his neck. He had no wish to drag Mickey into the investigation, but there was a possibility she was in danger.

Singh pulled up and they climbed in.

"Where can I take you, sir?"

Rowland sighed. "Metropolitan Police Headquarters, Mr. Singh."

Chapter Twenty-Five

DANCING IN THE EAST

Steady Ascendency of Jazz

That jazz was gradually superseding native dancing in China and Japan was the opinion of Mr. J. A. Andrew, who arrived at Melbourne aboard the steamer *Kamo Maru* yesterday after spending four years as dancing instructor at the Imperial Hotel, Tokyo; the Cathays Hotel, Shanghai; and the Hong Kong Hotel. Mr. Andrews, who is returning to England to act as manager for Miss Pat Sykes, undefeated ballroom dancing champion of Europe, said that the Chinese, particularly the young girls, were showing great aptitude towards the modern Western dances. Classes in the large hotels were attended by numbers of both sexes, many of whom had previously been exponents of native dancing.

In spite of the swing towards modern dancing, concessions had been made to native ideas by adapting musical scores to the native instruments.

—*The Age*, 19 May 1936

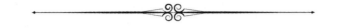

When Rowland Sinclair and Milton Isaacs arrived and requested an audience with the chief inspector, Randolph had no other engagements or pressing duties. Regardless, he insisted the Australians wait in the anteroom outside his office for forty minutes. It would, he thought, reiterate that he was not to be mistaken for a servant at their beck and call. In Randolph's experience, the Cathay's guests often needed to be reminded of that fact.

"What can I do for you, Mr. Sinclair, Mr. Isaacs?"

Rowland took one of the seats in front of the inspector's vast pedestal desk, Milton the other. "We've come across some information which we hoped might assist you in finding Miss Romanova's killer."

"What do you mean when you say you came across this information?"

"It is information we uncovered through our own investigations," Milton said impatiently.

"Your own investigations?" Randolph's voice rose. "On what authority do you gentlemen conduct an investigation in the International Concession?"

"We weren't conducting an investigation as such." Rowland intervened before the man could lose his temper. "We were merely alert to any facts that might relate to Miss Romanova's death."

Milton rolled his eyes.

"Why?"

Rowland's jaw tensed. "I discovered her body, Chief Inspector. That might be an ordinary occurrence in your particular line of work, but I find myself unable to not care about who killed the poor woman."

"Might I remind you, Mr. Sinclair, that you remain a suspect in Alexandra Romanova's murder?"

"All the more reason for me to care about establishing who really killed her, I should think."

Randolph stared at him. Finally he took up a pen and dipped it in the inkwell. "Very well then. What is it you wish to say?"

Rowland ventured the possibility that the taxi girl was killed by mistake.

"What exactly do you mean, Mr. Sinclair?"

"Perhaps the murderer intended to kill someone else."

"Are you saying you believe you were the intended victim?"

"Me? No. But perhaps Miss Higgins or Miss Hahn, or her sister for that matter."

"Miss Hahn?"

Rowland informed Randolph about the suite's previous occupants.

"What makes you believe Miss Hahn or her sister is connected with the murder?"

"I don't necessarily believe either is. I'm looking for any reason that a young woman might be brutally killed in my suite."

"Or perhaps you're trying to move the attention of the police from yourself."

"I'm not," Rowland said simply.

"That's all right then," Randolph sneered. "I'll just ignore the fact that the victim was found in your suite and that you were covered in her blood!"

Milton stood. "Look you—"

"Steady on, Milt." Rowland stopped the poet before he could erupt, then met Randolph's eye and held it. "I don't expect you to ignore it, Inspector. But neither do I expect you to ignore other lines of enquiry which might, in fact, bring Miss Romanova's murderer to justice."

"I applaud your determination to secure justice for a taxi girl. Exactly what was the nature of your relationship with the deceased?"

Rowland exhaled as he reminded himself to keep his temper.

"I danced with her and I found her body. I presume if you could prove I had done anything else, I would have been arrested by now."

"I wouldn't be in a hurry to presume anything if I were you, sir."

Rowland cursed furiously as they left the station. He nearly turned back to have a more frank word with the chief inspector. It was, unusually, Milton who advised restraint and caution. "He's just looking for a reason to throw you in gaol, comrade."

"Why would he want to do that?"

"Because cruelty has a human heart, and jealousy a human face."

"Blake," Rowland growled.

"Believe me," Milton persisted. "I know his type only too well."

"What flaming type?"

"The jumped-up little dictator type. Don't push him, Rowly. He probably doesn't have enough to convict you, but he might be able to lock you up for a while and..." Milton hesitated. "Wilfred isn't here."

Rowland's face clouded further, but he could not deny that his brother's influence might make matters easier now, even in Shanghai. He pushed a hand through his hair, frustrated. "You're right. I probably shouldn't get myself arrested."

Milton placed a hand on Rowland's shoulder. "Come on, mate. You've told him what we know, it's all you can do."

"For the moment."

"Yes, for the moment." Milton glanced at his watch. "Don't you and Ed have to go to this fancy party tonight?"

Rowland nodded unenthusiastically.

"Then we'll see if we can find Sergei Romanov tomorrow."

"We probably have time now if we hurry—"

Milton shook his head. "You'll be cutting it too fine, Rowly. Go do what Wilfred sent you here to do—Sergei will keep."

Rowland's laugh was wry. "Wilfred sent me here to do nothing. He made that very clear."

"Well, you should be able to do an excellent job then." Milton signalled Singh and the Buick. "We'd better head back so you can change. I believe your lot prefers to wear dinner suits while they do nothing."

The Paramount Ballroom was on Bubbling Well Road, just outside the French Concession. As it was in actuality a number of dance halls, the complex occupied a substantial part of the block.

"Andrew Petty promised to drop us home," Rowland told Ranjit Singh as the Buick picked its way through the congestion.

"I can wait, sir."

"This might take hours, Mr. Singh, and I don't see anywhere for you to park the car."

Edna agreed. "We'll go back to Kiangse Road with Mr. Petty. You go home to your wife, Mr. Singh."

Singh frowned. He wagged his finger at them. "Promise me you won't be tempted to take a rickshaw. The drivers all take opium—it's very dangerous."

Solemnly, Edna made the promise.

Rowland climbed out of the Buick and walked around to hold the door open for Edna. She took his hand and stepped out, the split of her cheongsam parting to give Rowland a glimpse of her thigh. She laughed as she noticed his gaze. "I've posed for you a hundred times, Rowly—you've seen my leg before. It's hardly cause for alarm."

Rowland nodded. "I assure you I'm not alarmed."

Edna entwined her arm in his. "Shall we make an entrance then?"

They walked into the building and were ushered by a doorman to the main ballroom on the ground floor. The massive hall embodied all the glamour and sleek style of contemporary fashion with a decadent flair of the previous decade. The Harlem Boys—an American jazz band—played in the ornate shell which formed the back of the stage. Round tables had been laid with white linen and silver for a banquet of many courses. A mezzanine level provided a surrounding balcony which overlooked the lower hall, and from which guests might watch the dancing or retreat to private conversations. Strings of flowers attached to the mezzanine hung over the tables, forming suspended centrepieces. The lighting was dim, the atmosphere charged, but not quite celebratory.

"Oh it's beautiful," Edna murmured, reaching out to touch a string of flowers. It seemed they were among the last guests to arrive.

Andrew Petty spotted them and approached with outstretched congeniality. "Sinclair! You're here at last. How are you, old man?"

Rowland shook Petty's hand and introduced Edna.

Petty took her hand and raised it to his lips. "We're going to be frightful bores and talk business from time to time, so do allow me to apologise in advance, Miss Higgins…though I suspect a young lady as enchanting as yourself will not be short of company if Sinclair is obliged to neglect you occasionally."

"Exactly the reason I'll be doing no such thing," Rowland replied pleasantly.

Petty faltered, and then he laughed. "Oh, I see. Very good, Sinclair, very good. But you may have to, I'm afraid. The Japanese chaps are determined to make a deal tonight." He showed them to their seats at one of the banquet tables. Despite Petty's insistence that Rowland would need a partner for the event, the other men at their table were unaccompanied.

Petty introduced Rowland to a number of Japanese businessmen, including Messrs. Akhito and Yiragowa, to whom the others seemed to defer. Standing dutifully behind each of their Japanese hosts was an interpreter—young men barely out of their teens, who were not introduced and who spoke only when translating words into and from English. The businessmen shared a military stiffness to their carriage and a slow formality to their speech.

Also at the table were Messrs. Masey and Lloyd-Jones of the Japan-Australia Society. Masey was young, no older than Rowland, and a representative of Johnson and Johnson. Rowland was already vaguely acquainted with Lloyd-Jones, who resided in Woollahra.

The table's numbers were completed by Herr Rabe of Siemens and Miss Violet Rutherford, who had come with Andrew Petty.

Rowland shook all the necessary hands and returned the bows of the Japanese gentlemen; Edna accepted introductory compliments with modesty and grace.

John Rabe, who was seated beside Edna, spoke English and so was able to engage the sculptress without the stilted conduit of translators. Rowland sketched him mentally. The German businessman had no particularly striking features. His forehead stretched to the crown of his head, and his upper lip bore the tidy, unremarkable moustache that was currently popular among men his age. His eyes were intelligent, assessing. The director of the local subsidiary of Siemens, a European company which dealt in industrial manufacture, Rabe and the Japanese seemed on familiar terms. Rowland pushed in Edna's chair as an army of waiters emerged in formation to serve the first course and keep glasses refreshed.

"Yiragowa has been charged by the Japanese government and a consortium of respected manufacturers to purchase wool on their behalf—the others all answer to him," Petty whispered into Rowland's ear. "They are keen to come to an understanding."

Rowland nodded, awkwardly aware that he'd been instructed to do anything but come to an understanding. Despite his best efforts to linger in social small talk, the conversation launched into business almost immediately. Fortunately, the need to use interpreters slowed the pace. Rowland said as little as possible whilst Andrew Petty waxed lyrical about the superior quality of Australian wool and the Australian businessmen spoke equally effusively about the friendship between Australia and Japan.

"You will not find a better price for your wool than that which we can offer, Mr. Sinclair," Yiragowa's interpreter said impassively.

"I have no doubt." Rowland glanced at Yiragowa. There was a hint of pride and expectation in the tilt of his head as the interpreter relayed the words. Regardless, Rowland offered no more. There was an exchange of Japanese which the interpreters did not convey.

In an effort to avoid direct questioning on the subject, Rowland invited Herr Rabe into the conversation, asking him about business in China.

Rabe spoke enthusiastically about the opportunities China could offer. In the background, the interpreters translated the conversation into Japanese.

"And how do you think the Chinese feel about the focus of the business world on their country?" Rowland asked, knowing the topic was probably not strictly appropriate for polite conversation, but hoping politics might waylay further talk of wool.

"My children and grandchildren were born here, Mr. Sinclair. I have tremendous sympathy for the Chinese people."

"Do you consider yourself Chinese, Herr Rabe?" Edna asked.

Rabe shook his head emphatically. "I am German in heart and mind. My first allegiance is to the Fatherland."

Edna's hand touched Rowland's arm under the table.

Rowland took a chance. "And the Nazis?" he asked in German. "Do they have your allegiance too?"

The interpreters murmured, confused. Clearly none of them understood German.

Rabe watched Rowland carefully and replied in German. "But of course. I am an organiser of the party in Shanghai. Like all loyal Germans, I love the Führer. If only the Chinese were blessed with a government like the Third Reich."

Petty looked flustered. "I say, chaps, I don't know if you realise the interpreters don't understand German...nor I, for that matter."

Rowland noticed a few couples on the dance floor and saw his chance. He stood and held his hand out to Edna. "If you'll excuse me, gentlemen, I might dance with Miss Higgins before the next course is served."

"I say," Petty said, surprised, "is that—"

Edna took Rowland's hand and stood. "I'd be delighted, Mr. Sinclair."

The Harlem Boys were playing a Lindy Hop when Rowland and Edna stepped out. The dance was not particularly well known in Australia, but they had picked up the steps while abroad a couple of years before. It took only a couple of tentative beats to find their rhythm on the spring-form dance floor, which suited the energy of movement. Conversation was, of course, constrained by the demands of the dance and the volume of the music so close to the stage.

It seemed the Hop was popular in Shanghai because by its end there were several more couples on the floor. And so Rowland and Edna settled into a slow jazz waltz within the privacy of a crowd.

Edna looked up at Rowland and smiled. "That's better," she said. "I was worried the conversation at the table was getting too serious."

Rowland grimaced. "The Japanese seem fairly intent on buying our wool," he said. "Perhaps I should just tell them that all business decisions are made by Wil."

"I'm not sure I understand why they are so determined to do business with the Sinclairs." Edna leaned back as Rowland led her into a series of turns.

"I suspect it's the influence of the Sinclair name they want. Petty seems to think the other brokers are waiting to see if Wil is willing to sell to the Japanese."

"Do you think he is?"

"I'm afraid my brother's business machinations are a mystery to me."

Edna's brow furrowed, her eyes fixed on his. "Herr Rabe. He's a Nazi."

"Yes."

"That bothers you."

Rowland sighed. "I suspect you can't be a German business-man nowadays without being a member. Rabe is probably like every other politically convenient, opportunistic businessman. If Germany was Communist, he'd be singing 'The Red Flag' with gusto."

"So you're not...you know?" Edna asked quietly.

Rowland looked down. The sculptress's cheek was rested against his lapel. He understood why she was worried. For months after their time in Germany, he had been unable to work or sleep. But he had learned to deal with those memories now. He was no longer crippled by it. "I'm perfectly all right," he said.

"Who do you suppose all these people are?" Edna asked.

"What do you mean?"

Edna glanced around at the hundreds of people in the hall, at tables, in alcoves, on the dance floor, and leaning over the balcony. "Are the Japanese hoping to do business with them all?"

"Many of them, I expect," Rowland replied. "Apparently there's serious talk of a trade embargo against Japan. I suppose they're trying to make sure they have what they need before it's imposed."

"So all these people have something they want?"

Rowland cast his eyes about the hall. "I suspect some of them are just people that go to dances," he said. "I saw Bernadine just now, and that chap Chao Kung—the Buddhist abbot. I wouldn't have thought either would have anything of interest to the Japanese."

Edna craned her neck in an attempt to glimpse Chao Kung. Rowland assisted her by lowering her into a dip so she could see the unusual holy man, albeit upside-down.

"Thank you," she laughed, as he pulled her up and finished the movement with a turn. "We probably should resume our seats before poor Mr. Petty explodes."

Rowland looked back at their table. All eyes were on them. He sighed. "One more number. The more time we spend here, the less time I'll have to spend trying to avoid committing Wil to anything."

Chapter Twenty-Six

TREBÏTSCH LINCOLN.
Return to Shanghai.

SHANGHAI—Refused permission to reside in Great Britain, America, Japan and European countries, the Abbot Chao Kung, better known in the western world as Trebitsch Lincoln who, in the course of a chequered career was a member of the British Parliament and later a wartime spy, returned to Shanghai last night accompanied by six Buddhist priests and one nun.

He is thoroughly embittered at his treatment at the hands of western nations, among whom he intended to spread the Buddhist faith. Refusing to see pressmen, he handed out a printed slip declaring that after years of experience with journalists, he was finally forced to the decision to refuse to see any of them in the future. "I am not interested in publicity," he added. "My work is to help suffering humanity through the doctrine of Buddha. You cannot help me and you certainly shall not hinder me."

He announced his intention of organising Buddhist

propaganda for distribution in European countries, using China as a base.

—*Western Mail*, 28 June 1934

As Rowland and Edna returned to their seats, the next course was being served.

"You're an excellent dancer, Mr. Sinclair," Violet said glancing resentfully at Petty.

"You and Miss Higgins make a very graceful couple," Rabe agreed. "The modern dances are too exuberant for me, I'm afraid. Mrs. Rabe must content herself with the occasional waltz."

Andrew Petty endeavoured to resurrect negotiations for the Sinclair clip. "Well done, Sinclair," he whispered. "Your feigned indifference is making them nervous. Bloody clever strategy. I suspect Yiragowa may be ready to raise their offer."

"It might be best to be indifferent for a while longer then."

"I don't think…" Petty trailed off as three European men approached and then stopped at their table. They were obviously known to their hosts, who stood and greeted them warmly without the aid of the interpreters. But it was Rabe's greeting that caught Rowland's attention.

The businessman stood. "*Heil* Hitler." Rabe clicked his heels and flapped his hand in a casual Fascist salute. The response was in kind, and the conversation which ensued, collegial, this time in German. Playful comments about what Mrs. Rabe would say if she knew he was dining with two such beautiful women. And then an enquiry about whether the Japanese had concluded their business.

Rabe cleared his throat and introduced Rowland Sinclair and the ladies. The Germans were presented as diplomats, representatives of the Third Reich, a fact which Rabe clearly felt recommended them. Rowland's reserve was marked but not beyond the explanation of a natural disposition. Only Edna was aware of the tension in his body. The Germans stayed a while longer, making jokes, being generally pleasant. They wished the Japanese wool buyers a good outcome before they departed for their own table.

For a while talk of wool was set aside as they ate. Eventually Petty returned the conversation to the Sinclair stockpile.

Yiragowa took up the negotiation declaring that he was willing to offer twice the market rate.

"Well that is a most generous offer—" Petty began.

"No," Rowland said.

Petty's head snapped round. "I beg your pardon, I thought you said—"

"I said no," Rowland's voice was calm and clear.

Petty whispered urgently into his ear. "Look, Rowland, I assure you that this is an excellent offer. I doubt they'll go much higher."

"It wouldn't matter if they did," Rowland replied. "The answer would still be no."

Lloyd-Jones scowled. "What exactly are you playing at, Sinclair?"

Masey stared at Rowland aghast. "Why?"

The Japanese wool buyers were talking amongst themselves—no interpreters were needed to translate their displeasure.

Petty was apoplectic. "For God's sake, man! What the hell are you trying to do?"

"I'm sorry, Andrew—I've decided not to sell the stockpile at this point."

"Sorry? We had an understanding!"

"No, I don't believe we did."

Yiragowa and Akhito were shouting now. The Germans, having noticed the commotion, were making their way back. Rabe stood and stepped away from the table to speak with them.

Edna grabbed Rowland's hand. "Perhaps we should go, Rowly."

Rowland nodded. He stood and thanked their hosts for what it was worth. The interpreter who translated, did so while cringing. Akhito barked a reply while Petty almost begged Rowland to reconsider.

"I'll be in touch, Mr. Petty."

Petty exploded, grabbing Rowland's shoulder angrily. "If you think I'm going to allow you to leave—"

"I wasn't asking your permission," Rowland said coldly.

"Let the boy go, Andrew."

Rowland turned. Alastair Blanshard. "Hello, Rowland."

"Do you know what this bloody fool has done?" Petty spat. "You'll regret this, Sinclair. I'll see that you do."

"Settle down, Andrew. There are ladies present." Blanshard smiled at Edna. "Good evening, Miss Higgins."

"Mr. Blanshard—hello. What on earth are you doing here?"

"That, my dear, is a story for another day. I believe you and Rowland were leaving. Don't let us delay you."

Rowland caught the advice in his tone, and whilst he did not entirely trust Alastair Blanshard, he took heed. He and Edna made their way to the foyer and waited briefly while one of the footmen fetched their coats.

"Mr. Sinclair!" Chao Kung pulled off his Tibetan skullcap as he approached and wrung it as he spoke. "I don't suppose you'd remember me. We were introduced at the soiree of Mrs. Bernadine Szold-Fritz."

"Good evening, sir." Rowland placed Edna's cape over her shoulders. "I'm afraid we were just leaving."

"I couldn't help but overhear that you have fallen out with the Japanese." Kung did not seem inclined to let them pass.

For a moment Rowland said nothing. "I see."

"I wondered perhaps if I might offer my services."

"And what services are they, Mr. Kung?"

Kung preened. "As a man of the cloth, I have connections of trust with the children of the sun, as well as the British and Germans. Perhaps I could assist you to sort out any misunderstanding."

Rowland smiled faintly. "Thank you, Mr. Kung, but I really don't think so."

"Allow me to assure you, Mr. Sinclair, I am a man of considerable influence. Surely it would be better to return to your brother having successfully concluded the business for which he sent you?"

Rowland's eyes narrowed. How on earth did Kung know what Wilfred had sent him to China to do? "No, I don't think it would, but thank you for your concern. We really must be getting on our way."

Kung gripped Rowland's arm. "Don't do something you'll regret, Mr. Sinclair."

Rowland looked down at Kung's hand. "I would caution you likewise, sir."

The abbot released his grasp. "Perhaps I could offer you a lift back to your residence in my motorcar. Where are you staying?"

"Thank you, but we have our own car," Rowland said coolly. He took Edna's hand. "If you'll excuse us, Mr. Kung?"

For a moment Kung hesitated, and then he pressed his palms together and bowed.

They slipped past him and through the door, stepping out onto Bubbling Well Road.

"What now?" Edna whispered.

"We disappear into the crowd," Rowland said quietly, "in case someone tries following us." Rowland adjusted Edna's cape, glancing back over her shoulder as he did so. "That chap Kung seemed rather too interested in where we were staying."

They weaved their way through a group of people clapping and laughing around a man with performing monkeys, as the creatures cavorted and begged for coins. Chao Kung scurried into the crowd after them, the monk's attire serving to clear the respectful from its path. It was not until Rowland and Edna joined a large group of Englishmen on the way to dinner that their attire and Rowland's height became less conspicuous, and the abbot fell behind and out of sight. The Englishmen and their ladies had obviously been taking pre-dinner drinks somewhere, and so they didn't seem to notice the Australians who'd insinuated themselves into their party.

After a couple of blocks, gaily traversed with the inebriated revellers, they found themselves entering a restaurant in one of the vibrant side alleys. The doorman waved in the group on the credentials of the gentleman at its head.

"We'll see about finding a telephone," Rowland said quietly as they were bustled in.

The restaurant was lit by candles and oil lamps. It was large enough to accommodate a band and dance floor, but with the number of people within it, there was barely room to move. The party had clearly been going for some time before their arrival. The clientele was mainly Western, though there were a few Orientals in the mix. Rowland could make out phrases of French and Russian and a little Italian in the multilingual babble. Waiters managed to negotiate the press of people with champagne and spirits. On the dance floor, couples moved together in a way that would have been a scandal in other establishments: entwined, enraptured, oblivious. It was warm in the restaurant, and perhaps for this reason, many patrons seemed to be in various forms of undress. Every now and then there were squeals and cheers as one of the guests removed some part of their attire. Rowland kept a firm grip on Edna's hand. It was not that they had never been to wild parties before, but that they had come to this one uninvited with no idea as to who else was there.

A young woman, naked to the waist, grabbed Rowland's lapel and made to kiss him. Surprised and apparently offended when he resisted, she demanded an explanation in inebriated indignation. "Don't you like me? Why are you being like that?"

Rowland declined her advances as courteously as he could, but it seemed the would-be seductress was taking his lack of interest somewhat personally. Her anger became tearful and loud. He made a futile attempt to calm her. Then Edna reached up and kissed Rowland herself. He responded without reserve, without any thought of defence. When the sculptress finally pulled away, the spurned stranger had vanished.

Edna laughed, rubbing the lipstick off his lip with her thumb. "I'm sorry, Rowly. I thought she might go if she thought you were spoken for."

Rowland stared at her, having in that moment forgotten completely about the naked girl.

"Rowly?"

"Yes...of course. Thank you. We should get out of here before someone notices we're not actually on the guest list."

Rowland asked a passing waiter about using a telephone, but making himself understood over the din of celebration was a challenge. Eventually the man gestured that he should wait and headed towards a small set of stairs in the corner.

"My God! You're a doll!" The accent was American. A gentleman who'd lost his jacket and whose tie hung loose about his neck. "You wanna come upstairs with me, sweetheart?"

"No, thank you," Edna said calmly.

"Oh, come on!" The American moved to seize Edna around the waist.

Rowland stepped in between them. "The lady said no."

"Gentleman's choice, buddy. It's the rules. We share and share alike." He grabbed for Edna. Rowland caught his arm. The American swung with the other.

The dispute exploded more than escalated, and it seemed the American had friends. They came quickly to the fray. The fight was brief and intense, and Rowland lost quite decisively. He was thrown out into the alley.

As he struggled to his knees, his first thought, his only thought, was Edna. Where the hell was she?

The alley was deserted.

Rowland closed his eyes, trying to steady a spinning word, attempting to recall exactly what had happened. He remembered being pulled away from Edna and slammed up against a wall while three men laid into him. She'd called his name, but in the crowded darkness he could not see her. They'd dragged him out and thrown him into the side street.

Light from the establishment's shopfront spilled into the head of the alley, allowing the shadow to be cast. A man in robes. The figure moved as Rowland looked up. "Kung!"

Rowland staggered back to the restaurant's entrance. The doormen barred his way.

"I'm afraid this is strictly an invitation-only event, sir."

Rowland tried to explain. The doormen refused to hear him. Frustrated and beginning to panic now, Rowland charged the door. And then he was on the ground again. One of the doormen produced a gun and pressed the muzzle against Rowland's chest.

"You'd best move on, sir," he growled. "Your young lady probably has."

Recklessly, furiously, Rowland refused. Somewhere a woman screamed.

"Rowly!" Edna's voice.

She appeared suddenly from the darkness of the alley and attempted to push the man with the gun away from Rowland. "How dare you! Leave him alone—"

It was hard to know what the zealous doormen might have done if two Rolls Royce limousines had not at that moment pulled into the alley, momentarily dazzling them all with their headlamps.

Startled, the doormen stood back. The gun was holstered hastily.

The doors of the first motorcar opened, and six burly European men climbed out and waited. A uniformed chauffeur alighted from the second vehicle and opened the rear door of the limousine. Du Yuesheng stepped out.

Rowland looked up into Edna's face. She was close to tears. "Rowly…"

He sat up slowly, painfully. "Ed, thank God! How did you—?"

"The waiter," she whispered. "He took me out through the kitchen after they threw you out."

Rowland embraced her. "I'm so sorry. I should never have—"

Du Yuesheng cleared his throat impatiently.

Rowland rose gingerly to his feet.

Du turned to his chauffeur and barked orders in Cantonese. The driver bowed and translated his master's instructions into Pidgin for the benefit of Rowland and Edna. "Mister wanchee go home? Zongshi say my tek."

"I think he's offering to have his driver take us home," said Edna.

Rowland hesitated. "Thank you," he said to Du Yuesheng. As unlikely as it sounded, accepting a ride from a Shanghai gangster seemed the safest and most convenient course of action in the present moment.

Du signalled, and one of the men who'd arrived in the first Rolls Royce opened the door and motioned Rowland into the back of the vehicle. Edna climbed in beside him.

The chauffeur slid open the partition. "Where to?"

"Cathay Hotel side," Rowland replied slowly, attempting to reply with what pidgin he'd managed to pick up.

"Rowly, are you sure—?" Edna began.

Rowland took her hand and nodded. He did not want Du Yuesheng to know where they were staying, if he could help it. By the time they reached the Cathay Hotel he would have recovered his breath enough to walk the couple of blocks to Kiangse Road.

Du Yuesheng's chauffeur was talkative. He did not seem to mind that his passengers understood very little of what he was saying. Edna took the trouble to nod and smile into the rearview mirror from time to time; Rowland was preoccupied with the pounding in his head. Edna asked him for his handkerchief as she opened the inbuilt drinks cabinet. She moistened the cloth with the contents of one of the crystal decanters and then pressed it gently to his temple. It seemed the newly healed injury inflicted by Sergei Romanov's violin had reopened.

Rowland flinched. The alcohol with which Edna had dampened his handkerchief stung on contact. He wondered fleetingly if he had time to pour some into a glass instead.

"Rowly—"

"I'm all right, Ed," he said quietly. "My pride's more bruised than anything else."

"It's not your pride that's bleeding, Rowly."

"No," he said. "That's definitely my head."

She said nothing for a moment. "What do you suppose that place was?"

"Some kind of nightclub. I expect there was a gaming room or an opium den up those stairs." Rowland's eyes clouded. "If anything had happened to you, Ed…"

"Nothing did." She pressed his hand. "They forgot about me the moment the fight started. I was terrified they were going to kill you."

Rowland smiled ruefully. "No, they weren't that committed to the task."

The Rolls Royce pulled up in front of the Cathay, and they disembarked.

"*Yáyà nong.*" Edna thanked the driver in Shanghainese, an effort which seemed to delight him. He waved and honked as he turned the motorcar around and headed back towards the Garden Bridge. They waited till he was out of sight.

"We'd better go in," Edna said.

"Into the Cathay?" Rowland asked. "Why?"

"We'll ask Mr. Van Hagen to have one of the hotel cars take us to Kiangse Road." She reached up and brushed back his hair to check if the cut on his brow has stopped bleeding. It had, but the area was bruised and bloody. "All things considered, it might not be wise to walk."

Rowland nodded. Kiangse Road was only a couple of blocks away, but his current state of dishevelment did make him somewhat conspicuous. They could also not be sure that they were not still being followed. Edna took his arm. She walked slowly, and accustomed to usual briskness of her step, he guessed she was still concerned about him. "Stop worrying, Ed. I was a boxer, remember? I know how to take a punch."

She looked at him critically. "Yes, I suppose you must."

He laughed. "Come on, let's find Van Hagen. I should probably cash another cheque anyway."

Chapter Twenty-Seven

AID TO COURTING

A Book Was Once Written

ABOUT 70 years ago, according to a classic which was published then, *The Art of Courtship*, there was no such thing as equality of the sexes in the business of wooing and being wooed, which in those days was called, "Winning the fair object of his affections."

..."If the now hopeful suitor is invited to a party," the book says, "at which the loved one will be present, he can take the bull by the horns, and send her some flowers with the written request that he hopes to have the unspeakable pleasure of seeing Miss X honor his unworthy self by wearing them in her corsage that evening."

—*Sun*, 5 November 1933

Milton opened the red door and regarded them with both relief and shock. "Bloody oath! He moved quickly to lend Rowland his shoulder as Edna stepped inside. "What the devil did you do to Rowly?"

The sculptress ignored him.

"Who's here?" Rowland asked, having noticed the black Singer outside the house.

"You have a visitor."

Rowland groaned. "Randolph?"

Clyde limped out into the hallway. "Actually no." He put his arm around Edna, relieved. "You're a sight for sore eyes, Ed—we thought... Good grief, Rowly, are you all right? What on earth happened?"

"I'll be fine. Who's here?"

Clyde stepped aside so Rowland could proceed into the drawing room. "You should probably see for yourself."

"Sinclair! Where the in the name of God have you been?" Alastair Blanshard stood as they came in. "Look at you! I thought I instructed you to go home!"

"Good evening, Mr. Blanshard. What an unexpected pleasure."

"Don't be absurd, Sinclair, I'm not here for tea and tiddlywinks!"

Rowland eased himself into a chair. He rubbed the back of his neck. "What can I do for you, Mr. Blanshard?" he asked wearily.

Edna telephoned Dr. Rubenstein, ignoring Rowland's protests.

"Suppose you start by telling me why you look like you've been run over by a flaming rickshaw." Blanshard said, rolling his eyes as Edna asked the physician to attend.

Rowland recounted the fracas at the nightclub.

Blanshard leant forward in his seat. "Are you sure?"

"Sure of what?"

"Sure that your present condition is the result of an altercation over Miss Higgins's honour."

"What are you suggesting?"

"Kung—that chap who calls himself an abbot, was once Mr. Trebitsch-Lincoln, Member for Darlington in County Durham. He has at various times been wanted by His Majesty's government for international espionage. Before his current incarnation as Buddhist holy man, he was working with Fascist sympathisers in Europe until he betrayed them too. I noticed you were speaking to him."

"He's a spy?"

"He likes to think so...but more of a mercenary whose allegiances are for sale."

Rowland told Blanshard the essence of their conversation with Kung and of the shadow he saw in the alley. "I was a little groggy, but I'm sure it was him."

"Who exactly was this fellow who propositioned Miss Higgins?"

Rowland shrugged. "I think he was already in the restaurant when we arrived. I don't know who the chap was—some drunken buffoon who thought he could take liberties."

"How big was he?" Milton asked, looking Rowland over.

"He had friends."

Blanshard shook his head. "For pity's sake, boy, was it truly necessary to start a brawl? This is Shanghai. You have to expect a certain lack of inhibition."

"It was his lack of manners to which I objected."

"Blast it, Sinclair, you can't go about swinging first, particularly now! I would have thought what happened in Germany..."

Edna returned to the drawing room with a tray of tea and one of Harjeet's coffee cakes. She handed Rowland the compress she'd made up in the kitchen, and poured him the first cup of tea. "Couldn't this wait till morning, Mr. Blanshard?"

"No, unfortunately I don't think it can. Time is our enemy."

Clyde's groan was audible.

"Where's Wing?" Rowland asked, noticing his absence for the first time.

"He took take the night off—visiting relatives or some such thing."

"He won't be back till the morning, but he laid out your pyjamas and fresh suit before he went." Clyde was obviously amused by Wing's continuing efforts.

"Who is this fellow Wing?" Blanshard demanded.

"Rowly retained him as a translator and guide," Milton replied. "As far as we can tell, he lays out Rowly's clothes for his own entertainment."

"Wing? An Oriental, then? Where did you find him?"

"He was the butler provided to us by the Cathay."

"Good of Sassoon to send him with you." Blanshard scowled. "Though a security guard might have been more useful. Is he trustworthy?"

"Yes," Edna said definitely.

Rowland agreed. Wing might be a Communist in hiding, but that probably made him more trustworthy than less.

Milton moved the cup of tea Edna had made for Rowland aside, and set down a glass of gin instead.

"What exactly are you doing in Shanghai, Mr. Blanshard?" Rowland winced as he reached for the glass of gin. Now that they'd stopped moving, the parts of his body that had taken the worst of it were beginning to ache. Nothing, however, that a good night's rest would not address if he could just get Blanshard to leave.

"I'm taking in the sights, Mr. Sinclair." Blanshard regarded Rowland thoughtfully. "What made you turn down the Japanese? From what I understand, their offer was generous."

"You turned them down?" Clyde said, surprised. "I thought Wilfred said—"

Rowland did not ask how Blanshard knew what the Japanese had offered. The man was a spy, after all. "The Japanese are working with the Nazis."

"What makes you think that?"

Rowland told him about the German diplomats who'd graced their table.

"This is Shanghai," Blanshard said carefully.

"It was not a chance encounter," Rowland replied. "Nor a mere public civility. The Germans were aware of the Japanese offer."

Blanshard sighed. "So I am to understand that you will not deal with anyone who has a sympathetic or friendly association with the Germans."

"With the Nazis," Rowland corrected. "No, I will not." He undid his bow tie and unfastened the button of his bloodied collar. "Look, Blanshard, the truth is I wasn't authorised to accept the Japanese offer anyway. Wil wanted me to mark time until he has the chance to deal with the issue himself. I just got sick of playing games."

"Were you authorised to refuse the offer?"

"Not specifically, but Wilfred will agree with my reasons," he said, not really sure that would be the case.

"I see." Blanshard's tone was sceptical. "Look, Rowland," he continued more gently. "I know you have good reason to distrust the Germans, but business deals are not made in isolation. There were many other deals relying on the Sinclairs being willing to do business with the Japanese despite talk of an embargo... deals which may, in fact, have prevented the embargo ever being imposed. There are a great many people with substantial fortunes at risk."

"Are you suggesting I accept the Japanese offer?"

"No. That matter is ultimately between you and Wilfred. However, I do need you to understand the danger in which you've put yourself and your companions. This is Shanghai. Business dealings here are not always polite. Coercion, extortion, and retribution are as commonplace as drinks before dinner." Blanshard drained his tumbler of whisky. "It's my recommendation that you all go home immediately."

Rowland glanced at his companions. "Regrettably, Mr.

Blanshard, the murder of Alexandra Romanova means that I, at least, cannot leave."

"And I suppose Miss Higgins and the gentlemen won't leave without you."

"That's right," Milton replied.

Blanshard rubbed his chin and directed Milton to top up his whisky. "Tell me about this murdered taxi girl."

Rowland detailed what they knew about Alexandra.

Blanshard stood and moved to the window. "I'll see what I can find out." He moved the curtain aside and peered out. "How did you get home?"

"What do you mean?"

"You said you sent your driver home. How did you get from this restaurant in the alley to here? I expect you know that both taxis and rickshaws are dangerous for various reasons."

Edna told Alastair Blanshard about the timely arrival of Du Yuesheng. "He had his driver take us home."

Blanshard looked at Rowland aghast. "You told Shanghai's preeminent gangster where you were staying?"

"No. We had the chauffeur deliver us to the Cathay, for what it was worth. But considering you found us, I expect Master Du will be able to do so too."

"Right then!" Blanshard put down his glass, frustrated. "May I implore you to jolly well do whatever necessary to get out from whatever suspicion you're under, and then leave Shanghai before you get yourselves killed!"

The first creak was loud enough to stir Rowland. He lay abed, unsure what exactly had woken him. It was still very dark, no hint of dawn, and his sleep had been exhausted without dreams to jolt him into consciousness. It had been midnight before Rubinstein left after inserting a precautionary stitch and reassuring Edna that Rowland was not seriously hurt. It was still too dark to make out the face of his watch, but Rowland doubted that he had been asleep long. Certainly not long enough. A second creak and he was out of bed, wincing as he was reminded sharply of the battering his body had taken a few hours before. Even so, he didn't pause, stepping into the hallway to investigate the noise.

Edna jumped, clamping her hand over her mouth to stifle a scream. A candle wobbled precariously in the holder she held in the other.

"Ed." He whispered in case Clyde and Milton had not already woken. "What are you doing?"

"I heard a sound downstairs." She peered down the stairwell. "I was going to look before I woke any of you—to make sure I wasn't imagining things."

Rowland shook his head. "Wait here," he said. "I'll go down and check."

"I'm not letting you go alone—"

"You need to stay here and wake Clyde and Milt if it happens that there is an intruder," he said quietly but firmly.

"Rowly—"

"It's probably nothing," he said, aware of the familiar scent of her rose perfume. "That fool Blanshard's just made you a bit jittery with his dire warnings."

Reluctantly, she handed him the candle. He made his way down the stairs and tested the back door first. It was secure. The kitchen seemed undisturbed, the dining room too. Rowland walked through the ground floor checking every room. There was nothing. It was as he was about to check the front door that he heard something. It took him a couple of seconds to realise it came from outside the door. He relaxed—probably a stray dog… or a cat. There seemed an inordinate number of cats in Shanghai. He released the bolts on the red door and swung it open. Kiangse Road was not silent, even at this time. A few rickshaws, two or three parked cars, a group of men gathered about a lit brazier in the space between the buildings directly across the road, but there was no dog or cat. There was, however, something on the doorstep.

Rowland picked up the bouquet, scanning for any sign of who might have left it. No one.

He frowned, bringing the flowers in and re-bolting the door. Edna had, by then, come down.

"Rowly, Ed…is that you?" Clyde peered down from the top of the stairs.

"Yes."

"Is something wrong?"

"No. Ed thought she heard something."

Clyde grunted drowsily. "Bloody Blanshard!"

"Go back to bed, Clyde," Edna said. "It was nothing."

Another grunt and Clyde did as she suggested.

"What's that?" Edna asked Rowland.

"Flowers, orchids I believe." He handed them to her.

"Who are they for?"

"You, I expect. People don't generally leave flowers for men—even in China."

"There's no card," she said, almost to herself.

"It's probably Kruznetsov getting overexcited again."

Edna bit her lip. "Maybe." She didn't sound at all certain.

"Should we put these in water?"

"No." She placed the bouquet onto the hall table. "I'll throw them out in the morning."

Rowland was a little surprised by the vehemence of her reply. "Are you all right, Ed?"

"Yes. I just don't think they're from Nicky."

"Why?"

She shivered.

"Come on, you're cold."

Edna did not return to the attic where she had been sleeping but followed Rowland into the bedroom he normally shared with

Wing. That in itself did not alarm Rowland in any way. It was the sculptress's habit to visit the men she lived with at odd times of the night, seized with enthusiasm for an idea, or rage against some inequity, or simply because she could not sleep.

"You get under the covers," Rowland instructed, concerned that she was still shivering. It was not a cold evening. He left the candle on the dresser, pulled a chair up to the bed and sat down, waiting for her to confess what was troubling her.

"I know who sent the flowers." She pulled her knees up and wrapped her arms about them. "I think—no, I'm sure it was Bertie."

"Middleton? We left him in Sydney."

"I know." She took a deep breath. "Last year, after what he did, I told him I never wanted to see him again." She looked up at Rowland. "He was so angry, Rowly."

Rowland tensed. "What did he do?"

The sculptress looked panicked for a moment. She forced out the words. "He came to the house. I told him to leave and he refused."

Rowland waited as she lowered her gaze.

"He wouldn't let me leave," she whispered. "He said I belonged to him, he wouldn't let me go...and that he'd see you off. And then when you were stabbed, I thought..."

"That wasn't—"

"I know, but for a while I thought he might have... He promised he'd never let me go, that he'd see me dead first." She closed her eyes. "I'd never seen that side of him. He smashed the clay sculpture I'd been working on...not in a fit of temper but slowly, piece by piece while I watched. Rowly, he was so angry." She shook her head. "I thought he was going to... He scared me."

"I'll kill him." Rowland's eyes darkened, almost black in the flickering candlelight. "I will kill the—" He took Edna's hand, words lost for a moment in fury. "Why didn't you tell us?"

"Milt was recovering from that horrible accident—he still

wasn't able to even walk—and you'd just been stabbed, Rowly. And you were getting married. It seemed so trivial. I didn't want you, any of you, worrying about me." She spoke quickly.

Rowland remembered then how winded and fragile she had seemed when she'd thought him heartbroken over the rejection of Jemima Roche. He had been too focused on getting Egon Kisch to Melbourne; perhaps he had wanted it to be about him... He hadn't asked. God, he hadn't been there, nor Clyde. And Milton had been laid up... He was livid with Middleton and now furious at himself. He should have known there was something wrong; he should have asked.

"I wasn't really hurt, and there were more important things going on than Bertram Middleton. I should have realised he was—" Edna swallowed. "I've known him for years, Rowly. I didn't ever think he could—"

Rowland put his arms around her and held her fiercely. But as angry as he was, he knew that rage was not what the sculptress needed from him. He waited for her to speak again.

"He turned up when I went into the city the next day. I looked up and there he was. He begged me to forgive him."

"Did you?" he asked hoarsely.

She shook her head. "He wrote to me almost every day, sent me gifts—I sent everything back." Rowland could feel tears, hot and wet against his chest, as he felt her breath against his heart when she spoke. "He began putting his letters in envelopes with no return address, so I'd open them before I knew they were his. He turned up at odd times when I was out... He always seemed to know where I was. And he'd leave flowers on the doorstep with no card."

Inwardly, Rowland cursed. He recalled Mary Brown speaking to him about flowers left at the threshold of Woodlands House, complaining that it was untidy and highly improper. He had not thought much of it—there were many men who brought Edna flowers, and his housekeeper was wont to think everything, bar church, improper. "You didn't say a word."

"I felt safe," she said. "I thought he'd stop eventually, and I felt bad that I'd hurt him. But now...here. What if he's here, Rowly?"

"If Middleton's here, it'll be easier for me to have a few words with him." There was flint in Rowland's voice.

"I'm being silly," she said, wiping her face with her sleeve. "It's a bunch of flowers, not a basket of snakes. Bertie would not have come all the way to China—not with a new job at the *Sydney Morning Herald.*"

Rowland took a handkerchief from his pocket and handed it to her. "You're not being silly. I'm glad you finally told me."

Edna smiled wanly. "Mr. Blanshard's warnings have made me jumpy. It was probably Nicky leaving flowers. He probably just forgot to leave a card."

Rowland thought the count too formally mannered to leave flowers on a doorstep, let alone without a calling card, but on that he said nothing.

She pulled out of his arms, wiping the wet patch on his shirt with his handkerchief. "I'm sorry, Rowly. I should clear out of your bed and let you sleep."

He shook his head. "I'm not going to sleep. You take this bed."

Even in the dying candlelight, Rowland could see a flash of unguarded relief in her face, suppressed quickly. She was frightened, no matter what she said. "What are you going to do?" she asked.

"I'm staying right here," he said. "The chair's perfectly comfortable."

"Oh, Rowly, you can't sleep in a chair."

"I'm not going to sleep, Ed."

"It's still hours till morning."

"I need to think." He smiled and kissed her hand. "Milt and Clyde are in the next room—if you listen carefully, you can hear Clyde snoring—and I'm right here. You sleep. We'll deal with all this in the morning."

Chapter Twenty-Eight

WOMEN AND OPIUM

Many women in China who are addicted to the opium habit are now receiving special treatment at the Lester Hospital, Shanghai, and hopes are entertained for their recovery. In nearly every case where women have applied for admission in order to break the habit, there has been a satisfactory care. The medical officer at the hospital, Dr. A. W. Towers, points out, however, that "they" bear pain and discomfort extremely badly and often; though we get them over the difficult habit of taking the drug, there remains a serious danger of relapse unless something can be done to strengthen moral fibre.

—*Newcastle Morning Herald and Miners' Advocate*, 4 May 1936

Rowland answered the tap at the bedroom door before any subsequent taps could awaken Edna.

"Clyde," he whispered. "Good morning."

Clyde glanced first at his friend before his eye was caught by the sculptress stirring in Rowland's bed. His brow rose more hopefully than askance. Had Rowland finally convinced Edna to love him? Had she finally realised how much Rowland Sinclair adored her? If so, Clyde was not so Catholic or pragmatic that he would not celebrate the breakthrough with all of his heart.

Rowland motioned him outside the door. Though he had spent most of the night watching over Edna, the depth of his anger pushed all weariness aside. Quietly he told Clyde what had happened.

Clyde's wrath moved Rowland's anew. "He did what?" Clyde was aghast. "I'll tear his arm off!"

"You may have to wait your turn," Rowland murmured darkly. He told Clyde about the flowers left on the doorstep.

"Do you think that bastard's in Shanghai?" Clyde asked.

"I wouldn't have thought he'd have means for the fare, but who knows? He might have followed us here."

Edna peered into the hallway. "Oh, there you are. What are you both doing out here?"

"Rowly was just telling me what happened last night."

Edna smiled. "He spent the night in a chair; we don't have to get married."

Clyde responded by embracing her. "For pity's sake, Ed, why didn't you tell us?"

"Because I would have been lonely with the three of you in gaol."

The enduring mumbles of conversation finally woke Milton, who stumbled out of his bedroom and demanded to know why they were having a meeting in the hallway.

With a little coaxing, Edna told him everything she'd told Rowland the night before. In the light of day, the flowers seemed less threatening, the likelihood that they were from Middleton more remote. But still, the extent of Bertram Middleton's behaviour elicited much the same reaction from Milton as it had in Rowland and Clyde. There was hurt as well as anger in the poet's voice. "How could you not tell us, Ed? Didn't you know we'd—"

"I'm sorry." Edna's voice cracked. "I thought he'd stop. I didn't want to talk about it. I didn't want to think about it. None of you ever liked him, and I felt so, so stupid."

Rowland put his arm around Edna. "Look, it's done, Milt. We know now. Let's work out what we're going to do."

Clyde sighed. "I'm going to brew coffee."

"I'm going to kill Middleton," Milton snarled.

Rowland nodded. "Both good plans. The coffee first, perhaps."

Edna shook her head firmly. "You sleep for a couple of hours, Rowly. We'll wake you for breakfast when Harjeet gets here."

Clyde and Milton consumed two pots of coffee while discussing what they would do. Edna drank tea. Despite their mutual anger, the men tempered their language and kept talk of Middleton in check for Edna's sake. For her part, the sculptress was not unduly concerned by the threats they'd made on Middleton's life, certain that neither of these men was a murderer, regardless of the provocation and despite what they said.

She was less unsettled than she'd been the evening before, less sure that the bouquet had been left by Bertram Middleton, and a little shy that she had been so distressed. But only Rowland had seen that, and he was asleep. From Clyde and Milton, the sculptress kept the depth of the panic that had seized her in the middle of the night.

The three of them examined the bouquet without success for any clue as to who might have sent it.

"They're probably from Nicky," Edna repeated.

"We should try and find out if Middleton is in Shanghai," Milton said. "If he is, we can deal with him directly."

Harjeet arrived, letting herself in with the key Rowland had given her. She was, as usual, full of news and exclamation and seemed within moments of her arrival to fill the house with the aroma of baking. Rowland woke to the sound of her voice scolding Ranjit for something or other. The couple hours of sleep had cleared his head. He washed, dressed, and shaved quickly. He was still a little tender but determined now to deal with the matter of Bertram Middleton immediately. Downstairs, Rowland spoke to Harjeet about Blanshard's warning, allowing her the opportunity to leave his employ and whatever risk that entailed. She shooed him out of her kitchen lest his nonsense make her cakes fall. Ranjit, if anything, seemed excited.

"So from whom exactly do you expect this threat, sir? We should be ready for the enemy! Perhaps I could fortify the entrances."

"I doubt anyone will lay siege to the house, Mr. Singh."

"One should be prepared, sir."

Rowland sighed. "Mr. Blanshard seems to believe that the threat is widespread." In the light of day, he was inclined to dismiss Blanshard's dire warnings as hysterical. But the thought of Edna gave him pause. "Someone left a bouquet of flowers on the doorstep last night."

Singh frowned. "There were no flowers when I departed for home."

"No, they would have been left much later than that. After Miss Higgins and I returned."

"That Russian fellow—"

"Perhaps...but maybe not."

"Wing Zau?"

"Possible, I suppose, but I very much doubt it."

"Does Miss Higgins not like flowers?"

"She'd prefer to know who left them."

Singh nodded thoughtfully. "I shall keep a watch, Mr. Sinclair."

They decided over a late breakfast to renew their efforts to find out what happened to Sergei Romanov. It was Ranjit who suggested that Romanov might have started the fire himself to mask an escape of sorts.

Edna was dubious but Clyde agreed. "If Kruznetsov is right, then perhaps Alexandra's murder was the result of a falling out between crooks. Perhaps he was afraid his partner in crime would leave him for Rowly."

Inwardly Rowland wanted to reject the idea out of hand. But Clyde and Milton had always accused him of being too easily manipulated by women in distress, too ready to believe in them. The failing had nearly seen him married a few months before, so perhaps they were right. "It's possible," he conceded finally.

"Romanov may well have died in the fire, whoever lit it," Milton pointed out. "We'd better establish if they discovered any human remains before we start searching for him."

"How are we going to do that?" Edna asked sadly. "We're not his family—we can't demand the information."

Rowland glanced at his wristwatch. It was still early. "I'll ask Mickey Hahn," he said. "Surely the newspapers will be able to find out if the fire resulted in any loss of life."

"I'll come with you." Edna stood. "Mickey's apartment is only a block or so from here. If we hurry, we can catch her before work."

Milton nodded. "You two do that. Clyde and I are going to send a telegram."

"To whom?"

"The *Sydney Morning Herald*. It should be fairly easy to find out if Bertram Middleton has taken up his post."

"He will have," Edna said quietly. "I'm quite sure the flowers were from Nicky."

"Let's make sure," Rowland replied.

So the Australians parted ways. Clyde and Milton took Singh and the Buick as Emily Hahn's flat was almost no distance to walk.

A Chinese boy answered the door. *"Nóng zō,"* Edna said haltingly, continuing in Chinese pidgin. "Catchee Missy Hahn?"

"Who you, Missy?"

"Mr. Rowland Sinclair and Miss Edna Higgins."

"You waitee. Yes?"

"Can do."

The boy disappeared and then returned to the door to admit them. Mickey Hahn's flat was small and airless. The sitting room contained two worn couches with a low table between them. An opium pipe and a book on the works of Sappho had been left on the table. Mr. Mills sat on the sideboard, eating an orange and watching them with dark beady eyes. It was a few minutes before Mickey herself emerged in pyjamas and a Chinese silk dressing-gown. "Rowland, Edna, hello! What a wonderful surprise!" She turned back to the boy and snapped, "Catchee tea, chop chop!"

The boy nodded vigorously and ran from the room. Mickey admonished Mr. Mills for making the sideboard sticky with orange juice and offered Rowland and Edna seats. "You must excuse me my slothfulness... I'm afraid I was quite late home last night." She closed her eyes and smiled dreamily. "Xunmei took me to a dingy little place on the banks of the Huangpu—more authentically China than all the ballrooms in Shanghai. Of course, now I'll be frightfully late for work."

"We won't keep you long," Rowland promised.

She waved away any concern. "They don't seem as bothered about punching the clock here," she said. "I'll still have time to get my stories out before I meet with Victor for drinks."

The boy brought in a tray of tea and set it down beside the opium pipe.

"What can I do for you, Rowland? Before you say anything, you should probably know that Bernadine and I have fallen out so I cannot intercede with her, if that's what you want."

"It isn't." Rowland took the cup of tea she handed him, wondering if it was the attentions of Shao Xunmei that had come between Mickey and the society doyenne. "We were hoping you might make an enquiry for us." He told her about the fire at the Chinese butchery above which Sergei Romanov lived. "Do you suppose you might be able to find out if he actually died in that fire?"

"The butchery on Nanjing Road?"

"Yes."

"Well I don't need to find out. I know. I covered the story for the *North China Daily News*." She took a sip of tea and sighed contently. "They didn't find any remains. In fact, they now suspect that Mr. Romanov set the fire."

"Well, that's good news," Edna said. "Not about him being suspected of arson of course—just that he's alive."

"It's rather unlikely that you'll find him, though," Mickey warned. "People disappear in Shanghai all the time. It's a good place in which to vanish."

Rowland finished his tea. "We should allow you to get ready for work."

"Did Bert find you?" she asked suddenly.

"Bert?"

"Middle-something. He's just started as a foreign correspondent with the paper. He's from your part of the world—only been in Shanghai for a few days."

Startled, Rowland glanced at Edna. She choked on her tea and then hastily put the cup and saucer down.

"He seemed a bit homesick, so I gave him your details. Thought the company of fellow Australians might cheer him up. He was so pleased, I thought he'd call on you straight away."

Edna smiled tightly. "He may have come by when we were out."

"Oh, that's a shame. But I'm sure he'll try again."

They walked back, arm in arm, but silent. Rowland was, if truth be told, staggered by Bertram Middleton's gall. Though they had never progressed beyond an acquaintanceship, he'd known the journalist almost as long as he'd known Edna. Rowland was aware that he found it hard to be fair to any man who sought the sculptress's heart, but he had never liked Middleton. Still, he had not believed the writer capable of threatening Edna, let alone pursuing her to China.

"What do you think?" he asked as they walked into the house.

She shrugged. "I'm glad that it turns out I'm not being hysterical. I've never thought of myself as prone to hysteria."

"You're not," he said firmly.

Edna kicked off her shoes and curled into one of the armchairs in the drawing room. Rowland glanced out of the window at Kiangse Road before he sat down. "Middleton's here, and now—thanks to Mickey—he knows where we're staying."

"Yes." Edna pulled off her gloves distractedly. "Mickey wasn't to know."

"As soon as Clyde and Milt get back to stay with you, I'm going to go have a word with Middleton. I promise you he won't come near you again."

Edna was quiet. Simmering. Suddenly she pulled her gloves back on. "There's no need to wait."

"I'm not leaving you here alone."

"No, you're not. I'm coming with you."

"What? No."

Her eyes flashed angrily. "Rowly, I am not in any way, shape, or form afraid of Bertram Middleton. I will not be afraid of Bertram Middleton. We'll simply call in at the *North China Daily News* now and tell him that he is not welcome on our doorstep. That this grand gesture of his is futile, and that he should go home and finish writing his stupid boring novel!"

"Ed."

She took his hand. "I know you want to protect me. You and Clyde and Milt. But I can protect myself. And I think Bertie needs to know that I'm making this decision, not you."

Rowland shook his head. "I don't really care what Middleton needs."

"I can't believe he followed me to China—how dare he!" Her face was hard now, her words vehement. "I want him to know that I hate him, Rowly, and that it's nothing to do with you." She slipped her shoes back on. "Step lively, we're going to have to walk to the Bund."

Chapter Twenty-Nine

COURTSHIP

...Although we live in a "modern" age, and courtship is short and swift, and usually ends with an indifferent "Will you marry me?"—an adherence to the beauties of the "old-fashioned" mode of courtship would, I think, make life far more interesting and enjoyable.

Why not make your courtship delightful and happy by being tactful and original, and thereby create impressions which will linger long?

The theme of this article comes from the "Centenary, Life, and Times of Daniel O'Connell," published in 1875. This work says in part:

"Certain observations of O'Connell on the manner in which courtship should be carried on serve at once to illustrate the profound astuteness of his mental constitution, and the mode in which he doubtless conducted his own courtship. 'It is injudicious on the part of a lover,' he said, 'to offer marriage at an early period of his courtship. By this precipitation he loses the advantage which female curiosity must otherwise afford him, and, in sapping his way to her heart, discards a powerful auxiliary. He may be tender and assiduous, but should not declare himself until the lady's curiosity is awakened and piqued as to his intentions. In this way he awakes in her heart a certain interest concerning him which he may forfeit the moment he proposes."...

—*Sydney Morning Herald*, 1 November 1934

Edna spoke to the receptionist on the ground floor of the *North China Daily News* building. She gave her name and requested a meeting with Mr. Middleton.

The young woman made a terse phone call via the switchboard, and then directed Edna and Rowland to the elevator.

"First floor, desk at the back," she said, her attention already elsewhere.

When the elevator doors opened, Rowland and Edna emerged into what looked like a disordered typing pool, rows of desks clouded in a smog of cigarette smoke from the midst of which typewriters hammered a torrential rhythm. They passed an empty desk—the brass name block identified it as Emily Hahn's—and made their way to the desk in the final row.

Bertram Middleton's smile faded as he saw that Edna was not alone.

He opened his arms to embrace her, dropping them only when she stopped out of reach. "I say, did you get my flowers?"

"I did." Edna kept her voice low. "I came to tell you not to leave any more."

"I know I should have stayed to give them to you myself but—"

"No, you shouldn't have come at all."

Middleton's voice became cold. "I sold everything I had, threw in my job to come here, to be with you."

"And I told you I didn't want to see you again! Neither here, nor in Sydney. Stay away, Bertie."

"You don't mean that!" Middleton's voice rose. "It's pre-wedding jitters, that's all. Every bride gets cold feet."

Heads began to turn. The tap of typewriters stopped.

"We're not getting married, Bertie."

"I won't take no for an answer, sweetheart."

Rowland had had enough. "Yes, you will."

"You can't scare me off, Sinclair!"

"The lady said no, Middleton. Come near her again, and you shall not find me so amiable...in fact I'll—"

"Rowly!" Edna placed her hand on his arm. "Let's go."

Middleton accused Rowland of defaming him, of turning Edna against him through slander and lies, and he threatened legal redress. Rowland bit back any response and followed as Edna walked away.

Perhaps such altercations were not uncommon at the *North China Daily News*, for the other journalists returned to their desks and their cigarettes without a word, and the typewriters resumed tapping once again. Edna took Rowland's hand as they left.

"I nearly lost my rag, Ed," he admitted.

She smiled. "There's nothing to be gained by threatening to kill him, Rowly."

"I didn't."

"You were about to."

"I... Yes, I probably was."

Clyde and Milton were back at the Kiangse Road house when Edna and Rowland returned. They had discovered that Bertram Middleton was no longer at the *Sydney Morning Herald*, but that discovery had of course been superseded by Mickey Hahn's revelations that morning. Milton was somewhat put out that they had confronted the journalist without him, and disappointed that Rowland had not taken the opportunity to "knock his block off once and for all."

It was Edna who demanded they change the subject. "I have no intention of ever thinking about Bertram Middleton again. We need to focus on finding out who killed Alexandra and how we're going to find Sergei."

"Are we sure he's not dead?" Clyde asked.

Rowland told them what they'd learned from Mickey Hahn; that Romanov might well have died, but not in the fire.

"So how are we going to find him?"

"Would Mr. Carmel be able to help, Rowly?" Edna asked. "Lawyers have to locate lost heirs, witnesses to crimes, and such—he might at least know where to start."

Rowland nodded. "You're right. Carmel might be able to help."

"We probably should let him know about recent developments anyway," Clyde added.

Harjeet came in with a plate of the syrupy cake she'd been baking that morning, insisting they try it. Clyde, Edna, and Milton complied enthusiastically, while Rowland telephoned Carmel and Smith.

"I was under the impression that the poor chap had perished in a fire," Carmel said when Rowland asked him to do what he could to find Sergei Romanov.

"No. It seems he either got out or he was not there when the fire started."

"I see. Yes, of course. I'll do whatever I can." A pause. "Now suppose you tell me about what happened at the Paramount. I understand there was a disagreement."

"Who—"

"This is Shanghai, my dear boy. Word gets about quite quickly."

Rowland gave the solicitor his account of what had transpired during the meeting with the Japanese.

A sigh. "I've always advised against informal meetings. It's so easy for misunderstandings to occur when people are socialising as well as conducting business."

"There was no misunderstanding," Rowland said. "There were too many Nazis in the company of the gentlemen from Japan for my comfort."

"There is no trade embargo against Germany, Rowland."

"Even so." Rowland was tempted to confess that he'd never been authorised to enter into a contract with the Japanese. But there was no point now.

"On reflection, Rowland, could you have perhaps been a little rash? Wilfred might not agree—"

"Wilfred won't countermand my decision." Rowland spoke with more confidence than he felt.

Carmel tried to reason with him. "The proposed embargo is to do with the Japanese invasion of Manchuria. It has absolutely nothing to do with the Germans. I really think—"

"It's done now."

"I'm sure if you were to—"

"I won't."

Carmel exhaled. "Very well. But will you allow me to intercede with the Japanese to see what I can do to minimise any offence that might have been taken."

"Please do," Rowland replied wearily. "To be honest, Mr. Carmel, I am much more interested in finding Sergei Romanov than whether I hurt the feelings of some wool buyers."

As a precaution, Rowland told the lawyer about Bertram Middleton and his flowers, as well as what had transpired that morning at the *North China Daily News*. "I don't want him coming near Miss Higgins again."

"Well, there may be prudent means of achieving that, Rowland," Carmel replied. "That's why you employ me. I shall be ready to fend off any allegations from that quarter."

"I'm not particularly concerned about what he may allege, Mr. Carmel. Can you do anything to keep him away from Ed?"

"Can you prove he sent the flowers?"

"No."

The lawyer sighed. "I'll see what I can do, but we haven't got any basis for a formal complaint."

There was someone banging on the red door when Rowland hung up.

"Sinclair. Sinclair! Open up!" Andrew Petty's voice.

Rowland opened the door. Petty was still in his dinner suit, though it was noticeably dishevelled now. He reeked of whisky and sweat. "I demand an explanation!"

Rowland grimaced. "Come in, Andrew."

"Oh…hello, Mr. Petty," Edna said as Rowland brought the broker in.

"I've come to talk to—nay, to plead with you, Mr. Sinclair."

"Perhaps you should have some coffee first."

"Do you know how many months I've been working on this deal with the Japanese!" Petty shouted.

Rowland said nothing. His friends retreated discreetly to the kitchen.

"Wilfred would have recognised the benefits and accepted the offer!"

"Look, Andrew," Rowland said. "You seem…tired. Perhaps we should have this conversation later."

Petty's voice became conciliatory. "Rowland, you're not the first young man to say something impulsively under pressure. Mr. Yiragowa will understand. He has a son your age; he knows what young men can do in the heat of the moment."

Rowland shook his head. He was aware that he could not retreat from "no" to the neutral position his brother had directed him to maintain. God, he wished he could speak with Wilfred, and restore the manoeuvring and intrigues of trade to his keeping. "I'm sorry if you had other expectations, Andrew. But changing my mind is out of the question."

Petty exploded into a lament about betrayal and prejudice and economics. He called Rowland a few names and wept. Rowland assumed, hoped, the man had been drinking and so allowed him to rant without reaction. In the end, he and Clyde helped Andrew Petty into the Buick and asked Singh to deliver him home. There were other telephone calls that morning, from the members of the Japan-Australia Society and a few other businessmen that Rowland had not met, all talking about the importance of trade between Japan and Australia and the potential ramifications of Rowland's "misstep."

Victor Sassoon also telephoned. It seemed that Chief Inspector Randolph had questioned Mickey Hahn that morning and the tycoon was displeased.

Consequently when someone knocked on the red door again, Rowland was wary. It was Wing, for the first time since Rowland had known him, not attired in Western style, but in traditional Chinese robes. He seemed in high spirits.

"Good morning, sir. How was"—he trailed off as he noticed the bruises and abrasions on Rowland's face—"the ball."

"Decidedly awkward."

"Is there anything I can do, sir?"

"Actually, yes. We'll be leaving in the next day or so."

Wing looked puzzled, and then his face brightened. "You are no longer a suspect in the murder of Miss Romanova?"

"I'm afraid I am," Rowland replied. "I don't propose to leave Shanghai. Just to take another house."

Edna looked sharply at him. "This isn't because of Bertie, is it? I told you, I'm—"

"Not at all," Rowland replied. "I'm afraid Victor Sassoon is withdrawing his hospitality."

Milton pulled a face. "Old Victor's rather protective of Mickey Hahn, all things considered."

"He wouldn't be the first bloke enslaved by a woman who won't have him," Clyde said, shrugging.

"What has this got to do with Mickey?" Edna asked.

Milton told them about the discovery that Mickey had occupied the Chinese Suite at the Cathay before them, and Sassoon's insistence that they keep the information to themselves.

"You don't believe Mickey killed Alexandra?"

"Why not?" Milton shrugged. "She was there, and she probably has access to Sassoon's master key..."

"But why would she?"

"Maybe there's more to her relationship with Sassoon than they're letting on. She could have been jealous... Sassoon's eye may have wandered in Alexandra's direction...or maybe she and Sassoon were in it togeth—"

"It's possible that Alexandra was murdered by someone who mistook her for Mickey." Rowland interrupted Milton's run of speculation. "In which case, Mickey could still be in danger, which is why we mentioned it to Randolph."

"In direct contravention of Lord Victor's orders," Milton growled.

"I've asked Mr. Carmel to find us another house," Rowland said. "Or a hotel that isn't owned by Victor Sassoon."

It took Gilbert Carmel only hours to find the mansion on the Avenue Joffre in a district known as Little Russia, though technically it was in the French Concession. They were by the next day able to move in. The grand colonial building had been built by a Parsi merchant who'd obviously done well with the China dream. Also on the block were three smaller houses, designed for each of the merchant's sons, which were connected to the main house by covered walkways. The grounds had clearly once been a showpiece of sweeping lawns and flower beds—indeed the bones were still there—but the lack of a full-time gardener was apparent. The estate was, of course, far too large for the immediate needs of the Australians, but it had been available on short notice.

"What happened to the family that lived here?" Edna asked the caretaker who let them in.

"The family has moved to Hong Kong, Madam," he said. "They intend to return some day."

Milton inspected the massive sitting room with its parquetry floors. It was furnished, but sparsely so for its size. "We could have a game of cricket in here, Rowly."

Rowland laughed. They had often used the ballroom at Woodlands House for that purpose.

"There are dozens of cricket clubs in Shanghai, if you would like to attend a match, Mr. Isaacs," Wing suggested helpfully.

"Wouldn't be a challenge without chandeliers to avoid." Milton bowled an imaginary ball.

Harjeet was already stocking the kitchen pantry, which she declared was much better appointed than the one on Kiangse Road. There were enough bedrooms to make sharing unnecessary, and the entire property was surrounded by a high iron fence. The house also came with three servants: an old woman and her two daughters, who had kept house and worked as *amahs* for the previous owners, and who occupied the adjoining servants' quarters.

Discovering who killed Alexandra Romanova was more urgent now. It seemed that doing so was the only way to convince Randolph to relinquish Rowland as prime suspect, the only way he could leave Shanghai as anything but a fugitive. And regardless, Rowland still wanted justice for the taxi girl. Finding Sergei Romanov was, Rowland believed, the first step to any hope of that.

"We're in Little Russia," Edna suggested. "Perhaps we should try asking at the restaurants and businesses here. Surely he would go to his own community for help."

"Maybe." Rowland frowned. "Except that it was members of the Russian community that were defrauded by Alexandra."

"What about this chap that she was seen with?" Milton said. "The one the band at the Cathay bashed our friend Wing for asking about. Perhaps we should try and track him down... Surely the band will be back by now."

Rowland nodded. "Ed and I will call in at the Cathay now. You chaps see if any of the merchants in Little Russia remember Sergei." He extracted his pocketbook and gave the poet several banknotes. "In case their memories require inducement."

"Check if anyone's been to the Cathay asking after us," Clyde said, scowling. Danny Dong's cousins had not yet found them, and he was becoming a little concerned that the old lady's remains would not be claimed. The chest, which was her current place of rest, had once again been stowed under Clyde's bed, which was compromising his own rest somewhat.

Wing grabbed his hat and made to follow Rowland.

"You'd better go with Milt and Clyde, Mr. Wing. They're more likely to need a translator, and the gentlemen in the band might not be entirely happy to see you again."

Chapter Thirty

CHINESE JUNK ON STAMP

An interesting stamp I have seen is the 10-cent stamp
of the Republic of China; in it is shown the picture of an
old Chinese junk, which is a symbol of ancient China.
In the background is seen a railroad bridge over which
is passing a train. This is evidently intended to show
the desire of the newly formed republic for progress.
—William Parkinson (11)

—*Sun*, 15 October 1922

The band members were at rehearsal in the Jazz Club. The venue
was closed to patrons until the afternoon. Fortunately Van Hagen
was not at the reception desk, and Edna was able to gain them
access by claiming she'd left her wrap in the club the previous
evening and sought to retrieve it. The young man in Van Hagen's
seat seemed flustered by the burdens of the position and the

various calls on his attention. After confirming that no one had called looking for them or Mrs. Dong, he let them into the Jazz Club and then excused himself to attend to the complaints and demands of other guests.

Rowland and Edna took seats in front of the stage without interrupting the musicians. The band seemed to enjoy having an audience, however small. When the ragtime number finished, the Australians stood and clapped. The musicians bowed and accepted the applause in good humour.

"What are you folks doing here?" the band leader asked. "This here is just a rehearsal. Y'all come back tonight for a real show."

"We were hoping we might speak with you," Edna said.

"Well, well, we got ourselves the prettiest autograph hound in Shanghai!"

Edna laughed. "Oh no, I'm not collecting autographs."

The saxophonist put down his instrument and grinned. "Then what can we do for you, mam?"

Rowland leant back against a table. He saw no reason to interrupt. Clearly the musicians were more interested in speaking with Edna.

The double bass player asked Edna whether she cared to step out with him for a drink. The saxophonist protested that he had been about to issue an invitation himself.

"Actually we wanted to speak to you about a friend who may have stepped out with one of you. Miss Alexandra Romanova."

The saxophonist tensed. "You weren't no friend of Alex's, I would have noticed you."

"No, I wasn't," Edna admitted, "but Rowly was."

The band gave Rowland their attention for the first time. "Rowland Sinclair. How'd you do?"

"You and Alex were cutting a rug the night before she died." The pianist swivelled on his stool to face Rowland.

"Yes."

"You sent that uppity Chinaman?" the trumpet player accused.

"No, I didn't. But Mr. Wing is a friend of mine," Rowland replied evenly.

"I'm sure Mr. Wing didn't mean to offend you," Edna said.

The double bass player laughed and waved his thumb at the saxophonist. "Virgil here put him in his place, good and proper."

Edna placed her hands on her hips and scowled. "Yes, well that was uncalled for. Poor Mr. Wing was simply trying to find out what had happened to Alexandra!"

Rowland felt a surge of love for the loyal sculptress, though he braced for the confrontation to escalate in the face of her admonishment. But Virgil seemed abashed.

"I reckon I did overreact," he said. "Things here were awful tense with the police asking questions and everybody talking about a murderer in the Cathay. I might have been a bit jumpy."

"Why?"

"Because, Mr. Sinclair, I am a black man. And Shanghai ain't quite that different from everywhere else."

Rowland nodded slowly. "Fair enough."

"But you did know Alexandra?" Edna pressed.

"Sure. We knew her."

"Were any of you in love with her?"

Rowland was, of course, accustomed to Edna's propensity to be direct, but the Americans were caught off guard. They vacillated amongst themselves and then Virgil spoke. "We all liked Alex—she was a terrific gal—but none of us were sweet on her."

"We used to keep an eye on the taxi girls. Sometimes a wise guy would think buying a dance ticket entitled him to take certain liberties, if you know what I mean."

"Do you remember any wise guy approaching Alexandra in particular?" Rowland asked.

The saxophonist shrugged. "There was an Englishman I told to clear off. High and mighty type."

Rowland groaned inwardly. There were thousands of

Englishmen in Shanghai. "High and mighty" didn't really narrow the field. "Did Miss Romanova borrow money from any of you?"

"Yeah, but we didn't mind. Poor kid didn't have a brass razoo. We slipped her a few dollars every now and then."

"Did she ever say why she needed money?"

"We can't all afford to stay at the Cathay, Mr. Sinclair. She probably needed to eat."

Edna shook her head, ignoring the dig at Rowland. "She was trying to borrow money from a number of people—it had to be for more than groceries."

The musician shrugged.

"I don't suppose any of you gentlemen have any idea about who might have wanted to kill Miss Romanova?" Rowland asked.

The musicians glanced at each other, and then the band leader shook his head. "Some of the taxi girls lived life dangerously, but not Alex. She always remembered where she came from."

"Did you know she once claimed to be a Russian princess?" Edna ventured.

"Maybe she was," Virgil said. "She sure didn't look like no ordinary dame. And she had all the airs and graces you could want."

The double bass player looked Rowland up and down. "They found Alex in your suite?"

"Yes. I found her."

"Did you kill her?"

Rowland met his eye. "No. I have no idea what she was doing there."

The musicians glanced at each other once again. "Alex loved looking around the premier suites," Virgil confessed. "Sometimes she'd get one of the room boys to let her in just so she could see how people like you lived. She said it made her feel at home. She never took anything or did any harm. Just looked."

The Public Garden on the northern end of the Bund was bordered by the Huangpu. European in style, the garden had originally been reserved for the foreign community, but the restriction had been lifted several years before, opening the park to all comers. Tight buds hinted at colour in flowerbeds set in verdant lawns.

Edna hooked her arm through Rowland's. He hadn't said a great deal since they'd left the Cathay. "A penny for your thoughts, Rowly."

He shook his head. "Alexandra only had to ask me if she wanted to see the suite," he said. "I would have shown her through and made sure she wasn't killed in the process."

Edna leaned into him. "I wonder why she didn't just ask."

"Hotel rules perhaps," Rowland mused. He wondered if the taxi girl had, for some reason, wanted to see his suite before she met him for tea. Perhaps it was the appointment itself that had made her curious about the Chinese Suite on that particular day.

"We don't know for certain that that was why she was there," Edna said.

Rowland nodded. "That's true, but it's the first possible reason we've found for her presence in our suite." He paused. "If she was there by chance, then perhaps she wasn't the murderer's target."

Edna could feel the tension in his arm. "If someone was trying to kill me, Rowly, they haven't tried again."

"As far as we're aware," he added.

"Should we go and see Inspector Randolph?" she asked. "Tell him why Alexandra Romanova might have been in our suite?"

Rowland thought for a moment. "Let's wait until we've spoken with Milt and Clyde. They may have unearthed something worthwhile."

Edna grabbed his hand and looked at his watch. It was still early. She pulled him towards the pleasure boats and junks moored at a nearby jetty. "Come on then. Milt and Clyde won't be finished asking after Sergei for hours, and you need to take your mind off murder for just a little while."

Rowland glanced dubiously at the ramshackle craft, but he had never been able to refuse the sculptress anything. Edna selected the junk, lamenting the absence of her camera.

"Where to, Missy?" the junk's captain directed his question at Edna as Rowland stepped on board.

"Anywhere and back again." Edna took Rowland's hand and jumped onto the deck.

The captain bowed and nodded and then cast off, sailing them down the Huangpu, past the great buildings of the Bund. They did not have the river to themselves, of course, and the captain worked the rudder from the vessel's stern to manoeuvre through the large ships and fishing craft, while he pointed at various landmarks along the way. Rowland removed his jacket and placed it on Edna's shoulders as the wind whipped up across the river waves. He was reminded of the morning they arrived in Shanghai and had beheld the city in all its glory from the water.

For a while they forgot about Alexandra's death and the trouble that had besieged them since their arrival in the Far East, talking instead as artists about the lines and shapes of Shanghai—Chinese lettering echoed in the flicking curve of the pagoda, the contrast of moon gates against geometric fretwork, the red and black and gold of dragons and buildings and fabric. They ate fish and rice cooked on deck by the crew; they struggled with chopsticks and pidgin, laughing and being laughed at. Edna charmed the sailors with warmth and interest, despite her lack of local language, and Rowland sketched. It was nearly twilight when the junk returned to the Public Garden.

"*Yáyà nong,*" Edna thanked the captain and the small crew in halting Shanghainese as Rowland paid the man twice what he asked.

The captain laughed at Edna's pronunciation and bowed. "*Xiá yà nong.* Bye bye, Missy."

The Australians disembarked and headed back towards the Cathay in no particular hurry to end the afternoon's reprieve.

The shadows lengthened, and the first lights of evening life in Shanghai were lit. Workers spilled out of office buildings, and the Bund became congested. Rowland waved away spruiking rickshaw drivers—they would call Ranjit Singh to collect them from the hotel.

They became aware of the police presence at the Cathay before they entered the hotel foyer.

"I wonder what the devil's going on," Rowland murmured as they stepped through the rotating doors.

Van Hagen was at the reception desk. Visibly nervous, he cleared his throat as they approached. Amongst the people awaiting service at the desk, a saffron-robed priest caught Rowland's eye. "Kung!" He moved towards him.

"Stop right there, Mr. Sinclair." A young policeman placed himself between Rowland and the reception.

"Officer." Rowland nodded politely. "What can I do for you?"

The doors to Victor Sassoon's private lift opened to reveal the man himself with Mickey Hahn on his arm. Neither moved, watching the proceedings from within the lift.

"I'm afraid I'm going to have to ask you to come with me, sir." The constable stepped towards Rowland.

"What? Now?"

"Yes, sir." Two more constables flanked the first.

Rowland glanced at Edna. "Where exactly would we be going, gentlemen?"

"Police headquarters, sir."

"And can you tell me why you wish me to accompany you?"

The constable licked his lips. "My orders are to bring you in for questioning."

Rowland frowned, irritated. What could Randolph want to ask him that he hadn't already?

The constable read into Rowland's silence, squaring his shoulders and lowering his voice. "If you refuse, my orders are to arrest you for the murder of a Mr. Bertram Charles Middleton."

Edna gasped.

Rowland placed his arm around her shoulders. The movement ignited the policemen into action, batons drawn. They dragged him away from Edna and restrained him.

Rowland tried to tell them that he was not refusing to accompany them, that they'd not known that Bertram Middleton was dead. The policemen were unmoved and remained determined to keep him away from Edna, to whom they seemed to believe he posed a danger.

"Are you all right, Miss?" the constable asked. "Did he hurt you?"

"Of course not!" Edna tried to reach Rowland. "Let him go!"

"It's all right, Ed," Rowland said, afraid the overzealous policemen might decide to arrest her too. "Telephone Gilbert Carmel. Let him know what's happened. He'll sort it out."

Chapter Thirty-One

LARGEST IN WORLD

Ward Road Gaol

In Shanghai

A gaol to house 8000 criminals must be huge, and inside the walls of Ward Road Gaol are buildings that would look large even in one of Melbourne's main streets. Walking through courtyards, along lines of cells, and through the workshops with Captain Wall, the prison governor, our party took three hours to make its tour—and then we saw only a part of the gaol.

Most of the prisoners are Chinese, dressed in wide, shapeless trousers and straightjacket, blue, white or khaki, according to the length of sentence, and marked with bright colored badges to show the type of crime that brought them there.

A few are White Russians, who have sunk to the economic level of the poorer Chinese. White Russians, too, are the tall guards who march along the walls or stand guard on the central watchtower.

—*Barrier Miner*, 15 January 1938

———————————◦◦◦———————————

Chief Inspector Randolph strode into the interrogation room.

"Sit down, Mr. Sinclair."

Rowland did so. The inspector assumed the opposite seat. A junior policeman sat to his right with a notebook and pencil poised. "Can I ask where you were last night, Mr. Sinclair?"

Rowland gave the address of the house at Kiangse Road.

Randolph's eyes narrowed. "We have been informed that you no longer reside at Sir Victor Sassoon's house on Kiangse Road."

"I did until this morning, Inspector. You asked me about last night."

Randolph took a briar pipe from the pocket of his jacket and took his time filling and lighting it.

"Very good, then. I believe you and Mr. Middleton were involved in something of an altercation yesterday."

"I'm not sure I'd call it an altercation."

The chief inspector opened the file before him and glanced over it. "Several witnesses report that you argued with Mr. Middleton, and that he threatened to bring charges against you."

"For defamation."

"So you admit that you and the deceased argued?"

"Yes, we did." Rowland tried again. "How was Middleton killed, Chief Inspector?"

"How did you know that he had been killed?" Randolph's eyes gleamed triumphantly.

"I was arrested for his murder—it seems a reasonable conclusion."

The constable smiled faintly as he took notes.

Randolph carried on, his face darkening with his mood. "Mr. Middleton was shot as you well know, Sinclair. You put two bullets into his skull!"

"No. I didn't." The detail of the accusation was startling. Middleton had been executed. "I don't even own a gun."

"A gun is easy enough to procure. Perhaps your friend Du Yuesheng provided the weapon." Randolph all but shouted touché.

"A dozen people heard you argue with the deceased. Several witnesses state that Mr. Middleton believed you were a violent man, insanely jealous of his relationship with Miss Higgins and capable of anything."

Rowland took a breath. "I argued with Mr. Middleton, but that was the last I saw of the man, and I assure you, he was very much alive."

Randolph opened another folder. The exercise was theatrical for it was clear he knew what was written in the copious notes on the pages within it. "Would it surprise you to know, Mr. Sinclair, that the deceased came to see me two days ago? That he provided the International Police with certain information pertaining to you."

"And what information would that be, Chief Inspector?"

"You have quite the chequered history with the law, Mr. Sinclair. I believe you were arrested for the murder of your own father the year before last, December 1933 to be precise."

"Those charges were withdrawn, as I'm sure you're aware."

"But no other person was subsequently charged?"

"That's correct."

Randolph's brow rose. Rowland pulled back a surge of irritation. He knew the chief inspector was attempting to goad him.

"You haven't asked why Mr. Middleton brought this information to our attention."

Rowland shrugged. He could guess.

Randolph continued. "Mr. Middleton was concerned for the

safety of his erstwhile fiancée, a Miss Edna Higgins. He believed you to be a dangerous man."

"Miss Higgins was never his fiancée!" Rowland stopped himself. Sharing his opinion of Middleton would not help matters now.

There was a barely discernible smile on Randolph's face. "But you know all this, don't you, Sinclair? That's why you murdered Bertram Middleton—to silence him."

"No, it's not."

"Perhaps you had some other reason for shooting Mr. Middleton?"

"I didn't shoot him."

"What happened to your face, Mr. Sinclair?"

Rowland had forgotten about the bruises on his face. He answered honestly, though he knew that the story of the brawl would do him no favours.

"So you reacted violently because the gentleman wished to dance with Miss Higgins? Are you usually so volatile when Miss Higgins is involved?"

"He did not ask her to dance. Whatever he asked, she refused."

"Hmmm." Randolph made some notes.

Rowland checked his wristwatch. Where the hell was Gilbert Carmel?

Edna telephoned the offices of Carmel and Smith for the third time.

"As I told you previously, Miss Higgins"—the secretary's voice was weary—"Mr. Carmel is in Nanking. We are trying to contact him, and we will endeavour to send another solicitor to assist Mr. Sinclair."

Edna replaced the receiver, frustrated, and gave up the public telephone to the next person in the long line waiting to use it.

She made her way back to Clyde and Milton. The modern waiting room of the International Police Headquarters was large and well appointed. Indeed, if not for the presence of uniformed constabulary, one might have been forgiven for mistaking it for a hotel foyer. Even so, the space was tainted with tension, with worry and panic, as people waited to give statements or to ask after friends and family who had come to the attention of the Shanghai Police.

The Australians and Wing Zau had come to give statements to alibi Rowland Sinclair. They were received politely, if a little indifferently, and directed to wait while the prisoner was being interrogated. After five hours their patience began to wear.

Edna took a seat beside Clyde. Milton paced.

"Are you sure they arrested him, Ed?" Clyde asked for the umpteenth time. "Surely they just brought him in for questioning?"

Edna shook her head. "No. They definitely arrested him. He was in restraints."

"But they haven't even—"

"We're not in Sydney, Clyde. God knows how they do things here."

Clyde rubbed his face. "Carmel picked a bloody wonderful time to leave town! How the hell are we supposed to help Rowly without him?"

Milton stopped mid-pace in front of Edna. "We've got to do something. What did they tell you about Middleton?"

The sculptress swallowed. "That he's dead... Someone murdered him apparently."

"Who found him? Where? Was there—"

"I don't know, Milt." Edna began to break down. "I don't know."

Clyde put his arm around the sculptress and cast a warning glance in Milton's direction. "We need help," he said. "No one's going to talk to us."

"Where exactly is Carmel?" Milton demanded.

"His office says he's attending to a client in Nanking," Edna said wanly. "They said they'll send someone as soon as they can."

Milton cast his eyes up to the clock on the station wall. "Perhaps we should go to Nanking and find him..."

Clyde shook his head. "Oh, mate, you're not talking about a one-horse town in the outback. I expect tracking down one man in Nanking might take months."

"What do you think they're doing to Rowly?" Edna asked distractedly.

Clyde glanced at Milton. "They'll just be questioning him, Ed. This isn't Germany."

The poet's patience reached its end. He stalked over to the reception window and demanded an audience with Chief Inspector Randolph.

The constable who peered back through the opening seemed surprised. "I'm afraid the chief inspector went home a couple of hours ago, sir."

"Went home?"

"It's nearly midnight, sir."

"But we've been waiting to give our statements—"

"I am sorry, sir. Someone should have told you to come back tomorrow. I'm afraid there's no one available to take your statement."

"But what about Rowly—Mr. Rowland Sinclair? He was falsely arrested—"

The officer stifled a yawn. "Mr. Sinclair has been remanded to custody pending trial."

Rowland removed his wristwatch, tiepin, and cufflinks and placed them onto the tray with the contents of his pockets, including his notebook. He was allocated a prison uniform and instructed to strip and put it on. All this was done under the eyes of stone-faced warders. They placed his suit in a paper bag with his other effects, and marked the bag with the number 6419, which appeared on the left breast of his prison tunic.

Rowland maintained a determined outward calm as he donned the coarse convict attire. Randolph would realise soon that he had arrested the wrong man. Carmel and Smith would sort it out and, hopefully, keep Rowland's companions from trying to break him out.

There were four other men being processed—all Chinese. The warders were predominantly naiks—Indians Sikhs who appeared to answer to the handful of British guards. A sallow Englishman with more hair beneath his nose than on his scalp, watched too closely. "Well, well," he said as he caught sight of the swastika-shaped scar on Rowland's chest. He commanded Rowland to stop so he could inspect it more closely. Rowland's skin crawled, but he did as he was instructed.

"What is that, felon?"

"An old injury." Rowland buttoned the prison shirt. He heard a snigger, but by the time he looked up, the warders were sober and expressionless, and he could not tell which of them had laughed.

The other warders addressed the Englishman as "Mr. Whitely, sir!"

It was Whitely who read out the rules of Ward Road Prison, who showed Rowland the long baton that his men would use against any prisoner who approached them without permission, who made it clear that Rowland Sinclair was now an animal in his zoo. It was not a conversation because prisoners were required to maintain absolute silence. Any transgression of the rules would be punished severely. Rowland said nothing, but he met the warder's eye, and that, it seemed, was enough to enrage the man, who gave him a taste of the baton for his insolence.

The blow cracked across his shoulders. Rowland staggered forward only momentarily. Instinct told him it would be dangerous to fall in this place, at the mercy of these men, and so he righted himself immediately. He moved his gaze down, casting his fury away from Whitely. But not before he noticed the smug satisfaction in the warder's face.

They were taken to the cell blocks then. Whitely led the way, turning occasionally to make some comment about criminal bloodlines, to the obedient titters of the naiks. Rowland had heard taunts about Australia's convict heritage before—he had, after all, attended boarding school in England. He realised that Whitely was trying to provoke him into doing something for which retribution would be swift; and so he kept his own temper in check. This was part of the orientation, no doubt, a demonstration of power and powerlessness.

The prison blocks were multi-storey. Dull eyes watched them from the cells along the walkway as they passed, raising hackles on the back of Rowland's neck. There was a pervading stench of men and fear and despair, and aside from the sound of their steps, it was silent. Still, Rowland did not give way to panic. He was on remand—Carmel would ensure he was released soon.

The cells were small—cages designed for a single man. A glazed and barred window was located on the wall at a height above most heads, and the floor was bare, cold cement. A spittoon and a latrine bucket were consigned to one corner. Each cell was used to confine up to three men in a six by eight foot space.

Whitely stopped and banged on the bars of a cell with his baton. Two prisoners moved to the back of the cage. Only then did Whitely unlock it.

"Welcome to your new home, felon," Whitely sneered. "Prisoner 3782 thoughtfully hanged himself in the isolation cells last week to make way for you." He brought his face close to Rowland's, his breath foetid. "The bastards on death row are often a bit eager to meet their maker after a while in here...the yellow ones mainly. Occidentals are made of sterner stuff generally, but we'll see." He used the baton to push Rowland into the cell and locked it after him. "There you go. Right cosy. I'd be careful of

4566 though—tuberculosis. Might finish him off before we can hang him."

"Ward Road Gaol—they call it the City of the Doomed. It is not a good place." Wing Zau's voice was grave.

"Well it would hardly do to call a prison Buckingham Palace," Clyde said in an attempt to keep everyone calm. "Let's not lose our heads."

They had returned home to regroup. Ranjit Singh had driven them back from the police headquarters and showed no signs of abandoning them for sleep. "I have a cousin who works in the prison as an assistant warder. I will speak to him and explain that Mr. Sinclair's incarceration has been a dreadful mistake!"

Clyde nodded. "Thank you, Mr. Singh. It will be a comfort to have someone who can check on Rowly." He placed his palms on the table. "In the meantime, we'll have to do what we can. We'll call on Carmel and Smith first thing tomorrow. Insist they find Carmel and get Rowly released or bailed or deported. And we'll send a telegram to Wilfred."

"It will take Wilfred weeks to get here," Edna said desperately. "We can't wait—"

"Carmel and Petty may not be Wilfred's only contacts in Shanghai. He might know someone else who can help us."

"Blanshard!" Milton exclaimed. "Surely Blanshard can help us."

"We don't know how to reach him," Edna said. "Rowly had his details."

"Did he write them down anywhere?"

"In his notebook perhaps, but he has that with him."

"With any luck Blanshard will contact us," Clyde said. "The man's a spy after all—he probably already knows what happened."

"You've not given me a task, Mr. Jones," Wing said. "I would like to help. What can I do?"

"I can well imagine," Singh muttered.

Wing snapped. "What do you mean by that, you odious, self-righteous fool?"

"I followed you the night you went to your family function! They did not look like family, the men you met!"

"You followed me?" Wing grabbed the chauffeur's lapel. "How dare you!"

Singh pulled back his own fist.

Clyde grabbed Singh; Milton, Wing. Suspicion from the first and simmering dislike unleashed, and it was all the Australians could do to keep them apart.

"Stop it! Both of you!" Edna demanded, standing between them. "What are you talking about, Mr. Singh?"

"I knew he was up to something." Ranjit Singh pointed at Wing. "I have been keeping an eye on him, following him when I could. Last night he meets a European at a bar in the French Concession, and then this night Mr. Sinclair is arrested!"

Edna turned to Wing. "Who was this man you met, Mr. Wing?"

Wing said nothing for a moment. And then, quietly, "A comrade."

"You're a Communist?" Milton said, releasing his grip on Wing.

"I was," he said carefully. "But there are no longer any Communists in Shanghai."

"And this man?"

"A Russian. A red Russian. I asked him if he knew of Alexandra Romanova...if his people were responsible for what happened to her."

"A likely story!" Singh scoffed. "Why would you do this in secret?"

"Because I wanted the truth."

"What did he say?" Edna asked.

"That people like Miss Romanova—fraudsters—only helped the Communist cause."

"You didn't mention anything…"

"I had already told Mr. Sinclair that the Communists in China did not care about Miss Romanova. I met my comrade only to be sure…and he made me sure."

There was silence as they considered Wing's story. Even Singh said nothing. Milton spoke first. "I believe him. It makes sense."

Clyde nodded. "As much as we still need to sort out what happened to Miss Romanova, Rowly's been arrested for Middleton's murder now. That should be our priority."

"I will do anything," Wing said immediately.

"You need to get to police headquarters at first light. Stay there and make a fuss until they take your statement." Milton pointed a finger at Wing. "You shared a room with Rowly last night at Kiangse Road, he's wearing the suit you laid out for him—that, comrade, is what we call an alibi."

A knock on the door and Edna ran to answer it. Perhaps the mistake had been realised, and it was Rowland returned to them. She opened the door.

"Mickey…"

Sassoon's Rolls Royce and chauffeur were waiting in the driveway. Mr. Mills tugged on the gold leash which attached him to his mistress.

"Oh, Edna, I'm so glad you're home. I wanted to come and offer my condolences." Mickey Hahn walked in, releasing Mr. Mills to explore.

"Your condolences?"

"For Mr. Sinclair's arrest. For what happened. I can't believe it, can you? He was so handsome and charming."

"I find it hard to believe he was arrested," Edna said uncertainly. She invited Mickey into the sitting room where the others were gathered.

Mickey took a seat. Clyde lit her cigarette. None of them were really sure what she was doing there.

"You must all be so devastated. Of course you never suspected...I never suspected—"

"Miss Hahn," Clyde interrupted. "Rowly didn't kill anyone. His arrest is a travesty."

"Oh." She looked around at each of them, seeing no doubt in any of their faces. "I'm here as a friend, of course, but if you'd like to talk on record—"

"No, we wouldn't."

Mickey sighed. "Victor told me I shouldn't come, but I feel responsible. I told Rowland about poor Mr. Middleton. I had no idea that—"

"How did Bertie get a job with the *North China Daily News*?" Edna asked.

"The same way I did. He walked in and asked." She beckoned Mr. Mills to her lap. "I ran into him outside the Cathay. Actually he was asking questions about the murder of Miss Romanova. Mr. Van Hagen was giving him short shrift as you may imagine. I guessed he was a fellow journalist on the trail of a story. He bought me a drink and told me he'd just arrived from Sydney, Australia. He was hoping to write a story on the taxi girl to sell to local paper and land a job. I told him he didn't need to write a story first and took him to the *North China Daily News* with me."

"And they took him on your recommendation?"

"More Victor's."

"Why would Victor Sassoon recommend him?"

"To stop him investigating Miss Romanova's murder—it's bad for the hotel. Bert had letters of recommendation from Australia too...the usual sort of thing." She studied Edna. "So you knew Bertie. You didn't mention it when I told you about him."

"Mr. Middleton and I were no longer friends. I was surprised that he would come to China."

"Was he looking for you?"

"Yes, I believe he was."

"Can you think of anyone here who would want to kill Bertram Middleton, Mickey?" Milton asked.

Mickey paused. "No. No one that I'm aware of. Bert was a little serious, but he seemed to rub along with everybody quite well." They could almost hear her thinking, aside from Rowland Sinclair.

Edna appealed to the journalist. "Rowly didn't kill anyone, Mickey. Could you talk to Sir Victor...see if he'll help Rowly?"

Mickey's face softened. "I'm sorry darling, I don't think Victor would help."

"Why not?"

"If Mr. Sinclair did not kill Miss Romanova, then everybody in the Cathay that night is still suspect. That's not good for business."

Chapter Thirty-Two

CITY OF DREADFUL NIGHT

SHANGHAI

Shanghai—"In one of the countless night dancing halls an American sailor slaps a Japanese dancing girl. She dashes a glass of water in his face, then cringes in a comer. Men interfere.

"INFURIATED the sailor yells: "I'm three times seven and white—see? No yella woman in all Asia can do that to me!

"A marine policeman enters the scene Cheerfully and vigorously he belts the sailor over the head with his club. Afterwards he drinks glass of beer and remarks: 'Aw, I don't beat 'em any more'n I'd expect to be beat up if I was them.'

"From the prison in the French Concession the news percolates through that four working men have died under torture.

"And from the Chinese military court in the Chinese city comes the news that a girl student, arrested by the

British police in the Y.W.C.A. as a Communist, has died under torture.

"One of her hands was burned off, but still she would tell no names of her comrades."

If you feel romantic about China. If you don't want your romance shattered, don't read Agnes Smedley's "Chinese Destinies." But if you can face stark truth, vividly reported, if you want to know the life of the Chinese people—not the polished upper classes and intelligentsia, but the people—here it is.

—*Daily Standard*, 26 December 1934

Prisoner 4566 coughed again, a rattling, hacking cough that ended in a splutter into the spittoon. Aware that Whitely had stationed a warder outside the cell to ensure the new prisoner observed the rules, Rowland suppressed an instinct to ask if the man was all right. Instead he watched as the emaciated Chinaman stumbled back to a thin blanket on the cement floor. Almost as soon as he lay down 4566 heaved and coughed yet again.

Unable to do nothing, Rowland leaned over and covered the sick prisoner with his own blanket. The man looked weakly at him in wordless surprise and gratitude. The third inhabitant of the cell watched, drawing his blanket more tightly around his shoulders.

Rowland sat with his back against the brick wall. It was cold and he now had nothing at all to soften the cement. But he was in good health, and he reasoned, unlike his wretched cellmates, he would not be there long. He expected Carmel was already unleashing legal fury against Randolph.

The night passed slowly, silent hours broken only by stran-gled coughing and the painful wheeze of a man fighting for every breath. Rowland played over in his mind the crime of which he had been accused. He wondered who'd want to shoot Middleton—other than himself and his companions, of course. From what Rowland had been able to glean from the chief inspector, Middleton had been shot at close range, executed. But surely Middleton hadn't been in Shanghai for sufficient time to make such mortal enemies.

He worried about his friends, concerned the accusation could be extended to them.

At some point, when exhaustion finally overcame all else, Rowland dozed briefly against the wall. He was startled awake when the cage was unlocked. Whitely stood over him. "Where's the blanket you were assigned, felon?"

Rowland looked across at his cellmate. His voice was a little hoarse after not speaking for so long. "I gave it to him. Though I expect he needs a doctor more than a blanket."

"There will be no trading or commerce in provisions," Whitely snarled.

"There was no trade or commerce—I simply gave it to him. The poor chap's dreadfully unwell."

Whitely poked the sick man with his baton. "So you persuaded the white man to give you his blanket, did you, yellow dog?"

"He said nothing!" Rowland said angrily. "I gave him the blanket; he was too weak to refuse."

"I see." Whitely studied Rowland for a moment and then walked out of the cell. He sent two naiks in to drag Rowland out into the walkway. "No prisoner is to have anything not allocated to him by the prison authorities."

"For pity's sake, the man needs urgent medical attention! He's coughing blood."

"You need to learn who's in charge, felon."

Rowland flared. "Look, you sadistic bastard—"

Whitely struck him with the back of his hand. "In here, I am your keeper." He signalled his men. The warders forced Rowland onto his knees, facing the cell, and ordered him to grab hold of the bars.

Whitely leant down and whispered into Rowland's ear. "You are a beast in my zoo. An animal who will take what he is given." He straightened and stepped back. "Ten," he said.

Rowland never saw which of the warders delivered the blows. Ten times, the long baton fell upon his back as the other prisoners watched in silence. Ten stripes for daring to show humanity in the city of the doomed.

When it was done, Rowland was gasping and incoherent, his knuckles white on the bars. But Whitely was not yet finished. "Isolation cell," he said.

The naiks dragged Rowland to his feet and to a rubber-lined cell. They left him there in the darkness.

"I'm afraid Mr. Carmel has been unavoidably detained in Nanking." The solicitor's secretary was apologetic but firm. "We have wired him, and we trust that he will be back in a few days."

"A few days!" Edna said horrified.

"As an interim measure, we've sent Mr. Murray to represent Mr. Sinclair."

"Who's Mr. Murray?"

"One of our most promising new solicitors."

"With all due respect to young Mr. Murray, we need someone with a bit more than promise," Milton said. "What's Mr. Smith doing?"

"Mr. Smith?"

"Of Carmel and Smith."

"Mr. Jerimiah Smith, our founding partner, has been dead for more than a decade."

Edna tried. "Mr. Sinclair is in Ward Road Gaol, Miss Stevens. While we're waiting for Mr. Carmel to return, Rowly is in prison. We just want someone to help us get him out now, please."

"I'll have Mr. Murray telephone you as soon as he gets in," she said primly. "May I tell him that you'll be home to receive it?"

"There will be someone home," Clyde said coldly as he handed her the message to be wired to Wilfred Sinclair. It seemed woefully inadequate to explain the extent of the trouble in which they found themselves. He wished he could clarify more, tell Wilfred how events had managed to spiral so out of control, but in truth, he didn't know. As far as he could tell, none of them had done anything extraordinary or reckless. And yet, here they were. Clyde could only imagine how Wilfred would react to the news that Rowland had been arrested for the murder of one of Edna Higgins's suitors.

They walked out of Carmel and Smith's chambers disappointed, frustrated, and more than a little panicked. Clyde cursed. "What is that idiot doing in Nanking?"

"To be fair," Edna said, "Mr. Carmel was not to know that Rowland would be arrested. And Carmel and Smith are not criminal lawyers."

"Well perhaps we should find Rowly some criminal lawyers," Milton said sullenly. "'Cause as far as I can tell, Carmel and Smith are doing precious little to get him out of prison."

Clyde nodded. "That's not a bad idea. Wing might be able to help us find a lawyer who knows how things work over here."

They made their way to Foochow Road and the Central Police Station. Wing Zau was having his statement taken when they arrived.

"Oh thank goodness," Edna said. Surely Rowland would be released as soon as the alibis were given.

She and Clyde and Milton lined up to do the same, for what it was worth. The desk sergeant, a Scotsman, took their affidavits.

"So you'll release Mr. Sinclair?" Edna pressed once their statements were complete. "There're no grounds on which to hold him now."

"That's not entirely true, Miss Higgins," the policeman said calmly. "Your statements will certainly be considered, as will all the other evidence, in determining Mr. Sinclair's guilt. Alibi evidence, while certainly probative, is just one part of the evidence."

"But surely you could bail him, pending trial?" Milton asked.

"Mr. Sinclair was determined a flight risk. He was denied bail." The sergeant smiled comfortingly at Edna. "You've done everything you can, Miss. You may as well go home and let the law run its course."

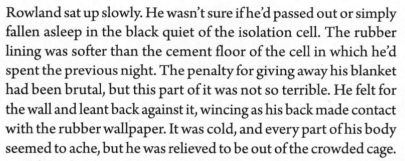

Rowland sat up slowly. He wasn't sure if he'd passed out or simply fallen asleep in the black quiet of the isolation cell. The rubber lining was softer than the cement floor of the cell in which he'd spent the previous night. The penalty for giving away his blanket had been brutal, but this part of it was not so terrible. He felt for the wall and leant back against it, wincing as his back made contact with the rubber wallpaper. It was cold, and every part of his body seemed to ache, but he was relieved to be out of the crowded cage.

After what seemed an age, the window on the door of the cell was opened. The shaft of light that fell on his face was harsh after the darkness. The door opened too now, and a naik walked in and shut the door behind him. Once again it was dark.

Rowland tensed.

The warder flicked on a torch. He squatted beside Rowland. "Mr. Sinclair?"

Startled by the use of his name, Rowland nodded.

"I am Amrith Singh. Ranjit and Harjeet are relatives of mine. Are you all right?"

"Yes."

"You were punished?"

"Yes."

"After punishment, prisoners are supposed to be taken to the infirmary."

"I wasn't, but I'll be all right."

"I will tell Ranjit. You're shaking."

Rowland looked at his hand under the torchlight—he hadn't realised. "It's the cold, I expect."

Amrith nodded. "It's too risky to bring you a blanket." He reached inside his jacket and pulled out a flask. "Try this—it may be warming."

Rowland took a swig. The brandy was bracing, its effect immediate and soothing.

"I'd leave it with you," Amrith said apologetically, "but it will be bad for both of us if Mr. Whitely finds it."

Rowland drank again before he returned the flask. "Thank you, Mr. Singh. Can you tell me if my solicitor has arrived—Mr. Gilbert Carmel? Surely, even here, they must allow me to see my lawyer!"

Amrith shook his head. "Yes, they must. But Ranjit says there has been a problem locating your lawyer."

Rowland cursed.

"Your friends wish you to know that they will find a way to get you released. I will tell Ranjit that I saw you." Amrith stood and switched off his torch. "I will bring food next time I come."

Rowland tried to find the least uncomfortable position he could. Perhaps it was the brandy, but he felt calm. With any luck he would see out his time at Ward Road Gaol in isolation, away from the notice of Whitely and his thugs. The cell smelled damp, the air within it stale. Occasionally he heard scratching—rats perhaps, or the ghosts of desperate men who been held in this cell over the years. The darkness pressed down on his face as if it wanted to get inside him.

The passing of time became difficult to judge. It seemed like hours, it seemed like days. But, in truth, Rowland had no idea how long he'd been confined to the isolation cell when the door began to open again.

Whitely shone his torch directly into Rowland's face. Rowland blanched, dazzled by the strong light. It was a moment before he could focus. The warder strode into the cell. He was followed in by four men—three Sikhs and another Occidental.

"Stand up!" Two men heaved Rowland to his feet. Whitely shoved a prison tunic into his hands. "Change your shirt, felon."

"Why?" Rowland asked bewildered, unsteady.

Whitely's hand moved to his baton.

Rowland backed away. He unbuttoned his shirt, fumbling, as his hands were stiff. He winced as the coarse fabric took dried blood with it. The new shirt was identical in all respects but for the letter *E* emblazoned where the breast pocket might have been. Rowland had no idea what Whitely and his thugs were playing at, but he was in no position to refuse.

Andrew Petty's car was parked at the gates of the mansion on Avenue Joffre when the Buick pulled up. When the gates were opened, the Rolls Royce followed them into the grounds.

"I'm afraid Rowly isn't here, Mr. Petty," Edna said as they all stepped out of the cars.

"Yes, I realise that." Petty shook his head. "He's been falsely accused and summarily incarcerated by Shanghai's pitiful excuse for British justice."

Edna glanced at Milton and Clyde, unsure how Andrew Petty knew.

Petty cleared his throat into the silence. "I know you're busy so I'll get straight to the point...I've good news."

"We could certainly use some."

"I've come to tell you that Mr. Yiragowa is willing to use his influence with the members of the Municipal Council to have Rowland released."

"Really?" Edna's face lifted. She glanced excitedly at her companions. "Can he do that?"

"This is Shanghai. The support of a business partner carries weight, and as you may be aware, the Japanese are increasing their influence on the Shanghai Municipal Council. Most of the other members are Britons so the thought of a white man in Ward Road Prison will not sit well. The Americans are—"

"But Rowly isn't doing business with Mr. Yiragowa and his colleagues," Edna interrupted.

"I am confident we can remedy that." Petty smiled reassuringly. "I took the liberty of sending Wilfred Sinclair a telegram this morning. Given Mr. Yiragowa's generous overture, I'm sure he'll direct Rowland to do the right thing."

Clyde snorted. "I don't like your chances, Mr. Petty. Wilfred Sinclair is not likely to take extortion kindly."

Petty inhaled sharply. "How dare you, sir! Mr. Yiragowa is making this offer as an act of kindness, in recognition of the friendship between Australia and Japan, and despite Rowland's rash and offensive behaviour! Something he was goaded into by his unsavoury political associations no doubt."

Edna folded her arms. "What exactly do you mean by that, Mr. Petty?"

"It's no secret the Communists are anti-Japanese. Neither is it a secret that Rowland Sinclair is keeping company with Communists."

"How did you know to find us here, Mr. Petty?" Milton asked evenly.

For a moment Petty faltered. "My good man, one does not hide by renting a mansion."

They did not invite Andrew Petty in, waiting till he'd climbed back into the Rolls Royce before they entered the house.

Alastair Blanshard looked up from his newspaper as they stepped into the drawing room.

Edna gasped. "Mr. Blanshard!"

"Did I startle you, Miss Higgins?" Blanshard stood. "Forgive me, but I think you'll agree that this is not the time to be waiting on niceties."

"Yes, of course, Mr. Blanshard."

Blanshard shook hands with the gentlemen. "Well it seems Mr. Sinclair has got himself into a spot of bother."

"Can't you get him out?" Clyde cut straight to the point.

"What would you have me do, Mr. Jones? Storm the prison?"

"If that's the only way."

"Let's hope that it's not." Blanshard waited till Edna had taken a seat and then sat down himself. "Rowland was, I believe, arrested for a murder unrelated to the taxi girl."

Edna nodded. She told him about Bertram Middleton.

Blanshard frowned. "And you're absolutely sure Sinclair didn't take matters into his own hands?"

"Yes." Milton replied emphatically. "We've all given our statements as to Rowly's whereabouts the night Middleton was shot."

Blanshard pressed his palms together thoughtfully. "Unfortunately, your credibility as alibi witnesses is compromised by your friendship with Rowland. It would not be difficult to convince a jury that you would all happily perjure yourselves for him."

"Yeah, we would," Clyde agreed. "But what about Mr. Wing? He shared a room with Rowly that night."

Blanshard regarded Wing for a moment. "Mr. Wing is both Rowland's servant and Chinese."

"Dear God, what are we going to do?" Edna was beginning to despair.

"Can you think of anyone who might have wanted to kill this fellow Middleton?"

Edna shook her head. "No. He'd only been in Shanghai for a few days. He barely knew anyone."

"Aside from Mr. Sinclair and yourself."

"Aside from us, and the people he worked with at the newspaper, I expect."

Blanshard paused. "Has it occurred to you that perhaps the entire purpose of Middleton's murder was to put Rowland Sinclair in the frame?"

"Why would anyone want to frame Rowly for murder?"

"I'm not sure." Blanshard rubbed his palms together now. "But perhaps it's a line of enquiry that will prove fruitful for Rowland's lawyers."

"If we could find the flamin' lawyer!" Milton said, frustrated.

"What do you mean?"

Milton told Blanshard about Gilbert Carmel's untimely absence.

"Do you know the name of the client he's representing in Nanking?"

"No, why?"

Blanshard shrugged. "I wonder if the timing of his absence was not accidental."

"You're suggesting that whoever killed Middleton is a client of Carmel and Smith?"

"What better way to frame a man than to ensure his lawyer is out of town when he's arrested?"

"But why would anyone want Rowly in prison?"

"As I told Rowland, there are many fortunes hanging off what the Sinclairs do."

Dread lodged like a rock under Edna's heart. She appealed directly and desperately to Blanshard. "Mr. Blanshard, you have to help us. Please."

Blanshard leaned over and placed his large hand on her arm. "Now, now, my dear. Don't upset yourself. Rowland is on remand—he is probably unhappy, but he is not, for the time being, in imminent danger." He stood. "In the meantime, I'll make some calls to my associates in Nanking. I think it's high time Mr. Carmel returned."

Chapter Thirty-Three

SHANGHAI GANG WAR
CHICAGO METHODS USED
POLITICAL CORRUPTION

(Special to *The Daily News*)

The most realistic representation of Chicago gang
wars is occurring in Shanghai, where there is kidnapping, gun-running and opium-smuggling, to the
accompaniment of a police motor pursuing desper-
adoes as a result of pistol battles in streets, says the
Manchester Guardian's correspondent at Shanghai.
The police declare the movies are a potential influence
and the crime wave is sweeping even the International
Concession. The American Club, numbering special
police among its members and situated opposite the
central police station, might be regarded as ultra-safe,
yet the club's rich Chinese steward, owner of a chain
of food-shops, found a motor car at a side door and
was invited to take a ride to an unknown destination.
He disappeared for weeks and only returned after the

payment of a ransom of 10.000 dollars (£1000). He is now always accompanied by a bodyguard of two Russians, a number of whom are General Koltchak's ex-soldiers licensed by the police for protection of Chinese merchants. The ex-soldiers find this profession a lucrative one. They live as members of the merchant's family and accompany him in evening dress when he goes out to dine. There were rumours that the bodyguards were too intimate with the gangsters, but this theory was dissipated by the slaughter of three in daring kidnapping raids, one dying from the effort to save his employer's daughter, who was murdered in broad daylight.

Shanghai is also copying Chicago's political corruption, prominent gangsters controlling vice centres being powerful in politics.

—Daily News, 19 June 1931

In the harsh electric light of the prison walkway, the clock showed ten minutes past two. Rowland wasn't sure if it was night or day. In fact, he wasn't sure what day it was. The corridors were deserted. Perhaps it was two in the morning. He assumed he was being taken back to the cell in the general block. Whitely led the way. A silent entourage of warders surrounded Rowland, shoving him along to keep pace. Three more men had joined them outside the isolation cell. It seemed an excessive number of guards to move a sole prisoner from one cell to another.

Whitely appeared in high spirits. He made jokes and talked of standing drinks when the shift was done. Rowland kept his eyes down.

Whitely stopped at a door which was no different from the others in the prison, aside from being marked with the letter *E*. He unlocked it and strode through the doorway. Rowland was pushed in after him. The light switch was pulled, and Rowland found himself in a large, windowless room. A narrow stairwell in one corner led to a floor below. It took Rowland a moment to recognise the industrial structure on the other side of the room. A wooden scaffolding—gallows. Instinctively he recoiled.

"What am I doing here?"

Whitely smiled. "That's between you and your God. We've come to hang you."

"I'm on remand." Rowland could feel the cold sweat breaking on his brow. "I haven't been convicted, let alone sentenced!"

"Well I'll be buggered!" Whitely feigned surprise. He poked the E on Rowland's shirt. "And yet you're wearing an execution shirt. Terrible mistake, but understandable."

"You're mad! That's murder!"

"Oh no, felon, it's you who are the murderer. We are just administering justice."

Rowland tried to break away, but the warders converged to seize and hold him fast. They secured his hands behind his back and dragged him up onto the scaffold. Rowland fought but it was useless. The naiks had obviously dealt with men in these circumstances before. Even so it took four of them to restrain Rowland Sinclair and force him onto the trapdoor of the gallows.

"Once we cut your body down, you'll fall through to the morgue," Whitely said, grinning. "It's a very modern and convenient design."

Rowland swore at him. "You won't get away with this, Whitely!"

Whitely held up his palms. "But I won't even be here, felon. I'm going to leave you in the hands of the able gentlemen on the scaffold." He cupped his hand behind his mouth and whispered loudly. "The darkies often make mistakes like this. I know we let them believe they're British but one can only expect so much." Whitely left via the stairs. Four of the warders followed him. The others remained at the gallows.

Rowland thought feverishly. Surely this could not be happening.

"Would you like a blindfold?" The naik's question was almost casual.

Rowland shook his head. "I have not been sentenced to death," he said clearly, trying to meet the man's eye. "By God man, I haven't even been tried."

"Not by a court."

"Why are you doing this?"

Hands gripped each shoulder to hold him in place. "If you accept it, it will soon be over. But if you struggle, you'll choke slowly."

The noose was slipped around his neck from behind and adjusted so that the knot sat at the top of his spine. "If you want to pray, start now."

"Go to hell!"

"Any last words?"

Rowland thought of Edna. But those were not words he could trust to a man about to kill him. Panic was taking hold now. He felt dizzy.

One of the warders moved to grip the long lever beside the gallows.

Rowland's entire body was taut. His heart pounded and the blood roared in his ears.

The lever was pulled. The trapdoor released. And he dropped.

Ranjit Singh relayed the news his cousin had given him.

They were silent, shocked. It was a relief to hear of Rowland, to make this contact, however indirect and small, but hearing of him also somehow made their predicament and his situation more real.

"He's in isolation?" Edna's voice trembled.

"Yes, but he's doing well," Singh assured her. "Obviously he's not afraid of the dark, and Amrith believes he may be better off there."

"Why?"

"He won't come to the notice of the guards. Amrith will smuggle some food for him."

"Why should he want to avoid the guards?" Milton asked sharply.

Ranjit elected not to tell them what the guards at Ward Road did to relieve boredom, what had already happened to Rowland Sinclair. There was no point in distressing them more than they were already when nothing could be done. "The general prison population is rife with tuberculosis. He is less likely to get sick in isolation."

"We have to get him out," Milton said. Unlike Clyde and Edna, the poet had seen the inside of a prison. He guessed what Ranjit was leaving out.

For a moment, Rowland thought they'd succeeded and he'd fallen into hell. Dead men surrounded him, their faces twisted into grotesques, limbs stiff. And laughter, screeching scornful mirth. Hoots and cheers. Whitely's laugh louder than the others. Then the realisation that he was not dead but that the men beneath him were. Rowland recoiled, bucking though his hands were still secured behind him. He rolled off the pallet of bodies onto the cement, where for a moment he lay gagging and retching. The noose was still around his neck, the rope never connected to the gallows.

One of the warders hauled him to his feet. Rowland's knees

buckled. In what may have been an unexpected act of kindness, the warder removed the cuffs so that Rowland could use a nearby rail to keep himself upright as his stomach heaved uncontrollably.

"Bloody oath!" Whitely slapped his thigh and wiped tears from his eyes. "The look on your face! That never gets old."

Rowland stared at the corpses piled on the pallet. Executed by hanging or disease and neglect, and then in a final indignity used to break his fall in some cruel schoolboy prank. God! He gripped the rail trying to catch his breath.

Only Whitely was still laughing now. "You really thought—" He slapped Rowland on the back like they were old friends.

Rowland ignited, turning and launching himself at the man. It was hard to know why exactly the other warders held back, why they allowed Rowland to break Whitely's nose before they raised their batons and pulled him off.

Ranjit Singh's Buick pulled up outside the house of Du Yuesheng. Milton and Wing Zau climbed out. The poet had elected to keep his plan from Clyde and Edna, but it had been necessary to bring Wing into his confidence. It had taken them over a day to be granted an audience with the *zongshi*. Rowland had now been in prison for three days, and there was still no sign of Carmel.

"I'm sorry to drag you into this, comrade," Milton said, clapping his hand on Wing's shoulder. "I know full well it's dangerous, but I can't talk to Mr. Du without you."

Wing straightened, pushing out his chest. "I want to help. I am grateful to you for the opportunity to do so and for your trust..." He glanced back at the Buick and Singh. "But I'm not sure I understand why you haven't confided in Miss Higgins and Mr. Jones."

"I'm about to ask a gangster for help, comrade. I assume his methods will be less than legal, and to be honest, I don't care."

"But Miss Higgins and Mr. Watson Jones will?"

"They might… Women and Catholics can both be awkwardly moral. I didn't want to take the chance."

"Zongshi will require something in return for his help."

"Yes, I expect he will." Milton glanced at Singh. "But we need to get Rowly out of Ward Road."

Singh rested his elbow on the open driver's-side window and looked up at them. Since their near altercation, he had been less hostile towards Wing. "Yes. I think it is necessary. The City of the Doomed is no place for a man like Mr. Sinclair."

"Right." Milton adjusted his cravat. "Onward then. Men may come and men may go; we'll go on forever."

"Well said, Mr. Isaacs!" Wing fell in beside him.

Milton smiled wistfully. "Rowly would probably have wanted to give Tennyson the credit, you know."

Of course, Milton could not know what Wing said to the various circles of security around Du Yuesheng, but whatever it was, it did gain them an audience. As he did the first time they met the taipan, Wing kowtowed. Milton watched, allowing Wing to observe whatever proprieties and pay whatever deference was necessary. For Rowland's sake, the poet too would have happily dropped to his knees, but the kowtow was more complex than that and the risk of giving offense by doing it improperly, too great.

Milton spotted Kruznetsov among the security guards who maintained a circle around Du. Neither he nor the Russian gave any sign of recognition.

Du Yuesheng sat on a wide carved chair with scrolled arms and no back. He spoke before either Milton or Wing had uttered a word.

"Master Du wishes to know if you are here about Mr. Sinclair," Wing translated.

"Could you ask him what he knows about Rowly's situation?" Milton replied warily.

Wing obliged and the *zongshi* spoke again.

"He knows Mr. Sinclair is in Ward Road Prison. He knows he was arrested for the murder of another foreigner."

"Tell him that Rowly didn't kill anybody."

To that, Du Yuesheng did not react. He spoke again.

"He knows that Mr. Sinclair refused to do business with the Japanese."

Milton was startled. How would the gangster know that? Why would he raise it?

"Master Du wishes to know if Mr. Sinclair will change his mind."

Milton shook his head. "No. I don't think so."

Du Yuesheng studied the poet before he replied. His eyes were calculating and cold, and there was something vaguely chilling about his tone.

"Master Du says he will help Mr. Sinclair."

Suddenly Milton was unsure. Du Yuesheng was a gangster, a murderer. Had he just procured a kind of help that Rowland himself would never countenance? Was he compromising Rowland in his desperation to help him? "Ask him what he plans to do, Mr. Wing."

Wing's eyes widened and he swallowed, but he translated the question.

Du seemed amused.

"Master Du says he will send his lawyers to the British Court to have Mr. Sinclair bailed immediately."

"Tell him that's already been attempted."

"He says it has not. Zongshi says the bond is likely to be substantial."

Milton nodded. "Rowland will be able to repay him in full as soon as he's released."

Du waved the promise away.

"Would you ask him what he wants in return for his help?" Milton ventured.

Wing licked his lips nervously and asked the question.

Du's response was short.

"Master Du says he requires nothing."

"Why?" Milton said before he could rein in his surprise. The question did not apparently require translation.

The gangster smiled as he stated his reason. "Du Yuesheng is Chinese."

Edna reached the door before the shuffling *amah*. The old woman glared at her with such baleful ferocity that the sculptress wished she'd not responded to the knock. She opened the door.

"Mr. Carmel!" Relief and joy followed surprise in quick succession. "Oh Mr. Carmel, I can't tell you how wonderful it is to see you."

"Not a moment too soon, I gather!" Carmel kissed her on each cheek. "I'm so sorry, my dear. I feel wretched, truly wretched! To be away when Rowland truly needed me...I don't know if Wilfred will ever forgive me! If I'd had the slightest inkling—"

"Well, you're here now, Mr. Carmel."

"Yes, indeed I am. The office tells me that young Murray was given the case file in my absence, but it seems he was a little out of his depth. This has been rather a cockup, I'm afraid. Fetch your coat, my dear—you can tell me exactly what happened on the way to the courthouse."

"Clyde..."

"By all means bring Mr. Watson Jones, Mr. Isaacs too. I daresay Rowland will need his friends about him after what he's been through."

"Milt and Mr. Wing stepped out this morning. I'll just call Clyde and let Harjeet know where we're going." She stopped to smile at the solicitor. "I'm just so glad to see you, Mr. Carmel. Do you think we could possibly have Rowly back today?"

"You just leave it to me, my dear. I shall insist upon it! I shall invoke Blackstone, Coke, and Locke, issue a writ of habeas corpus, and remind them of who Rowland Sinclair is. By the time I am done, they will not only release our beloved friend, but they will apologise!"

Chapter Thirty-Four

VALUE OF BATHS AND POULTICES

Poulticing is simply putting a hot bath on a particular spot, with the idea of soothing pain or inflammation by the local applications of warmth and moisture. The poultice may be made of various materials: bread or starch or rice flour, or bran, or linseed meal. It should always be applied as hot as it can be borne, and should be frequently changed, no poultice being of any value after two or three hours. The surface of the skin is often vaselined before the application is made. The poultice should be larger than the area to be covered, and so that the heat may be retained, it should be spread thick on a piece of linen, of which the edges have been turned in a little way on each side to prevent any portion escaping. A layer of cotton wool under oiled silk should cover the poultice, and a broad flannel bandage to keep it well on. In applying a poultice to the chest the nipples should not be covered over if possible...

—*The Courier Mail*, 31 August 1935

When Gilbert Carmel of Carmel and Smith arrived at the British Court, there was some confusion. It seemed that lawyers claiming to represent Rowland Sinclair had arrived as the courts opened to demand his release on bail. Carmel was outraged. "I am Mr. Sinclair's legal representative. Why, this is preposterous—they are kidnappers no doubt. The hide of them—to snatch the poor fellow from Ward Road Gaol itself!"

It was not until Milton and Wing emerged that it became clear that there was no elaborate plot to abduct Rowland. Carmel remained somewhat affronted that Milton had seen fit to replace him. The poet apologised. "We could not reach you, Mr. Carmel, and we've never laid eyes on Mr. Murray. You must understand, we were getting desperate."

"Yes, of course. The timing was very unfortunate, but I'm here now."

"I'm sure Mr. Soo will be happy for you to take over."

Edward Soo shrugged. "Bail has been granted," he said, unruffled. He nodded at Milton. "Please convey my regards, and those of Master Du, to Mr. Sinclair."

Milton thanked him, and for a moment they all watched as Du Yuesheng's lawyer departed with two junior solicitors trailing behind him.

"What did you do?" Clyde turned on Milton.

"It doesn't matter what I did," the poet replied firmly. "Rowly's been bailed. We can pick him up from Ward Road."

"What did you promise Du in return for his help?"

"Nothing. He wanted nothing."

"I'm not sure enlisting the help of a man of Mr. Du's reputation was wise, Mr. Isaacs."

"We couldn't reach you, Mr. Carmel," Milton reminded him.

Carmel sighed. "Indeed, the fault is mine. Forgive me."

Edna interrupted. "Can we please just get Rowly?"

Carmel nodded, smiling suddenly. "Yes, we should be there to collect the dear boy and celebrate this first victory. To the automobiles, my young friends!"

Shortly thereafter, Singh's Buick and Carmel's Packard drew up and parked outside the release gate of Ward Road Gaol. Unable to contain their impatience, the Australians climbed out and stood by the massive wooden gates. There was a small door in the gates through which, Carmel had informed them, Rowland would be allowed out.

Several minutes passed.

Clyde and Milton returned to the Packard to discuss the delay with Carmel through the window. "Could something have gone wrong, Mr. Carmel?"

"Perhaps Mr. Soo did not file the application properly." Carmel frowned. "Still...it all seemed in order when I spoke to the clerk." He checked his pocket watch. "Releases are generally quite punctual affairs."

"Could Randolph have—bloody hell!" Clyde broke off as the door finally opened and three men emerged.

Two were Sikh guards. They supported Rowland between them.

"Rowly!" Edna reached him first. "My God, what have they done to you?"

Rowland was damp and hot to touch.

The naiks did not release him until Clyde and Milton's shoulders had taken the place of their own. Clearly Rowland could not stand unaided.

"Good grief, comrade, you're burning up," Milton said.

Ranjit Singh stepped out of the Buick and spoke to the guards in Punjabi. Carmel too left his vehicle to assess the state of Rowland Sinclair. The lawyer was furious. "You tell Mr. Whitely that I will not let this lie!" he bellowed at the guards.

Rowland tried to speak, but he was shivering quite violently.

Edna reached up to touch his face. She tried to speak, but horror stole her words.

"Put him in the motorcar," Singh said. "I'll take him straight to hospital."

Carmel shook his head. "No, absolutely not. Hospitals in Shanghai are no more than reception rooms for mortuaries. I would not let one of their doctors treat my dog! Let us not have retrieved the dear boy only to hand him into a different kind of danger. Take Rowland home. I'll meet you there with a doctor."

Harjeet took charge the moment they returned with Rowland, pausing only a moment in her horror at the state of him.

"He has a fever," she said, testing his forehead. "It's no wonder in that filthy place." She instructed Milton and Clyde to draw him a bath of tepid water and to take his clothes for Ranjit to burn. She told Wing to listen for Carmel and the doctor while she pounded herbs for a poultice and sent Edna to find Rowland's pyjamas and fetch extra pillows.

Taking comfort in her maternal practicality, they did as they were told.

Rowland, for his part, was ill enough to be thoughtlessly compliant. He barely registered the fuss around him. "I'm all right," he said when he realised how worried they were. "I've just caught some kind of chill." He was thankful to wash the grime and decay of the prison cell from his body, to put on his own clothes, and to lie on clean sheets in a bed. He didn't notice the shock and fury of his friends when the welts and bruises left by the batons were revealed. His mind wandered to the men with whom he'd briefly shared a cell, but he couldn't hold the thought.

He felt Edna's hand stroking the hair away from his face, and he breathed the soft scent of her rose perfume. Milton told him something about Du Yuesheng, and Clyde asked him about the livid bruise on his neck.

"Must have happened when they hanged me... I think the rope snagged on one of the bodies for a while..."

Clyde glanced anxiously at his watch, concerned by the delirium.

Harjeet brought in a fragrant spiced tea made of roasted coriander seeds. She called it "Kothamalli" and insisted Rowland drink, if only a couple of sips. He gagged on the first mouthful, but Harjeet persisted and he kept down the second. It was hot and honey-sweet, brewed with ginger. It soothed his throat and he thought he felt better.

Gilbert Carmel arrived with a Frenchman he introduced as Dr. Henri Le Fevre. The physician chased them out of the room so he could examine his patient in private. They took Carmel into the cavernous drawing room. Milton poured the lawyer a drink. Carmel drank deeply and looked so utterly dejected that Edna moved to sit beside him on the settee.

"You mustn't blame yourself. You weren't to know that Rowly would be arrested."

Carmel patted her hand. "You must not worry about me, my dear. Not when Rowland is lying on what might be his death bed."

"Death bed?" Edna pulled back, shocked.

"Did I say death bed? I meant sick bed... It's been a difficult day. Forgive me, my dear. I'm a little weary, that's all."

When Dr. Le Fevre emerged he was sombre. "I suspect Monsieur Sinclair has contracted pulmonary tuberculosis at Ward Road."

Edna gasped. Tuberculosis could be as much a life sentence as any the courts of Shanghai could hand down.

Carmel sighed. "I was afraid of that."

Milton stood. "Tuberculosis? Are you sure?"

"Mr. Sinclair has a very high fever, he complains of chest pain and is coughing blood."

"I didn't notice any blood."

Le Fevre's response was not without compassion. "It was evident in my thorough examination. I am quite certain of my diagnosis."

"We have to take him home." Edna's voice was unsteady.

"I'm afraid Monsieur Sinclair cannot travel now," Le Fevre said gravely.

"Even if he were well enough, he cannot leave Shanghai," Carmel added gently. He hesitated and then went on. "I think it's only fair to warn you that Chief Inspector Randolph is already taking action to have Rowland's bail revoked. Apparently Rowland assaulted a warder while he was incarcerated."

"They can't do that—not when he's so ill!" Edna was close to tears now.

"Ward Road Gaol is equipped with an infirmary," Le Fevre advised.

"I'll bet," Milton replied bitterly.

Carmel took a deep breath and lifted his chin. "Rest assured, my friends, Inspector Randolph will not be unopposed. I shall meet him on every legal battlefield, but..."

"But what?" Milton demanded.

Carmel shook his head. "It would be easier if Rowland had friends of influence."

"Wilfred's contacts—"

"Have been alienated by this business with the Japanese."

"Excuse me, gentlemen." Edna stood to leave.

"Where are you going, Ed?"

"To see Rowly."

Le Fevre shook his head firmly. "No, Mademoiselle Higgins. Mr. Sinclair has pulmonary tuberculosis, a highly contagious disease. We must move him to a private chest hospital as soon as it can be arranged."

"I'll need to speak with him," Carmel objected. "To take instructions, for what it's worth."

Le Fevre was unhappy with the notion. "You do so at your own risk, Monsieur Carmel."

Carmel waved away the physician's warnings. "It would be a small price if I can compensate for letting the poor boy down." He rubbed his face. "Dr. Le Fevre, would you be so kind as to make arrangements for Rowland to be admitted to a private sanatorium? Spare no expense—I will cover it personally."

"Steady on," Clyde interrupted. "Is moving him necessary?"

"I assure you, Mr. Watson Jones, he will get the very best of care."

"Does Rowly know that he has tuberculosis?"

"Not yet," LeFevre replied.

Carmel rose. "I'll tell him," he said grimly. "I can speak to him about his defence, reassure him and apologise."

"We'll come with you," Edna said. Clyde and Milton stood hastily.

"If you are all going to ignore my advice and risk infection"— Le Fevre made no attempt to mask his irritation—"then I must insist you visit one at a time. Do not get too close, and leave the window open. But let me warn you that Monsieur Sinclair is fevered and not at all lucid."

Carmel rolled his eyes. "Yes, yes, noted. If you'll make the necessary arrangements with the sanatorium, Dr. Le Fevre, I must speak with my client!"

Gilbert Carmel went into the sick room first. When he emerged twenty minutes later, he was visibly distressed. He grabbed Edna's hands. "Oh my dear, our friend is more unwell than I expected— quite affected by delirium and, I suspect, anxiety over the case against him. He is justifiably angry with me—refuses to believe he's ill. I fear I've lost his confidence. He seems to believe that there are conspiracies against him."

"That doesn't sound like Rowly," Edna replied. "It's only the fever speaking, Mr. Carmel."

"I don't want you to be upset if he says anything harsh, dear girl."

"Harsh?"

"He seems to believe that you enticed that poor fellow Middleton to follow you to China in order to make him jealous, that Mr. Watson Jones stole his car, and that Mr. Isaacs is a card cheat."

Edna stepped back shocked, hurt. "Rowly said that?"

Carmel's face softened. "Oh my, now I've upset you. It's nonsense of course…a passing madness he will not remember tomorrow."

Le Fevre shook his head. "I did warn you, Monsieur Carmel. Monsieur Sinclair is not in his correct senses. The medication I have administered can have the unfortunate side effect of inducing paranoia and aggression." He checked his pocket watch. "God willing, the sedative will begin to take effect soon, and he will cease to be so needlessly agitated."

Edna nodded tightly. "I promise I won't take any notice of what he says."

The sculptress set her shoulders and let herself into the bedroom, closing the door behind her. She ignored Le Fevre's advice, sat on the bed, and took Rowland's hand. It was warm; his eyes seemed a very bright blue. "Rowly, how are you, darling?"

He turned away to cough. "Ed—thank goodness. Tell those idiots I've just got a cold," he said hoarsely.

She smiled at him, pressing his hand to her cheek. "Dr. Le Fevre's taking you to a hospital where you can get proper care."

He shook his head. "I'm not sure he's a doctor, Ed."

"Why do you say that?"

"He seems to think I have tuberculosis for one thing!"

"Oh Rowly, you just have to do what he says and get well. Mr. Carmel will take care of Inspector Randolph—you're not to worry."

Agitated, Rowland tried sit up. "No, don't trust him!"

She kept a firm hold of his hand. "Mr. Carmel will keep Inspector Randolph in check, Rowly."

"Not Randolph—" The effort of sitting up started him coughing again.

Edna held him. "Rowly, the medication is muddling your thoughts. You must try to stay calm."

Le Fevre opened the door. "I thought I told you not to get too close to him," he said, frustrated. "Are you trying to get infected, Miss Higgins?"

The spasm of coughing took Rowland's ability to speak. Edna ignored the doctor as she rubbed his back and spoke soothingly. "You just get well, Rowly. Leave everything else to us."

"Mademoiselle Higgins." Le Fevre held open the door. "For your own sake, you must leave."

"Let me settle him first," she said defiantly. "When he's resting quietly, I'll leave."

Le Fevre exhaled, exasperated. "You are taking a dreadful risk, Mademoiselle Higgins!" He stalked out, slamming the door.

When the doctor entered the drawing room, Milton and Clyde were discussing the necessity of a sanatorium with Carmel.

"Absolutely, it is necessary, gentlemen," Le Fevre said. "I know you wish to stay with your friend, but I want only to save Monsieur Sinclair's life. He is gravely ill. And he is contagious. He cannot be left here."

"Having Rowland confined to a sanatorium will be a significant argument against the revocation of bail," Carmel added. "At all costs, my friends, we must avoid Rowland being returned to Ward Road Gaol."

"On that we agree," Milton said.

"I'll go with him," Edna said, entering the room now. "To the sanatorium." Her eyes bore the signs of tears hastily brushed away. "It's the best solution."

"That's not—"

"If I'm going to get sick, I will have already been infected by now, anyway," the sculptress said resolutely. "I understand that it's the fever speaking, but Rowly doesn't trust either of you gentlemen. I can at least get him to cooperate with his own recovery. I will not let him think we are abandoning him, even if he thinks… whatever he thinks."

"My dear," Carmel said softly. "Dr. Le Fevre has arranged the very best of care, but I'm not sure the facility will be able to accommodate a…visitor."

Clyde intervened now. "Actually, I don't think it's such a bad idea." He turned to Carmel. "It's a private hospital, you say? Surely they can be persuaded to let Ed stay with Rowly. In any case, we would not send Rowly anywhere that we can't visit."

"But Miss Higgins will be putting herself in very great danger of infection!" Le Fevre threw his hands in the air. "*Comment suis-je censé aider ces idiots?*"

Edna smiled. Clearly the physician did not realise she spoke French. "You just help Rowly, Dr. Le Fevre. And allow us to do the same."

Chapter Thirty-Five

TUBERCULOSIS
Sanatorium Treatment Best

Health Department's Advice

The medical officer of the Tuberculosis Division of the Health Department (Dr. John Hughes) in a recent address emphasised the absolute necessity of rest in treating tuberculosis, pointing out that the only place where such rest can be obtained under suitable conditions is in a sanatorium.

Outside a sanatorium a person is living in a community where his friends and relatives are living irregular hours, leading a life of pleasure, and the example set makes him envious, and he throws caution to the wind.

—Armidale Express and New England General Advertiser, 1 August 1938

The Denville Sanatorium seemed more like a grand villa than a hospital. It was on the very outskirts of Shanghai, in what seemed to be the countryside, where the fresh air would help Rowland's lungs and the quiet would allow him to rest. The grounds were gated. The room to which Rowland was taken was on the third floor. It was large and furnished in Chinese style with a bathroom attached; the walls hung with long banners bearing paintings of village scenes and dragons. He was stretchered up to the room for fear the stairs would prove too strenuous in his current state. Le Fevre had given him a strong sedative in any case, to make the move easier.

"The hospital only admits two or three patients at a time," Le Fevre explained. "It allows each patient to be given the utmost round-the-clock care, and it means it can accommodate Mademoiselle Higgins in one of the spare rooms."

"A big place for two or three patients," Clyde commented.

"It is very expensive," Le Fevre replied. "But it is the only facility which would allow Mademoiselle Higgins to remain."

"I'll bet," Clyde murmured. He suspected that Le Fevre was not above taking advantage of the situation to turn a healthy profit. But perhaps that was unfair. In any case, money was the least of their worries right now, or any time really.

For a few hours, the three of them and Gilbert Carmel sat in the room while Rowland slept fitfully under the effects of the sedative. The large windows were left open in deference to Le Fevre's dire warnings. A Chinese orderly came in with a tray of tea and pound cake, and nurses and Le Fevre himself came in to check on Rowland, but otherwise the hospital was as quiet and restful as promised.

To distract them all from worry, Carmel told them tales of old Shanghai, the rise of men like Sassoon, the intrigues and scandals of the city.

"How long have you lived here, Mr. Carmel?" Edna asked, her eyes still on Rowland.

"Since just after the war," Carmel replied. "I can tell you it was not easy at first to do business with those I'd fought in the trenches against." He followed Edna's gaze to Rowland. "I understand Rowland's suspicion of the Germans—I shared it once, but I realised years ago that it was time to move on, to let the wounds of war heal. It's one of the great advantages of Shanghai... It's a place where the old empires come together to build a new world indifferent to national prejudices."

"Rowly's suspicion of the Germans is nothing to do with the Great War." Milton took issue with the lawyer's romantic vision. "And Shanghai is hardly indifferent to national prejudices. The servants are Chinese, the taxi girls Russian... I've not seen a white man pulling a rickshaw, only riding while some half-starved, barefoot native pulls him along the road!"

Carmel nodded. "We are not perfect, Mr. Isaacs, but I find that in business all things are equal. Old enemies shake hands and make fortunes together."

"Yes, of course, fortunes."

"The free market is blind to race and class, Mr. Isaacs."

"The free market is blind to many things, but not race or class, Mr. Carmel."

Carmel sighed. "Perhaps you are right." He stood to leave. "As much as I would love to spend the afternoon defending Shanghai, my dear young friends, I must prepare Rowland's defence and ensure that that bloated chief inspector is not successful in having his bail revoked." He took Edna's hand and enclosed it in both of his. "You keep an eye on our boy, my dear, and I shall return this evening."

"Thank you so much for everything you've done, Mr. Carmel."

"I only hope it is enough," the lawyer replied before he left them to it.

"We should probably go too," Clyde said eventually. He was not happy about leaving Rowland and Edna, but the hospital seemed secure.

"Now?" Edna asked. "Why?"

"We can't leave Rowly's fate to Carmel and the courts of Shanghai," Milton replied. "And now we've got to work out who killed Bertram Middleton as well as Alexandra Romanova."

"What are you going to do?"

"I wish I knew, Ed." Clyde shook his head. "But we've got to do something. Rowly won't survive Ward Road Gaol again."

"Surely Wilfred—"

"We haven't heard from him," Milton replied, frowning. "It's odd…but who knows what's going on back home. Wilfred could well be busy overthrowing the soddin' government again."

Clyde laughed. "The Lyons government are his lot, Milt. Wilfred doesn't need to overthrow them." He sobered. "Maybe there's just nothing he can do this time."

"Mr. Kung, the Buddhist priest, was in the foyer of the Cathay when Rowly was arrested," Edna said, remembering. "In fact I'm sure I've seen him there before."

"Perhaps he's staying there." Clyde bit his lip thoughtfully. "We can try asking Van Hagen—see if it leads anywhere."

"We picked up Sergei Romanov's scent just before Rowly got arrested and everything went to hell." Milton took his hat from the post on the end of Rowland's bed, where he'd hung it. "One of the restaurateurs in Little Russia thought he saw Sergei pan-handling in some place called Blood Alley. We might start there."

"Blood Alley?"

"Yes, these places never seem be to be named High Street."

"Be careful, please."

They embraced the sculptress. "We'll be fine. You just make sure Rowly follows the doctor's orders."

"And don't you get upset about anything he says," Clyde added. Le Fevre had obviously told Clyde and Milton about Rowland's accusations. "When my cousin Clarice contracted measles, she ran through Batlow naked, screaming that the water was poisoned."

Milton agreed. "Tell him not to worry. We're not going to let him go back to gaol—whatever it takes."

———————————————✧——————————————

Ranjit Singh drove Clyde and Milton to the Cathay, where they claimed to have an appointment with Chao Kung. Milton described the abbot for good measure. Van Hagen informed them curtly that there was no guest of that name or indeed that description currently registered at the hotel. Milton slapped his forehead, lamenting that they had missed him and asked if Kung had left a forwarding address. Van Hagen checked his register and reported testily that there had not been a guest of that name at the Cathay that year.

And so the Australians left with only the knowledge that whatever the reason for Kung's presence in the Cathay's foyer, it was not because he was staying there.

Singh took them back to the house in Little Russia to pick up Wing Zau before driving them all to Blood Alley, a short road just off the Bund. The street was within the border of the French Concession, between Rue du Consulat and Avenue Edward VII, and was officially named the Rue Chu Pao-san. It was a precinct of low bars and dives, brothels and opium dens. There were many such districts in Shanghai, but Blood Alley was legendary as the most seedy of all. Early evening saw the short street move from a sinister languor to a kind of degenerate vibrancy. Sailors on shore leave, in search of comfort and vice, moved in uniformed packs for safety, though they leapt eagerly into the frequent brawls. Singh was not at all happy about their intent to seek Sergei Romanov in Blood Alley. "I should accompany you, but it would be foolhardy to leave the motorcar unguarded here."

Milton smiled. "Despite appearances, Mr. Singh, Clyde and I have not always been gentlemen of means."

"Indeed, we still have no means," Clyde pointed out.

"Blood Alley is not so different from Darlinghurst back home. You can rest assured we are perfectly accustomed to the business that goes on here."

"The chap we spoke to said he'd seen Sergei panhandling outside the Palais Cabaret," Clyde said, pointing out the theatre across the street. "So we'll begin there." He glanced at Wing apologetically. "We may need to speak to some of the girls who work there. Milt and I can deal with the ones who speak English, but you'll need to sweet-talk the others, Wing old mate."

Wing Zau seemed uneasy, but he nodded. "Of course. My words will be honey."

Milton patted his shoulder. "Attaboy!"

The entrance to the Palais Cabaret was choked with American sailors in their bellbottom whites trying to catch the next show. Some were distracted from their purpose by the painted women who called their wares from the corners and alcoves. The mood was festively salacious, loud American voices, laughter, and swagger. Milton, Clyde, and Wing checked the rows of hawkers and entertainers for Sergei, but there was no sign of the Russian.

They spoke to the girls who leant against the wall with one knee bent. Milton and Clyde struggled with pidgin, compensating with gestures that were greeted with giggles and guffaws. Wing had more success speaking Shanghainese and then basic Russian to glean that a man of Sergei's description had set up a game of chance outside Maxim's Café.

He signalled the Australians, and they left the theatre for Maxim's. There was again no sign of Sergei. They took a table inside so Wing could question the waitresses. Clyde and Milton watched on amused as he made jokes and paid compliments in a language they did not understand, but in a manner that made his meaning plain. Finally, after taking a flower from the vase on the table and handing it to one of the young women, he turned to the Australians triumphantly. "He's at George's Bar. Apparently that where he spends his winnings. She says he did well today, so he'll be there for a while."

"Well done, comrade!" Milton placed a generous gratuity on the table for the helpful waitress. "Tell her thank you."

They made their way then to George's Bar, pausing only by the Buick to inform Singh of their progress. George's catered to a more subdued clientele than nearby Finnemore's or the Silver Dollar. Its patrons were committed drinkers, uninterested in whores or dancing. The tall stools along the mahogany bar were already taken by the regulars, except for the couple on either side of a tall, unkempt Russian. As they got closer, they understood why. Sergei Romanov reeked.

"Bloody hell," Milton muttered, turning his head and taking a deep breath as if he intended to hold it from then on. He took the seat beside Romanov and signalled the bartender. "A bottle of your best vodka for my friend."

Romanov looked up slowly, started, and pulled back abruptly. By then Wing and Clyde had him surrounded.

"Sergei," Milton said calmly. "You have nothing to fear from us, mate. We're here to help you."

Romanov's eyes were wild with terror as he looked frantically about the bar. The barman glanced over. The other drinkers seemed to sink lower into their shoulders.

Romanov tried to run. Clyde grabbed him. "Steady on, Sergei. Don't you remember us?"

"Where is she?" Romanov said. "The girl. Is she dead too?"

"Who—Ed? Do you mean Ed?" Milton asked. "No, Sergei. She's fine, safe…but," he added thoughtfully, "if we're going to keep her safe, we'll need your help."

"No, no, I cannot help."

"You have to." Clyde grimaced. "For pity's sake, Sergei. You smell like you've been sleeping in a swamp."

The bartender put the bottle of vodka Milton had ordered on the bar. "You know this man?" he demanded.

"Yes," Milton replied, handing him several banknotes.

"Then get him out of my establishment. He's putting off the customers."

Clyde placed his hand firmly on Sergei's shoulder. "That's not a bad idea. You look like you could use a proper meal."

Milton held the bottle of vodka tantalisingly just out of Romanov's reach. "How about it, Sergei? Will you help us? Will you let us help you?"

"The other one," Romanov said. "Sasha's rich foreigner with blue eyes—is he dead?"

"No."

"Then I come."

They flanked Romanov out of the bar in case he changed his mind and bolted, for the Russian still seemed anxious and wary.

"Sorry about this, Mr. Singh," Milton whispered as they bundled the pungent man into the back of the Buick. Wing took the front seat, and the Australians sat in the back with their guest. Milton gave Romanov the bottle of vodka to keep him calm. Singh drove as fast as he could back to the grand house in Little Russia.

Rowland opened his eyes. He swallowed. His throat was sore. He didn't feel well, but he felt better than he had for a day or two. It took him a little while to recall where he was. He turned his head looking for Edna, the last thing he remembered.

"Hello, Rowland. So glad to see you awake."

"Mr. Carmel..." Rowland's voice was strained but steady. "Where's Ed?"

Carmel smiled. "I asked the lovely Miss Higgins if I might talk to you alone for a moment. She was kind enough to oblige." He took off his spectacles. "Rowland, I have some worrying news. The chief inspector is trying to have your bail revoked. Apparently you assaulted a warder, occasioning actual bodily harm."

"I see."

"I understand that you were provoked. Making a man believe he's being hanged is…well, just not British. And I'll make that case, but it's unlikely we'll be able to get any of the warders to corroborate your side. Dr. Le Fevre has serious concerns that, in your current condition, you will not survive reincarceration."

Rowland's brow furrowed but he said nothing.

"I know young men are heedlessly brave and reckless with their own lives, but you must realise that if you are convicted, your friends will be implicated. They may even be prosecuted."

Rowland eyes darkened. He moved to sit up.

"I don't want to distress you, my boy—not in your condition—but I do want you to really consider whether your vendetta against the Germans is worth alienating the only people who may be able to help you now. Randolph's so-called evidence is circumstantial. With Mr. Yiragowa's assistance, we can have these charges dropped, at least long enough for you to leave China."

Rowland pressed the heels of his hands into his eyes as he tried to think clearly.

Carmel exhaled. "I don't know if you are aware of this, but your dear brother Wilfred saved my life twice during the Great War. I consider it my duty and my privilege to save yours in return. Please…I beg you to allow me to do so."

Rowland looked up. The lawyer was emotional, fraught. Rowland shook his head. "Let me talk to my friends…"

"I'm afraid there is no time for that. I really must urge you to act now. Please, Rowland. I cannot tell Wilfred that I failed to protect you."

"You honestly believe selling the Sinclair wool to the Japanese will keep me out of gaol?"

"I do. I think it's the only way to proceed. For your sake and that of your friends."

Rowland took a deep breath. He glanced at the clock on the

wall opposite his bed. Nine in the evening. "Can you draw up a contract by morning?"

Carmel leaned forward. "Yes, yes, of course."

"Draw it up and I'll sign tomorrow."

"Where the bloody hell have you been?" Alastair Blanshard was distinctly unhappy.

"We could ask the same." Milton was not going to be bullied.

"Who in God's name is that?" Blanshard said as a clearly inebriated Russian stumbled through the door with an empty vodka bottle in his hand. "And what is that unholy smell?"

"The answer to both questions is Sergei Romanov," Clyde said.

"God! Has he been hiding in a cesspit?"

"Perhaps." Clyde took the empty bottle out of Romanov's hand. "We're not going to get anything sensible out of him right now."

"Allow me, Mr. Watson Jones." Wing stepped forward to take Romanov's arm from Clyde. "A gentleman's gentleman is experienced in the art of treating excessive consumption and inducing sobriety. Come along, Mr. Romanov."

Wing pulled Romanov's arm over his shoulders and tried to guide his stagger towards the stairs.

"Allow me to assist you, Mr. Wing." Singh rolled up his sleeves and took the Russian's other arm. The stench brought tears to his eyes. "Perhaps we should start by putting him under a shower."

Holding his breath, Wing could only nod. Fortunately Romanov's inebriation had reached a point of compliant stupor, and so they were able to coax him up the stairs.

Clyde and Milton took Blanshard into the drawing room, telling him quickly about the state in which Rowland had emerged from Ward Road Gaol. Blanshard listened gravely.

"So Carmel came back?"

"Yes. We thought you'd used your contacts to fetch him."

Blanshard shook his head. "No, my contacts in Nanking couldn't find him. I did, however, discover the name of the client for whom he was acting. It appears Mr. Carmel also represents Andrew Petty."

"Petty? Are you sure?"

"Petty let it slip himself."

Milton swore. "Would Andrew Petty have known about Bertram Middleton?"

"Carmel might have mentioned it to him." Clyde checked his watch. It was late, but the lawyer had promised he would not rest until Rowland had been exonerated. Perhaps he was still in the office. "We should ask him. I'll telephone to let him know we're on our way."

Chapter Thirty-Six

Rest For Tuberculosis

I was visiting an ex-heavyweight amateur boxing champion who was a patient in a tuberculosis hospital. He looked so well that I told him he didn't look like a T.B.

"Well," he said, "I am one all right. I'm lying on my back for a year, then sitting up for six months, then up and around the grounds for another six months, and then home."

He was not only a good fighter or boxer, but he loved to fight, and yet he was willing to remain absolutely quiet for two years in order to get well.

...It is rest that allows the protecting scar tissue to form slowly yet surely.

When rest by simply lying down is not sufficient to allow the protecting wall to form, then other means of resting the lung—cutting the nerve that moves lung, injecting air into the pleural cavity in which the lung lies—may be used.

However, for the great majority of patients, simply resting for long period brings about the cure.

—*Northern Star*, 21 January 1935

Le Fevre snapped shut the doctor's bag as Edna walked into the room.

"Mademoiselle Higgins. I've just given Monsieur Sinclair a sedative to help him sleep. I'm afraid he will not be lively company, but rest is vital to his recovery."

Edna smiled. "I might just sit with him till he drifts off." She smoothed the covers on Rowland's bed. He mumbled a drowsy greeting. "How is he?" she asked Le Fevre.

"Quite unwell," Le Fevre said disapprovingly. "It's imperative he rests." The physician regarded her almost accusingly.

"Of course. I won't stay more than a couple of minutes. And I won't say a word."

"I shall return tomorrow morning. He should sleep till then."

"Thank you, Dr. Le Fevre."

"Good night, Mademoiselle." The physician tipped his hat and walked out. Edna waited until his footsteps faded before she closed the door. She relaxed a little. There was something about Le Fevre that unnerved her.

"Rowly!" she said, startled to find him sitting up when she turned from the door.

He moved his finger to his lips and beckoned her over. Opening his hand he showed her the pills Le Fevre believed him to have swallowed.

"Oh Rowly, you have to take your medication," she whispered.

"I haven't got tuberculosis, Ed. Just a bit of a chest cold. Do you know where my clothes are?"

"Why?"

"We have to get out of here, and I really don't want to walk the streets of Shanghai in my pyjamas."

"What? Rowly, be reasonable. You're ill."

"Ed." He took her hand. "Le Fevre is a fraud, a charlatan."

She tested his forehead for a fever, some cause of delirium. He was warm but not particularly so.

"Rowly, you've been so ill. You don't know what you're saying."

"I'm not that ill. This diagnosis of tuberculosis is positively absurd."

Edna clasped his face between her hands and spoke slowly. "You're not a doctor; Le Fevre is."

"He hasn't so much as taken my temperature, Ed. He's done nothing but sedate me!"

"Perhaps he is experienced enough to tell without a thermometer…and darling, he's just trying to keep you quiet so you get the rest you need."

"There's nothing but a revolver in that bag of his—I got a glimpse of it when he was pretending to examine me."

Edna stared at him. "A gun?"

He nodded. "And nothing else."

She exhaled slowly. "Right then. Mr. Carmel told us he was a specialist…"

Rowland took her hands from his face and pressed them to his lips. "I'm not entirely sure what Carmel is up to, what Le Fevre's told him. He seems convinced that unless I deal with the Japanese, I'll die in prison. I've told him to draw up an agreement, that I'll sign it."

"But—"

"I don't intend to go through with it, Ed." He stood carefully. "I just needed him to leave, so we could leave." Though he still felt quite weak, he was sure on his feet. "Perhaps you should leave first, Ed. You're not a patient. You could tell them you were meeting someone for dinner and just leave—"

The sculptress shook her head. "I made such a fuss about staying with you, they'd be suspicious. And I'm not leaving you, anyway." She opened the cupboard and took out the dark grey suit and freshly laundered shirt they'd brought in when Rowland was admitted, though they hadn't expected him to need them for several days. Rowland changed as quickly as he could. It was possible that one of the "nurses" would come in to check if Le Fevre's pills had taken effect.

Edna helped him slip on his shirt, still shocked by the black bruises which covered his back and shoulders. He'd still not told them what had happened to him. She wasn't sure he ever would.

"How do you feel?" she asked, studying him anxiously. Whether or not he had tuberculosis, he had been ill when they'd collected him from Ward Road. She buttoned his shirt gently, being careful not to pull the fabric against his injuries. "I'm not sure you're well enough to do this."

Rowland pulled a handkerchief out of his back pocket and turned away to cough. "It's a chest cold," he said when the paroxysm finally abated. "If we were in Sydney, you'd tell me to quit complaining and stop being such a baby." He ran his hand through his hair in a vague attempt to tidy it.

Edna helped him with his tie and then his jacket before she turned off the light and opened the curtain to look out. "So how are we going to do this?"

"Le Fevre believes he's sedated me, and convinced you that I'm dangerously ill. He probably won't have expected us to try and walk out. With any luck, the night staff will be taken by surprise and not know what to do."

Edna looked at him sceptically. "You want to just walk out?"

"I don't think there's any other way."

"We could get a message to Milt and Clyde, or the police." Edna was not fooled by his refusal to bend to pain. "They're going to try to stop us, and you're in no condition to fight or even run."

There was a movement of light at the window. Rowland looked out to see Carmel's Packard come through the gate. The chauffeur got out and opened the rear door. Looking down on the dimly lit garden, it took Rowland a few moments to recognise the gentlemen who climbed out with his lawyer: Yiragowa and Akhito. Le Fevre emerged from the front passenger seat, and the party proceeded briskly into Denville Sanatorium. "What the devil are they doing here?"

Edna took his hand. Any doubts that he was completely lucid were long allayed. Rowland's manner was urgent, but there was nothing fevered or hysterical about it. "What now, Rowly?"

Rowland opened the door. They could hear Carmel and his guests below. He beckoned Edna out into the hallway and closed the door after her. Rowland scanned the long corridor. All the doors along it were closed. They tried each in turn. Loudening footsteps on the stairs counted down the time. All but Edna's room were locked. They slipped into it. A poor hiding place but their only option. Rowland hoped it might give them enough time to slip past.

He kept his ear to the door. "The moment they step into my room, we'll make a break for it," he whispered. He could see Edna's eyes in the darkness. Large. Worried. "I'll be all right," he promised.

They waited.

Le Fevre's voice was first. Brusque, annoyed. "I told you before, I had to sedate him, or the girl might have noticed he was improving... He might have realised."

Now Carmel. "We'll stick his head under a cold shower if we have to. The Japs are suspicious; they want to see him sign."

"He might not cooperate."

"Leave it to me. I'll talk him round. Our friend Whitely did his job, and Rowland has already agreed to sign. The poor boy, bless him, is not particularly bright."

"What about her? Sinclair's tart."

"Don't worry, I'll take care of her."

The click of a latch being turned, and the voices stopped. This was their chance. Rowland counted to three and opened the door. He stepped out into the barrel of Le Fevre's gun.

Chapter Thirty-Seven

Hygiene
THE DAILY BATH.

The necessity of a daily bath from a health point of view is, I trust, too well understood to need any explanation from me on the subject, but many men do not realise that not one of the least benefits to be derived from a bath is the rubbing which should follow it.

Such an opportunity of promoting the circulation should not be lost, for it is only when the blood is healthy and circulates freely that all the organs of the body can do their work in a satisfactory manner.

The surface of the skin being freed from the perspiration and greasy deposit thrown off by the sebaceous glands is more susceptible to properly applied friction than at any other time. The skin should be thoroughly dried before it is rubbed; if left moist, evaporation will go on, and a certain amount of heat will be abstracted from the body. It adds greatly to the comfort of the bather to have a large Turkish sheet at hand, which will keep the body covered during the process of drying.

The towel used for the purpose of friction should be fairly hard and quite dry.

A thermometer should be placed in the water before taking a bath, for it is impossible to test the temperature accurately by any other means.

—*Queenslander*, 12 March 1898

"Move back, Monsieur. Say not a word."

Rowland did so. He kept Edna behind him.

"Gilbert," Le Fevre called with just sufficient volume. "Step this way if you please."

Le Fevre forced Rowland and Edna back. Carmel came in and closed the door behind him. He pulled the light switch.

"You must forgive the good doctor," he said, frowning at Le Fevre, who lowered the gun. "He is a little fanatical about quarantine. Surely you weren't planning to leave? It would be reckless in the extreme to do so while you are still gravely ill, not to mention contagious."

"I haven't got tuberculosis and you know it!" Rowland said angrily.

Carmel shook his head sadly. "My dear boy, that's the fever speaking." He turned to Edna. "Talk to him."

Edna's voice was calm. "Why are you back here, Mr. Carmel?"

Carmel swallowed and smiled broadly. "I bear good news, my dear young people. Mr. Yiragowa was delighted you've come around, Rowland. He was keen to deal with the formalities, and I thought that the sooner we could despatch his influence in your aid, the better. We cannot risk you being incarcerated again. The next time they hang you, it won't be a hoax."

Edna glanced sharply at Rowland, but she said nothing. This

was not the time. Whatever went on in Ward Road, he would tell when he was ready.

"Am I to understand that you were going to take me to Mr. Yiragowa at gunpoint?" Rowland asked staring coldly at Le Fevre.

"Henri is a little overzealous when it comes to doctor's orders I'm afraid." Carmel's laugh was hollow. "Since you're up and dressed, what say we go down and do this deal, dear boy? We'll all sleep a great deal easier knowing you won't be dragged off to Ward Road."

"Aren't you afraid I'll infect them?"

"It's your welfare that concerns me, Rowland. And that of your friends. We talked about the danger in which you're placing them by refusing help."

Edna shook her head. "Rowly, don't—"

Carmel sighed. The explosion of movement caught them by surprise. Le Fevre moved on Rowland. Carmel seized Edna, dragging her away. Rowland froze. A sharpened blade, a bayonet, was pressed against Edna's throat.

"Don't make a sound, dear girl," Carmel said quietly.

"And don't you try anything, Monsieur." Le Fevre jabbed the revolver's barrel into Rowland's temple.

Carmel was sweating, his face suffused as he spoke to Rowland. "Don't make me do this again, you spoiled little bastard."

Clyde returned the telephone receiver to its cradle. The operator had not been able to raise anyone at Carmel and Smith. Clyde had called the Denville Sanatorium, but, so far outside visiting hours, he was told only that Rowland was resting quietly and Edna had long since retired.

The sound of a baritone from the upper floors reminded him about Sergei Romanov. "Let's see what Romanov has to say for himself before we try to hunt down Petty," he said, taking the stairs two at a time. Milton and Blanshard fell in behind him.

The Russian was still in the bath, singing an aria from Mozart's *Don Giovanni* as if he was centrestage at the Royal Opera House. The Australians blanched as Romanov chose that moment to rise from the water in some dramatic flourish. He stood in all his naked glory like an ungainly Aphrodite emerging from the waves. Milton applauded. "Well done, Sergei. You don't need a violin."

Romanov bowed.

"For pity's sake, give the man a towel," Blanchard growled. "Cover your shame, man!"

Perhaps it was the effects of drink, but Romanov clearly felt no shame. Eventually, however, he was persuaded to don one of the embroidered silk dressing-gowns Edna had bought to take back for Rowland's mother. It was possibly inadequate for the purpose, but a significant improvement on nothing.

With Clyde and Milton assisting Wing and Singh, Romanov was eventually out of the bath and covered to some level of modesty. They coaxed him downstairs to the kitchen where Harjeet had prepared chicken pies and black coffee. Once he had eaten, Romanov was a great deal more cooperative and conversant, and they began their questions.

"Where have you been, Sergei?"

"Here, there. I stay out of sight. It is hard for a bear."

"Why, Sergei?"

"Because he tries to kill me. Because he burns my house."

"Who?"

The Russian shook his head.

"Why does someone want to kill you?"

"Because I know Sasha was working for him. Much money he promised, but I know she displeased him."

Milton sat down beside Romanov. "What was this man paying her to do, Sergei?"

Romanov wiped his mouth with the back of his hand. "She

was to seduce a married man—that is all." He swigged the coffee. "Married men are the most easy to seduce, she would say, but he was not married."

"Who wasn't married?"

"The man she must seduce…and then he seduces her." He pounded his chest. "She began to think that perhaps this blue-eyed foreigner would be her prince."

"Rowly? Do you mean she was employed to seduce Rowly?"

"But he was not married."

Clyde threw his hands up in the air. "He's still drunk! He's not making any sense."

Blanshard rubbed his chin thoughtfully. "Rowland replaced his brother, did he not?"

Milton could see where he was going. "And Wilfred is happily married."

Blanshard nodded. "Married men have the most to lose with an affair." He took a seat at the scrubbed kitchen table. "Could Miss Romanova have been hired to seduce Wilfred Sinclair?" he asked.

Romanov began on another pie. "I don't know names. I remember married man. I told her it was not right, but she said it would mean enough money to send her boy to school in America."

"Her boy?"

"Mikhail…everything she does for Misha, to give him the life the Bolsheviks stole."

"And where exactly is Mikhail?"

"Sasha sent him to school in Nanking, but that was not enough." Romanov shrugged. "Misha must go to America, she say."

Blanshard clicked his fingers in front of Romanov's face to get his attention. "Who was this man who hired your sister to seduce a married man?"

"An Englishman. I saw him only once."

"You saw him?" Milton said. "Then you'd recognise him."

"Da." Romanov scowled. "He knows I did not die in his fire.

He comes looking for me. But Sasha's clumsy bear is not stupid. He knows how to hide."

"You say this man tried to kill you?" Blanshard asked.

"Da." Romanov broke into a string of exclamatory Russian.

Clyde poured him more coffee. "What did this bloke look like, Sergei?"

"An ordinary man…smart, rich. And bald. Hairless on his head."

Milton tensed. Petty had a full head of hair. "Bald? Are you sure?"

"Da. He touched his head like so." Romanov patted his own thick mop. "Like there might be hair there somewhere. *Lysyy durak!*"

Milton stood. Clyde paled. "My God, that's Gilbert Carmel."

"Again?" Rowland stared at Carmel as he held the blade against Edna's throat. And the realisation that this man had killed Alexandra Romanova surged cold in his veins. "Let her go—I'll do whatever you want. Please."

"Yes, you will." Carmel's voice shook. His head gleamed with perspiration. "You will go downstairs with Dr. Le Fevre, and you will smile and bow and sign whatever they put in front of you."

"Fine—but she comes with me."

"I think not."

"I'm not leaving her with you."

"If you sign the agreement, do your part, then I won't be forced to hurt her."

Rowland knew Carmel was lying. The lawyer couldn't let them go now, no matter what Rowland signed. He played for time. "You weren't forced to kill Alexandra Romanova, but you did anyway."

Carmel exploded. "For pity's sake, Sinclair, don't be such a bloody fool!" He dropped the bayonet away from Edna's throat, using it to remonstrate as he spoke. "The girl was working for me from the outset. She was a tart, hired to compromise your upstanding brother, but you turned up instead, and she got ideas. Fancied she might snare a wealthy husband instead of doing what she'd been hired to do. The little tramp went up to your suite to try it on for size, for God's sake!"

"She liked to look at the first-class suites," Rowland said. "She wasn't—"

"Henri overheard her making that message for you. He took the disc from her, but the cunning little minx gave him a blank one. Oh yes...she intended to tell you, all right, to earn your love and gratitude by betraying me! I couldn't allow that."

"But Wilfred—"

"I might have misrepresented the facts a little there. He didn't save my life; I saved his." Carmel's knuckles were white on the bayonet's handle. "And how does he repay me for his miserable life, for the happiness and wife and children that came with it? I ask him to come to Shanghai, and he lets me down, sends his idiot Communist brother in his place."

Rowland's eyes darted back to Edna. She was rigid. He wanted desperately to snatch her away from Carmel, to protect her, but he could not risk her to a skirmish.

"Did you kill Bertram Middleton, Mr. Carmel?" Edna forced sound through terror.

"Yes." Carmel laughed. "Rowland told me about the man himself. I couldn't believe my luck. I telephoned and made an appointment to meet him that evening." With his free hand, he pulled an imaginary trigger twice. "It was surprisingly simple, much easier than the Russian girl."

Rowland felt sick. He'd as good as signed Middleton's death warrant. Though he despised the man, this was different. "Why do you need me to sell wool to the Japanese?" Rowland asked.

"Because I advised some very dangerous men that the Sinclairs would sell to the Japanese. And they made investments accordingly. Your obstinacy, my boy, is set to ruin me. Now I suggest you go before Mr. Yiragowa becomes anxious."

"Not unless Ed comes with me." Rowland swallowed, aware of how dangerous the lawyer was. Their only chance, ironically, was with the Japanese businessmen. "I won't leave her with you."

"Would you rather watch me cut her throat, Rowland?"

Rowland's mind worked furiously for some way of putting himself between Edna and Carmel's blade. He tried to keep the lawyer's attention on him. "If you do that, Mr. Carmel, then all this...the murder of two people, all your elaborate planning—it's all wasted, because I will sign nothing."

Carmel flicked the bayonet. Edna gasped as it nicked her throat. A bead of red trickled onto the blade. Le Fevre grabbed Rowland before he could lunge towards the lawyer. "Will you say that when she's bleeding, Rowland?" Carmel demanded.

"Do not move, Monsieur," Le Fevre whispered. "He will not hesitate."

Rowland froze, and for a moment there was only fear and horror, eyes locked and breaths held. The screech of tyres startled them all. There were cars at the gate once more, a horn was sounded now, and for just a pounding heartbeat, Carmel turned. Rowland took the chance that Le Fevre would not shoot and lunged, seizing Carmel's wrist and forcing it away from Edna's throat. Rowland brought Carmel to the ground and pounded the lawyer's hand against the wooden floor in an attempt to loosen his grasp on the bayonet. He shouted for Edna to run, but Carmel slammed his forehead into Rowland's temple. Rowland weakened, dazed, and Carmel brought the blade up between them. Edna screamed.

Le Fevre opened the door and ran out into the hallway. Realising that Edna was still in the room, Rowland rallied, blocking Carmel's arm before the blade could be plunged into his chest. Even so, Rowland knew he was fading, now coughing and battling to breathe.

"Rowly!" Milton's voice from somewhere in the house. Edna cried for help.

Still Carmel did not pull back, crazed, focused only on driving the bayonet home. Desperation more than strength was all Rowland had left.

Edna was trying to pull Carmel off when Milton burst into the room. He grabbed Carmel's arm and forced it back, blade and all. Then Clyde threw himself into the fray. The bayonet skittered across the wooden floor. Rowland rolled away, gasping for air and coughing blood.

Chapter Thirty-Eight

Etiquette of the Handkerchief

Mrs. Jefferson Davis is the "New York Journal's" distinguished authority on etiquette. Recently she discoursed on the etiquette of legs, informing her lady readers that it was very bad form to sit with the legs crossed. Now the wearing and carrying of the pocket handkerchief claims her attention. She says:

"The handkerchief is one of the most necessary articles of the modern wardrobe. But etiquette demands that, in spite of its usefulness, it should be kept out of sight. The inconspicuous use of the handkerchief proves the refined man or woman. The misuse of the handkerchief indicates lack of breeding as much as faulty grammar or gaudy dress.

"The etiquette of the handkerchief for a man, although very important, is also very simple and direct.

"Don't use a handkerchief as if signalling an enemy with a flag of truce. Don't display a handkerchief in a breast pocket as if it were an advertisement. Don't in full dress wear it tucked in the waistcoat as though its sole purpose was to protect the shirt front. Don't on a hot day wear a handkerchief tucked inside a collar, like a bib. Gaudy handkerchiefs are considered as bad taste for men as women. It is no longer correct for a man to carry a large silk handkerchief. The proper handkerchief is fine white linen with a half-inch hem and a tiny embroidered initial in the comer. When necessary to use a handkerchief in public, always do so in the quietest, most unobtrusive manner. The fashionable multitudes have never become used to the bugle blast some people blow."

—*Yackandandah Times*, 27 July 1900

Chief Inspector Randolph surveyed the sorry gathering before him, trying to ascertain what exactly had occurred from the babble of accounts. As a precaution, he had placed everyone, including Edna, under arrest, confining them to various rooms in the sanatorium, while he waited for more vehicles to transport the prisoners back to the International Police Headquarters.

The Japanese businessmen were furious, alternately demanding immediate release and the attendance of the consul and lawyers.

Rowland coughed again. The rally in his health had, once the immediate danger was over, subsided, and he felt wretched. He left it to Edna to explain to the police what had happened. From the guarded office, Gilbert Carmel was shouting with all the force and volume of the law, claiming that he was the victim of a deranged, homicidal client. Le Fevre was as yet unaccounted for.

Alastair Blanshard lit a cigarette. He introduced himself to Randolph. "Might I have a private word, Chief Inspector?"

For a moment it seemed Randolph might refuse, and then he relented.

Rowland watched the exchange. He wondered if Blanshard had pulled some sort of rank. Perhaps international spies outranked the local police. He realised that he had never ascertained what exactly Blanshard was doing in Shanghai.

Edna returned from giving her statement, ignoring the young policeman who tried to direct her to wait in another room. She went immediately to Rowland's side. "Haven't they seen you yet?" she asked, placing a hand on his forehead. "Rowly, you're running hot. You should be in bed."

He looked at her throat. "Did he—"

"Just the tiniest scratch, Rowly."

"God, Ed, I'm sorry. If I thought he'd let you go, I would have signed over everything I own."

"Oh, I know that. You did the right thing." She took his hand in hers. "Mr. Carmel would have killed me the moment you stepped out of the room. He couldn't very well allow either of us to live."

Clyde and Milton sat down opposite Rowland.

"So Carmel was behind it all?" Clyde handed him a glass of water. "Why?"

"Money, I suppose. I expect he always knew the Sinclairs were unlikely to preempt the embargo." Rowland swallowed painfully and drained the glass before he went on. "But he'd promised his clients that we would, so he hired Alexandra to compromise Wil."

"To blackmail him."

Rowland nodded.

"But then you turned up, so he decided to kill her instead?"

Edna pushed the hair gently back from Rowland's face. "Alexandra wanted to tell Rowly the truth. She might have told him she wanted out of the scheme, or Le Fevre might have told him about the message he overheard her making for Rowly. Mr. Carmel couldn't allow that."

"Bloody hell, the poor girl... What about Middleton?"

Rowland rubbed his face. "That's my fault," he blurted. "I told Carmel about Middleton in case someone from the *North China Daily News* made a complaint. If I hadn't—"

"Don't you dare feel guilty about Bertie," Edna said fiercely. "He got caught up in this because he followed us here! Because he was trying to..." Her lip trembled. She wiped her eyes, furious that after everything that had happened that day she would be reduced to tears over Bertram Middleton.

Rowland wrapped his arms around her. "I'm so sorry, Ed."

She broke down then. Rowland held her as she sobbed into his chest. Clyde and Milton waited, without a word, for Edna's tears to expend. They were shocked, but it was not a loss that they could grieve. Though he was sorry for his part in Middleton's end, Rowland could feel only sadness for the wastage of a life. He had never liked Middleton particularly, and his recent treatment of Edna had transformed years of studied neutrality into open hostility. Even so, Middleton had been murdered. Callously and brutally. And it seemed right that at least Edna, who had loved him occasionally, should weep, that there should be tears, however confused.

A throat was cleared pointedly. Rowland looked up.

Chief Inspector Randolph nodded brusquely. "Would you care to come with me, Mr. Sinclair? If we take your statement now, we can release you to see a doctor as soon as possible. I understand you are unwell."

Rowland was surprised by the new conciliation in Randolph's manner. Nevertheless, he hesitated, reluctant to leave the sculptress.

It was Edna who drew away. "You go, Rowly."

Clyde and Milton agreed. "We'll keep an eye on Ed, mate. You tell them what Carmel's been doing."

Rowland took the handkerchief from the inside breast pocket of his jacket and handed it to Edna. "It's clean. I always carry two of these."

She laughed through her tears. "It's just as well."

Chapter Thirty-Nine

Influenza Convalescents

One of the worst features of influenza is its weakening effect after recovery. Careful attention to diet, early bedtime, and freedom from overexertion are obvious rules for the convalescent, but sometimes more than that is required to build up the strength which has ebbed since the illness.

Those who have no great faith in the ordinary tonic will often take a homemade cordial, especially when it is based on eggs—the lightest, most nourishing, and most easily digested of foods. The following egg tonic is recommended: Take 6 eggs, which should be straight from the nest, and not more than two days old. Wipe them thoroughly, and put them in an earthenware basin. Pour the juice of seven lemons over them, and let them stand for 18 hours until all the shells are dissolved.

Turn them over occasionally, and take care that the eggs are covered with the juice of the lemons. Then when the eggs have absorbed all the juice, beat them up well, strain the mixture, and add a quarter of a pound of Demerara sugar, half a bottle of Jamaica rum, shake well, and bottle. The cordial is ready for use in a day or two. One liqueur-glassful should be taken in the middle of the morning with a biscuit.

An egg cordial which needs less preparation is made as follows: Take the yolk of an egg, beat it well with three spoonfuls of castor sugar, and add a spoonful of port wine.

—*Mercury*, 11 October 1934

"How are you feeling, comrade?" Milton walked into Rowland's bedroom wearing a jacket of red and gold silk brocade he'd bought in a Chinese boutique.

Rowland winced. The jacket hurt his eyes, which until then had been the only part of his body which didn't ache.

Milton frowned. "You look like death warmed up."

"Then I look better than I feel."

"O World! O Life! O Time! On whose last steps I climb..." Rowland closed his eyes. "Clearly Shelley understood."

From the armchair by his bed, where she'd spent much of the time he'd been ill, Edna rolled her eyes. "You were much more stoic when you had tuberculosis."

"I never had tuberculosis."

"Well, you complained less when I shot you."

"That was just a bullet," Rowland replied, smiling weakly.

"Yes," Milton agreed, leaning on the scrolled foot of Rowland's bed. "For pity's sake, Ed, the man has a cold!"

Edna laughed. Now that she was sure Rowland wasn't dying, she was determined not to give him unwarranted sympathy. "Come on, Rowly, get dressed. There are a legion of people who want to talk to you about wool."

Rowland groaned. He was still congested and his body ached, though nearly three days of bed rest had improved him greatly. Dr. Rubenstein, who had taken over his care, such as it was, from Le Fevre, was confident that he did not have tuberculosis. "A severe chest infection," he confirmed. "More uncomfortable because you are beaten and bruised—which is why there is pain when you cough. It will subside with time and rest." And substantially, it had, though Rowland seemed uncharacteristically content to lie abed. His reluctance to claim recovery was probably not unconnected to the commercial furore that had arisen in the wake of the revelations about Gilbert Carmel, and the expectation that Rowland be involved in its resolution. The venerable members of the Japan–Australia Society had already enquired several times after his health, assuming that Gilbert Carmel's criminal activities had rendered his refusal to contract with the Japanese null and void.

Chao Kung had offered his services in resurrecting relations between Rowland Sinclair and the Japanese wool buyers. It was only the man's status as a cleric that had prevented Clyde from throwing him out. Milton, as always less influenced by the considerations offered to religion, escorted Kung from the premises, explaining exactly what the abbot could expect should they ever see him again.

Sir Victor Sassoon had also called personally to extend his apologies and that of the Cathay, and to invite them to return to either the hotel or his house on Kiangse Road. They declined though they bore Sassoon no ill will.

Clyde strode in, scowling. He had just been to the Cathay once again in the hope of finding that Danny Dong's cousins had called, but there had been no message or enquiry. He was beginning to worry that he would have to take the old lady's bones back to Australia. He handed a telegram to Rowland. "Wilfred," he said. As they had sent most of their previous telegrams to Wilfred through Carmel and Smith, it seemed none but the first, sent through the Cathay, had actually been despatched. And Wilfred's telegrams demanding to know why Rowland had not reported as instructed had also not been passed on.

"I wired Wilfred through the Cathay yesterday." Clyde grimaced. "He might have quite a lot to say."

"No doubt." Rowland read through the telegram with one eye closed, flinching every now and then. He placed the page on the bedside table. "I told him I was the wrong person to send."

"Well, I expect you showed him." Milton grinned.

Clyde sat down and pulled the chair up to Rowland's bed. "What now, Rowly?"

Rowland shrugged. "Wil wants me to sell the Sinclair stockpile to the British. Their offer isn't nearly as generous, but he thinks it might be to the only way to"—he picked up the telegram and read from it—"put the uncertainty I've generated in the market to rest."

"That's so unfair!" Edna protested. "This is hardly your fault. Gilbert Carmel is Wilfred's old friend!"

Rowland nodded. "Make sure you include that in your next telegram, Clyde."

Clyde snorted. "That'd be poking a brown snake. I feel a bit sorry for Wilfred, to be honest."

"For Wil?"

"Carmel was his mate; they served together. Apparently he saved the blaggard's life and named his son after him. Carmel planned to entrap Wilfred so he could blackmail him, until you turned up in his place. One helluva betrayal."

Rowland nodded thoughtfully. Clyde was right. Knowing how much Wilfred cherished his family, Carmel's plans seemed chillingly personal and cruel. Rowland had trusted Carmel without question because he knew Wilfred did. He glanced at the telegram, wondering now if there was more pain than anger in the missive.

Wing Zau entered bearing a tray of green tea. Sassoon had offered to reinstate him at Cathay once he'd finished his employ with Rowland Sinclair. Wing had declined, having decided to hang out a shingle as a private investigator. Indeed he and Ranjit Singh, reconciled now, intended to embark on the endeavour in partnership.

Clyde had tried to talk them out of it. Milton had recommended the "very instructive" works of Conan Doyle. And Rowland had invested financially in the venture.

Rowland drank the tea while Wing showed Edna the camera he'd purchased for surveillance. Between Harjeet and Wing, he'd been plied with every cold and influenza remedy ever concocted. Wing had obtained various powders and herbs from a practitioner of traditional Chinese medicine, most of which Harjeet had thrown out. Still, there were some that had met her approval and which she added to her own remedies and potions. Rowland learned that it was easier to imbibe without resistance and just trust that he wasn't being poisoned. The occasional tonic was so laced with brandy or rum that he didn't care what else was in it. Not green tea of course, it tasted like hot water.

Harjeet came to the door now. "There's a gentleman to see you, Mr. Sinclair—shall I tell him you are not receiving visitors?"

Rowland groaned. Another member of the Australia–Japan Friendship Society no doubt.

"Rowly's very ill." Edna didn't look up from her book. "Why, with the sniffles and everything, it's amazing he's survived this long."

"You're an unfeeling harpy, Edna Higgins," Milton declared.

Harjeet clicked her tongue. "I will ask the gentleman to come back tomorrow."

Rowland thanked her. Tomorrow was early enough to deal with untangling the mess Carmel had left in his wake.

But the reprieve was short-lived.

"Don't be ridiculous, woman, there's nothing whatsoever wrong with the boy!" Alastair Blanshard barged past Harjeet and strode into the room. "Good Lord, man, have you got some dreadful disease after all?"

Rowland sighed. "No, I'm just malingering. Good morning, Blanshard. What can I do for you?"

"You can tell me why that turbaned fool who drives for you is following me around?"

Rowland glanced at Wing. "Mr. Singh is following you?"

"Yes, he's been traipsing after me all morning. About as subtle as a bloody brick in the back of the head! Suppose you tell me why."

"I have no idea. Did you ask him?"

"He said it was a coincidental encounter."

"Perhaps it was."

"Nonsense. Now you tell me what he's doing, or I'm going assume he's an assassin and shoot him!"

Wing's head snapped up. "Allow me to apologise, Mr. Blanshard. Mr. Singh is not an assassin... He was simply—"

"Doing his job," Milton finished.

"What part of his job involves following me about?"

Milton shrugged. "I retained the gentlemen of Wing and Singh to find out what you were doing in Shanghai."

Blanshard was outraged. "You were spying on me?"

"Ironic, isn't it?" Milton was unrepentant.

"It's my fault, Mr. Blanshard." Edna smiled sweetly as she confessed. "You see, Milt and I wondered what you were doing here, and since Mr. Wing and Mr. Singh were establishing an investigation agency, I suggested they look into it...as practice."

"And what did they report?" Blanshard demanded indignantly.

"Oh we didn't report to Miss Higgins!" Wing declared. "We couldn't tell a lady where you'd been!"

Milton started to laugh. Edna nodded. "As you can imagine, Mr. Blanshard, it was quite vexing."

Rowland smiled. "Good Lord, Blanshard, what on earth have you been doing?"

Blanshard glared at Wing. "I was making enquiries on behalf of His Majesty's government."

"In sing-song houses?" Milton was clearly less concerned about protecting Edna than Wing had been. "Lots of sing-song houses. Too many for a single, lonely man." The poet winked. "Have the princes been up to no good again, then?"

For a moment Blanshard said nothing, his hand flexing at his side. Milton stepped out of reach as a precaution. "My enquiries do not concern the king's sons," he said finally.

Milton's horror was contrived. "The king? Who would have thought—"

Blanshard eyed them all coldly. "Mrs. Simpson," he corrected. "It appears she spent some time in the Far East."

Rowland's brow rose. They had come across rumours when they were in England about the king's eldest son and the American divorcée. Clearly the liaison was now causing enough concern to send secret service to China to investigate her past.

"Speak of this again, and I will arrange to have each and every one of you shot."

Accustomed to Blanshard's regular threats to shoot people, they did not react particularly. They did drop the subject, but only because they were not especially interested in the reputation of Prince Edward's latest paramour. Blanshard spent some minutes railing about the temerity, the impudence and incompetence of Wing and Singh's attempted investigation.

Milton made some sort of amends by pouring the disgruntled spy a drink.

Rowland used the lull in Blanshard's fury to thank him for his help. "Lord knows how long we would have been held if you'd not had a word with Randolph."

Clyde nodded. "I still don't know how you managed to

convince the chief inspector to despatch his men out to the sanatorium in the middle of the night."

Blanshard smiled. "I told him Rowland Sinclair had kidnapped Miss Higgins. He was so keen to rearrest you that he called out every available man. Of course I set him straight once the scene was secured."

"Wasn't he angry?" Edna asked.

Blanshard's smile broadened. "Oh yes."

"I'm in your debt, Mr. Blanshard," Rowland said quite sincerely.

Blanshard studied his whisky for a moment. "I have always felt bad about leaving you in Munich—that terrible business with the Brownshirts. I'm glad I was able to assist this time. But"—he looked up and met Rowland's eye—"you may not always have a king's man conveniently on hand. It may pay you in the future not to be so bloody minded when it comes to the Nazis. As much as I detest everything they stand for, it does look like they're here for a while. You may need to learn to deal with them."

Rowland lay back with his hands behind his head. "Not for all the tea in China."

Epilogue

OUTED BY BMA EX-CONVICT
IS NOW QUACK
SAYS SOUND MAN HAS T.B.

Diagnoses Tuberculosis of Throat from
Drop of Blood taken from Earlobe
ABRAMS' APOSTLE—HANDS OUT DISEASES

SUPERVISION of the public health, which, in the last analysis, is the greatest asset of any community, is evidently very fox in Sydney town. A case in point is that of George Frederick Hewer, ex-gaol-bird, ex-B.M.A member, who is raking in a fat living at 'Adyar House,' in Bligh-street, with the aid of an American electric system, which, after having been investigated by high medical authorities from all parts of the world during the last ten years, has finally been pronounced 99 percent quackery. 'Dr.' Hewer diagnoses at great expense to his clients all sorts of complaints, and that some of them don't exist within the patient's body is evidenced by the fact that two of *Truth's* investigators, during the past fortnight, have been along to the doctor's sanctuary at Adyar House and have been diagnosed as suffering from physical ills which existed only in his imagination...

After his release from prison—early in 1924—the doctor was struck off the list of members of the British Medical Association, and, faced with this serious handicap, evidently he decided to do what nearly all discredited members of any profession have done since the world first knew professions.

He resorted to quackery, and in that way he is getting his living today at the expense of trusting fools who are unacquainted with the fact that the medical system with which he has thrown in his lot has become long since a hissing and a byword among reputable citizens. He became an apostle of the Abrams system and established the clinic of electronic medicine at Adyar House.

—*Truth*, 29 April 1928

Dr. Henri Le Fevre turned out to be George Frederick Hewer, who had been struck off the list of members of the British Medical Association. He was not French, though he spoke the language quite well. When captured he confessed to being the man whose voice was on the recording left by Alexandra Romanova, though he denied any part in her murder. With no evidence that he had done anything other than misdiagnose Rowland Sinclair, and attempt to deprive him of his liberty, he was eventually released without charge.

After it was revealed that he had been retained by Gilbert

Carmel to ensure Rowland Sinclair's stay at Ward Road Gaol was particularly unbearable, John Whitely was investigated for corruption, but in the end no action was taken.

The junior lawyer "Murray" who had been assigned the defence of Rowland Sinclair in Carmel's absence was shown not to exist. Carmel and Smith was a firm made up of Gilbert Carmel and his faithful secretary.

Gilbert Carmel was charged with, and eventually convicted of, the murders of Alexandra Romanova and Bertram Middleton, and the attempted murder of Rowland Sinclair, as well as a litany of lesser offences. All charges against Rowland Sinclair were dropped.

With his sister's killer caught, Sergei Romanov came out of hiding and began to bathe regularly once again. He allowed Rowland Sinclair to replace his violin and returned to teaching the instrument to the children of wealthy Shanghailanders. Occasionally he worked for Wing and Singh Private Investigations.

Alexandra Romanova's son, Mikhail, was sent to school in the United States as his mother had wished. The expenses of his education were met by Rowland Sinclair.

Emily "Mickey" Hahn continued her unconventional relationship with Shao Xunmei, supporting herself by writing for *North China Daily News* and the *New Yorker*. By 1936 she had achieved her ambition of becoming an opium addict. After the fall of Shanghai in the 1937, Hahn signed a document declaring herself Xunmei's second wife under Chinese Law and, in doing, saved his printing press from confiscation. She eventually left Shanghai in 1939, but her experiences in China became the foundation of a long and brilliant career which saw her author more than fifty books of fiction, history, memoir, and reportages as well as innumerable articles.

When he'd recovered enough to do so, Rowland accepted Shao Xunmei's invitation to dine with the Celestial Hound Society, a group of Chinese artists and art-lovers who favoured the Parisian school. Thereafter the Australians encountered Xunmei often in Mickey Hahn's flat on Kiangse Road, where they would discuss poetry and politics, art and gossip. It was probably a sign of Milton's esteem for the Chinese poet that he did not attempt to steal his verse.

Du Yuesheng (Big-Eared Du) continued to wield power both official and illicit in Shanghai until the Japanese invasion of 1937. He offered to fight the Japanese by scuttling his fleet of ships in the Yangtze River to prevent their advance, but eventually fled to exile in Hong Kong. He returned to Shanghai after the war, but his influence had waned with its citizens, who felt he had abandoned the city.

Intermittently during the remainder of their time in China, one or the other of the Australians would see Chao Kung, fleetingly, though he did not approach them again. Born Ignacz Trebitsch to an Orthodox Jewish family in Hungary, Kung had operated as a double agent in the Great War. He worked his way into the extreme right-wing militarist fringe groups in Germany and Europe before betraying them by selling their information to the secret services of various governments. In China he worked for a number of warlords before, yet again, transferring his loyalties in 1937 to the Empire of Japan.

Despite his loyalty to the Nazis, John Rabe became a hero during the 1937 Japanese occupation of Nanking, during which he worked tirelessly to establish the Nanking Safety Zone. He sheltered approximately 200,000 Chinese citizens from slaughter during the massacre.

Sir Victor Sassoon, the 3rd Baronet of Bombay, lived in Shanghai until 1941, when the war forced him to leave. After the Chinese Communist Revolution in 1949, he divested his assets in China and retired to Nassau in the Bahamas.

Danny Dong's cousins eventually called at the Cathay to collect their grandmother. It was with significant relief that Clyde handed over the chest he had watched over. Even so, the Australians accompanied the remains back to the village outside Nanking in which Mrs. Dong had been born and in which she would be finally interred amongst her ancestors. There they enjoyed the humble hospitality of her grateful grandchildren, toasted Danny Dong with hot rice wine, and saw a little of what Mickey Hahn called "the real China."

The Sinclair stockpile was sold to a British consortium of wool buyers. The rumours of international trade sanctions against the Japanese for the illegal invasion of Manchuria never eventuated. The member countries of the League of Nations had important trading links with Japan and were consequently unable to agree on the precise nature of sanctions. Australia actively pursued a policy of appeasement, and while it did enter into a trade war with Japan in 1936, the restrictions had nothing to do with Japanese activities in China.

Wilfred Sinclair never sent his brother to trade wool again.

Alexandra Romanova's body was eventually released and laid to rest in Shanghai. Her funeral was attended by only handful of mourners, including her brother, her son, and four Australians. Whoever she once was, she died a taxi girl, far from the land and the past she loved. But there were tears for her in China.

Her widely praised standalone novel *After She Wrote Him* has been chosen as a "Target Recommends" book for 2020 and Apple's Best Book of the Month for April 2020.

ABOUT THE AUTHOR

Award-winning author Sulari Gentill set out to study astrophysics, ended up graduating in law, and later abandoned her legal career to write books instead of contracts. When the mood takes her, she paints, although she maintains that she does so only well enough to know that she should write. She grows French black truffles on a farm in the foothills of the Snowy Mountains of New South Wales, which she shares with her young family and several animals.

Sulari is the author of the award-winning Rowland Sinclair Mysteries, a series of historical crime novels set in 1930s Australia about Rowland Sinclair, the gentleman artist cum amateur detective. The eighth in the series, *A Dangerous Language*, was published in the United States by Poisoned Pen Press in June 2020.

Under the name S. D. Gentill, Sulari also writes fantasy adventure, including The Hero Trilogy: *Chasing Odysseus*, *Trying War*, and *The Blood of Wolves*.